MW00931753

Copyright © 2021 Elora Morgan

ISBN-10: 9798758437056

Contents

Content Expectations Including Triggers

The Beyond the God Sea trilogy matures with the protagonist.

Beyond the God Sea: Betrothed (Book I) is YA.
Bound by Dark Waters: Wed (Book II) is Dark/Mature YA.
Borne to Salt and Sin: Fated (Book III) is New Adult and includes explicit, spicy content.

<u>**Potential Triggers**</u>:
The Upper YA material in Book II is darker and more mature, especially surrounding the bully prince and the sexual expectations of Zaria's arranged marriage. While there is little-to-no explicit content, the themes and challenges within this story are more appropriate for older teen readers. **As Zaria straddles the line between Young Adult and New Adult, so do her experiences.**

Mild swearing, consumption of alcohol, thoughts of self-harm, and issues surrounding the topics of sex, violence, abuse, and trauma are present.

Part One

Bend to Endure

Chapter 1

We flew at a gut-wrenching speed away from the boy I loved.

"Kirwyn!" I sputtered, still choking on seawater as violent spray from the waves smacked my face. "Turn back! Let me go!"

Boats couldn't move that swiftly. Hearts couldn't hold that much agony. It was unbelievable and unbearable all at once.

Strong hands pulled at my shoulders and snaked around my waist. Hands I did not know or want to touch me. I scanned the surface but I couldn't find Kirwyn's head or either of our boats. *How long was I under the water? How fast were we moving?*

"He's gone, girl, let it go," said a deep voice behind me.

"Don't torment her," another voice chided. "Your shot missed. The boy made it back on his boat."

Shot?

"You're the only one tormenting her with false hope," the first, doom-filled voice replied.

"Kirwyn," I breathed, scanning the seascape. Nothing caught my eye amidst the black waves. My knees buckled and I slumped to the bottom of the strange, large vessel. The mechanized roar of the so-called engine droned, hurting my ears. Artificial light flooded the hull, paining my eyes.

The speed at which we raced, the seawater in my lungs, the white-hot agony in my heart...

...the knowledge that we were headed somewhere *else,* somewhere *new...*

All of it became too much to bear. I retched onto the slippery floor, dry heaving until I fully vomited the meager contents of my stomach onto someone's dark shoes. Possibly the man holding back my hair.

"That's it, you'll feel better, get it all out," the man soothed, and I recognized him as the one who claimed Kirwyn made it back to his boat.

Did he? Please, Keroe, please help him.

Those dark, scuffed shoes were the last thing I saw. I might have even collapsed right on top of them when I blacked out.

#

Blue-gray predawn muted the sky when I woke. Not with promise, like the day I found Kirwyn on the beach – but opaque with thick clouds, concealing the future. Only dull gray stretched endlessly, foreboding nothing good would come of it. The cry of dinbirds told me we were near land, though I hadn't yet sat up in the boat to look. My wedding dress had irreparably torn, hanging off my body in tatters. My head ached and my stomach rumbled, though any thought of food made me ill. The pain low in my bladder screamed for me to find a place to pee, soon.

Despite my aching body, I couldn't muster the nerve to look beyond that opaque sky.

If I looked, that made it true.

Other land existed.

Kirwyn was… gone.

"We shouldn't sneak her in like this," someone said. "Safety in numbers. The crowds would have been the best course for protection."

"This was the agreed-upon alternative if the Black Passage flooded. These damn shenanigans cost us time and now it's high tide. We'll never make it into the castle through the tunnel now."

Strange accents, I thought. More like Kirwyn's, but not quite. *You have to look, landdammit,* I scolded myself, pushing down the creeping fear. *Be strong. Remember your vow.*

"Where's Kirwyn?" I demanded, hoarse. I pushed myself into a sitting position and swallowed the lump in my throat. "Who – who are you? Take me back."

Blinking, I realized I sat in the bottom of the largest boat I'd ever seen -- white and slippery, made of some material other than wood, and without sail or paddle. Three strange men looked down at me. Their faces weren't like mine, but they weren't quite like Kirwyn's either. It was hard to put my finger on; the differences were subtle. Lips smaller than I was used to seeing or noses a shade bigger... all features assembled with a slight variation in alignment. Each man wore similar black attire, more akin to Kirwyn's odd clothing than our own tunics, but altogether distinct from both.

"Easy..." said the man I'd vomited on the night before. He was exceedingly tall, had a mop of soft brown hair, and deep smile lines crossing his pale face. "We're here to help you, to escort you to your new home. I'm Tolas. This is Raoul and Singen." He pointed to a short man with a long, coarse beard as Singen and a beardless man with a long gold necklace as Raoul.

Was I expected to make polite conversation? Was this a joke? I'd happily tear these men to pieces with my bare hands if I got the chance.

Would I?

"I'm here to help you," Tolas repeated, lines deepening around his mouth as he smiled warmly. "To learn our ways and your place here."

13

"Take you back to what?" Singen interrupted gruffly, stroking his beard. I recognized his as the same deep voice from the night before, claiming Kirwyn didn't make it. "He's long gone either way. And don't get any ideas. There's no getting off this island."

"If we ever get back on it," mused Tolas, staring at something in the distance.

You have to look, I scolded. *You can't escape if you're too afraid to even* look.

I took a deep breath and stood on shaky legs, following Tolas's gaze over the side of the boat. As I rose, my mouth fell.

This can't be real. A dreamland.

I blinked, rapidly, covering my mouth as I gasped.

Land. Other land.

Green and mountainous and sprawling farther than imaginable. My heart sped to behold it. Directly ahead of our boat sat a palm-lined cove. Rising in the distance, I could see what I assumed to be a palace like our own, and yet, nothing like it. The formidable structure, built of gray stone, perched atop a sheer cliff. It was a marvel of architecture and engineering no one would believe. Cascading down windows and climbing up stone, half the structure dripped with vines, flowering in every color. Rows of bushes and potted trees decorated windows and balconies scattered throughout towering walls.

"It's awe-inspiring to newcomers," Tolas sighed, standing beside me and sharing my view, as if seeing it through my eyes. "Everyone feels the same when they first look upon it, not just Elowans."

Forgetting for the moment that I wanted to murder him, I breathed, "Is this... the Isle of Lights?" It couldn't be real. With each blink of my eyes, I anticipated the grand illusion shattering when I next opened them.

"Some call it that," Tolas said gently.

"No one calls it that," Singen snapped.

"Her people do," Raoul shrugged. "Those who know, anyway."

"We call our home Rythas," Tolas said.

"Rythas," I mouthed the funny word. I could feel Tolas studying me, but I couldn't tear my eyes from that towering, floral palace. *Were they taking me there?*

"High Spire," Tolas nodded at the imposing gray structure. "It's – all of this – was built on an ancient fort, soon after the Great Decline. Inspired by anything fantastical that suited Osvaldo's taste and could be crafted with unchecked power and the unlimited labor of those fleeing the wars on the mainland. But don't dismiss it as folly. Times have changed, but mainlanders with means come to enjoy what we've built here. Our beauty's our survival."

Mainlanders, High Spire, Rythas. Was it all

true? Everything Kirwyn said?

My breath came short and shallow as I asked, "Do… people live here? Are you a… clan?"

How big? How many people? Could I escape?

Tolas nodded and for the first time I truly scrutinized his strange face. It seemed an honest one. These three men tried to kill Kirwyn. They'd taken me. They were my enemy. *But this one,* I thought, *maybe he could be useful -- or even trusted, someday.*

"Both clan and country." Turning, Tolas pushed aside his dark vest-shirt, revealing his right shoulder blade. My eyes rounded seeing the black mark upon his skin: a crown and, beneath it, a key.

Just as Kirwyn said.

"Is it true that you saw him?" I whispered, heart pounding in my chest. "The boy coming for me. Did he make it back to his boat?"

Tolas smiled, sadly. "I don't have the best eyesight. Too much time reading books, I'm told. But I believe so."

I swallowed the lump in my throat. Were Tolas's words enough to hold out hope?

They'd have to be. They were all I had.

Don't cry, I warned myself. *And don't fight them, not openly.* That had been my mistake with my mother and Nasero. I had to be smarter now -- despite every part of my body screaming to jump into the water and swim far away.

"How many bullets are left in that gun?" Raoul asked Singen, indicating the weapon he'd fired at Kirwyn.

"Two. We need more guns. Doesn't Grahar understand we need more guns? War will be here any day now. When's that twat Mal-Yin coming anyway?"

My ears pricked. *Mal-Yin.* Kirwyn had said that name our night together in Lover's Cove. I felt the lump re-form in my throat.

"He's Mal-Yin, he'll come when he's good and ready and no parade of preening young girls is going to entice him any sooner," Raoul replied.

"But they will certainly entertain him while he's here," Singen sneered.

"Forgive them," Tolas said archly, casting a pointed look at the two other men. "Such matters aren't for your ears... yet. We'll give you a chance to become accustomed to our ways before you take part in any royal business."

"This was damnable foolishness," Singen cursed between clenched teeth. "Pomp and pageantry were the ways to bring her in, not cloak and dagger."

"Don't scare the girl," Tolas admonished.

"I'm not afraid," I lied, my firm voice turning heads in my direction. I squared my shoulders. "You think this would be the first attempt on my life? I'm no stranger to people trying to kill me." That part was true, at least.

"Kill you? Nah. No one wants to kill you. They just want to kidnap you for the ransom money," Singen said. Looking at Raoul, he instructed, "Keep your sword ready." Then he jumped over the side of the boat, splashing into the turquoise surf. Raoul and Tolas followed his lead, swinging over the rail and into the water.

"Allow me," Tolas offered, reaching his long arms into a cradling motion.

I didn't move. *Was touching now permitted?*

"I'm sorry," he said, mouth twitching as he read the indecision in my eyes. "Please, let me help you out of the boat." Tolas tucked one hand behind his back, formally, the other still extended, offering me assistance in stepping down.

The only way out is through.

I clenched my jaw and put a hand in Tolas's, feeling a little better to find what seemed liked genuine kindness in this fearsome place. Maybe I could make an ally of him, convince him to help me find Kirwyn.

If he's alive... oh Keroe, please let him be alive... then I'll find him. Somehow.

I forced myself to smile. "Thank you," I said, jumping into the surf beside the tall man. "It's nice to meet someone kind here."

Tolas returned an eager smile. *Yes, he could be an ally.*

Singen led us up the small inlet and it was

obvious why we couldn't dock elsewhere. Rocks rose like walls to our left and right. The beach itself was nothing more than a tiny cove. My heart skipped a beat and the hair on my arms stood on end with my first few steps on new land, strange land. Yet so far, except for the palace, it didn't look too dissimilar to my own. I recognized the same tall, swaying palm trees, the familiar call of dinbirds. But knowing it was *not* home, my skin pricked and my mind repeated, *this can't be happening.*

Quietly, the four of us stalked through the brush and up the steep incline, concentrating on our footing.

You could run, said a voice in my head. *Take your chances in the forest. So what if they catch you? The worst that can happen is they drag you back.*

Don't do it, scolded another voice. *Play your part until you find sure escape.*

But my muscles tensed as I readied to sprint. I was younger. Maybe faster. I could do it.

I heard a rustle to my right and my stomach flipped, as if deep in my bones I already knew the threat. In a flash, Singen pointed his gun and Raoul raised his sword.

The familiar whistle of an arrow cut through the air, accompanied by the sick *twack* as it embedded itself deep into Tolas's skull, tallest out of our group and standing right beside me.

For the second time in my life, a man was

killed instantly, right before my wide eyes.
     This time, I did not scream.

Chapter 2

I did pee myself, just a little.

Maybe a lot.

In my defense, I hadn't been given the chance to relieve my bladder all night. When the shot flew, I gasped and fell, pressing my body flush to the dirt. The act had the unfortunate consequence of soaking the front of my dress.

As horrific as it was to see Tolas's life end abruptly – and with it my plans for befriending him - I did not weep. I only wished the arrow had hit Singen, since he was the one who tried to kill Kirwyn. A boom, same as the night before, rang out from the bearded man's gun. Birds took wing in a frenzy and a man yelped and fell.

"Stay down!" Singen yelled, scanning the trees -- though Raoul and I certainly didn't need to be reminded.

Was I going to die in this strange land? Never

see Kirwyn again?

Singen left us trembling in the dirt, combing the tree line stealthily, kneeling to examine the ground every few feet. Sweat pooled beneath my armpits and my hands shook. Finally, the bearded man circled back to us. "We're clear for now," he declared, voice low and commanding. "Let's move and be quick about it."

Tucking my head, I rose to a sitting position while Singen trudged over to where the attacker had fallen. "Shame he's dead," he said, kicking the body. "Won't get any information out of him this way."

"Are you alright?" Raoul asked, as I gaped at Tolas's corpse. I could only nod.

"Well, it can't be an inside job or else he'd have had a gun," Singen mused.

"Unless they want us to *think* it's not an inside job," Raoul countered. "Too much of a coincidence, finding us here, now. Come on. Let's hurry."

Just like that? I thought. *Your friend died and we just... moved on?*

"Y - you said no one wants to kill me," I muttered, still staring at Tolas's body.

"That's why it's him with an arrow in his head and not you," Raoul said, gently. Sensing my hesitation, he explained, "He stays where he lays. Palace officials will need to investigate. Don't worry, we'll be safe at High Spire and once we root out this kidnapping plot, all will return to normal."

I blinked. *Normal? None of this is normal.*

#

Dazed, I followed Raoul and Singen through dense forest. When we reached a clearing in the trees, I caught my first glimpse of the massive palace up close. I grasped the nearest tree trunk, knees buckling, craning my neck up to take in its full height. It wasn't just a castle; it was a community. Gray stone walls encircled the structure and broad stone pathways crisscrossed the open area leading up to the walls. The grandest feature was the front itself, rising behind sprawling gardens. A fountain of water bifurcated one enormous staircase, cascading down the steps. Atop stood tall doors I assumed to be the front gates.

Raoul caught my frightened stare. "High Spire. You'll be safe there."

"Is that where the... prince lives?" I asked. I realized I didn't even know the name of my betrothed. I didn't care.

"Jullik Doreste is the young king," Raoul corrected. "The heir uses the term *young king,* regardless of his age. It serves as a firm reminder of who's next in line for the throne. Only his siblings go by prince or princess." Surveying the paths before us, he shook his head. "Too many people are going to see you... like this."

"Well, we can't get in through the Black Passage now and we can't keep her out here all day," Singen snapped, itching his beard.

"We'll take her through the Bone Gate." Stepping in begrudgingly for Tolas, I supposed, Raoul turned to me and said, "It's nearest and the least populated."

I didn't want to go into that castle. I didn't want to go home, either.

I no longer knew where I belonged.

I swallowed, thickly. Everything before me felt like too much to take in, making me long to rest my head and close my eyes. To sleep, and wake to find it had all been a dream. I wanted Kirwyn beside me again, like the night we spent together. My hands ached to touch him, to feel his warm skin. My body yearned for the comfort of his strong arms wrapped around me.

"Put this on," Raoul said, tossing me a red swath of cloth previously tucked into his back pocket. "Cover your head and face."

I did as I was bid. *Bend,* I thought. *Bend or you'll break.*

Singen snorted, "Like no one's gonna notice that gown."

Raoul shrugged, turning to me as I tucked the last of my hair under the scarf. "Stay close to us."

Or what, I thought? *What harm could befall me that you haven't already brought upon my head or plan upon bringing?*

#

Too often during those first few steps I swayed on my feet, fighting rising panic. *A man died. He was alive and poof, now he's dead.* Each time I made us stop Singen tensed, bringing his hand to the gun strapped at his waist, as if more kidnappers would appear any minute. Stealing glances at passers-by only made my anxiety worse, so I kept my eyes down, telling myself there would be plenty of time to study the people later.

By the time we neared the community, I'd gone into a place deep inside myself. My mind closed off, like it had received too much information and couldn't process it all at once.

I'll think about it later. When I'm alone. They have to leave me alone somewhere in this strange place to clean up. Don't they?

"Where exactly are you taking me?" I asked, eyes downcast, walking in a trance-like state.

"Relax," Singen ordered, which infuriated me. *He* certainly wasn't relaxed. "We're taking you to your room."

How much farther? I longed to be by myself, to release the stinging tears and figure out a plan to find Kirwyn. *He has to be alive. He has to be.*

We wound through fantastical, stone-cobbled streets, up into the castle of High

Spire itself. I kept my gaze trained on my feet, avoiding eye contact, per Raoul's advice. When I couldn't climb any more steps, I removed the uncomfortable wedding sandals and walked barefoot over cool, smooth stones. From the corner of my eye, I picked out pillars and statues and clothing so unlike our own. Long, sheer, colorful swathes of cloth. Unfamiliar voices and accents shouting and laughing – all the noise so much louder than at home. Strange smells assailed my nose – intense citrus and pungent spices and heady flowers. And beasts! Impossible, enormous, hoofed beasts, like Kirwyn's tales. I dared not glance at more than their massive legs, mesmerized by the *clop-clop-clopping* as they walked slowly past, dragging wheeled wooden carts.

Five guards joined us at the so-called Bone Gate, a set of double-doors at least two stories high, and Singen finally stopped reaching for his gun. The new men also wore loose black pants and shirts, some with colorful sashes. I didn't speak to any of our escorts, and no one spoke to me, though I could *feel* their curious glances.

Inside the castle, the crowds thinned, though I heard servants scurrying about so I kept my head covered. When I felt like we couldn't possibly wind through any more halls, we came to an abrupt halt in a cool, echoing corridor.

"Dammit," Raoul cursed. I could feel our small group tense in unison and I instinctively tensed along with them, straining my ears to hear what caused the alarm. "That's Juls. Dammit, he can't see her like this. Cover the girl."

A school of minnows darted across my gut. *Did he mean my intended?*

From the far end of the hall, I heard the clattering of footfalls. Guards' bodies pressed around me, shielding me.

I wanted to laugh. I had to bite it back because if I started, I feared I'd never stop.

You want to hide me? I thought. *Do you think I care what I look like? What this prince – young king, whatever – thinks of me?*

Peering between my broad-shouldered escorts, I could make out the young king's party moving perpendicular to ours. They wore colorful, loose pants and tunic-vests. Some donned sashes around their waists, some wore metal breastplates. The brilliance and variety were unlike anything I'd seen at home and I openly gawked.

Move, Zaria, I scolded myself, fisting the folds of my wedding dress. *Act, seize control, do* something. *Don't let everything be on everyone else's terms.*

I tapped a guard on his shoulder. Even after all I'd been through, the act of willingly touching another male felt strange, bold. As bold as what I was about to do.

The man turned, curious. For the first time, I met his eyes.

"Let me pass," I commanded. When he refused to budge, I raised my eyebrows, ignoring the minnows in my stomach.

I'm your young queen, I thought. *Whatever that means.* I gave him my haughtiest stare and prayed some bravado, however false, worked its way into my gaze.

It did -- the soldier stepped aside and I slid forward.

Singen growled, clenching his jaw, but didn't stop me. Raoul smacked his hand over his eyes, but he didn't protest either. *Interesting.* As I broke away from our small party, one of the young king's guards noticed me and stilled. The rest quickly followed.

Gulping, I lowered the silk from my head.

My knotty hair hung in clumps down my back. Whatever face painting my mother's maids had colored the night before had long since washed off -- or worse, smeared. My wedding dress was filthy and torn, hanging limp from my body. Since I'd removed the aching shoes, I now approached barefoot, feet caked in dirt.

I'd long since lost my crown.

I was pretty sure I reeked of body odor, urine and *worse...* the mud staining the hem of my gown smelled suspiciously like animal dung of some kind.

Whatever lovely, ethereal bride was supposed to be presented to this young king had vanished, leaving behind a filthy, foul-smelling creature who looked as if she'd rolled around in dirt and crawled through a latrine.

I hope you don't like what you see, I prayed. *And send me away.*

My heart pounded so hard against my chest that I imagined the entire hall could hear it. My head screamed with a thousand questions about this strange land and my role in it. None of this felt real; I continued on as if I dreamed it. But I kept my back ramrod straight, shoulders squared, head high. Proud, like a tree. *I was built for the sea. There was no greater honor.*

I had to make the right impression, despite my haggard appearance.

You only get one chance to set the tone of how you'll be treated here.

Wherever here *is,* I thought.

Everyone stared as I walked alone across the hall to approach the young king. I tried not to let my greedy gaze divert to the strangeness surrounding me.

As the guards parted respectfully, I saw him.

About the same age as Kirwyn, but skinnier, less muscular. His skin was light brown, and his eyes were a deeper, richer shade. His brown hair fell straight to just below his ears, though most had been tied back in a loose goat's tail.

I supposed he could be called handsome. He wasn't old or obese or hideous – at least, not on the outside. The young king stared at me, initially wide-eyed, then suddenly relaxed, as if remembering himself. His gaze swept the length of my soiled gown and back up to my dirt-stained face.

I was surprised he didn't speak. I supposed he expected me to do so, having approached alone, obviously intent.

What did I want to say? I hadn't thought that far ahead.

I'm pleased to meet you, now send me back?

No, civil. *I had to wear a guise of civility. And command. I had one shot to seize it.*

I licked my lips. "Prince... Jullik? I mean... young king?" I was disappointed to find my voice wasn't as assured as I'd hoped. It came out weak, questioning. I swallowed and tried again.

"I am Zaria, the... chosen braenese." *Your chosen wife?*

"We were ambushed on the way here." *Wherever here is.*

"One of the men escorting me has been murdered. Tolas. He needs to be..." I faltered. *Given a funeral at sea,* I wanted to say. But I didn't even know where I was, let alone what happened in this strange world, after death.

"...Put to rest," I finished quietly, and not nearly as strongly as I wanted. But at least I had taken control of what I could while the guards cowered at my back.

When the young king didn't reply I felt my palms sweat, but I lifted my chin again. A long moment of silence passed, during which he studied me curiously and I chewed the inside of my mouth.

Jullik flicked his gaze to someone behind me -- for confirmation of what I said, I guessed. He quickly looked back at me.

Had I acted inappropriately?

Well, if I'd already broken some royal protocol I wasn't even familiar with, I might as well keep going.

"You're staring," I remarked, hoping it sounded like a reprimand, even though I shifted my weight nervously. *This is preposterous. I'm not marrying you,* I thought. *I don't even know you.*

Do you even want to marry me?

Everyone was listening, watching us. My guards to my back, his guards to his.

Perhaps it *was* reprimanding, because Jullik's eyes widened slightly.

"My apologies," he said stoically, evenly. "I'm a bit taken aback. I was told to expect someone... more..." he struggled to find the right word, "...reserved."

"Well, I was told to expect a god," I shot back.

My stomach flipped and I wished I hadn't been so rash. I folded my lips between my teeth to prevent further speech. *Now I'd gone too far.*

Jullik's deep brown eyes widened further, full lips parting slightly. Then he suddenly laughed, startling me.

"My apologies *again,*" he said, this time with sincerity. "I suppose we're not making a very good first impression on you. First you're attacked and then I insult you."

I blinked, transfixed by his accented voice. He spoke in buttery, dulcet tones -- but not falsely. Not as if to sell sugar-coated lies like I'd heard at home. When he laughed, it touched his eyes.

He was not what I expected.

I couldn't be what he'd imagined.

The sea swallowed me and spit me back up and I certainly looked every inch the bedraggled foundling. *I* couldn't be making a very good impression on *him,* either. And I needed to make a good impression if I hoped to convince him to help me.

I supposed I *did* care what he thought.

One of the guards coughed, jarring Jullik out of his musing. He straightened and his tone became formal once more. "Please see the chosen braenese to her quarters." He gave me a sharp nod and said, "We'll see you tonight."

With quick steps, Jullik and his group resumed their walk, heading purposefully down the corridor.

"At least Laz wasn't here," Raoul mumbled,

as the guards shuffled to my side. "We'd never hear the end of it."

Who's 'we?' I wondered, staring at the young king's back. *What was happening tonight?*

Chapter 3

For the remainder of the walk through the fantastical, floral palace, I held my head high. What was the point in hiding any longer? I'd staked a claim, presented an image I planned on holding onto. *The cool, confident queen-to-be.* A façade to hide behind.

Only my eyes darted left and right, soaking up the strange beauty of arched courtyards and painted walls. I gaped freely at all I beheld: thick glass upon windows, impossibly-carved statuary, bright clothing, man-made fountains and an explosion of plants and flowers in every nook. Like a floral dream of the First Feet. Except it wasn't the past, it was real and *now.* I yearned to tell someone, everyone, back home. Tomé especially.

Guards escorted me into a sprawling bedroom with cream and seafoam accents, unlike anything in my world. My *old* world. Floor cushions dotted the floor, but unlike home, a table and chairs sat to one side, as if for dining in one's own chambers. The space was large enough to accommodate a long-but-narrow sofa, gilded along the wooden frame. Even the bed was a marvel to behold, unusually large and draped with soft blankets. Many tall, glass windows lined one side of the room.

"We'll leave you here to rest," Raoul said cautiously, as I quickly crossed the tiled floor and peered out one of the windows. My stomach dropped just looking at the distance to the rocky shore below. I'd never been so high before. I couldn't sneak out of here. "If you need anything, there's a guard just down the hall."

I didn't miss Raoul's implication. *Don't do anything stupid.*

I'd be a liar if I said the thought hadn't crossed my mind. But I wouldn't. Not when Kirwyn might still be alive. At the agony sweeping through my chest like a tidal wave, I corrected myself. *Not when Kirwyn* is *still alive.*

The moment everyone left me alone in the sprawling room of cream-and-seafoam trimmings, I tore the remainder of my dress from my body and unhooked my mother's conch-pearl-and-diamond necklace, my one trinket from home. I couldn't force myself to throw it out the window; I placed it on the ivory-colored bedside table. Then I threw myself onto the unbelievably soft, massive bed and wept shamelessly until I fell asleep.

#

A knock on the door jarred me awake. Snapping my eyes open, I'd momentarily forgotten what had happened. It returned in a sickening rush.

I wasn't home. This wasn't my palace. Kirwyn was... gone.

Grabbing a sheet to cover my body, I sat up in the large, springy bed.

"What do you want?" I called out, expecting Singen or Raoul.

Instead, a female voice replied. "I want to come inside. Is that alright?"

I paused. "I – guess."

The door opened to reveal a girl a few years older than me. She possessed an impressive cascade of dark curls she'd pinned up in sections with glistening, gold combs. Her attire was more like that of the young king's guards: a short tunic with decorative metal. Unlike an Elowan dress it wasn't white; but colorful, silken. Like me, she was broad-shouldered, but where my muscles were long and lean from swimming, hers bore more definition. From her larger physique and the dagger strapped to her waist, I wondered if she belonged to some sort of Steel Guard.

The girl raised her eyebrows at my disheveled appearance, yet she grinned, wide. "Hello. My name is Yesmoré, with a *J*." Her accent matched everyone else's in this strange land.

I blinked.

"It's spelled with a *J*, but it's pronounced with a *Y*," she explained, studying my blank face.

Should I give her my name? Does she already know? Why is she here?

"Mhm," she hummed, rocking back on her heels. "Am I moving too fast? I just wasn't expecting to be your companion. Tolas's death was rather sudden. Everyone calls me Jesi anyway," she said, taking the liberty of spinning a wooden chair backwards and straddling it. Folding her arms across the chairback, she explained, "In Tolas's place, I'm here to help with your transition."

I finally found my voice. "Who attacked us? Why?"

Jesi shrugged. "I don't know. Officials will investigate. It's possible it's part of this kidnapping plot, I suppose."

Jesi's face was painted as mine had been for my wedding. Her lips were full, her eyes were big and brown, and her wild curls spread out beyond the width of her shoulders and fell in a glossy cascade. She was undeniably pretty and yet something about her was different than the people of my island. I noted her oval face was slightly longer than an Elowan's, the bones in her cheeks and line of her jaw were unusual...

but the rest of it was hard to put my finger on. It was simply a type of face I hadn't seen before, just like Kirwyn's, just like the men on the boat, just like everyone in this strange land.

"It's… uh, nice to meet you Jesmoré," I whispered. "Help me transition how?"

She grinned, shaking her head. "Call me Jesi. *Yes, si.* Just don't make any jokes about it, trust me, I heard them all by the time I was seven. And you don't know how crass the boys in the Mid-Spire can be. You'd think my mother could have thought it through, but then, if you'd met my mother, you'd see she hardly thinks beyond the day ahead."

Catching my wide-eyed stare at her rambling, Jesi continued, "Anyway, what I mean is, help you learn our way of life. I imagine – I've been *trying* to imagine – what it's like from your perspective. Everything must be a shock to you. Honestly, we're a bit of a shock to mainlanders, even. That's part of the appeal. I'm here because we thought you could use a guide, a friend."

"Who's *'we?'* I don't need any assigned friends."

After I'd said it, I wished I could take the words back. *Idiot. You're not going to get off this island by making enemies.*

Jesi closed her eyes and shook her head, seemingly frustrated with herself. "That didn't come out right. I'm better with swords than words. Let me try again. I'm interested in learning more about you. The thing is, I know what it's like to be an outsider. At High Spire, if you're not a Doreste or a Glinn, you're never really in the inner-circle."

I frowned. Was she trying to help me because she genuinely cared about doing her job well or because she wanted to be a part of some inner-circle and saw me as her entrance? I cocked my head, wondering, *how could I use either to my advantage?*

I didn't know. This was harder than I thought. What irritated me even more was the unwelcome idea that *my mother would know.*

"Who are you then, if not a Doreste or a Glinn?" I asked, skeptically. "What's your second name?"

"Last name," Jesi corrected. "First and last. I'm a Tash. Jesmoré Tash. You won't find my family here, I'm the only one at High Spire. I can't claim to be smarter than Tolas, but I know enough to teach you what you need to know about life here. And I'm very experienced in combat. I can teach you to defend yourself, too. That will be fun. Everyone in Rythas should learn to fight a little, even kings and queens."

"Fight?" I repeated, blinking.

Jesi held up her hands, grinning. "You're not going to become a master. That takes years that you've never had. But I can teach you a little self-defense." Jesi rolled her eyes. "Just don't tell King Grahar. He'd find it unseemly, I'm sure." Jesi looked back at me, intensely. "On Elowa, you were the protected. Here, you must become the protector."

"Where *is* here?" I demanded, fisting the sheet. "I want to see a map. Do you have a map?"

"Oh, we've got plenty."

"Let me see them."

Jesi cocked an eyebrow. "We'd have to go to the library. Don't you want to get cleaned up first?"

"No, I want a map." My pulse sped at the thought.

Jesi folded her arms. "You're having dinner with the Dorestes tonight," she said. "Night's feast, that is. You can't go looking like that. I have to … you have to… be presentable."

My stomach dropped at the idea of dinner, but I replied slowly, "I'll tell you what. You show me a map and I'll clean myself up to be as presentable as you like."

Jesi threw back her head, chuckling. "Are we negotiating?" Her laughter was so deep and infectious, I couldn't help but flash back a *very* nervous smile. She nodded. "Okay, I can take you there. You're going to spend a lot of time in the library anyway. But as soon as we're done, you'll go into a bath."

"Deal," I agreed, my heart beating faster at the promise of holding a map.

"And put on a robe," she said, giving me a pointed look. "I'm not taking you up there in a sheet."

#

I did accept a robe, not unlike a Mystic's garb; though short, like a tunic. Jesi led me up into a tower at the opposite side of the square-ish fortress-castle. More relaxed in her presence, I stopped trying to conceal my gawking at everything we passed and allowed myself to absorb the splendor -- but nothing could prepare me for the library. My mouth fell as I tilted my head back, taking in the towering height of bookshelves lining every wall. Thin windows circled the top of the tower, notched on either side, perhaps as arrowslits. Sunlight beamed through the openings and enchanting dust motes floated in their light like magic sparkles.

How could this exist? Tens of thousands of books in all shapes and colors and sizes; thick tomes overstuffed the shelves and piled high atop the many tables. So many books I could *smell* them. If Tomé ever set foot in the room, he'd never leave. We'd find him asleep in here.

I could finally picture how Kirwyn grew up in a place like this. No wonder he knew so much about everything.

He's got to be alive, I told myself, rubbing the skin over my heart, as if I could clutch the organ, soothe it. *I would know, I'd feel it if he weren't.*

A large, hanging map dominated one wall. My feet carried me over to it as I stared, slack-jawed. "Is this real?" I asked, caressing the giant paper.

"Yes. This is current. Older versions exist over there," Jesi said, indicating another section of the library. I blinked and shook my head, tracing my fingers over the outlines of utterly massive islands. If someone had given me a blank scroll and bid me draw anything I desired, asked that I conceive of such wonders, I still wouldn't have imagined anything like it.

"Where are we?" I breathed.

Jesi came close beside me. "Here." She pointed to a tiny island, at least, tiny compared to the large landforms. "And this is Elowa," she said, pointing to an even smaller one.

Continents, Kirwyn had called them. *No sea monster, no ice wall, no giant waterfall, no tidal pool.* Was everything he said true?

"How can this all exist?" I marveled. "It's so big. It can't be real."

I moved my fingers to the nearest continent, heart pounding. "Is this the mainland?"

"Mm-hm," Jesi hummed.

Kirwyn's home. Anxiously, I scanned the region nearest for a notation of Fort Cuttle, where Kirwyn said he'd been headed before the storm hit his boat, but I couldn't find it. I looked for the other place he mentioned – El Puerto en Blanco. I wasn't sure of the exact spelling, but I didn't see anything close.

"It's a lot, but don't worry. I'll teach you everything you need to know," Jesi said, moving her hand to angrily stab another island nearby. "Most importantly, this is Oxholde." A harsh edge infected her voice and she locked a fiery gaze on me. "This is why we fight. They attack our lands and take our people. Grahar thinks another war is coming and he's right. They've been too quiet lately. They're planning something big. Soon."

Gullbumps ran up my arms. I wobbled over to the nearest chair and sat, head in my hands. War? I knew of war; we'd told tales at the story gatherings of imaginary lands and battles. But I'd never been threatened by such violence before.

Jesi came close and audibly sniffed the air above me. "Look, there's plenty of lessons in store for the future. We couldn't cram it all in one day if we wanted to. We should get back to your room and get you cleaned up."

When I didn't move, Jesi said, "You can come here every day, I promise. In fact, you have to. The king wants you up to speed as quickly as possible. Mornings for reading or court observation, afternoons for exercise or field study throughout High Spire. Then you'll bathe and dine with the royal family each night, keeping the king abreast of your progress."

"And if I don't want to follow this schedule?" I asked, teeth clenched. I didn't like being told what to do, especially not by these people.

Jesi's smile wavered. "We can tweak it if you want to. If you'd rather do more physical things during the mornings and read in the afternoons?"

I sighed and mumbled, "No, it's fine." Honestly, I was dying to get my hands on any of these books. It was a fantasy come true. *And it doesn't matter how I arrange a schedule. None of it will get me off this island. Unless... unless there's something in this library.*

I chewed my lip, unable to get a clear read on Jesi. Would it always be this way, forever? Suspecting secrets and lies behind every word? The gift from my mother and from home?

"Are you marked?" I asked Jesi.

"Marked?"

"Do you have a tattoo on your shoulder?"

"Of course," Jesi replied, sweeping aside her dress to show me. It was the same black image Tolas bore: a crown with a key beneath. The image made me shudder. *Would I be marked too someday?* I didn't want to be branded; I wanted to be a freeborn, like Kirwyn. *Had my aunt been marked when she was sent here?*

"Where is my aunt?" I asked, disappointed when my voice quaked for some reason. "I've never met her. Do you know Alette?"

Jesi blinked rapidly, fluttering long, dark lashes. Her hand reached out to touch my shoulder, but when I flinched, she stopped. "I'm sorry. I didn't know... how much you knew. Alette's here, or she was. Grahar sent her on some mission to the mainland. I know she was reluctant to miss your arrival, but she'll return in a week or two."

I folded my arms and studied Jesi's oval face. She didn't have to bring me to the library, and when she'd tried to console me, it was a spontaneous act of kindness. "Why are you being nice to me?" I probed, wondering if I could *ever* trust again. "Because you were assigned to me or... is it something else you want?" *Are you using me, like everyone else does?*

Jesi sucked in a deep breath, exhaling loudly. "Look. You're right to be suspicious. Not everyone here is your friend. But what I've told you is true. I've been curious about you, and I know what it's like to be an outsider at High Spire. I swear to you, I have no ulterior motive other than helping you learn."

I eyed her suspiciously, "So being the young queen's confidante doesn't come with any benefits?"

Jesi tossed her long hair back and crossed her own arms. "Can you fault me for enjoying that it's a step up and not down? But just because I have ambition doesn't make my friendship insincere."

"That's just what a clever liar would say," I replied, narrowing my eyes and thinking of all the times I'd suspected Kirwyn.

If only I'd listened to you…

Jesi laughed, deep and throaty. "I've never had time for lies. You want honesty? You smell like horseshit. I'm tempted to burn the sheets you already slept in and this robe along with it. And you look as bad as you smell. So let's get back to your room where we can fix both."

#

As Jesi rifled through an antechamber filled with strange clothing, I clung to the edge of my mattress like an anchor, watching the last of the sun's light disappear out the glass-encased windows. I didn't want to have dinner with the young king. That night or any other.

After a bath – similar to my own back home though in a much larger tub - I waited on the bed, trying not to throw up.

How could I escape and find Kirwyn? Sailing to his mainland had to be step one. That's where he'd go. *Unless… he came here, to find me? Did he even know where I was?*

From the closet-room, Jesi carried an old world gown – *new world,* I corrected myself. *Current world.*

"Something pretty for your first dinner. How about the blue?" She held up a long dress of azure, parting down the center to reveal a swath of turquoise, cut from a softer, shinier cloth than the outer layer. Along the bodice, gold and silver stitching decorated the seams. It reminded me of the sea by Queen's Beach where I'd first found Kirwyn, and I bit my lip to keep from crying. What was the point in weeping for home? I didn't want to go back there. It was a land of lies, with family who traded me like the catch of the day.

With Jesi's help, I slid the dress over my head, but it felt like a cage. The garment wasn't ruffled and cumbersome like my wedding gown, but I wasn't used to material grazing my shins and hindering my steps. The thin, almost-sheer strips of cloth parted to allow movement as I walked, but I couldn't help but think it would be easier without material hanging all the way to my ankles, threatening to trip me. What was the point?

"How do you normally style your hair? I'm sure we can do better than when you met the young king this morning," Jesi remarked.

Well, it could hardly be any worse. And I see news travels fast in this castle.

"I don't care if he likes my hair or not," I snapped. "It's fine as it is."

Jesi licked her lips. "We typically wear more ornamentation here. Would you mind if I at least put something in it?"

I shrugged, which was all the encouragement she needed to open a drawer chock-full of sparkling treasures. One alone would be invaluable in Elowa. Jesi secured one side of my hair up with a silver comb not unlike her own and fluffed the rest. When she lifted colored tools, similar to those my mother had used for my wedding, I backed away.

"I do not want to be painted," I insisted. Not for *him,* this boy I never agreed to marry. Catching her grimace, a sudden thought occurred to me. "You're being judged on me, aren't you? On my presentation? I'm your responsibility."

Jesi let out a deep breath. "Kind of."

I sank back into my chair. "Fine. Do whatever you have to do. But I'm doing it for *you,* not *him.*"

I meant it. So far, I didn't dislike Jesi, despite her bluntness. I didn't trust the feeling – yet. But I *wanted* to. If I could get a better read on her, talk to her more, I could pelt her with the million questions swirling around my head and screaming for release. *How many people live here? How was this castle built? Where are the docks?* But for now, I thought it wiser to hold my tongue; to watch and listen. Showing her how much I desperately wanted to know answers to everything gave her power over me. And I needed to claim power, not give more of it away.

Jesi grinned. "I appreciate that. You'll like it. I'm as talented with a brush as I am with a blade."

"And modest, to boot?" I mumbled the quip and Jesi laughed, baring large, white teeth. She seemed to laugh *a lot.*

"Can't be bothered. Much like dishonesty, I've never found it worth my time," she replied, swiping on some powder. As Jesi piled on colors, curiosity got the better of me. *It wouldn't look natural if I didn't ask* some *questions,* I reasoned.

"I'm confused. Are you a servant or a Steel Guard?"

"I'm a warrior," Jesi beamed, unoffended by my question. "I'm part of the palace guard. With Tolas gone, the king thought it better that your closest companion be someone trained to defend you. That I'm good with makeup is a lucky bonus."

"What's it like here? What's the mainland like? I heard-" my voice cracked. I swallowed, then continued. "I heard it's on fire, full of warring clans."

Kirwyn's face floated through my mind and a pang shot across my heart.

Wait for me. I'll find you.

"Sometimes I think it's a miracle we exist amidst all the chaos," Jesi replied, turning my face left and right, to inspect. "Other times I think the truly amazing thing is that no one created more clans like ours before. When the sky is the limit, why did all the cities of the past begin to look the same?" Jesi asked, rhetorically, I assumed. I certainly had no answer. "They'd raze forests and pluck trees and pave roads and it's as if they intentionally wiped the beauty from the land, intentionally sought to distance themselves from anything resembling a state of grace. I don't know how much better things were then than they are now. Less warring clans, for sure, but the life that endured wasn't much worth fighting for. At least, to me. I'd rather live now. Then again, I'm lucky enough to live here."

She turned me around to face a gazing glass much shinier, much more reflective than those I was used to. It was like my wedding day all over again. I was me, transformed into a prettier version of me.

"And you," Jesi declared, "Are lucky enough to be queen."

Not if I can help it.

"Lord, I'm good," she grinned. "You're going to stop hearts tonight."

I rubbed clammy palms against the silken dress, meeting her eyes in the gazing glass. "What's he like?"

"The young king? He's grand. Rythas loves him. I'm sure you will too. He's not at all like his father, he takes after his mother. She died years ago. It doesn't hurt that he's good-looking. No one should have that much power, poise, *and* pretty in one package. Everyone's always known he's to marry you, but I'm sure girls are going to be jealous anyway."

"Are you?" I asked, holding her eyes in the gazing glass.

Jesi chuckled. "Not my type."

"Does he want to... marry me?" I chose my words carefully. The last thing I wanted was everyone watching for me to manipulate him or waiting for me to escape. "We've never even met until today."

Jesi hesitated and her pause intrigued me. "Juls will do what he's expected to do, of course. You could do a lot worse, for a husband. He's, well, everything a king should be."

I stared at my reflection in the gazing glass. Was I everything a queen should be? Certainly, no. Certainly, one of the first requirements should be to love the king.

I love Kirwyn. My heart twisted, remembering his clever green eyes, his soft lips kissing me, his deep voice whispering in my ear...

I took a steadying breath, rising from my chair.

Just as Kirwyn swore no god could keep him from me, I vowed no king could keep *me* from *him.*

Chapter 4

"*The young queen.*"

The man I assumed to be King Grahar greeted me too casually, too jovially. Tall and dark-haired with graying temples, he looked about ten years older than my own parents. Fine lines wrinkled sharp, watchful eyes as he spoke. He was leaner than both my parents but radiated no less power in his rigid carriage. "This is my son, your betrothed, the Young King Jullik."

Sweeping my eyes to Jullik, I again took in the same noble-looking boy I'd encountered in the hall. He was dressed more formally for dinner in a deep purple-red vest of some sort and loose trousers. Like his father, a thin crown rested upon his head. *Yes, pretty,* I thought. Jesi was right; there was something pleasing and majestic about him. Even I could admit that, despite wanting nothing to do with him.

"And this is my other son and Jullik's twin,

Prince Lazlian."

I moved my gaze *up,* taking in the height of a twin who could not be identical. Prince Lazlian resembled his father, right down to the keen, cutting gaze. His brown hair was just slightly shorter and wavier than Jullik's, his cheekbones were higher, and his thin lips became even more crooked with the sneer twitching at the corners. He might not have been any skinnier than his brother, but his height gave him the illusion of a slimmer appearance. Where Jullik's vest remained buttoned to his neck, Lazlian's was unbuttoned halfway down his smooth, brown chest, revealing a long silver necklace, from which dangled a silver key.

Jullik's features might be described as beautiful, but there was something displeasing about Lazlian's face -- and his insolent expression only worsened it. I doubted anyone called him handsome. The sneer he fought to stifle told me he didn't think highly of me either.

You are all my captors, I thought furiously, forcing myself to offer a smile. *I hope war does come to your land. And I hope it takes you from it.*

Grahar pointed to a chair – an order to sit on one side of a long, rectangular table. The king took a seat at one head and Jullik took the other. The sullen-looking Lazlian sat across from me.

Every detail of the room – the tufted chairs, the painted ceiling and tiled floor – was more extravagantly crafted than anything in Elowa. Silver and glassware shone upon the wooden table like a treasure hoard from the First Feet. Unable to restrain myself, my fingers stroked the soft burgundy material of the chair's seat beneath me. All of it was a marvel I longed to share with Tomé.

"I heard you had an eventful journey," King Grahar remarked, breaking the awkward silence with an equally awkward statement.

What did he know, or think *he knew, about Kirwyn?*

I licked my lips to buy time. *Journey?* I wanted to shout. *You mean kidnapping.* I'd been pulled from everything I'd ever known and thrust into a new world. How could it be anything *other* than eventful?

"It's been quite a shock," I replied. My voice, thankfully, remained devoid of venom but I couldn't keep the trepidation from my tone.

It was easier speaking to Jullik alone, than facing off against three older men, all at once. Perhaps the king knew that and purposefully intimidated me in such a manner. Perhaps it didn't even cross his mind. He was difficult to read, and I now knew better than to judge by appearances.

"Do you like what you've seen so far?" Jullik asked, leaning forward on his elbows. His lips turned down in a contemplative frown. "I know you don't have much of a basis of comparison. But do you think you could like it here?"

"I – I..." my heart picked up speed. I didn't want to cause trouble for myself by responding honestly to the loaded question. But every part of me wanted to scream, *no, I don't belong here! Let me go back.*

I plastered a stiff smile on my face and forced myself to say, "I haven't yet seen much of this, um... land... but so far it is very beautiful, my-"

I faltered. *How should I address him? My... betrothed?*

Oh god, what a horrible farce to maintain, to play kind to my kidnappers... and for how long?

"-my young king?" I finished with a question.

Jullik grinned. "Call me Juls, please. Everyone does. As are you as well, I might add." Juls smiled and quickly corrected, "Beautiful, I mean. As you are beautiful, as well."

The compliment came so easily I blinked, studying his face for a lie. But Juls appeared honest, earnest even. From the corner of my vision, I caught Lazlian roll his eyes and I may have even heard a soft snort.

"No need to woo her, brother," Lazlian said, voice laden with contempt. "She has to marry you whether you beguile her or beat her. You don't even have to lay with her after she pops out a few heirs."

Shamed and enraged, my cheeks flamed.

"Lazlian," the king warned, voice low and deep. Lazlian shrugged but said nothing further.

"No one is beating anyone," Juls said sharply, giving his brother an irritated look. His words helped soothe my nerves somewhat, but the fact that we were even having this discussion made my stomach knot. Before the awkward silence could extend, Juls turned to me and changed the subject.

"I'm told you enjoy swimming."

"Everyone enjoys swimming?" It came out like a question because truly, his remark made no sense. I enjoyed breathing, too. What was the point of mentioning it? *Was it different here?*

Juls leaned forward, as if he conspired or shared a secret. "Laz sure doesn't."

Lazlian flashed a smile so false I could see through it from a mile away. "Don't like messing up my hair," he replied.

He's hiding something, I noted, clinging to any information I might be able to use in my favor.

Servants appeared, laying strange foods upon the table. The roast chicken -- skin crisp, golden, and dripping with juices -- was apparent enough. But other meats and vegetables swam in pots of unfamiliar sauces of every color. The smells hit my nose and might have been mouthwatering but for there being so many different ones at once. They overwhelmed me and turned my already-upset stomach. I rubbed the silk of my dress against my sweaty palms, stealing glances at Juls throughout.

This has to be the most awkward meal in history. You want to make me a part of your family and I want you all to disappear forever.

I blinked at an incredibly sharp knife upon the table and my fingers twitched. I could pocket it. Protect myself. *I used to carry a knife when I visited Kirwyn.* I almost cried at the memory. I'd never really had any intention of using it against him, not after the first few days.

But these men -- I could stab one of them now. Not Juls; he seemed too nice, despite his being the best target. But his father, maybe. Would I be sentenced to death, or could I escape somehow?

Maybe I'd be killed on the spot.

Would death be so bad? Worse than this?

I huffed, knowing I'd never do it. I wasn't a killer.

Instead of grabbing the knife, I reached for the closest morsel of food – a fluffy roll -- only to find it heavier than I expected. It must have been stuffed with cheese or paste of some kind.

King Grahar turned to me and asked *much* too casually, "Speaking of heirs, are you fertile yet?"

I nearly choked up the small corner of bread I'd motivated myself to swallow. *Impossibly, things had gotten more awkward.*

"*Father!*" Juls cried out, smacking his hand on his forehead.

"Am I - what?" I sputtered, flushing all over again.

"Have your cycles come about? Elowans are a bit behind the curve in... maturing."

"I- I don't understand," I said, stupidly. I *did* understand, really. I just couldn't believe we were having this conversation.

"He wants to know if you bleed, if your body ripens with the moon," Lazlian interjected, mouth twisted cruelly. "So that he can start breeding you to my brother and get the beautiful grandchild of his dreams." At the last part, Laz held up his glass, as if toasting in celebration.

I felt a fish flop in my gut – both by Lazlian's tone, and, more importantly, the idea of bearing children. *Someone else's children. Not Kirwyn's.* Above all, at *this* point in my life. I wasn't ready for that yet.

My cheeks burned. "I...I..."

Lazlian studied me with narrowed eyes. "She hasn't," he declared.

"Father. Laz," Juls warned, sternly. He looked back and forth between the two men. If the king was insulted by his son admonishing him in such a manner, he didn't show it. He showed very little beneath that steel veneer. "We won't discuss these matters. Zaria is my bride. I will decide when to-"

"Breed her, brother?" Laz offered.

"When to broach such matters," Juls corrected, exasperated. "This isn't appropriate for her. For any of us."

Juls turned to me, smiling stiffly. "I apologize for my brother. We might be accustomed to speaking more freely than Elowans are used to. I know you're more conventional... ah... conservative..."

"She eats insects, Juls," Lazlian scoffed. "And wears the same dirty rags every day. Don't make it sound like they're the proper ones over there."

I slammed my fist on the table, surprising even myself, and shot to my feet. The move certainly wasn't proper, but then, neither was the way Laz spoke. My legs burned with the urge to run out of the room -- though I had no idea where I'd go.

"Insects are plentiful and they're nutritious. Only a fool would eschew their value."

Juls hurriedly rose to his feet, matching me, ready to intervene. King Grahar watched us all calmly, biting into a leg of chicken.

"And I happen to like my tunic. More than this... this... monstrosity I can't even move in!" I slapped my arms against the airy panels of silk, sending them up in a puff of air and letting them float back down softly.

"Are you going to let her talk to you that way throughout your marriage?" Lazlian asked his brother, as if I weren't there.

My heart skipped a beat. I was entirely alone in this strange world. If Juls decided to silence me, to control what I said, what recourse did I have?

To my profound relief, the young king shifted reproachful eyes back to Laz. "Yes. If I've earned it. What I won't allow is for *you* to talk to her that way."

Glancing between the two boys I was suddenly struck with deep gratitude that Juls was the first-born twin; that I was not promised to his dreadful brother, who clearly despised me.

But, landdammit, Laz managed to provoke me when I'd sworn to appear yielding.

"That's enough," Grahar ordered, tiredly. He placed his chicken leg on his plate and raised his cup of wine, taking a sip. "Juls, escort the young queen back to her room. Lazlian, let's try to remember our manners, shall we?"

I stomped out of the room without waiting for Juls, uncaring if I was rude. They certainly were. And I despised these men; why should I concern myself with what they thought of me anyway?

Because you'll never find Kirwyn if you don't

make allies, came the answer. *And it appears you already have an enemy.*

Lazlian's cruel eyes flashed in my mind. They reminded me of a lizard's or some cold, unfeeling creature.

"I apologize," Juls said, darting after me. He offered a dashing grin. "It seems I'm doing an awful lot of that lately."

Halting, I sighed through my nose. *I need him to like me so I can persuade him to let me go.*

"No, I apologize. I shouldn't have stormed out like that. If I'm going to... be queen here... I will control my temper better. I'm just... this is all really... sudden. Please understand that I've been through a lot in the past-"

Day. Oh, Keroe, it had only been one day. This time the night before I'd been reaching out, screaming for Kirwyn across the waves. How had so much changed in so little time?

"I understand," Juls said, smoothing back a section of his dark hair behind his ear. He focused large, brown eyes on me and spoke pointedly. "I think it could be we understand each other in a way no one else does."

I highly doubt that, I thought. But I returned his hopeful grin. *Why did he have to be nice? Why couldn't he be a monster, like Laz?* The more I spoke with Juls, the less I thought I could stab him.

Who was I kidding? I couldn't hurt anyone. Not fatally.

Chivalrously, Juls walked me through the wonderous stone corridors back to my bedroom. But he didn't speak. The journey was just as awkward as our dinner. *Do you even want to marry me? Can you send me back?* My mind screamed the questions so loudly I almost thought he could hear them. Stiffly, Juls deposited me at my door and my stomach dropped when he paused.

Is he going to try to kiss me or something? Instinctively, I pulled back my head.

But he simply said, "Goodnight," then dipped his own head in a cross between a nod and a bow before leaving.

With a sigh of relief, I slipped into my room and closed the door.

I can't do this, I thought. *It's a nightmare come true.*

Faces appeared in my mind. My mother's, Nasero's, Kirwyn's. Out of nowhere, a sob tore through my chest and ripped past my lips. I raced to the nearest window, climbed onto the ledge, and stared into the dark, churning waters below. I looked far out in the distance, as if I could see Kirwyn in the blackness. I looked back down at the rocks. They beckoned, offering a solution.

All this would be over, came the wild thought, *if I jumped.*

My mother would be sorry for what she'd done. No strange prince would ever touch me. I wouldn't be forced to hurt anymore.

So easy. Just let go...

If Kirwyn hadn't made it, maybe we'd be reunited.

But if he had...

But if he hadn't...

My fingers clutched rough stones as I rose into a squatting position. I belonged to the sea. Wild-eyed, I stared at the waves -- dark and churning, swirling and crashing beneath me...

Suddenly, two strong arms snapped tightly around my waist, frightening me so much I almost lost balance and toppled forward.

"Are you crazy, girl?" Jesi cried, yanking me back hard enough to scrape my legs against stone. I hadn't even heard her approach. "Do we need to put bars on your windows?"

"I - no!" I cried.

"What were you thinking?"

"I just-" The tears I'd held back suddenly spilled forth. "I was just sad for a moment, that's all." I sounded pathetic and I hated myself for it.

"You didn't look just sad, you looked suicidal," she growled, easily hauling me back. "Just - get on the bed. Stay there. Don't move."

"I won't," I said, still sobbing as I climbed under the covers. The dam broke and words poured out. "I'm not going to jump. I just miss the sea. I'd feel better if I could swim. I don't... want to be here. Please don't tell anyone."

Curling into a ball under the bedding, I drew my knees to my face and hid, sniffling pathetically.

Jesi was quiet for a moment. "I know," she said, finally. "It's not a secret. Goddamn Grahar. He could have brought you here and let you choose your own nobleman."

"It wouldn't have mattered! I don't want any of them. I – I want someone else."

I instantly regretted the confession. I shouldn't trust Jesi, I shouldn't trust anyone. But I *needed* allies, I couldn't do it all on my own.

Another pause. "So it's true?" she whispered. "I heard there was trouble when they picked you up."

"Can I trust you?" I asked, too desperate to stop the pointless question. No one would ever say 'no.' But I needed someone to talk to and Jesi *felt* safe. I couldn't explain it. "You won't tell anyone?"

"I told you," Jesi sighed, giving me a look with her hooded eyes. "I don't have time for lies. But I'll make you a deal. You can trust me as long as you promise never to do that again. Don't go near that window. Not like that. Deal?"

I rubbed my runny nose, unsure where the strength came from when I quipped softly, "Are we negotiating?" But having Jesi to talk to already felt like a weight off my shoulders. I wanted to confide in her so badly. What was the worst that could happen? The Dorestes already knew the truth.

Jesi sat down on the bed beside me -- near, but not touching.

"Jesi," I quaked, licking a tear off my lips. "There's a boy..."

I told her about Kirwyn, starting with the day I found him on the beach and ending with the shot from Singen's gun. The scattered candles throughout my room burned low by the time I'd finished. Wide-eyed, Jesi took a deep breath and exhaled slowly, as if she'd journeyed alongside me the entire time on Elowa. I stared at her for confirmation that she'd help me, that she'd keep my secrets. Or at the very least, not taunt me about everything I never knew or what Kirwyn and I shared.

It felt like an eternity passed before she let out a low whistle and declared, "Yeah... you're kind of screwed."

For some reason, her bluntness made me laugh, even as new tears sprung. "Yeah, thanks. I don't even understand why I'm *here.* Why me? Why are Elowans different?"

"Mm, it has something to do with your genes. Your ancestors were a part of the OE Program, Optimal Election." She sighed. "I'm not a historian, Tolas would have been much better at this. Alette can tell you everything when she returns." Yawning, Jesi rose. "I won't tell anyone about your boy, but it's late. I need to get to sleep."

I shook my head. "I can't sleep in this strange place."

It wasn't just the Dorestes. It was kidnappers and talk of war and being so alone. I had no choice when I'd been too exhausted to move that morning. But now... with the creeping shadows and otherworldly furnishings... everything seemed poised to attack. The only good thing about my room was I could hear the sea if I opened my windows.

Jesi paused. "Go to bed. I'll stay and sleep on the sofa."

"Thank you, but..." I couldn't help myself from asking again, "why are you being so nice to me?"

"I'm not," Jesi snorted. "It's my job to look after you. Plus, I don't trust that you're not gonna jump out that window. After hearing your story, can't say I blame you. So I'm doing this for me as much as you."

Jesi plopped heavily onto the long, narrow sofa, tufted in cream and painted gold on the edges. I laid my head back upon my fluffy pillow, watching the flame from the last taper flicker and die. It was so late, neither of us had changed our clothes.

"Besides," Jesi spoke into the darkness, "I told you. I know what it's like to be an outsider." She said nothing further and her light snore came minutes later.

Don't cry yourself to sleep, I scolded, alone on the strange bed. *You swore you'd be brave.*

But with no one to watch or judge me, I stared into the darkness for a long while, clutching the sheet and mouthing Kirwyn's name like a prayer.

Chapter 5

"**M**orning, sunshine," Jesi said, sweeping her arms in a wide arc as she dove to the floor, stretching. She'd tied her long curls up and out of the way. I lay abed, shading my eyes against the light. *I don't feel the least bit sunny. I feel like I might be sick. Or scream and never stop. I would like it to rain. Keroe, make it pour today, please.*

"How are you awake this early?" I moaned.

"I've got endless stamina." She smiled, baring her large, white teeth as she lunged into another stretch.

So did I, I thought. *Before. In the sea. If I knew a swim was in my future, I'd get up. Or if he were here, somehow. How many mornings did I wake early and run to my cave, wanting to see Kirwyn and not wanting to admit it?*

"Can we go to the beaches this afternoon?" I asked, dragging my knees to my chest. "Once we're done in the library?"

I'd feel stronger if I could touch the ocean and beg the Sea God for help. Even after all I'd been through... I couldn't help but believe *something* existed down there, beneath the waves. I couldn't deny I felt a special connection to the murky depths.

Abruptly, Jesi stopped stretching. "Actually, I've been instructed not to let you leave High Spire. Not to leave the castle, really. Grahar doesn't know who wants to abduct you, and until we root out the plot, he wants us to stay put."

I groaned, fighting panic. Jesi's words made the castle even more of a cage, closing tighter around me. I'd never escape if I couldn't explore the grounds. I needed to learn where the docks were located, how to operate the strange boats, who guarded them...

Jesi mistook the dread on my face and quickly added, "Don't worry, whoever wants to abduct you isn't competent, at any rate. We've known about their plot to collect ransom money for *months.* That is, moon cycles as you call them."

My heart sank. *You've known but haven't caught them. So how long would I be trapped here?*

"Don't you want to head up to the library anyway?" Jesi suggested. "You'll be free to read. I want to freshen up. You might not be used to makeup, but the rest of us indulge in a morning routine."

Heavily, I slid from the bed. She was right. The smartest thing I could do now was find the location of Fort Cuttle and the library was the best place to start.

#

"I'll only be gone a few minutes, okay?" Jesi said, warily, wanting to slip back to her room to clean up. "You're not going to do anything stupid? There's a guard just outside the door."

I shot her a look, plastering a sarcastic smile on my face. "Books make people smarter, not stupider."

Jesi snorted. "Depends on the book."

I rolled my eyes, fingers itching as I scanned the dark, towering shelves. "I'm fine. I just want to read." *Not cry,* I warned myself. *You will not cry.*

She gave a tight nod and departed. Alone in the cool, fragrant room, I raced to the section Jesi pointed to the day before, the one with old maps. An entire alcove overflowed with books, scrolls, and spare pieces of parchment unlike the dried palm leaves we used in Elowa.

My stomach dropped. *So many.* Why? Landlines didn't change. Did they?

Kirwyn, I thought, grabbing one map after the next and piling them on the floor to peruse. *Where are you?*

#

"I see you like maps," Jesi observed, startling me. *She's good at sneaking up on people.* Then again, I'd gotten lost in all the books surrounding me as she'd taken much longer to prepare for the day than she'd said. Perhaps near an hour had passed. Jesi had donned her usual soldier's garb but restyled her long curls and applied red paint to her lips.

"I just want to understand the world," I sighed, spreading my hands. It wasn't a total lie. I couldn't confess I'd frantically piled books and papers in a circle around me to desperately search for markers that might lead to Kirwyn. But nothing made sense. According to the documents, landlines *did* change and very few bore dates, so I couldn't understand the chronological order to any of it. Regardless, no papers mentioned the places I needed.

"Why isn't it consistent?" I asked, frowning. Elowa didn't shift, not like this. The only cartographic update we'd had in my lifetime was the Felled Tree marker I used in my second pageant.

"Well," Jesi sighed. "This is why Tolas would have been more help." She plopped down on the floor next to me, lifting the closest map. "Ah, okay. This shows old coastlines. Sea levels rose, changing the shape of land, the outlines." She picked up another, cocking her head and grimacing. "This... I don't know. Looks like someone documented clans at one point, but none of these are in existence any longer."

The sea rose? Keroe claiming more for his kingdom?

I pointed to an enclosed section of the library behind a locked steel door. "What's over there?"

"The Forbidden Texts?" she shrugged, disinterested. "Think it's mostly math and science stuff from long ago."

Coquina clams raced up my spine. People didn't lock up things for no reason. *Something to figure out – later.*

I licked my lips, debating whether or not to ask what I really wanted to know.

"Jesi, have you heard of a place called Fort Cuttle?"

"No. Why?"

"I heard... my mother mention it once. I wondered if it had anything to do with Elowa."

Jesi flipped her dark curls over her shoulders, shaking her head.

Here goes nothing. "What about El Puerto en Blanco?"

She laughed. "The Blank Port? How'd you hear about *that?*"

"I... same. I eavesdropped on my mother talking to our High Mystic one day."

It wasn't a very good lie, but Jesi chuckled too much to notice.

"It's a myth," she said. "Like the fountain

of youth. A story parents tell their children at night. A fantasy ship on a mythical dock that carries those who find it to a hidden, southern utopia."

My heart sank, but I argued, "Some thought the First Feet were a myth, too. And not only did they exist, they *still* exist. You're here. This -" I waved my hand around, "is all here."

"True," Jesi agreed. "But as much as I love it here, we're no utopia."

"But this southern place isn't either," I quickly countered. "I heard you're required to provide three years of indentured servitude in exchange for passage."

Jesi stilled. "What else did you hear?"

"That's it, I swear. That's all I know."

Her eyes narrowed. "Don't make my life more difficult, okay Zaria? I'm not trying to make yours more difficult, I'm trying to help. You're a fool if you try to escape. And you're an idiot if you believe in El Puerto en Blanco."

"That's not - I – I -" Suddenly, my stomach growled, saving me from replying. The vulgar sound made Jesi laugh.

"I forgot to feed you. Come on, on your feet," she grinned. "I'll take you to my favorite courtyard. And since we can't leave for... I don't know how long, it's the next best thing to being out and about."

\#

I sucked in a breath as we entered the courtyard; a garden, in the middle of the fortress. One man-made fountain tinkled from its center, flowers climbed the walls – hummingbirds flitting from blossom to blossom – and the ceiling opened up to a bright sky. Providing shade, fruit trees grew wherever I turned, especially those heavy with dangling pink and green mangoes.

"It's enchanting," I gasped, in spite of myself. Ruthless captors were supposed to have dark and dirty dungeons. Not a garden fit for a god. Not a library out of a dream.

Not, I titled my head, studying Jesi, *a friend amongst the strangeness.*

I ran my hands through the cool waters of the tiered fountain while Jesi requested servants bring us refreshments. Under the punishing sun, she tied her hair upon the top of her head and suggested we sit beneath a tree, for shade.

"Strawberry and mint tea," Jesi explained, when a young girl quickly returned with a tray. She poured the cool liquid into little glasses, like our own treasured artifacts from the First Feet. Bright pink cakes lined another tray, dotted with tiny, sugared leaves. Following Jesi, I put one of the leaves in my mouth. It was *incredible.*

"What is this?" I asked, reaching for another.

"Crystallized mint. You've never had it before?"

I shook my head. "I've had candied violets but they weren't this good. This is sweet and refreshing at the same time."

Jesi smiled and took a large gulp of tea. Bees buzzed nearby, lured by the sweets perhaps, and I heard the quiet chirp of colorful birds. Tentatively, I took a bite of one small cake. I'd eaten almost nothing but a crust of bread the night before and my hands nearly shook from the lack of sustenance. But the idea of partaking in food made me fear I'd be condemned to stay in this strange land, like a fairytale I'd once heard.

"It's not poisoned," Jesi snorted, cocking an eyebrow.

Smiling with embarrassment, I shoved the whole thing in my mouth and picked up another spongey, pink cube.

"I've had guava cake before, but it never tasted like this," I remarked. "Everything is so different here... but then, sometimes, it's the same... but different."

Jesi snorted again at my ineloquence. She leaned back against a tree, folding her arms beneath her head.

"I've got good news," she said, "At least, I think you'll see it as such."

Instantly, I raised my guard. I didn't know why. She'd said "good," after all.

"Grahar is having an emergency meeting tonight with the Assembly of Elites in the war tower. That's his advisory council." Jesi shifted, withdrawing the dagger strapped to her waist and toying with its point. "They've received reports that Oxholde is building something, some kind of weapon to attack. So your dinner with the young king has been cancelled."

"Oh." *Good.* "Praise Keroe."

"That's another thing," Jesi said. "We don't worship the Sea God here. Well, we do if it's convenient."

I blinked. "What god do you worship?"

"All of them. None of them. Depends on the situation and who's doing the worshipping. Anyway, you're going to have to get comfortable with the royals before your gala," she advised, noticing the relief upon my face. "There will be a presentation party for you in the next few weeks. Everyone who matters will be invited."

I tried not to groan. I failed.

"A party? But what about this war you said is coming?"

"Don't worry about whatever it is they're doing. Oxholde will attack, they always do, but you're safe here. Nothing can take down High Spire. Not unless the Spades attacked, of course. And the treaty ensures they won't."

Spades. Another clan Kirwyn mentioned -- slavers. They had a treaty with slavers?

"Has there been any news on who killed Tolas?" I asked. "Is it connected to the kidnappers or not?" I'd been thinking it over and it didn't make any sense. If someone wanted to kidnap me, why kill Tolas when Singen was the one with the gun? Unless the archer just shot the first man he saw?

"Could be Oxholde is after you," Jesi mused. "But then, wouldn't they want something more than ransom money? Could be a mid-level family here, but then who'd be so bold? It could be an upstart mainland clan that needs gold, but why not kidnap someone closer to home?"

Jesi stabbed a small cake with her dagger, lifting it to her mouth and taking a bite. "Grahar worries it's a plot within his court, though he can't figure out the motive. You have to understand, his taking you for his son wasn't a popular move. Any family with designs on bringing you into their ranks had their hopes dashed. Any family with schemes to marry one of their daughters to Juls had their plans shattered upon the rocks. Grahar could have made two nobles happy and fostered support among two strong families. Instead, he hoarded it all for himself and pissed off a lot of people."

Though I didn't blame Jesi, I gritted my teeth at the way she spoke of me. A bargaining chip, an offering, a pawn.

Everything I'd vowed not to be any longer.

Maybe I didn't have to be passive…

"Jesi," I asked excitedly, sitting up straighter, "what if we let them?"

"Let who?" she asked, furrowing her brow.

Staring at the babbling fountain, I worked out the plan as I spoke. "What if we let the kidnappers take me. Let them *think* they'd caught me unaware. But really… we'd be laying a trap. Maybe I could pretend to get lost, or we could stage a fight, or I could act as if I'm trying to give you the slip. Create some reason I'd be alone. When in reality, you'd be following close behind. You could watch, track us, and find out where they take me. Then you could rescue me and we could capture *them*."

My heart beat faster. *This,* I thought, *this is the type of cleverness I needed. When I'd vowed to the storm and the sky that I'd outplay everyone -- this is the type of plot I needed to hatch.*

Jesi's already-large eyes bulged out of her head. "You're crazy if you think I'd just let you get captured. You're insane. Do you know what the Dorestes would do to me if they found out I purposely put you in danger? I don't even want to think about it! I can't even think about what they'd do if you were caught on my watch and I'd taken every precaution against it!"

"Well then, let it be my fault!" I argued. "I tell you I have to pee and run away instead. Make you blameless."

Jesi shook her head. "No, no, this is insane.

Stop talking. You're going to get us both killed."

I folded my arms, sinking back with a huff.

After a moment of silence I prodded, eyes glowing with anticipation, "But what if I *don't?* What if it works? Think about it. I'll be free from having to worry about kidnappers -- we all will. And you, Jesi, you'll be the one who saved me, who captured them and rooted out the traitors within the castle. You want to be respected and rewarded with inner-circle privilege? Think about it Jesi."

It was Jesi's turn to fold her arms. "There she is," she declared, mouth forming a tight line.

"There who is?" I asked, confused.

"The Elowan schemer in you. Your mother's daughter." Jesi shook her head, half-smirking, half-scoffing. "Braeni breed for it or something, I swear, and it looks like you know what you're doing. Elowans have a reputation as master manipulators, making everyone in Rythas jump at their command."

"What are you talking about? *You're* manipulating *us.* Rythas sets the rules; our entire island is under *your* thumb!"

"Really? You've got every citizen here in a tizzy for some village weavings or Elowan almonds or some other stuff you send over in tribute boats. You've elevated everything you produce to god-level status, so that all it takes is a boatload of carvings and one Daughter of Elowa and *we're* expending all our resources to protect *you*. Who's manipulating who?"

I closed my gaping mouth, blinking. That... wasn't right. Was it?

"Does that mean you'll help me?" I asked, changing the subject.

"It means I'll think about it."

"Alright," I said, twisting my hair off my sweaty back and knotting it at my neck. "Let's go back to the library then. For tonight, I'm content to spend the rest of the evening reading. I want to know everything there is to know."

Everything that can help me escape this place and find Kirwyn.

Chapter 6

"Only thing worse than a fool bounding for trouble is the bigger fool who follows her," Jesi mumbled, scowling. She walked close beside me, pretending not to notice my wide and wandering eyes as we weaved through the outskirts of a sprawling market.

Three agonizing days of confinement, toiling in the marvelous library or staring at my bedroom walls, helped persuade her to try my plan. But the prospect of glory twinkling in her eyes told me her true motivator. That Rythasian warriors would risk their lives for valor was a concept I was beginning to understand. Each night, Jesi and I dined alone in my chambers - though I couldn't motivate my stomach to tolerate much more than crusty bread – and she slept on my long, elegant sofa.

I didn't see Juls or his family the entire time.

"Look, I *think* I know how we can sneak

out of the castle," Jesi had admitted the night before. "But once we do it, we won't be able to do it again. Meaning, don't make my life difficult, okay?" she commanded, giving me a pointed look. "And it's going to cost a guard his job."

"What do you mean?" I had asked.

"There's a guard named Carrington by the Garden Gate. He's got a crush on Tianca, bad," Jesi had said, flipping her dagger as she spoke. "If we slip him a forged note that she wants to meet asap... I suspect he'll abandon his post and we can slip out. He's already been warned once. He'll be sacked for sure this time. Are you okay with causing someone to lose their job?"

I chewed on that for a minute, squashing rising guilt. "Well, it wouldn't really be *us* causing it. It's his own fault for choosing his crush over duty. And better to expose such a weakness in the guard anyway -- safer for everyone, right?"

Jesi shrugged, "Fair enough."

She was right – it had been surprisingly easy to persuade the guard to abandon his post with her forged note. To be honest, as we slipped through the Garden Gate, I thought more about how this plan cost *me,* than Carrington. *Once I used this out, I couldn't use it again.*

Jesi kept my dress simple and my hair and face partially covered by a white shawl. When we reached the outskirts of the market and hadn't been spotted by any officials, she purposefully tugged strands of blonde hair to poke out at the base of my scarf – a beacon of sorts. Finished, she shook her head and moaned, *"I'm* going to get sacked for this – or worse."

"You've known about this plot for many moon cycles and haven't thwarted it yet," I pointed out, as I'd done so many nights in my chambers. "Do you want to be locked up in that fortress for months on end, in the hopes that something changes?"

As we walked, I purposefully turned my head in all directions, drinking in the boisterous jostle of people, the bizarre market wares, the unfamiliar accents and smells. The sheer variety of body shapes, height, and facial features dazzled me. I longed to tell everyone back home, to shout from the Mystic's dais that we were all being lied to, that wonders beyond our borders existed.

Then again, how many people knew and chose to ignore it?

Finally, I saw Kirwyn's beasts up close. Hairy and majestic with large, glazed eyes. Men and women rode astride their backs, just as he described.

"You look like prey," Jesi observed, eyeing me with a sidelong glance.

"All the more believable that I'd get caught," I returned. We'd gone over this argument *several* times, late into the night. It was why I wanted to do it now, before this so-called presentation party. The fact that I didn't know my way around and the evident truth that everything captivated me only served to make me look like easy quarry. I didn't have to act; High Spire at the height of day sent my pulse racing.

"Lord, what am I doing?" Jesi groaned, closing her eyes. "Making bait of the braenese. I'm going to hang for this."

"It's going to work out. I trust you, Jesi," I insisted. *Maybe not yet with all my secrets, but with my safety,* I thought, eyeing her well-defined biceps and the collection of daggers strapped to her body, some hidden beneath her clothing. Jesi couldn't request a coveted gun without drawing attention to our plan, but she'd come armed to the teeth. And while there hadn't been enough time to train me on using any advanced weaponry, she'd brought out books for me to at least identify the types and styles.

"Don't you trust me?" I asked. I knew she didn't *yet,* but I could tell she wanted something badly enough that "rescuing" me might acquire; money or glory or status within the inner circle.

"Maybe. But it's *them* I don't trust. Not because they're clever, because they're not. Fools make foolish mistakes that could get us all killed. That includes us now too. We're idiots," she grumbled.

I couldn't blame her for second-guessing our plan. She risked much more than I did.

"I know you don't want to be locked up forever in that castle with me," I said. "So we outwit them. This is the first step to freedom."

The first step to finding Kirwyn. Or helping him find me.

Coming to the end of a long, odorous row of stalls hawking familiar fish and other oceanic creatures, I announced loudly, "I have to go to the bathroom."

Jesi refused, shaking her head, while I gestured and argued in return.

"I have to go – now," I insisted, after we carried out our mock-debate for at least a minute.

Narrowing her eyes, Jesi finally pointed toward the trees, motioning long enough to hope someone spied on us. I nodded vigorously. I'd go where she told me. Then I'd run. If Grahar was right and kidnappers lurked just around the corner, I might be lucky enough to get caught. Jesi would secretly follow, from a distance, ambushing the criminals.

Just run, like a rabbit through the wood, I thought. *Easy enough.*

Still, my legs turned to jelly as I ducked beneath the cool canopy of trees, wading into unfamiliar brush. I could hear the sounds of the market, muted under the squawk of birds.

Squatting, I made as if I did what I supposedly came to do, though I nearly fell right into the dirt, balancing on my shaky legs.

Was this an insane plan?

But I couldn't stay locked up in the castle. I'd never find Kirwyn.

My heart rabbited, racing against my chest, pounding to get free.

You can do this, I urged. *You are rather good at getting caught, at least.*

Alright, Zaria... run!

I darted off in the direction opposite the market. Faster and faster, trees a blur, uncaring when branches lashed my skin. I thought only of putting distance between me and that hateful castle and it felt *wonderful.* For a few glorious moments, I didn't care if anyone abducted me or not. I'd already been taken; what worse fate could be in store? I hoped I'd get caught or that I could run forever... until I hit the beach, stole a boat and... well, I didn't know how to work one, but I couldn't think about that now. As my feet pounded the dirt, tears, somewhere between joy and fear, pricked my eyes. I might have grinned like a madwoman.

That's when I heard the hoofbeats.

"Cut her off at the stream!" someone yelled.

I didn't believe it. *Had it worked?*

Thump-thump.

Oh, Keroe, yes. Someone was coming!

But Jesi didn't have a horse-beast. If they took me, she'd have to follow on foot. *Could she?*

Thump-thump. Closer now. I clenched my jaw. Too late. She'd have to track me or...

"Stop!" A large man astride a brown beast darted out, blocking my path as he reared his horse to an abrupt halt. He aimed a crossbow at my head; a weapon I recognized from one of Jesi's books.

I sucked in a breath. *I thought they only wanted ransom money?*

Behind me, another man approached, reaching down to grab me.

"Get on," he demanded.

Stalling, giving Jesi time to catch up, I cried, "Who are you? What do you want?" I didn't fake the terror in my voice.

The man with the crossbow snarled, "We want you to keep your mouth closed and get on the horse." He wore Rythasian clothing, but his accent was unfamiliar. His head was shaved and colorful tattoos crossed his neck and shoulders.

I looked up at the man with the extended hand. I was as petrified of mounting the beast as I was at being taken by these strangers. Like his companion, this man's head was shaved, but he bore no chest markings and he was skinnier, smaller, allowing more room on a horse.

"Do as we say and we won't hurt you," he

promised.

"Or don't and get shot," the bulkier man added, gruffly.

"Don't shoot me," I pled. *Where was Jesi?* Unable to stall any longer, I reached for the extended hand. The smaller man yanked me up onto the horse's back -- with inelegant wiggling and adjustments on my inexperienced part. Once righted, we took off and I was torn between feeling disgusted at being pressed so close to my abductor and terrified at the breakneck speed at which we rode. Despite both, mad-like exhilaration shot through my chest as I watched the trees fly by.

Maybe I'll fall off and die or maybe they are going to kill me.

My only regret was that my dying would endanger Jesi.

Landdammit. My escape plan definitely had a flaw. I didn't owe Jesi my allegiance, but I liked her. If I ran away, how would the Dorestes punish her?

The long game, Zaria. Play the long game, came the answer.

#

So much pungent malodor assaulted my nose, I couldn't distinguish the stench of man from horse. The farther we rode, the more fear knotted my stomach. *Would Jesi find us?* Finally, a dilapidated shack appeared, half-hidden by overgrowth. The large, bald man halted his horse and dismounted.

"Where are you taking me?" I demanded, déjà vu washing over me. "Who are you?"

No, not a feeling. This *did* happen already. I'd asked these same questions of a different set of strange men only days before. Mad giggles burst through my lips. *Was this my fate, to get kidnapped over and over, eternally?* Once the maniacal laughter started, it wouldn't stop, even as the man helped me off the horse, giving me a quizzical look. The stranger's touch burned my skin, but I laughed through it. Only ducking under the splintered doorway into the shadowy, spider-webbed shack sobered me.

No, I told myself sharply. This time *was* different. This time, *I* was in control.

As long as Jesi tracked us.

I gulped, catching shiny, black bugs darting under floorboards too quickly for me to identify. The shack contained a table and two chairs so splintered I wondered how they stood upright.

"Sit," the large man with the crossbow ordered. "We're taking a two-minute break, that's all." He raised his chin in the direction of the other man. "Get what we need."

Slowly, I sat, but only because I wanted to reserve my strength. I watched the skinny man busy himself with rummaging through bags, stuffing food and water into a faded, green sack. *Supplies. We were headed somewhere, maybe far. Was two minutes enough time for Jesi to find me?*

Only if she'd ridden a horse as well. She would have had to borrow or steal one, I reasoned.

"Did you kill Tolas?" I whispered, reaching for any conversation to stall our departure.

"Who?" came the gruff reply from the tattooed man.

"My... guard. From the beach."

"We haven't killed anyone," the skinnier man said, firmly.

"'Cept we might kill you if you try to run away," the larger man added.

Would he? Maybe. The smaller man seemed less inclined to murder... but the gleam in this one's eye told me he liked violence.

Did he notice me noticing? Was there a tantalizing fear in my own expression? As I stared, it was as if something caught his attention and motivated him to stalk toward me. I didn't like his hungry look. I leapt from the chair and backed away.

"What are you doing?" I demanded.

"She came to us too easy," the large, bald man said, speaking to his companion and not me. "How do we know it's her and not a decoy?"

"Have you ever seen a girl who looks like that before?" the first man cried. "How would they get a decoy to look like an Elowan princess?

Look at her!"

"I am looking," the man stalking toward me replied. "I want to look more."

My knees momentarily buckled; I didn't mistake the threat in his words. *What had I got myself into?*

Mind racing, chest heaving, I backed away until I hit the wall. "You said you weren't going to hurt me," I reminded him.

Don't touch me. If you touch me, I'll scream, I'll kill you. I searched the shack for a weapon, but only the tattooed man held anything I could use. No, even if I got my hands on the crossbow, I didn't know how to work it.

"Stop it," the skinny man across the room warned. There was too much pleading in his voice to comfort me. "You know we're not supposed to touch her."

"But no one said we couldn't *look*," the larger man countered, stalking closer.

I pressed into the wall of the old shack, blood roaring in my ears. My muscles coiled. I'd fight, even though I knew I couldn't overpower him. *I'll go down fighting.*

The *slam* made my eyes pop open – I hadn't even realized I'd closed them.

Jesi.

Everything happened rapidly; she'd burst into the room and thrown her dagger at the man. He was faster than he looked – she only struck his arm, sending the crossbow clattering to the floor as he grunted and ducked. Jesi threw a second dagger but it missed, embedding into the wall behind him. Quick and smooth as a fish darting under water, the man bent down, retrieving the weapon and pointing it at her, forcing Jesi to half-hide behind the flimsy, swaying door before she could grab another dagger.

A tidal wave of hysteria rose in my chest. I had no time to think or do anything except throw myself in front of Jesi on the wild hope that the tattooed man wouldn't shoot me. I squealed involuntarily, closing my eyes again as I used my body to shield her –

When the bolt didn't hit, when the man hesitated, I popped my eyes open.

I hadn't been shot. I acted almost without thinking again when I lunged at my abductor in a desperate gamble that he didn't want to hurt *me.*

Though he might be provoked to kill me to defend himself...

...Not a heartbeat later I slammed into his solid torso.

I took the fearsome man down to the floor only because he was thrown off-balance in trying to hold the crossbow, to not injure me, and to defend himself all at the same time. I yelped as my elbow hit something hard and my knees banged the floor.

Before we could struggle, Jesi swooped

beside me, tearing the crossbow from my abductor's hands and plunging her dagger into his heart with deadly force. Another dagger into his throat quickly followed. Blood sputtered from his open mouth. Still half entangled with the man, I made a noise resembling a gasp and a gag, pushing myself off him.

In a flash, Jesi's left arm shot up, aiming the crossbow at the remaining, quaking man in the corner. To my shock, her other hand seized my throat and squeezed. Wide-eyed, I clutched at her fingers but couldn't dislodge her grip.

"What the hell were you thinking?" she demanded, keeping her eyes on the man in the corner. "Do that again and I'll kill you myself!"

Before I could attempt some fumbling response that I was saving her life, she released me, bringing both hands to her weapon and shouting at the shaking man, "Don't move!"

The thin man didn't listen. He lunged for something I couldn't see and Jesi let an arrow fly. Aiming low, she intentionally hit his thigh and he fell with a yelp.

But he didn't stop. The man's fingers quickly unflapped his bag, withdrawing something small and dark.

I froze, recognizing a gun.

This time, Jesi angled herself in front of me, aiming the crossbow at our assailant.

If he tried to shoot us, she'd shoot him.

Stalemate.

Or so I thought.

"I'm not going to hurt her," he wheezed. Sweat glistened on his face. "We were never going to hurt her."

"Didn't look like that to me," Jesi shot back with a deadly calm – calm I certainly didn't feel. In fact, the room started to spin.

The man's finger moved – tightening on the trigger mechanism?

"Don't be a fool," Jesi snarled. "The rest of the guard is minutes away. You can't escape us. Put down the gun."

The man blanched at the news. His gaze shifted to mine, giving me a long look, conflict raging in his eyes. "I wouldn't have hurt you," he swore.

Then, quick as lightning, he brought the gun to his own head and fired. A shot rang out – I was sure it could be heard for miles – as blood and brains splattered the wall to his left.

I screamed. It wasn't like seeing someone hit with an arrow. Not even close.

"What the hell!" Jesi cried. "What the…"

I kept screaming.

"Calm down," Jesi ordered, gripping my shoulders. "Zaria, you have to calm down, okay?"

"Oh my god!" I babbled, still shrieking and shaking all over. "Oh my god, oh my god."

Jesi flung the crossbow to the floor, charging

to the body. "Dammit. There's no one left to question. Either he was hiding something he'd die to protect, or he didn't want to be tortured. *Dammit.* We needed him alive."

"Tortured?" I whispered, between sobs.

Jesi bent down, examining his grotesque corpse. "You know a better way to get someone to talk? I had to make the threat; I didn't have a choice. He would have shot me and taken you." She cocked her head. "How'd they get a gun? They must have ties to someone powerful. At least this will help us trace it back."

Standing, she toed the body with her foot. "Dammit. I hope this didn't come from inside. Grahar might be more paranoid than ever," Jesi groaned, then clicked her tongue. "Maybe it ends here. They're not from Rythas anyway."

Snapping her gaze back to me, she pointed. "You're my responsibility, understand? You throw yourself in front of me like that again and *I* will kill you."

"I-"

Jesi cocked her head, eyes hard. "Or do you have a death wish?"

I stilled. Her question hit me in my gut. "I don't know," I breathed. *Did I? Could she blame me?*

"Come on," she huffed. "We've got to get back to High Spire and report this. You okay to ride?"

I nodded, despite my racing heart. I'd make myself be. I wanted to put distance between me and the shack as quickly as possible.

Chapter 7

We almost died.

Jesi killed my kidnappers instead.

And I didn't know if we'd be praised or punished.

It was insanity. But we'd pulled it off.

We rode through thick forest back to High Spire on the horse she borrowed to track me. Jesi and I spoke little, save the few times she asked if I was okay. Jesi took up more room in the saddle and she sat forward, requiring me to hold on behind her. I feared I'd fall aft, but I'd ride with her any day over either of those men. As soon as we made it back to the Garden Gate, commotion erupted. I'd been noticed missing. Guards – some angry and some relieved – separated Jesi and I. I was shown to my room to be examined by the healer and palace officials pulled Jesi to give a report.

Every time I closed my eyes, I saw the

grotesque image of the man's shattered head. I yearned for the privacy to bathe myself, but after the healer finished treating the cuts from my tree-lashing, other men and women invaded my room, this time to ask endless questions about my feelings, to make sure I wasn't traumatized by what had happened -- all without a hint of irony.

I'm no more traumatized now than by being here in the first place, I wanted to laugh, but I knew where that would get me. Thankfully, Jesi shooed them away when she returned, several hours later.

"What happened?" I asked, shooting to my feet.

She grinned, plopping into a chair and tossing one leg over the arm. "They're docking my wages which means I'll have less money to send home to my family, but I won't serve jail time and I'll probably get promoted."

I wrinkled my nose. "That doesn't make any sense."

"It doesn't have to, it's the law," she shrugged. "There's some command on the books about reduced pay for insubordination or something. Regardless of how what we did benefited everyone, rules are rules." Jesi's eyebrows rose. "Anyway, I've caught Navere's eye. He was promoted to Commander of the Guard last year and hasn't chosen his first, second, and third yet. Said he wants to watch us for a while before making any decisions."

"Jesi, that's great. I think."

"Plus, you're free to move about a bit more, now that we've caught your abductors."

"But what about whoever killed Tolas? They said they weren't behind it."

Jesi snorted, "And you believe them?"

I opened my mouth. I closed it.

"Navere thinks they're one and the same. If you prefer to convince him otherwise, be my guest. But you'll be jeopardizing your own freedom."

I shook my head.

"Anyway, Grahar isn't pleased with me but he's actually angrier at you, suspects you were behind it. Don't get on his bad side, Zaria. That's not a place you want to be."

I pursed my lips, looking down. She had a point. Playing a sweet, besotted braenese would be a better ploy, moving forward.

"Your dinners were to resume tonight, though you've now been excused on the pretense that you're recovering. *But,*" Jesi circled her finger as she pointed, "I think Juls wants to have dinner with you alone, to save you from his father's wrath."

"Alone?" I coughed. Sweat dampened my forehead, my armpits. "What?"

Jesi nodded, pointing downward. "Here. He's coming to your room tonight for a private meal."

I collapsed onto the enormous bed. Hadn't I been through enough for one day?

#

Clad in a silken pink dress with a golden bodice, I awaited the young king about as eagerly as I'd await an execution. The dress was pretty and not too provocative, save the loose pink straps hanging down my arms as if I'd just been ravished or was expecting to be. Jesi fixed a golden clip in the shape of a flower into my hair.

"You look gorgeous and you're about to have dinner with the future king," she chided. "Why do you stare as if you're facing oncoming doom?"

"You know why."

"I do. But I'm just reminding you that a thousand girls would kill to take your place. And nothing bad is going to happen tonight. It's just dinner. Juls is a good man, gentle."

Then why is he forcing me to marry him?

Servants came as night fell, lighting tapers around my moonlit room. Someone pushed the window wider, allowing the sea breeze and the briny scent of the ocean to float into the air. I shifted uncomfortably in my chair at the intimate, romantic set-up.

Jesi left me alone to wait, and I didn't have long before I heard the knock on my door.

At least he knocks, I mused. That was a good

sign.

Juls strode into my chambers, followed by four servants carrying large, silver trays. He wore a deep red tunic-vest and pants, similar to the last time I'd seen him, but with a different swirling design stitched beside the gold-ribbon trim. Leather sandals, not unlike an Elowan's, completed his attire. He didn't wear his crown or tie back his hair; it fell loosely just past his ears.

"Are you here because I'm in trouble?" I asked, bluntly.

Juls seemed taken aback by my question, eyes shifting to the servants. But he smiled. "My father isn't pleased that you put yourself in danger. I thought it best to let him calm down."

We stood awkwardly facing one another and I wondered what I was supposed to say or do. Did captives here often dine casually with their captors? Or was I a special case?

As servants laid the silver trays upon my bedroom table, Juls walked forward to eat, so I did the same. But even sitting alone with him, my mind warred with itself. How could I feign acceptance of this absurd marriage when every part of my body wanted to scream – *this is preposterous. We don't even know each other. I don't want to be here. Send me back.*

I forgot my schemes for a moment when the servants lifted the lids on the trays and I gaped at enough food to feed several families. Up until then, I'd dined mostly on bread and water, maybe a few sea grapes or those little guava cakes, if I felt weak.

"I didn't know what you liked so I brought everything the kitchens prepared today," Juls announced.

"What *is* all this?"

He began pointing and describing with authority each dish around the table. Only the oysters and spiced monkfish were familiar.

"What's that?" I asked, gesturing to large, brown slabs.

A perplexed expression crossed Juls's face, then he smiled. "Steak. Beefsteak. From mainland cows."

I shook my head, shrugging. Something else to look up.

He cut a piece of beefsteak and served me. "Try it," he urged, as if it were a normal occurrence for the future king to feed a –

-- *stranger*, I wanted to finish. But I wasn't just a stranger, was I? I was his bride.

I balled my hands into fists to stop from covering my eyes at the thought. But desperate, even crazier ideas followed. Once again, very sharp knives had been placed upon the table and my frenzied mind fantasized.

What if I grabbed one and sliced my own throat? What if I held one to his throat? Demanded release or threatened to kill the young king? What if I stabbed his neck, as I'd seen Jesi do earlier?

My gaze fell upon the column of Juls's long neck, searching for a vein. I watched his Adam's apple bob as he swallowed. I noted the dark hair grazing just below his ears.

After a moment, my eyes jerked abruptly to his, realizing Juls stared at me as intently as I stared at him. *Because I'm thinking about killing you,* I wanted to shout at the curiosity I read in his gaze. *Not because I'm attracted to you.*

Distracting myself from my flaming cheeks, I grabbed the silver fork provided to spear the beefsteak. My eyes widened when it touched my tongue and Juls gave a low laugh.

"This is amazing," I gushed, almost before I'd finished chewing.

Then, for the first time since I'd arrived – for the first time since my sham of a wedding feast -- I dug into a meal. Once I broke the dam by swallowing that divine piece of meat, I eagerly scooped up a little of everything until my plate was covered in glazed vegetables and green sauces and crispy, fried orbs of some kind. I nibbled pinkish rice with something called Huckleberry Dove. Everything was new, different, right down to the water which tasted of more minerals than our own.

After a few minutes, I noticed Juls's stillness. I froze, fork mid-air. "You're not eating."

"I'm watching you." His brown eyes danced.

I dropped my fork and sat back abruptly.

"Don't."

He cocked a one-sided grin. "Do I make you nervous?"

"No. Yes." I scoffed, "Who wouldn't be with someone staring at them while they ate?"

Juls leaned forward, his thick, glossy hair swaying with the act. A smile still played at his full lips. I noticed he had long, dark lashes. "Would it make you less nervous if I told you that you make me nervous too? You're very beautiful, you know."

I let out a sound that reminded me of the horses in the marketplace. "You're difficult to dislike."

He tilted his head, but the grin hadn't faded. "Are you determined to dislike me?"

I looked at my lap, blushing, then *immediately* scowled at myself. I was being forced into an arranged marriage everyone curiously refused to talk about. Wasn't it only natural I wanted to rip him and his family to pieces? Wasn't that the normal reaction? What right did he have to think I'd be persuaded to love him? A king's right?

A king's arrogance was more like it.

"Your brother is determined to dislike me," I lobbed. Lazlian's calculating glare flashed so strongly in my mind, I shivered at the memory.

"He's just over-protective," Juls said. "Takes on the older brother role."

"But you're the older brother," I said. "Jesi

instructed me on how it works here." *First-born girls aren't sent away in marriage bargains,* I thought. But I only repeated, "Unlike Elowa, females don't inherit the crown and you're the heir."

"Right." Juls's grin faded at the edges. "By a few minutes only."

A silence descended between us, and I couldn't determine what to make of it.

"We'll return to formal dinners soon," Juls said, taking a sip of water. "I can't save you from my father every night."

While delivered in jest, his words made me shudder. Juls noticed and quickly began talking, launching into a lecture on the inner workings of High Spire. The guards and servants weren't too different from our own, though they had modern weaponry – although, according to Juls, not enough. The noble elites were a lot like our Braeni. But the rest of the island thrived with a complexity and density unlike anything imaginable on Elowa.

"Long ago, we were like a Noah's Ark," Juls explained. At my blank stare, he clarified, "People fled the mainland and came here, bringing their various cultures with them. The more educated claimed the best land and the loftiest positions alongside Osvaldo. Those who fled the mainland wars without highly-coveted skills or knowledge were given safety and offered training to help build all this," he waved his hand. "Towns, farms, High Spire itself."

"Do people still flee the mainland to come here?" I asked.

Juls shook his head. "Not to live. We're not as secreted as Elowa, but only those who can afford it journey here. Their visitations are a helpful booster to the economy. You'll learn all about it, in time."

"What about the men who tried to abduct me today? Who are they? Did they come from somewhere else?"

"Yes. And the good news is, that means we don't think it's a plot from within. As long as you stay with Jesi, you'll be able to leave the castle. Swim," he smiled encouragingly.

"And bad news?" I probed.

Juls winced, twirling the stem of a wine glass. "We'll need to tighten security at the docks, as well as visitor restrictions."

Oh no. Meaning escaping to find Kirwyn will be even harder. Or having him sneak in to find me, somehow. If he's… alive.

Frustrated more than ever at the notion, I asked the embarrassing question everyone seemed to dance around. "When are we expected to… marry?"

"That's up to my father," Juls answered.

"But – you're the groom."

"He's the king."

A knock on the door suddenly sounded,

interrupting us.

"It's late," Juls declared, rising. "I should leave you to rest. Do you need the doctor – that is, the healer -- to return?"

Shaking my head, I stood, toying with the skirt of my dress. Painful awkwardness descended once more, and quickly. I reminded myself that I needed Juls to be on my side if I ever hoped for his help.

"Thank you for the incredible meal," I said, following the young king as he walked to my door. "I mean, the food."

That didn't come out right. "Not that it wasn't nice to talk – it was. I just mean I'd never had food like that before. I mean-" I sighed at my own babbling, closing my eyes. I opened them. "Is this..." *What you want?* I longed to cry. But it didn't feel, strategically, like the right question. "This is strange, isn't it?" I asked instead, smiling with what I hoped was a charming smile.

"Yes," Juls chuckled, turning to me. "But we're not doing so bad, are we?" he asked.

Whatever he read in my face caused his smile to fade. Another tense second passed. "Do you think you'll be well enough to dine with my family tomorrow?" he asked.

"I don't see why not," I replied.

Juls nodded curtly and reached for my door handle. He paused, turning back, as if he wanted to say something. For a moment my heart pounded, wondering if he'd ask me if any of this was what I wanted.

Should I answer honestly? Which was better to help me escape?

But then he changed his mind and quickly left.

I stared after him, my stomach tingling with a peculiar twinge as sweat broke out on my brow. I wondered if the weird feeling was due to conflicting emotions arising from my not *entirely* hating Juls, warring with my simmering desire to knife him and everyone in the castle.

I was very wrong.

Chapter 8

Darkness enveloped my bedroom when I woke, my throat sore and scratchy.

What time is it? I wondered.

My head felt heavy; perhaps the start of a headache long overdue from one shock after the next over the last few days. Tossing onto my side, I tried to fall back asleep, but I ached everywhere.

Am I getting sick? My hand flew to my throat. *Yes, I think I am.*

As soon as I acknowledged it, it was as if the pain worsened. Or maybe it was me shaking off the vestiges of sleepiness. *What do I do?* At home, I'd call for Maz, my mom, or one of the other servants. But here... I didn't know these people. Who would I disturb in the middle of the night? Not Jesi. She'd watched over me the past four nights and after all we'd been through, she needed sleep.

Groaning, I sat up in bed, realizing I'd soaked the sheets with sweat.

I feel awful, I thought, dragging my knees to my chest and dropping my head onto them. *I'll just wait... wait until dawn... until someone comes into my room...*

#

"Zaria!" Jesi shouted. "Zaria, what's wrong?"

My eyelids protested at being opened, but I looked up at her from my position on the floor. The cool tile felt better, though I didn't remember when I'd pitched myself onto it. It also felt steadier somehow, less prone to shaking or spinning. *Yes, the floor is good,* I thought. *I'll stay here.*

"Zaria!" Jesi cried, pulling me back to reality.

"I don't feel so good," I croaked, closing my eyes again.

"Selcony!" Jesi cried. "Help! We need some help in here!"

A few moments later, I felt strong hands lifting me by my ankles and under my arms, carefully placing me back into my bed.

"Stop," I groaned. The motion made me want to throw up. I flopped like a fish to pitch myself back onto the cool floor, but I didn't have the strength. "I need a healer."

Jesi's cool hand touched my forehead, "My god, Zaria, you're burning up. Don't worry, the doctor is coming."

"Mmm…" I groaned, drifting off into blissful sleep.

#

Agony, *much* worse than before, hit me like a full-body slam the moment I awoke. My throat felt as if knives had scraped a path up and down the lining of my esophagus, then wedged themselves into the soft tissue, so that every swallow, every breath brought searing pain. My head throbbed as if someone had smacked the butt of a sword against it. My body burned like raging fires lit from within. And my stomach, *oh my stomach!* Unable to lift my head, I retched onto the pillow beside me, dribble hanging off my chin.

Deep, horrid groans sounded from my throat. Another time, I might have been embarrassed at the noise, but I was far from caring now.

"Where is the doctor?" someone cried. I must have only been out for a few minutes or the healer was very far away.

"He's coming, he'll be here soon!" someone else urgently swore.

I no longer cared if he came.

I no longer cared if I lived or died.

No, that was a lie. It hurt so badly – the betrayal from my family, losing Kirwyn, being forced into a marriage I did not want and now this sudden, excruciating torture in every part of my body... as ashamed as I was to admit it, I *did* care.

Because a part of me didn't *want* to live anymore.

#

Consciousness returned. Consciousness faded. I liked it better when it faded, liked the place of not feeling. No pain. Neither physically, nor the wretched agony in my heart, longing for Kirwyn's embrace. Hours may have passed, or days, I couldn't tell.

"She needs hydration," an authoritative voice ordered. "Pull whatever we've got. All of the reserves. Spade medications, anything Mal-Yin's smuggled in. Don't guess, just grab. I'll sort it out up here."

"What does she have?" someone whispered. "Food poisoning?"

"What *doesn't* she have?" the strong voice replied. "Food poisoning is likely the least of it. Did you inoculate her at all before bringing her here?"

Inoculate me? What did that mean?

I had no time to speculate when a sharp jab pierced my arm. I didn't like it, didn't want it invading my tender flesh. I hated blood, pain... the image made me woozy, I couldn't hold on...

Blissful darkness rose, like the black waves at night, washing over me again.

#

More hour-days passed. I tried not to feel them, tried not to exist, but agonizing, unwanted consciousness forced itself upon me more frequently. Sometimes cool rags pressed to my head, my cheeks, wiping sweat and bile from my face.

"If she dies... she can't," I heard someone say. "She *can't* die."

Thanks for discussing my death while I'm lying here on the brink of it. Sorry to disappoint you but I can, and in fact, may depart this world tonight.

The thought had appeal. I wouldn't have to marry this young king and I wouldn't even have to jump to the rocks. Death could carry me out right from the discomfort of my own bed.

"If we lose her... The other one is too young to marry. She can't give Juls heirs for another sixteen years at best. The king will never stand for it. This one's gotta live."

In my pain-addled fog, I didn't comprehend what the men were saying.

"Maybe if we bring her here, she'll mature earlier. Twelve, maybe thirteen? She could marry the young king in a decade if we're lucky."

Oh my god.

Jona. They're talking about Jona.

Even in my fevered state, my blood ran cold. My eyes popped open as I understood.

If I died, they'd take my baby sister in my place.

How... why didn't I think of that before? I was such a fool. I'd missed the obvious again, not understanding the scope of potential events; how all-encompassing and far-reaching consequences could be.

All revolving around me. Whether I lived or died.

My stomach churned. I was going to be sick again.

Sweet, innocent Jona. They'd make her go through a wedding charade and trade her to the Dorestes in my place. My baby sister.

Never. *Never.*

"Is she as pretty as this one?" a voice asked.

"How would I know? She's a baby."

I swallowed back my own vomit.

I couldn't let that happen. Gnashing my teeth, I narrowed my eyes at the dark corner of the room, as if I stared down death itself. Nostrils flaring, I vowed I'd *live.* My chest rose and fell in heavy breaths I tried to still, to not alert whoever spoke that I listened.

I won't let them take her, I swore.

My heart sank as another horrible realization struck.

Oh god. I'd never be free.

Even if I escaped, I'd condemn my baby sister to take my place. And even if I found a way to smuggle her out of Elowa, what then? Who'd be sacrificed next? A cousin? Another child of my mother's? The cycle would repeat, this generation and the next.

I whimpered softly, hoping no one heard. *Escape wasn't enough.* Rythas needed to stop taking brides from Elowa. Or Elowa needed to stop giving them. *Both.* It was so much larger than *me.* And not an endeavor in which I could possibly succeed, at least not alone. I couldn't change a clan, a country. Not *one,* let alone *two.*

I closed my eyes, focusing. If the problem was bigger than me; the solution, if there was one, would have to be as well.

What did I have? What did I possess that would help me or even qualify as an asset?

Nothing. I had no skills, no allies, no power, no fortune. I hardly even possessed any knowledge of the way the world worked.

Groaning softly, I wanted so badly to just give up and give in, to let the pain sweep through me and carry me away into the night.

But I saw her in my mind's eye. Jona's bouncy blonde curls, her drool-covered smile, her tinkling baby laugh, her tiny hands reaching up to hold me... that image was the only thing keeping me anchored. Jona, and girls who would come after her. I was all that stood between them and a dire fate.

"We're out of ivies," a voice suddenly said, coming close enough to touch the crook of my arm.

Was that some kind of plant-based medication,

I wondered? *But no.* Someone had wedged a permanent needle into my skin. I fought the instant shiver.

The men resumed talking about medications I didn't understand. I no longer cared. They didn't matter -- these guards or servants or doctors or whoever was in my room. They weren't going to make decisions for me, and I had bigger plans now. *Much* bigger.

I had no idea how to execute them. But everything hinged on the first step: staying alive.

I cleared my throat, forcing myself to sit up despite the spinning room. The men leapt back in surprise.

"Water," I croaked. "I'd like a glass of water."

"You're awake," a familiar voice sang.

Jesi. She was in the room, too? Focusing my vison, I caught her emerging from the far corner of my chambers. She'd been there the whole time, quiet and still enough to be a part of the furniture.

"How do you feel?" she asked, quickly closing the distance between us.

"Like one of those horse-beasts stomped all over me."

Jesi laughed, "That's good. You're making jokes. Bad ones."

Her strong, cool hand pressed to my forehead.

"I have good news. Your Aunt Alette is sailing back from the mainland soon. She's eager to see you."

Chapter 9

Anytime I opened my eyes, I saw her. Pacing the room or running through more push-ups or sit-ups than I believed a person capable. Other times, Jesi awaited on the bed itself, as if she knew I'd stir any moment.

Her presence and the stay it gave me -- the time to rest in bed and adjust -- almost made near-dying worth it. I wasn't forced to bungle through strange customs or uncomfortable dinners with the Dorestes. I'd been granted a reprieve.

Whatever Jesi brought to read that day, I listened to with rapt attention. *Knowledge is my power, my passage,* I repeated. As I convalesced, a plan formed in my mind.

Step one – soak up as much information as I could about the world and the ruling classes of Rythas.

Step two -- save myself. *By escaping? By*

pretending to go along with marrying the young king? I wasn't sure.

Step three -- find Kirwyn. *By getting off Rythas? How? Should I stay put in case he finds me first?*

Step four -- save everyone else. *By negotiating? By making allies?*

Another girl, a better girl, might have considered that sacrificing herself by going through with the wedding might be the strongest course of action. That with the power of being queen, she could find a way to save future generations.

If I hadn't met Kirwyn, I might have even been that self-sacrificing girl.

I wasn't any longer.

Unless... if Kirwyn had died... I didn't know what I was or what I'd do.

"More," I demanded late one night, after Jesi carried maps by the armful into my bed, spreading out each one on the covers before me. Never did I find Fort Cuttle or El Puerto en Blanco, but I studied clan territories, heart skipping beats whenever I hit a name Kirwyn mentioned.

Copperheads, Biohazards, Blackjacks.

"They mostly go by Spades now," Jesi corrected, shoving a book with pictures of Spade City under my bent head.

My fingers traced drawings of buildings taller than High Spire, sleek and shining; roads wide and smooth, and bodies crowding every corner.

And slaves.

I shuddered at the images. Backs of people marked with large "X's," just as Kirwyn said. I swallowed the lump in my throat. *If I had believed you, would we be together now?*

"Spades are monsters," I spat. "I don't ever want to go anywhere near their territory."

"Don't worry, we've got the treaty. They don't attack us," Jesi said, tossing one leg over the side of the sofa and wrinkling her nose. "They don't stop Oxholde from attacking us either though, and they're slavers too. Those heathens are coming any day now. I just hope I get the chance to kill enough of them before the battle's over. I've *got* to be in consideration for the top three now, and Navere will make me his first if I prove myself."

Jesi laid back to sleep on the sofa, still dressed. She fell asleep so quickly and easily it hardly mattered. I read until the bedside candle flickered out and died. Then I stared up at my moonlit windows, picturing Kirwyn's face.

Where are you? I asked into the darkness. *Do you forgive me? Are you coming for me?*

The question I couldn't ignore, the one that haunted me at night, surfaced.

Are you still alive?

#

Two guards trailed behind us as Jesi and I braved the outer roads of High Spire, heading toward the pleasure gardens. I'd been given a stay for Doreste dinners once more, as Grahar didn't want his son anywhere near me until he was certain I proved non-contagious.

Perhaps I needed to be ill more often.

I'd dressed for the day in the clothes Jesi chose: a simple green shift, soft and silken like all the dresses here. An ornamental collar rested atop, fastening around my neck and spanning my chest in a cross between a necklace and a breastplate, though certainly not thick enough to serve as real armor. The evolution of Rythasian customs was a curious thing. It seemed a handful began in genuine earnest, but I suspected had since morphed into lip service. Or else it was the other way around -- a few having initially formed in a more contrived manner having grown to hold deep value in the hearts of the people. I couldn't quite tell. Most rang true, yet it felt like some served as performance art for visitors.

"You'll be a Doreste soon," Jesi said, making idle talk as we strolled. "I don't think you'll get to keep your last name as your aunt chose. Ms. Elowa loves her husband of course, but she loves herself, too."

"What do you mean?"

"Your last name. It's customary you take

your husband's upon marriage, though not everyone does. You'll switch from Elowa to Doreste."

"But I don't have a last name," I pointed out.

"All the Elowan brides just use 'Elowa.'"

I frowned. "Zaria Elowa? That sounds ridiculous."

Jesi shrugged. "I'm sure you can pick something else as it's only a formality for the wedding ceremony. You'll become a Doreste and whatever you were before won't matter. Do you have a name in mind?"

Holt, I thought, heart pounding. *I want Kirwyn's last name if I have to pick a second one.*

I opened my mouth, then shut it.

If I chose his name, they'll only rip it away and it will hurt worse.

I never even knew Kirwyn had a last name until I found it in his book. I could picture him so clearly in my cave – the first day he'd attacked me and pinned me to the ground. Even now, I could almost *feel* his body pressed to mine, recall with clarity his woodsy scent. I think I fell in love with him on sight. *Or lust, as my mother claimed.*

"*I'm a freeborn,*" Kirwyn had said, later the day we met.

I turned to Jesi and the words were out of my mouth as soon as I thought them.

"Freeborn. I want to be Zaria Freeborn."

Jesi clucked her tongue, then laughed,

loudly. "You're looking for trouble, aren't you? The king won't like it. Are you determined to get on his bad side? But I guess he can't come up with a good reason to deny you, especially if Juls backs you."

We came to a slope in the cobblestone road; ahead, it opened into an area with tanks and cages. I quickened my pace to explore, forcing Jesi and the guards to follow.

"What is this place?" I asked, eyeing the glass displays, the pits, the tanks.

"La Menagerie de la Muerte," Jesi voiced, in mock horror. "King Grahar's great-grandfather gathered all the deadliest species he could find to make a macabre little zoo."

I recognized the aquatic creature in the nearest tank, with an alluring russet and white pattern on its shell. Sure enough, a plaque beneath it read "Cone Snail," bearing the same name we gave the poisonous creature.

"What's that?" I asked of the next display, holding a cute little frog.

"Poison dart frog," Jesi replied. "Very rare. Very deadly."

I strolled past displays of snakes, spiders, jellyfish and insects. A chill creeped up my spine, despite the heat. The last tank in the row contained an ugly Goodnight Fish. I flashed my teeth at it on instinct, as if the hated thing could see me, or cared. Hurrying out of the row and into an open pit, my jaw dropped to behold dark, scaled creatures right out of a nightmare.

"What are *those?*" I asked, shaking my head in disbelief at the huge reptiles. Even from our safe distance high above, I could see their otherworldly, slitted green eyes.

"Crocodiles," Jesi replied. "You've never seen any in Elowa? Even in the waters?"

"No," I breathed. "Thank Keroe."

I scurried away from those terrors to the adjacent, empty tank. The large reservoir was filled with a variety of sea-like formations at the bottom -- fake coral and rock-like grottos rising up from the floor. But nothing moved in the murky depths and the slight discoloration along the glass made me think the aquatic tank hadn't been cleaned in some time.

Cocking my head, I asked, "What's in there? Is it hiding?"

"No," Jesi replied, "It's missing."

"Missing?"

"We used to have a shark, but one day it simply went missing. Somebody probably stole it to sell or to use in medicine."

Shark? My blood ran cold.

"Sharks were hunted to near-extinction, mostly due to medicinal properties believed to be found in their oil and marrow. Particularly for cancer and fertility treatments, once birthrates began dropping. People still believe in the curative effects and hunt them today."

"Missing?" I repeated, breathless.

"Yeah, it's a bit of a puzzle because there's no way a common thief could pull off the heist. They'd need a large tank to transfer the shark -- if they meant to sell it live, which would have more value. And even if they just planned on killing it here and cutting it up to use or resell in parts, it still would be a ballsy endeavor for anyone to pull that off."

A cloud passed over the sun, thick and large. Coquina clams climbed up my spine. I knew the answer before I even asked.

"Jesi. When did the shark go missing?"

I held my breath, unmoving.

"Mmm…" she mused, "About a month or two ago."

My stomach dropped.

That was exactly when I'd had my first pageant and the shark mysteriously appeared in Wide Cove. I'd bet anything someone from Rythas had stolen it and found some way to deposit it there that morning.

Because I didn't have enough to worry about with war looming and the mystery of whoever shot Tolas and whoever tried to kidnap me and how I'd get off this landdamn island.

Someone wanted me dead. Someone powerful.

I let out a high-pitched laugh.

At least one thing's familiar in this unfamiliar land.

Chapter 10

A fortnight passed with the same daily routine. Jesi and I awoke and she either piled stacks of books for me to peruse in the library or she escorted me down to the king's hall to watch Juls on court days. I immersed in poetry, often reading in the enchanting courtyard Jesi showed me. It helped me feel closer to Kirwyn, knowing he'd read some of the same, growing up in his library. Though the more dramatic sonnets about love and longing suited my dark mood, one catchy poem by William Blake caught my eye, even though it wasn't about love at all. *A Poison Tree,* it was called, and reverberated with repressed rage.

"I want to read those Forbidden Texts," I told Jesi one morning in the library, eyeing the locked steel door. "Don't you?"

"Dry materials on science and engineering? No thanks. But if you want to read them so badly, just ask the keylord."

"What's a keylord?" I asked, snapping my book shut and giving Jesi my rapt attention.

"It's the next-highest honor, after ruling of course. More powerful than Commander, less powerful than the king. He keeps the keys to pretty much everything."

Before Jesi even said the name, my mind flashed to Laz's bare chest, remembering the strange silver necklace he wore, from which dangled a silver key.

Of course. Deflating, I asked, "It's Laz, isn't it?"

Jesi nodded, "You've noticed the necklace? He likes to flaunt it. It's just a symbol though. Laz keeps all the keys under his protection. Gate keys, manacle keys, keys to the war tower..."

"Of course he does. And he hates me." *I wouldn't be surprised if he was the one who tried to kill me.* "If he knows I want to read the texts, he'll deny me just to spite me."

Jesi threw her head back in a deep laugh. "He doesn't have a reputation as being a jerk for nothing."

Alright, I thought. *I'd have to find a way to get the key* without *asking. A task for another day.*

When Jesi and I weren't reading in the library tower, we sat in on Juls's court days. Grahar turned responsibility to the young king when he'd turned sixteen, surprisingly young.

Every few days, Juls sat his throne-like chair for those seeking an audience.

"When your long-awaited day arrives," Jesi whispered in my ear, as we watched on one side of the enormous king's hall, "you approach and pay respect-"

My eyes rounded as I observed a man twice Juls's age prostrate himself by bending to kiss the young king's sandaled foot. I couldn't help but compare the custom to my mother's rule – though thinking of her was something I tried very hard *not* to do. She might be a tyrant, but she didn't make anyone kiss her feet, and certainly not in a public act of subservience. Then again, not many were granted an audience at all.

"-and then you plead your case or make a request," Jesi finished. "Juls is very fair. You'll see."

"What is it you seek?" Juls asked the man.

"Permission to divorce," the man replied.

Beside me, Jesi sucked in a breath. "Ooh, I know him. His union bore children. Divorce is... kind of a crime, and it's especially taboo if the marriage was fruitful."

"State the reason," Juls instructed, tone level.

"I've... strayed. I've fallen in love with someone else."

Jesi winced again. "Even worse," she whispered. "Affairs are punishable offenses as well." Sighing, she added, "Although they're plentiful. It's complicated and a little hypocritical. Rythasians love love. And most want children, even if they're having trouble."

"Yet you have offspring?" Juls asked.

"They are older. Our chambers grew cold."

"So, you would burn down your whole house just to heat the bedroom?"

I couldn't tell if Juls asked the question rhetorically. The man didn't respond. The interesting analogy made me pause as well. I thought Juls would deny the seeker's request from the information Jesi provided, but he surprised me.

"Three months incarceration to think it over. If you still want a divorce once time is served, it's granted."

"Thank you," the man bowed, smiling, though he was ushered away by guards, seemingly to prison.

"What just happened?" I whispered to Jesi.

"Mercy," she replied. "Prison is standard for anyone wishing to leave a marriage. Since it's technically illegal, jail time must be served. It's a deterrent, and it also serves as a period for hot tempers to cool off. I thought Juls would give him a longer sentence, seeing as how they've had plenty of children, but," she cut off in a shrug, giving me a sly smile, "I guess he's feeling love all around today."

Every so often, Juls's gaze did slide to mine, and though his royal mask never cracked, a tension permeated the air between us. *He is good at this,* I had to admit, watching him render judgements with the grace of a man beyond his young years. And I had to wonder *– just as I often felt on display for his scrutiny, mustn't he feel very much on display for mine, right now?*

Frequently in the afternoons, Jesi and I swam – by far my favorite part of the day, even if I was only permitted near the coastline. I'd close my eyes and pretend I wasn't a captive in a strange land. Jesi swore she'd show me how to defend myself *after* my presentation party. "Can't risk bruising this pretty face before your grand debut," she said, pinching my cheek while I shot her a scathing look.

To prepare for that sweet terror, every night in my chambers we lit candles and Jesi showed me how Rythasian people danced. It wasn't at all like a simple village jig in Elowa. Jesi explained a dizzying number of styles for various affairs, ranging in formality from the *High Twine*, customary for the dreaded gala, to the informal *Sea of Flames* – whose wickedness I could glean from the way Jesi licked her teeth and grinned.

"Hold your partner's eyes," she instructed for the *High Twine.* "They'll anchor you when you're spinning, when all else will make you dizzy."

Each night, I tumbled into bed and stared

out my windows, clutching the sheet and imagining Kirwyn holding me, whispering soothing things, encouraging things, into my ear.

I refused to cry.

Crying meant he was dead, and that couldn't be true.

But every night I dreamed of Kirwyn. When nightmares plagued of him sinking to the bottom of the ocean, I'd wake in a sweat, ready to leap from my bedroom window and take my chances in the rocky sea.

I'd pull out the William Blake poetry book and recite that poem then. *A Poison Tree.* I didn't know why. Perhaps I was growing such a tree inside me. Either way, I read it until I'd committed it to memory:

I was angry with my friend:
I told my wrath, my wrath did end.
I was angry with my foe:
I told it not, my wrath did grow.

And I watered it in fears
Night and morning with my tears,
And I sunned it with smiles
And with soft deceitful wiles.

And it grew both day and night,
Till it bore an apple bright,
And my foe beheld it shine,
And he knew that it was mine,--

And into my garden stole
When the night had veiled the pole;
In the morning, glad, I see
My foe outstretched beneath the tree.

Chapter 11

"**N**o. Absolutely not. I'm not wearing this," I protested, as Jesi laid out my dress for the presentation party. My palms were sweating *before* I even saw my attire for the night.

The gown itself wasn't too unlike what women usually wore, but for one key difference. Typically, the layer of ornamental armor came up beneath the collarbone, covering most of the female torso, or fastened around the waist as a wide belt. The metalwork for this dress rose from the waist to right beneath a woman's breasts, almost pointedly lifting and cupping them. Even though fabric concealed the chest area, the attention drawn by the shape of the bodice made me blush.

"That's obscene," I said, throwing my hands in the air.

"I imagine some here feel the same way about your beloved tunic," Jesi shrugged.

I narrowed my eyes. "I can't wear that."

"You won't be alone. It's a popular fashion for this type of affair. I'll wear one too."

Groaning, I picked up the first layer, a deep scarlet silk. Not sheer, thankfully, but thin enough for plenty of definition to be seen beneath. Swathes of silk with varying degrees of transparency secured to the waist, so that airy red panels draped and waved, offering glimpses of a lady's legs as she moved. Two sheer sashes, also in scarlet and hanging to the floor, pinned to each shoulder, to flow behind a woman as she strolled or danced.

"Fine, okay. I just have to make it through tonight," I whispered, steeling myself.

"And there's a morning-after event tomorrow. A late brunch, just for the nobles. You'll be expected to appear."

Reluctantly, I shimmied into the landdamn dress and Jesi painted my lips a matching shade of red. She applied a dewy gel so my face glowed and glistened as I turned, catching the light. Lastly, she dabbled my eyes with black lines and lash-paint so minimal I almost couldn't see it. I was surprised by her restraint when everything else screamed *look at me.* But when I saw the effect, I understood. Nothing distracted from my mouth, already plump enough without color, the sirenesque lip paint made it stand out like a beacon.

Like a cry to be kissed, came the intrusive

thought.

#

"Don't leave my side." I squeezed Jesi's hand as she escorted me through High Spire toward the king's hall, the same room where Juls conducted court. True to her word, she dressed in similar garb, though her gown was a pale lemon chiffon and less ornate. I could hear the melodies of string instruments floating down the stone corridor. The elite of Rythasian society had been socializing for almost an hour already. *I just have to get through the first dance, that's all.*

"What if I trip?" I squeezed Jesi's hand harder.

"You won't trip, we've practiced enough."

"I'm no good on land, I never was," I argued.

"Is that really the case or is that what you always wanted to believe?"

"Now is not the time for your hard truths, Jesi," I groaned. "Give me the well-meaning lies."

"Wasn't made for it and I hardly think you of all people want to be lied to."

"Well make an exception, don't double down! I feel like a spectacle."

"That's the point."

"Ugh," I cried, tossing my head back. "You're impossible."

She grinned. "I think we have that in

common."

As we turned the last corner, my stomach flipped.

Juls waited at the end of the hall, fidgeting, regally dressed in a white tunic-vest and pants, each trimmed in silver. He wore a silver crown and slicked his hair back with some kind of gel or paste.

"I'll just go on ahead," Jesi said, releasing my hand and breezing past the young king to enter the hall from the back.

I gulped. I hadn't been alone with the boy I was doomed to marry since our private dinner.

"You look stunning," he said, his gaze quickly darting down and back up to my face, as if he didn't want to get caught looking.

"Thank you. You do too," I replied stiffly, positive every girl in the hall would think the same thing. Catching my gaze on a small box he held, Juls suddenly stepped forward and lifted it.

"It's customary for the groom to give the future bride a ring," he explained, opening it. "When you fell ill, I didn't get the chance. It should've been done before tonight."

One large, shockingly red ruby glittered between two smaller diamonds, like those in my mother's necklace -- the one I hadn't looked at since I'd taken it off my first day in Rythas.

"It's a promise to wed," he said, smiling his shy-but-dashing smile. "An engagement ring.

It's customary for a woman to wear it at all times. It goes on this finger," Juls explained, pointing to his own.

"Oh. Thank you. It's beautiful." Truly, it was, and now I understood why Jesi wanted me to wear red, a color I didn't particularly like. A color I'd now be forced to wear every day. In a ring I wasn't supposed to remove. For a marriage I didn't want.

The idea weighed heavily, like one more tie, one more leash to a land I longed only to escape.

"May I?" Juls asked. Gently, he lifted my left hand and slid the ring onto the finger nearest my pinky. I could only imagine the large gem getting in the way as I swam.

The gold band, designed for someone with more delicate hands, caught on my knuckle. The ring refused to budge no matter how Juls pushed, and fear fluttered through my stomach and across my chest, like the panicked beat of bird wings. As if *I* somehow failed by not fitting into the ring. I could tell he tried not to hurt my finger, but Juls wasn't going to give up either.

"You need to wear this before we enter," he insisted, furrowing his perfect brow. I wasn't sure what we could do when Juls met my eyes. Holding my gaze, he lifted my hand to his mouth and I watched, stunned, as he parted his full lips and sucked my finger – right at the knuckle.

This is... weird. Wrong.

I stared while his warm, wet mouth sent a tingle through my body. I couldn't help but wonder what Kirwyn would do if he'd witnessed this. He was possessive, but he wasn't foolish. *Would he attack Juls or bide his time, as I tried to do? Unless... what if he didn't care anymore?*

Juls tried again and, with difficulty, pushed the ring onto my finger.

I stared at the tether, a banding I was supposed to wear forever... and swallowed, hard. I possessed nothing of Kirwyn's, not a single item to remember him by -- not an article of his clothing, nor his book, nor even the knife he'd use to scrape his beard. Certainly, no jewelry. And now I'd be forced to wear this oversized red gem from another man, like a drop of dark blood upon my finger.

Juls held out his bent arm, a formal offer to continue.

"Shall we?" he said.

#

The entire king's hall bloomed with white flowers. The group of musicians I'd heard played their string instruments to one side of the crowded room. While plenty of drinks were provided, not a morsel of food could be found. My stomach rumbled at the idea of a long night without sustenance and my neck began to sweat at the sight of so many strangers gathered to watch me dance. I shifted uncomfortably, embarrassed, hoping I cooled down by the time Juls touched my sweaty back.

"Ah, the belle of the ball," Grahar proclaimed, as Juls and I walked discreetly through the rear entrance and over to a group of officials. The king wore a silver crown atop his black and ash head of hair. His smile touched his crinkled eyes and his relaxed posture told me he was in a good mood. Laz, dressed similarly to Juls, gave me a quick once-over, then turned back to his father.

"Our ships can't get close enough but they're up to something," Laz snarled. "Plus, they haven't attacked in, what, eight months?"

"Eight months, three weeks, and four days," Juls replied, drawing us forth to enter the conversation. Raoul and Singen, whom I hadn't seen since my arrival, made up the rest of the small circle.

"Is Mal-Yin coming tonight?" Singen asked.

"We don't need him," Raoul replied.

"We don't need *him*," Singen quipped. "We just need whatever he can give us."

"*Will* give us," Laz corrected. He didn't spare me a glance as he said, "Mal-Yin doesn't care about her little coming-out party. He'll come for the Fae fête. Can't pass up the decadence. But if we can install the solar panels-"

Grahar cut his son off with an icy stare and

firm wave of his hand. The king's voice cracked like a whip, silencing everyone. "No panels. We've discussed this. The tore forbids it."

Angrily, Laz tossed back a glass of some clear alcohol and shot me a dark look – as if I was the one forbidding whatever he wanted. Then he stormed off. In his wake, the men resumed their war-talk, but no one glanced in my direction, and I didn't follow the conversation about various defenses. After a few minutes, I caught Jesi nearby and slipped off Juls's arm to join her.

Raising my hand, I announced, "I have a ring of engagement."

She chuckled. "I see. I don't know that piece. They must have purchased it new for you."

"Is courting here always this awkward or am I just lucky?"

Jesi made a sound in the back of her throat. "You're going to be queen, so I'll go with lucky but knowing what I know about your past I know *you* don't see it that way."

"What is tore?" I asked, quickly changing the subject away from Kirwyn. I couldn't think about him if I planned on surviving the night without humiliating myself by bursting into tears.

"Tore?" she arched a brow.

"Grahar said the tore forbids the installation of sun panels Laz wants to put... somewhere."

"Oh, T-O-R-R," Jesi corrected. "The Treaty of

Red Ridge. We don't expand our technological capabilities and the Spades leave us alone. That's the deal. Laz is always itching to push the boundaries. We're allowed frivolity," Jesi moaned, rolling her eyes. "Faerie orbs for parties or string lights for the king's ship. But fortifying High Spire or developing weaponry is expressly forbidden."

Jesi bared her teeth, "War is coming though, I can feel it in my bones. It's all anyone here is talking about tonight. Oxholde is going to attack."

"War is coming and we dance?" I scoffed.

"Before and after battle is the best time for dancing," Jesi replied saucily, and even I wasn't so naïve as to miss her double meaning.

A sudden touch on the small of my back made me stiffen.

"It's time," Juls said, coming up close enough to whisper in my ear. I didn't like how it gave me gullflesh.

Right, okay. With shallow breaths I followed him to the center of the empty dance floor. *Why did it have to be empty?*

Juls rested one hand on my back, the other clasping my right hand, high and firm. He smelled of sandalwood and leather. I wondered if it was from his styling oil, a perfume like my mother wore, or just *him.* We were promised to each other by some ancient pact, yet we'd never even been physically close until that moment, and no one but me found that strange.

Juls flashed his dashing grin. "You can relax. I won't let you fall."

I returned a nervous laugh. I probably looked like a scared rabbit, though his words made me feel a little safer, despite my resistance.

The music began and Juls led the steps, twirling us around the floor with graceful ease. Of course, he didn't have to worry about tripping on a fluttering swath of silk. But I wasn't surprised to find him skilled at dancing. *The heir. The golden son.*

The eyes of everyone in the room burned into my back.

Every girl here must want to be me, I realized.

I felt their stares pinned to Juls, as well. Like he possessed an otherworldly force, commanding attention. Not for his size; he wasn't especially tall or strong. But for his regal, self-possessed manner. Like everything in the world came easily to him. Dancing with Juls *was* effortless once I forgot about my fluttering dress. He led, I followed. Easy.

It would be easy to dance with him like this every day, were I any other girl.

I locked onto his eyes exactly as Jesi instructed -- but they locked back, making my spine tingle. Juls's dark eyes were a cage -- anchoring me, holding me through dizzying, breathless spins -- but endangering me too. *A cage door can easily snap shut forever.*

I suddenly remembered how he sucked my finger and wondered if he was thinking about it, as well. When the last strains of music came, Juls brought my hand to his lips, placing a dry kiss upon my knuckles and giving rise to more gullbumps.

This is wrong, I thought. *I don't know where Kirwyn is. He could be hurt. And I'm dancing with strange boys who kiss my knuckles.* I turned, eager to disappear into the sidelines, but Juls gently grabbed my forearm.

"Wait. Laz is next. As my brother and keylord, he gets the next dance."

My face fell before I remembered to school it. I was about to flash a forced smile when Laz approached, wearing a similar expression of distaste, so I didn't bother. *The feeling's mutual,* I thought. Unlike his brother, Laz never wore a crown, but donned the same key necklace and silver bracelets from our awful dinner.

Limply, he held my hand, as if a weak touch was the next best thing to no contact at all. His other arm slid around my back, practically hovering over my skin instead of laying his hand upon it. He stood too far apart to be capable of dancing well; I knew that before we even began. But as we awkwardly twirled across the floor, I couldn't tell how much of it was due to Laz being a terrible dancer versus him wanting as much distance between us as possible. My only consolation was at that point, other couples began to dance and were more focused on their own appearances.

My nostrils flared, catching a strange scent on Laz's skin -- tangy, like blood. I knew that wasn't quite right, but it was close, and my imagination couldn't help but associate him with violence. I looked away, focusing on the other dancers -- a whirl of brightly colored dresses flashing by.

When I couldn't avoid it any longer, I shifted my gaze back to Laz. Unlike Juls's warm brown eyes, Laz's were a hazel I'd never seen before – wide patches of faded brown with lines of muted green beneath, and only a few flecks of bronze. It reminded me of dead or dying grass: thirsty, desolate. His eyes were scorched earth.

I jerked with the realization that Kirwyn's eyes were the *exact* opposite: a deep, lush green, full of life and enchantment.

How long was this song?

Laz stared back at me. Not at my eyes or face, but my lips specifically.

"What are you staring at?" I blurted.

"Your mouth. Although I'm not surprised Jesi gave you that color, given her family. It's the same shade they wear in the brothels."

My lips rounded into an "o" of surprise. I closed them, not wanting to draw more attention to my mouth. *Was he implying what I thought he was implying?* Jesi told me briefly about men and women of pleasure, one of High

Spire's main attractions.

"I'm not a whore," I gritted, keeping my voice low.

"You're not a virgin either, are you?"

My face burned. *What did he know?* "That's none of your business."

"No, it's my brother's business, and mine by extension. He should have returned any damaged goods, but he's too noble. My brother thinks it was young infatuation, a first love. That that boy hit you like a barbed arrow. Juls thinks it will cause more damage if we try to remove it. He believes it's better to leave it alone than to pull it out."

That boy. My blood ran cold to hear Laz speak of Kirwyn. I didn't breathe for a moment, as if his words fisted the airways above my lungs, choking off my oxygen supply.

He had no right. How much did they know?

"So tell me little queen, did it?" Lazlian's lip quirked. "Did it hurt when he pierced you?"

My cheeks flamed hotter at his unmistakable innuendo. *I guess that answers that question.*

"That's none of your business," I repeated. I could feel the heat on my skin, making my declaration markedly less fierce than I'd desired and practically writing the answer all over my face. *God, I wish this song would end.* But both Laz and I twirled, equally participating in the performance art, unwilling to reveal anything less than total self-control to a room full of people judging us.

"For an island full of secrets, you are remarkably bad at keeping them," he mocked.

"For an island with a royal court you are remarkably bad at possessing any courtly manners," I replied.

Laz shrugged, seemingly unaffected. "I don't find them very useful."

"Good thing you're not the young king, then."

In the deathly stillness of his face, I could tell I'd wounded him. But I didn't feel triumphant, at least, not for very long. My stomach twisted at the loathing in his glare. I braced for whatever came next, concentrating on my footing, on putting on a show.

"Whatever I am or am not will always be superior to what you are." Laz looked down at me, lips curling with revulsion, as if I were a filthy rat or decaying fish he'd been forced to touch. Voice laden with contempt, he declared, "I find you revolting. Make no mistake, even when you are queen, you will not be our equal. You will never be our equal."

I hated that my lip quivered. I had no comeback. I did the only thing I could do – swallowed the lump in my throat, jut my chin, and refused to let the stinging tears leak.

A good man would apologize at the outburst. A bad man would back off, seeing he'd won.

Confoundingly, Laz did neither. Only when

he'd so obviously beaten me did he suddenly firm his grip on my hand and my waist, holding me closer, like a proper dance partner. Not in apology or due to a *shred* of kindness, but to kick me while I was down.

We were close enough now that Laz could whisper near my ear, "Juls might be right about that arrow. It will hurt a lot worse coming out than it had going in." His words sent gullbumps down my neck. "But we'll rip it out."

At his threat, I saw red.

"I don't *want* to be your equal," I snapped, baring my teeth. "You're a goat's ass, Lazlian."

He chuckled, deep in the back of his throat. I reviled the sound. *"Horse's ass."*

"What?"

"We don't say goat's ass here. It's horse's ass or just ass."

"Yes, whatever. All that. You're all the asses."

My ears picked up the change and I jolted. The stupid song had ended, and we'd danced right into the next one without noticing. Abruptly, I yanked my hands from Laz's grip. Without bowing or formally departing, I stormed away, hoping I left him looking foolish on the dance floor. I scurried back behind the royal table and wedged myself into a shadowy corner. Pressing a hand against my racing heart, I committed to stay until my pulse returned to a normal rate.

Why does he hate me so much? I wondered.

Why did I make it worse? I'll never get the key now. And he's watching me. He knows I want to escape…

I saw a flash of yellow as Jesi hurried over to me.

"Thanks for the warning about the dance with Laz," I scowled. "So much for honesty."

"Zaria," Jesi whispered urgently, pulling me close by my bicep. "Someone is here to see you. Someone from Elowa."

"What?" I breathed, heart skipping a beat. The room suddenly faded. I forgot all about Laz or anyone else.

"It's not him," Jesi said, grimacing, as if reading my mind. "It's an Elowan. That's all I know. You've been excused to return to your chambers, but Grahar's not happy. He was in a good mood, and you managed to put him in a bad one again."

"*Me?* I didn't do anything. Who is it?" I repeated, clutching my neck, somewhere between elation and terror.

"I don't know. But you better go deal with it."

Chapter 12

I gasped, covering my mouth. *My mother, my father, Tomé, Maz* – of all the people I expected to see, she wasn't one of them. *How did she get here?*

Lida stood still as stone, chin high, right in the center of my room. I blinked a few times to make sure I saw correctly. Lida's belly was... flat, I realized with growing dread. *Where was the baby?*

"Are you - are you okay?" I asked. "How did you get here? Is Tomé with you? Is he okay?" The questions tumbled from my lips, even as a sour sensation rose in my gut, eyeing her stomach.

"No. And before you ask, he's no longer with us either." As Lida held her hand against her belly, I sucked in a breath. *A miscarriage?*

I didn't want to push, so I simply nodded and said, "I'm sorry, Lida."

We both stood quietly for a few moments,

sizing up one another. I watched her eyes sweep the length of me, analyzing my exotic red dress. Finally, I couldn't hold back from repeating, "How did you get here?"

"How did I get you out of the dungeons?" Lida countered, in her usual haughty tone. "His father. Guilt is a powerful weapon." Lida lifted her chin even higher. "And before you think of sending me back, know that that is not what I want, and I will use everything I have at my disposal to get what I want."

I blinked. *First of all, I don't doubt it. Secondly, send you back?* Honestly, I didn't want to admit it, but I was ecstatic she was there.

"I wouldn't do that," I swore. I didn't even know if I *could,* but I *wouldn't.* "Lida, I'm happy to see you."

Another tense silence grew between us. Maybe she wasn't pleased to see me, but she'd been given no other choice? Why had Grahar allowed it in the first place?

"Who was the father?" I asked gently, unable to bite back my curiosity.

Lida let out a puff of air. "Pentyr."

My mind raced back to Elowa. *The young Mystic?* I marveled. *I* knew *it. I knew he never intended a life of celibacy. Hypocrites, all of them.*

"After everything happened, I didn't want to be there any longer. I never did, but I never had a way until Pentyr got me out. Certainly not out of the kindness of his own heart. I think part of him was relieved to get rid of me. And just so you know, there's others who want me gone, in case you're thinking of sending me back."

I shook my head vehemently. "I'm not sending you back! But you... knew? About all this?" I asked, spreading my hands.

Holding my eyes with her shrewd gaze, she said, "I've always known a lot more than you, Zaria." This time, her declaration wasn't snobbish. Her eyes softened and Lida seemed uneasy. Instinctively, I braced myself.

"I think we should sit somewhere and talk. There's news from Elowa. Quite a bit."

#

Servants poured the customary strawberry-mint tea into little etched glasses. Chilled, for refreshment on another hot night. They set it beside a late-night snack – slices of coconut-mango bread -- though neither Lida nor I touched the food. We made a show of sipping the cool tea as we waited for so many ears to depart the room. My own presentation party continued at the opposite end of the castle, without me, much like my wedding feast on Elowa.

When the last servant closed the door behind her, Lida met my eyes and took a deep breath. "Tomé is unwell. Zaria, you have to get him out of there. Bring him here."

"Unwell? What do you mean? Is Marcin

alright? Before I left, my mother *swore* he was healing. Was that another landdamn lie?"

"Marcin is *physically* well. But he's changed. The experience... he's not the boy you remember. I don't know who got to him – his parents or the Mystics or both. But he's different. He refuses to see Tomé."

I frowned, wrinkling my forehead. "Then why aren't you asking for Marcin to come here? I don't understand. I don't even think I *can* bring anyone here, but wouldn't it be better if they both came?"

Lida shook her head. "Marcin refuses to hear talk of anything but Elowa. Tomé is a wreck. He needs to get out of there, be where he can be himself." She pinned me with her keen stare. "I know you understand."

I dropped my head into my hands, covering my eyes. *Was* no one *destined to be happy together?* Tomé and Marcin were the only ones who seemed to stand a chance, albeit secretly.

"I don't know what I can do," I told her, trying to figure out what I might use to negotiate. "Let me think about it."

When I finally looked up, Lida stared at me so hard I bit my lip, knowing another blow was about to fall.

"That's not all I have to tell you," she said, slowly. "Your boy, Kirwyn, caused quite an ordeal back in Elowa."

It was as if her words reached out and

wrapped a hand around my heart, first stopping its beat, then manually pumping it back to life. But for the intake of one shaky breath and the instant tears pooling my eyes, I froze. *Is she lying, like so many others?* I searched Lida's face but hers held only sympathy.

An eternity passed while I didn't breathe. I was terrified that any question would break the spell, the magic of this surreal moment -- as if talking would somehow make it not real, not true. I feared Lida would correct me, tell me I'd misheard her or that there'd been some misunderstanding. If I spoke and she broke my heart, it would destroy me.

"He's... alive?" I made myself whisper.

Lida's brow furrowed. "Yes, I - I thought you knew."

I'd never heard such a sound as tore from my throat. My body slumped, falling off the cushioned chair and landing on the floor. The next thing I knew, I was on my knees sobbing, completely helpless to stop myself, without any care that Lida sat near enough to watch. Soon I was laughing and crying and emitting the strangest noises as a feeling between hysteria and euphoria seized me. After a while, I heard myself repeating, *"He's alive, he's alive, he's alive."* Clutching my heart, I thanked Keroe for carrying him out or spitting him back up.

Alive.

One word from Lida changed my entire life.

You're alive, I thought. *You're alive and I love you and I'll find you.*

"I'm sorry," Lida murmured. "I thought you knew. I don't understand. What happened that night, at sea?"

I tried to speak and failed. I was rocking. Crying and rocking myself. Lida pressed a cup to my mouth, and I forced myself to drink great gulps of cool, fruity-herbal tea. I tried to pour myself another cup, but my hands shook so badly I dropped the pot. Luckily, it only hit the tray and not the floor, where the resounding crash surely would have called a servant into the room.

With the back of my hand, I wiped the tears from my cheeks. "He – there was gunfire and Kirwyn fell into the ocean. I didn't know if he made it back to the boat or if he drowned. I didn't know," I told her. "All this time, I didn't know, I didn't know."

I took deep breaths to steady myself, wiping more tears. "What happened? Please. Tell me everything that happened."

Lida chewed her lip. "I only know what Pentyr told me. Kirwyn snuck into the palace somehow, I have no idea how he did it. He kidnapped your brother and threatened to kill him if the High Braenese didn't give him what he wanted. I don't think he ever intended to hurt Gereth," Lida quickly added. Frowning, she said, "Unfortunately, I think your mother knew that too, so it wasn't as good of a bargaining chip as he'd hoped. I can't say for certain if she fully called his bluff though. All I know is a meeting took place and Kirwyn somehow negotiated getting help to leave Elowa. Your mother wouldn't take him to you, of course, and she wouldn't tell him where you'd gone. But she sent him off to the mainland."

"Where is he now?" I breathed.

Lida shrugged. "Somewhere on the North Continent."

I closed my eyes, sighing, picturing Kirwyn in my mind. I imagined him exploring a strange forest or looking out on an unfamiliar beach. Was he trying to rescue me? Could he even set foot here?

I have to find him if he can't find me.

Needing to get its rapid beat under control, I still clutched my heart.

You're alive and I'll find you. I just need to be smart about it this time.

"Lida... would you have told me all this if I intended on sending you back?"

She remained quiet for a moment. "I would have traded the information for your assurance not to."

I blew out a puff of air. "I understand."

"Zaria... there's something else I need to tell you. I wanted to make sure you were in the right frame of mind first and I don't know if

I've only made it worse."

I frowned, not appreciating yet another person in a never-ending string trying to manage me -- least of all her. But I let it slide because she held all the cards, and also because she brought me the best news I'd ever received in my life.

"It's about your father."

I sucked in a breath, bracing.

"He was ill for a long time and in the last few weeks, it worsened. He lost the battle. Your family buried him at sea a few days ago."

"That- that can't be right," I protested, stomach knotting. "My father was the embodiment of health."

"No," Lida shook her head. "He had something wrong inside. He knew. Your mother knew. They snuck in mainland medicine when they could, tried natural remedies…"

Soursop tea. My father claimed he loved the taste. He always had a cup in hand. But people often drank it for mysterious ailments.

"He's dead?" I whispered.

Lida nodded, solemn.

I waited for the grief to wash over me, to knock me back off my chair and onto the floor. It didn't come. Sadness for his death crept like a shadow across my heart, but… as I tried to sort it out, I realized I mourned the father I never had. The man who never let me close, who barely acknowledged my existence. I'd never known such a relationship and now I never would.

Was he in pain? What were his last words?

"There's one more thing."

I flicked my gaze back to Lida's face.

"You have a baby brother."

My mouth fell in silent wonder. My mother had her baby. I had a new sibling.

Lida let out a low whistle. "Your mother was further along in her pregnancy than she let on. The babe came a bit early but... he's not your father's. If there was any doubt when he was born with darker skin and large, dark eyes, your mother gave the finger to anyone whispering behind her back when she named him Naseroson. You can imagine the scandal."

I knew it. And I certainly could imagine. Broken vows on my mother's part, broken vows on the part of the High Mystic. No one would be gossiping about much else. The horrific image of Nasero shouting, drowning in that storm came to mind. *Did he know he was going to be a father? Did it bring him any comfort, in death, to know he left behind a piece of himself? Or was it worse to know he'd never hold his child in his arms?*

"Is my brother... healthy?" *A brother I'd never meet. Never touch. Now that I was finally allowed to touch, I'd been torn from him.*

Nasero and I had that in common.

"Oh yes," Lida replied, waving a hand. "And cute as a coquina."

I nodded wordlessly before a terrible question popped into my head. I wished I didn't think it, wished that I was incapable of speculating. I longed to go back in time to before I knew or suspected. For one brief second, my eyes fluttered closed, and I mourned the loss of that innocence, however unnaturally prolonged and false it was.

I opened my eyes. "When was my brother born?"

Lida scrunched her lips, thinking. "Ten days ago, maybe?"

"Who was there when my father died?"

"He died peacefully, in his sleep."

"With my mother," I declared.

Lida cocked her head.

I laughed, but it was mirthless. "I just... I can't. I can't help but wonder if she hastened his death. Knowing the baby was coming and that it wasn't his." I rose on tired, shaky legs and walked to the window, looking out at the churning waves below.

"You think Queen Pama murdered her husband?" Lida asked.

"I guess I'll never know," I sighed to the sea.

Another mystery, forever. Just like whoever killed Tolas and whoever wanted to kidnap me.

#

Jesi came to my chambers shortly thereafter. She'd changed back into the tunic-dress of the palace guard and eyed Lida with her hooded stare.

"I've been instructed to bring her to the king," she announced.

With both Jesi and Lida standing together, I saw the Elowan similarity. Lida's olive skin was a different shade than my own and her brown hair a dissimilar color, but our faces bore a distinct resemblance. The variations I used to notice had been exaggerated in my mind, without a wider basis for comparison. Lida, Tomé, Nasero, my mother, myself… there was something "Elowan" about our features. Alluring, wideset eyes and small, dainty ears and high, elegant cheekbones. Broad shoulders, lean muscles and long limbs – hardly anyone stood out as overly short or bald or hairy amongst our people, as individuals often did in Rythas. We bore a striking similarity to one another and collectively, those features were generally pleasing.

But why?

"Jesi, this is Lida. From Elowa," I said slowly, still frowning. "Why does Grahar want to see her?"

"To plead my case," Lida replied. "If you approved of my staying, he agreed to hear me out."

I chewed my lip, unsure what to make of Grahar's move. It seemed considerate or respectful even, for him to allow me to speak with Lida first. But then what did he want? Final say?

Jesi swung her eyes to me. "*You okay?*" she mouthed.

I nodded, but she knew something was wrong. *Should I tell her about Kirwyn? Could I trust her not to tell Laz or the king? Did they already know?*

Back straight, Lida walked out of the room first, forcing Jesi to follow.

"I'll come back and check on you, okay?"

I nodded again. *We'd saved each other's lives. I could trust her, couldn't I?*

Chapter 13

Jesi didn't arrive back at my chambers until the middle of the night, when I was already sleeping, so I never got the chance to tell her about Kirwyn. It took me forever to fall asleep as my thoughts raced from my mother to my father, and back to Kirwyn. More than ever, I longed to escape. I needed to learn the ways out of the castle. The locations of the docks. And, lastly, figure out how to steal and operate a boat. I could sail, using the sun or stars, to guide me to the mainland.

I'll see you again, I promised. *You're somewhere in that wildness.*

When Jesi and I both woke late the next morning, she pulled out yet another red dress for the afternoon affair.

"Do you have any Elowan tunics here?" I asked her, looking out my window to the sparkling waves below. Seeing Lida gave me an idea. Knowing Kirwyn lived gave me courage.

"Why? What are you doing?" Jesi raised her eyebrows and crossed her arms.

"I don't want to be paraded about today's affair in silk and satin and gleaming, fake armor. I want my old clothes. Do you have any tunics here?"

"The brothels have 'em," Jesi said, wryly.

"Ugh," I groaned, throwing up my hands as I imagined the reason. "Fine. Are they authentic?"

"No, but no one would know the difference."

"Can you get me one?"

Jesi scowled, tapping her fingers against her biceps.

"I'm sorry," I bit my lip. "Will I get you in trouble?"

"No, but you're going to get yourself into trouble. If you show up today in an Elowan tunic, it will cause a stir and Grahar will not be pleased. Are you determined to anger him? Because you've been doing a good job of it so far. He'll interpret it as a refusal to fall in line. He won't like it."

I knew my eyes twinkled as I shrugged. It was that same thrill of power coming over me as when I'd plotted to get myself kidnapped. "But what will the guests think?"

Jesi scrunched her lips and flicked her dark curls. "I honestly don't know."

"Well then," I grinned. "Only one way to find

out."

#

I gave my tunic a final tug, straightening it. "Any word on Lida yet?"

"She's been granted permission to stay. Grahar put her up in her own room somewhere. I don't know more than that." Jesi cocked an eyebrow at me. "I thought you liked our pretty dresses. You try to hide it, but I see you admiring the silks when you think no one's looking."

I ran a comb -- made from an actual tortoise shell -- through my knotty hair. "Alright, *sometimes.* But sometimes don't you just want to be comfortable?"

"That scratchy misshapen sack isn't comfortable at all," Jesi lobbed.

I squared my shoulders. "Well, I like it."

"Not as half as much as you like being stubborn."

"And with one act I get both," I grinned, pleased with myself. "Comfort and obstinance."

Jesi withdrew the dagger she kept strapped to her side. "I can't tell whether you're an idiot or the cleverest girl I've ever met."

I froze; her words were like a lash to my heart. *Kirwyn once said something similar to me. And I'd often thought the same thing about him.*

"Why does Grahar care so much about how I

dress anyway?" I asked, hurrying to finish my hair. We were late. "What's it to him, as long as Juls is pleased? And Juls likes me. So far."

I didn't really expect an answer. Certainly not the one I got.

"Grahar..." Jesi toyed with the blade, debating her words. "Thinks... you mean something to him. His wife died shortly after childbirth, you know."

I fluffed my hair – a long and loose cascade of blonde, no ornamentation. Just like I used to wear it. "I know how hard it is to birth twins. It's a difficult process on Elowa as well."

"No. Life's bitter irony," Jesi said, twirling her dagger as she often did. "Juls and Laz came into the world with ease, though Laz was small and sickly. Just over a year later, Fersanda – that's Juls's mother - had a daughter. It was a terrible ordeal. No one expected any trouble after the twins, but she got pregnant again when Juls and Laz were only a few months old so maybe it was too soon. Both she and the babe died, mere hours after her daughter was born. Grahar was devastated. Exactly three days following their deaths, news came from Elowa." Jesi pointed the dagger at me. "News of your birth."

I was born. So what? I shrugged my shoulders, sliding my feet into simple leather thongs.

"In his grief, I think Grahar connected those events in his mind. He lost his wife and daughter and only days later the chosen braenese arrives? There was no way he was going to give you up to another family, not after that. I think Grahar sees you as the daughter he lost. Or he sees you as solid breeding stock, to ensure *his* son doesn't lose any children. Or maybe even as the reincarnation of his late wife. I don't know, but he's always been fixated on having you as a Doreste. No one could persuade him from this course."

Of all the sad and repulsive things she'd said, I fixated on one. The same one Laz mentioned. Because Grahar certainly didn't treat me with the warmth of a wife or daughter.

"What do you mean, breeding stock?"

"Conceiving can be a problem," Jesi said gently, grimacing.

I stopped fussing with my tunic. My voice was hard. *"What do you mean?"*

"I mean, lots of people can't have children. It's rare on Elowa. But everywhere else... couples have about a one in four chance of being unable to conceive. Before the Great Decline, it was different. Well, it wasn't, but there were medical treatments people could seek for help. With the loss of that knowledge, infertility rates have held steady around twenty-five percent for, I don't know, hundreds of years. Usually, fertile couples produce more babies to make up for the lack in other pairings. Or one clan turns to warring with another. In

Rythas, it's not a huge problem for us in *general*. It's just... well, it's a huge problem for a couple, on a personal level, as you can imagine."

I sat on the bed, dazed. Suddenly, what Jesi had whispered about *unions bearing children* during Juls's court case made more sense.

"With the way my mom popped out babies she probably expected me to have future in the brothels or in marriage," Jesi said, wrinkling her nose. "I saw what *that* did to keep her down. If I'm going to sleep beside a weapon, I prefer to wield it myself." Jesi grinned at me as she finished, flourishing her dagger. She seemed to be expecting something but when I didn't reply, she added, "I have a lot of brothers. A lot of mouths to feed. That's why I send part of my wages back home to the eldest. He's more responsible with money than my mother."

"Oh," I said, still reeling. "I didn't... that's... I'm sorry. Couples are infertile in Elowa too, but it's very rare."

Jesi nodded. "I imagine Grahar would rather not gamble with the odds, as they are. If he can introduce Elowan genes to the Doreste bloodline, all the better. There have been cases where your lack of a large gene pool has led to some... issues, as you know. But usually, it's the other way around. The Dorestes have been uncommonly lucky," Jesi drawled, eyebrows raised. "Though some whisper of generations past having secret surrogates or the uh...

assistance of a virile third party." She cleared her throat and cocked a one-sided grin. "If you know what I mean. But nothing's been proved."

I grimaced. This entire conversation was too creepy. "So Grahar wants more children and is possibly fixated on a granddaughter? Why didn't he just marry me himself?"

I'd asked it rhetorically, but Jesi replied, "Maybe he would have, were it not distasteful to the nobles. Maybe he loves his son and would do anything for him. Who knows why Grahar does anything, really?"

"Ugh, that's disgusting." I ran a hand down my face, thankfully free of paint, and sat down on the bed. Once again, I saw how easily things could have been worse. I could have been fated to marry Lazlian. Juls could have turned out to be cruel, or ugly, or even just irritating and he was none of those things so far.

But that didn't mean I loved him, and I certainly didn't want children with him.

"I'm not..." I gave Jesi a meaningful look. "I haven't started my moon cycles yet."

"I know," she replied. "That's a good thing. It will give you time to get to know Juls first, before you marry."

I dropped my head into my hands, shaking it. "Jesi, *no.* I can't marry him. I can't make babies with him! I have to... Jesi, I have to leave here."

I felt the bed dip as she sat beside me. When she placed her strong arm around my shoulder, pulling me closer, I broke down. Outside of my mother and Kirwyn, I couldn't think of a single person who'd ever done anything like that before.

Tears came again, softly this time, but I still despised the weakness. "Jesi, can I trust you?"

"You can trust me." She squeezed my bicep. "I swear it."

I didn't know if that was true, but I couldn't bear it all alone and I knew I needed help to escape anyway. Slowly, I told her what Lida told me the night before.

"Can I truly trust you, Jesi?" I repeated as I finished. "You won't tell anyone?"

"Even if I didn't like you, which I do, I'm a sucker for love," she sighed, wistful. "This is Rythas. We're weaned on tales of passion and valor. Who here *isn't* a sucker for a good love story?"

I laughed, wiping my nose with the back of my hand. "The king."

I felt Jesi nod her agreement.

"Help me. Please. I'm not planning anything – yet. But I want to read the Forbidden Texts. I want to learn all the exits to the castle. I want to understand how the gates work. When do they open and close? Who guards them? I want to see the Black Passage. What is that? Can you show me?"

Again, I felt Jesi nod. "Okay. Let me look into the guards' new schedules and I'll show you. As long as you *promise* not to do anything without telling me first."

"I promise," I swore.

Chapter 14

Emerging into the small dining hall in my Elowan tunic, Grahar and Lazlian immediately fell into twin expressions of irritation, mouths set in firm lines, gazes dark. But Juls's eyes danced, and a smile played on his lips.

Even if I've angered the king, I've amused my intended.

Heads turned in my direction and whispers rippled through the intimate crowd, like a wind blowing branches on the trees, softly rustling leaves from one to the next.

Four tables had been set up to accommodate roughly ten guests apiece. Crossing the room, I smiled wide, as if unaware of anything out of the ordinary. "I'm sorry I'm late," I said, taking the empty seat beside Juls, who sat at one head of the table. The king sat with his officials, including Raoul and Singen, heads re-bent into whatever heated discussion they'd been having before I'd entered. Unfortunately, Laz was seated across from me. His nose twitched as he gazed upon my tunic, as if fighting another sneer.

Emboldened by our dance the night before or the unavoidable fact that his enormous ring was on my finger, Juls took my hand in his, giving it a soft kiss. I tried to relax against the instinct to yank it away. "You look adorable," he said, eyes glowing.

I made myself smile at the compliment, though adorable wasn't what I was going for. *Bold. Powerful. Beautiful, maybe.*

Plates and bowls of fruit, game, and warm, fresh bread were set upon the table. Laz speared a miniature, plump piece of meat and ate it while eyeing me with his sardonic grin, as if it were a challenge of some sort I didn't understand. Annoyed, I lifted my own morsel of tender meat and popped it in my mouth.

Juls leaned over to whisper in my ear. "That's a dove heart."

"What?" I asked, mouth half-full.

"Laz's favorite dish is hearts of mourning dove. I wouldn't suggest exotic cuisine, after your illness."

I spit the meat into my hands. After I'd grabbed a glass of water to wash out the taste, I blurted, "You eat dove hearts? I- I'm sorry. I didn't mean it as an insult, I'm just surprised." I supposed it was logical not to waste any part of an animal, but we never ate aviary organs in Elowa.

"No apology needed," Juls said, holding his brother's eyes. "Laz is just being an ass, as usual. Isn't that right, brother?"

Coquina clams crept up my spine and I straightened it. Juls meant to help, but all I noted was the fact that Laz ran and told his brother everything I'd said the night before, like an overgrown tattletale.

From the corner of my eye, I caught Raoul striding purposefully to our table. He tapped the young king on the shoulder and whispered, "Your father wants to speak with you."

"Excuse me," Juls politely announced, "there's been disturbing reports from Oxholde. I must go see what my father needs."

As the young king, he certainly didn't need to explain himself, but he did. Rising, he placed his napkin on his chair and crossed the room. I watched him go, delaying the moment I'd have to acknowledge that he'd left me alone with Laz.

Stretching back languidly in his chair, Laz sipped a glass of white wine. As usual, his open vest fell wide, revealing the dangling silver key. Even the way he sat -- smug, expectant -- seemed both contrived and like bait of some kind.

"Are you playing at being the insolent prince or are you actually the insolent prince?" I whispered through clenched teeth, angered by his stunt with the dove hearts. "Do you even know anymore?"

"What's the difference to you, little queen?"

I sat back, shrugging, grabbing my own glass of wine. I supposed there wasn't one. He'd treat me like a rat infesting his castle either way. *I'm never going to get that key,* I thought, staring at the taunting wink of silver on Laz's necklace, symbolizing the power to unlock those Forbidden Texts. I had no idea what was in that room, but I needed to find out, because it *might* contain maps to help me find Kirwyn. Otherwise, I'd be sailing off into the unknown with no plan.

I glanced up at Laz to find his face tight, almost scowling. I flushed, realizing I'd been staring at his chest. *Not because I'm looking at that vulgar display of flesh,* I thought. *Because I was focused on your key.*

Understanding what Laz thought only made my cheeks hotter and I tore my gaze to the side, too late understanding *that* act only made me look *more* ashamed. I fought the urge to hide my face. There was no way to explain my actions without making it worse.

At least Laz had finished eating -- he pushed off his chair and stalked out of the dining hall, leaving me in peace.

Alone, the rest of the lunch affair passed easily. I made small talk with an elderly woman who asked about my tunic – though I claimed its authenticity and certainly did not speak of its origins from the brothels. With everyone focused on eating, I spent the time observing the nobles as discreetly as I could. One girl, seated across the room, repeatedly stole glances my way. She had straight, dark hair and a thin frame. She hardly spoke to anyone and mostly looked down at her hands, shyly. But she peered at me so frequently, I made a note to ask Jesi about her later.

After lunch, Jesi and I returned to the library tower. To my surprise, Lida was there – although, knowing her, I shouldn't have been surprised at all.

"I've been granted permission to stay," she announced, without getting up from her chair. Unlike the night before, she'd brushed and braided her hair back into its usual style.

"How?" I breathed, sitting across from her at one of the long, dark tables in the room's center.

"Zaria, don't," Jesi warned.

"Don't what?"

Lida's gaze slid to Jesi. A tense pause filled the room.

"Yes, he's taken by me. But don't worry, I'm more of a gift for *her* than himself. He thinks she'll behave better with a friend."

It took my brain a few seconds to catch up. When I did, my face fell in shock.

"That's it," I slammed my fist onto the

table. "Everyone's been tip-toeing around me my whole life. Stop treating me like I'm a delicate creature that's going to burst into sobs if you speak plainly. Kir- that is, my friend told me plenty of things, you know." I jut out my chin. "*Taught* me them, too. So, I'm just as experienced as you both." *Maybe.* "Not to mention, I'm the one doomed to marry any day now so there's no point in treating me like a child. Stop it."

Lida and Jesi exchanged another look before Jesi crossed the library, disappearing behind the tall bookshelves.

"Are you okay?" I asked Lida. She nodded, waving me off as Jesi returned to drop a heavy tome on the table.

"What's this?" I furrowed my brow at the dark, title-less book.

"An education."

"In what?"

"What do you think?" Jesi mocked, opening the book to reveal a picture with *several* entwined people, making me instantly cough and flush. "You won't be childlike when you finish reading this, I promise. You should get ready for the next affair anyway. The Fae fête is less than two weeks away and it's ah... quite a celebration."

Jesi flipped a chair backwards, straddling it. "The fête isn't just for faeries. Anything goes, really; everyone dresses in costume. It's about the light and the dark, the dead and the living, the mortal and the immortal. Some events take place in the graveyard, some in the gardens. Some are reverent, mourning those recently departed and some are hedonistic, rejoicing in ah," she cleared her throat, arching a pointed brow back at the book, "the pleasures of living."

I slammed the book shut, clearing my own throat. "I'll look at this later. Tonight. In um... bed." My face burned. *Did that sound worse?*

"Listen, Zaria, this fête is important, it's not just frivolity. We don't know what Oxholde is up to, but we've had reports it's something *big*, something terrible. Grahar is actually worried High Spire itself might be threatened. I overheard him discussing plans for your safety – yours and his sons' – just in case."

My heart beat faster. *Did I want to be safe? Wasn't my enemy's enemy my friend?*

"Mal-Yin will be at the fête. Grahar hopes to seduce him. Occasionally, Mal-Yin smuggles weapons to help us. Depending on how generous he feels that day," she added with a wry grin. "Mal-Yin plays all sides, but for himself most of all."

Jesi stood and retrieved a very thin book from a nearby shelf. She flipped through until she found what she wanted, then slid the book to me.

"That's him," she instructed, as I stared at a picture of a skinny man in his mid-twenties.

His face was finely chiseled, his hair dark and short, and if the artist captured his likeness correctly, his eyes were dangerous.

He has mainland ties, mainland power, I thought. *Maybe he could be an ally. Help me find Kirwyn or intervene in gifting the Daughters of Elowa... somehow.*

"I know of Mal-Yin," I said, swallowing back the lump as I remembered my night with Kirwyn, when he mentioned the name. "I thought he sold wine?"

Jesi snorted. "Sure. Sure, he does. On the surface. Mal-Yin is someone you don't want to mess with. He's not a slaver, like the Spades or Oxholde, but horrific things happen to those who cross him."

"Like what?" I asked.

Jesi shook her head and tapped the book, "Let's stick with one shocking revelation at a time."

"Fine, whatever," I sighed. "Then tell me, who was that dark-haired girl at the king's table today? She was petite and had long, straight hair. Seemed pretty shy."

"Merie? She's Navere's sister," Jesi replied.

"The Commander? She kept staring at me."

"Oh. Yeah," Jesi said, wincing. "You might have... displaced her. In Navere's mind. He's kind of ambitious."

"What do you mean? I thought you said my marriage has been long-arranged."

"It has. But Juls and Merie were friendly at one time. I don't think there was any romantic affection between them, they were very young. But there was talk. I'm sure Navere hoped Grahar would break your engagement."

My mind raced with possibilities. "Has Juls ever had a say in any of this? Does he like her? Does he even *want* to marry me?"

Jesi wagged a finger. "I know what you're thinking but it won't happen. Trust me. Juls will do his duty. He wants to love you, I'm sure... wants for you to enjoy each other but... he'll do his duty either way. The young king isn't as romantic as you."

"*No one* is as romantic as Zaria," Lida chimed in, only half-paying attention as she turned the page of her book.

"Thanks," I said.

Without looking up, she replied, "Oh, it wasn't a compliment."

I shot her a look, which she didn't see.

"When can you start training me to defend myself?" I asked Jesi.

"Whenever you like," she replied. "That reminds me. Juls, the king, and the rest of the Assembly of Elites are back on the nightly meetings, so you've been spared dinners again. Don't take this the wrong way, but I kind of wish you weren't. Or at least I wish I was on that council to know what's going on. The intensity of these sessions is starting to worry me... and the idea that High Spire itself might be threatened... I'm not afraid to fight, but I want to know what we're up against."

Jesi's declaration sent a shiver through my body. Imagining strangers crawling upon our shores to attack - from yet *another* strange land – almost made me wish for Doreste dinners once more. Almost.

#

The next day, Jesi brought out a gown of bright mint and seafoam green, trailing to the floor and woven with golden thread. A bodice of gilded armor, heavier than usual, was placed across the front of the dress and secured with straps at the back.

"This was sent to you this morning. A gift to wear today."

I clenched my jaw. "I see."

I didn't need to ask who sent it. I'd begun a secret war, using clothing. I had a feeling if I wore my tunic again, the next dress sent up would be even heavier and more ostentatious.

Was this the right path? I wondered. *Or should I play it meeker?*

But to my surprise, when Jesi and I took a walk around High Spire that afternoon, I saw the king was too late. I spied the first white tunic on a young girl by the Garden Gate, making my heart leap.

Several more tunics appeared later that

evening. Some resembled the original Elowan, some had taken a Rythasian spin, with gilded belts or breastplates atop, or swathes of bright pink or green silks crossing the torso and tucked at the waist.

Something was happening that I couldn't quite figure out how to harness or use to my advantage, but I knew it was an asset, nonetheless. The people approved of me. Kirwyn lived, I lived, and no one tried to arrange a wedding – yet. Those were the most important things. Jesi was soon taking me on an intimate tour of the palace exits, and while I didn't have a plan to help Tomé, I'd think of something. I'd work out a way to escape to the mainland after that. Maybe Mal-Yin could be of assistance. Maybe with Kirwyn's help, together we could figure out how to stop the practice of bartering Elowan brides.

Early that evening, I stood on one of High Spire's many floral balconies overlooking the ocean. Clutching the balustrade, I smiled into the marine wind caressing my face. The sea sparkled like countless diamonds glittering upon the waves, like jewels from the sea kingdom I'd once unquestioningly believed hidden beneath the shadowy depths.

Standing tall, I breathed the briny, fortifying air.

Now I knew the truth.

The light can lie just as well as the dark.

Chapter 15

I rubbed my legs together as I awoke the next morning, only to find my thighs slick, wet. My eyes flew open and I laughed softly, embarrassed to remember the book Jesi gave me. I'd fallen asleep reading the scandalous tome and must have dreamed about it. Blushing, I sat up and threw back the covers to clean myself.

Bright red blood colored the sheets where I lay. I couldn't help it – I yelped. Staring at that shock of red, the truth was obvious. My moon cycles had come.

Jesi knocked a moment later, but I'd already leapt out of bed and raced to the bathing room, hysterical for no reason and every reason.

"Zaria," Jesi shouted, alarmed as she ran to the tub. If she hadn't seen the blood on the bedsheets, she couldn't miss it on my bare skin as I began washing.

"Jesi," I sobbed. "Don't judge me, I - I wasn't prepared... I always thought my mother would be here. I know I'm being ridiculous it's just... this is a horror." I met her eyes. "Do you know what this means? I can't bear someone else's children."

Jesi spoke softly, quickly. "It's okay. Listen, we'll clean this up. The king will know, everyone will know. Nothing is secret here."

I winced at the idea of strangers in my very personal business.

Kneeling, Jesi continued, "But I can get you something. My brother has... friends in Mid-Spire. It's an injection, okay? Like medicine. You take it once and you won't get pregnant for about a year. You'll have to take it again at that time if you still... if things don't change. But Zaria, you can never tell anyone. Grahar would hang me, I swear. Birth control isn't quite illegal but it's taboo, given the difficulty some have conceiving. Plus, if the king knew you defied him like that, he'd break something. A chair, your arm, your spirit, my life. Swear to me you will never tell anyone, okay?"

"I won't," I cried, wiping my tears. "Thank you, thank you. That makes me feel so much better."

Half-covering my eyes, I asked, "You don't think I'm an idiot for reacting this way, do you? I just always feel like I'm... so alone and everything is... too powerful for me to fight.

Like I can't stop these things from happening, forcing me into a future I don't want. Not moon cycles, of course, but what that means *here*."

Surprising me, Jesi laced her clean fingers through my bloody ones. She bent, touching her forehead to mine. "I don't know what we can stop from happening. But I promise you, you're not alone. Whatever is coming, I'll fight by your side."

I believed her; she already had. We fought and saved each other that day in the shed. Salty tears touched my tongue as I licked my lips and smiled. "Thank you."

"Let's get cleaned up, okay? And then we can do whatever you want today. Take the day off from studying. Will that make you feel better?"

"The gates," I said, immediately. "I want to understand how they work, learn the guards' schedules, and what this Black Passage is. Will you take me there today?"

"Okay," Jesi whispered. "Okay."

#

I was frustrated to find the Garden Gate, the Bone Gate and the King's Gate were heavily guarded at all times, whether open or closed. I could see why Grahar felt safely ensconced behind the thick walls of High Spire. Each of the massive gates was controlled by a wheel *and* stolen Spade technology, in a secure, lofted section high above the gates themselves.

Next, Jesi wound us down through the bowels of the castle to the Black Passage, where Raoul and Singen originally wanted to slip me discreetly into the fortress. The passage turned out to be a long, half-natural cave -- a corridor for small boats to sail in and out. The boat on which I'd first arrived would have been much too large, Raoul must have planned on switching when we neared. With the rise of tide, the passage flooded right to the ceiling. Unfortunately, guards were continually posted here as well – though less care was taken when the tide blocked the tunnel.

It was a slim hope, but the only possibility for escape I saw was sailing or swimming out of that passage near high tide. Deeply disappointed, Jesi and I returned to my room. She left me alone to stare out my window at the sea, only to pop back a few moments later, visibly cheerful.

"Family's here to see you," she announced.

"Who?" I asked, turning toward the door with my heart in my throat. I expected my Aunt Alette. Instead, a commanding, dark-skinned man walked into my room.

"Hello, Zaria. I'm your Uncle Saos." He flashed a wide, white-toothed grin reminding me so much of Tomé's it sent a pang through my heart. He was a strong, portly man, with a soft, round midsection, the likes of which I'd rarely seen in Elowa.

"By marriage," Saos clarified, striding forward. "I married your Aunt Alette when she came here."

Any misplaced affection I felt toward the man for his Tomé-like grin immediately dissipated. I gritted my teeth, slamming protective walls up around me.

"When she believed she was going to marry the Sea God?" I snapped, stepping away from him.

Saos threw his head back, laughing so loudly I jumped at the sound. "Not that she lets me forget it, either! You have her spirit, I hear. Not a moon cycle passes where she doesn't remind me. I swear I'll spend the rest of my life jumping through hoops to live it down. There should be a statute of limitations on such things." Saos came closer, speaking lower, "I think your aunt enjoys torturing me."

I blinked, unsure what to say as Saos straightened and turned serious. "But I swear to you, I wouldn't have married her if she didn't want to. You can ask her yourself. She'll be coming along any minute. I asked your aunt to let me woo her, to give us both the chance for her to make up her own mind. But I knew she couldn't resist," Saos winked.

He might have misread my silence when he patted his stomach and added, "I wasn't always this fat. Ah, I was a specimen in those days. And your aunt remains the most beautiful woman

I've ever seen. You have her look, young queen."

I hadn't even realized I looked to Jesi for guidance until she replied lazily, "He's harmless, I can vouch for him."

My cheeks colored. Was I that transparent?

"Everyone loves Saos, don't they, you charmer?"

Everyone loves the young king too, Jesi had said when I arrived. *That didn't make him my ally.*

Unoffended by my scrutiny, Saos rumbled a deep laugh, "Just like your aunt."

On cue, a woman slid into the room, and I recognized her as family immediately.

"Alette?" I whispered, eyes popping.

She looked more like my mother than me, though her body was soft and round, like Saos.

"I'm sorry, darling, I couldn't make my hair do what I wanted, and my best dress was soiled from our trip – we only just returned moments ago and came right over. I sent Saos on ahead to make sure you hadn't yet left for the day. Look at you!" my aunt cooed. "You're the spitting image of your mother."

Saos strode over to his wife, kissing her once. "I'll leave you two alone to chat." Turning to me one last time he winked again. "Pleasure to meet you. We've been looking forward to your arrival for a long time."

Jesi and Saos left my chambers together, but I couldn't stop staring at my aunt. It was like seeing another, slightly altered version of my mother.

"I have so many questions," I said.

#

Alette drank the cool tea – guava this time - and nibbled palm-sized pies stuffed with squab, plums, and raisins. We sat at my table, but I had no appetite.

"Aunt Alette, I don't understand. Why are we here in offering, like prized goats? Is it because we're different? Why are we different in the first place?" I asked, gesturing wildly with my hands as I spoke.

"How much do you know about genetics, darling?" she asked through sips of tea.

I shook my head, shrugging. Kirwyn mentioned that word, but he'd said so many unfamiliar terms I'd barely kept track, and Jesi spoke of the Optimal Election, but she didn't know much else.

"Let me start at the beginning," Alette declared, wiping an errant crumb from her pretty mouth – a mouth shaped just like my mother's, without the firm, hard-set line. "Those living in a golden age rarely know that they are, until worse times come along, and they look back and realize how good they had it. I'm sure it doesn't *always* feel wonderful to those living in such an era. But it can get worse, it can always get worse."

Though she spoke slowly, I hung on her

every word, unmoving.

"During the Age of Tranquility, debates about interference in human genetic engineering erupted. That is – the science of preselecting or altering the genes of an unborn child. That DNA is the building blocks to make you who you are. Scientists of this age were a *marvel.* They figured out numerous ways to modify these blocks. If a child was predicted to have been born missing a limb or with a crooked spine, the doctors could correct the code to prevent it. Or they could select the desired codes to create a child that it would never happen to in the first place. They could even go so far as to take a peek into the statistical probability of genetic outcomes in future offspring. Most people agreed this was a kindness. Do you follow me so far?"

"Um… a little," I lied. I'd waited so long, I needed her to go on. I could sort it out later.

My aunt took a sip of tea before continuing.

"The ethics grew murky around aesthetics. Who had the right to draw the lines, and where?"

She looked at me, but I had no answer. I didn't yet grasp the methodology behind the question.

"While the debates continued, the science persisted," Alette said. "In an increasingly competitive world, parents flocked to clinics offering an edge, opting to genetically select or engineer their offspring. One of the most renowned centers was in the southern regions of the North Continent, the Old America."

My aunt paused again, debating her words. Nervously, I rubbed the rim of my seat while she carefully returned the colored glass to the table.

"Beauty is a tricky thing to pin down. It's both objective and subjective. Certain aspects can be measured, can be timeless. Others are a matter of trends. For instance, studies have shown facial symmetry is proved as desirable amongst all cultures throughout time. But the configuration of other features may go in and out of style. Sometimes thick eyebrows are sought after, sometimes thin. Sometimes curly hair is in fashion, sometimes straight," absent-mindedly, my aunt stroked her cheek as she spoke. Her face took on a wistful gaze. "Do you understand?"

I nodded. We had trends in Elowa, the concept wasn't unknown to me.

"Late during the Age of Tranquility – before The Great Descent - when the old America was just breaking into warring factions, there were many who sought these scientific services to provide offspring with a desired set of traits, those dominantly favored at the time. These preferences for everything from the size of your nose to the shape of your chin were preselected by parents, guided by prevailing beauty standards and physician preference. The result being many children in that particular region began to look a lot alike. Regardless of ethnic background, a homogeny emerged – women with breasts the same size, men of the same height, and so on. And while trends come and go, no one disputes that these children – and much of their future generations – possessed an uncommon beauty. All the way down to the pronounced whites of their eyes, the length of their lashes, the strong, gleaming teeth. And such longevity... a glow on their cheeks to last unnaturally long as they aged, a tightness in their skin to hold well past the middle years."

Alette held my eyes, batting her own long lashes, once. "Elowans are their descendants. Such exquisiteness has been preserved by the isolation of her people, inter-marrying and breeding and creating more offspring with astounding beauty. It is the fairness of our faces that have become so prized amongst the Rythasian nobility – amongst all peoples, really. Not just beauty, darling, though it's most apparent. Everything from athleticism to artistic talent to problem-solving skills were carefully chosen as a part of the Optimal Election program."

"You make us sound... more than human," I breathed.

Alette smiled quizzically. "You'll find

yourself a bit of an oddity here, I must tell you. There are others like us, kin from previous marriages. But you and I are the only ones here now who were born on Elowa. To Rythas, it's an almost mythical place."

"But if it's so wonderful, why don't they go there? They're the ones keeping it a secret," I argued. "They like it, don't they? Penning us in like goats."

"Who it benefits most, who even started it, is debatable, my darling."

Alette bit into another squab pie and for a long time, I said nothing. Everything my aunt described was difficult to grasp. But now that I had a basis for comparison, I realized we *did* possess a distinct set of traits I didn't see as commonly in Rythas. Our eyes were bright and clear, our hair thick and shiny, our lips so full they almost formed a plump, pink circle – Braeni especially. There were probably a thousand tiny details I couldn't put my finger on that added up to giving Elowans a near-ethereal appearance.

"I don't understand," I began, tentatively. "I mean, I understand a little that our ancestors were formed to be special, somehow. But why are we all clustered together? How – how did we get there? You said this happened on the North Continent. So why do we all live in Elowa, having no contact with the outside world? And why am I here in offering, like a prized goat? And why could I never be touched?"

My aunt examined another squab pie, debating.

"You were raised under your mother's rule. Things are different in a matriarchy. The men in Rythas can be... territorial. Several generations back, a braenese came to be married having little interest in her husband, having formed an attachment beforehand. When the husband found out, he went mad with jealousy and had the Elowan man who touched his wife, slain. In his rage he jeopardized the secrecy and separation as well."

I fought the urge to pull my hair and scream, settling on a huff instead.

"As to why we first came to Elowa... I've done more research into the subject than anyone and I still don't know. It's a mystery." My aunt said. "Nor do I know why the eldest daughter is given in an arranged marriage. It's just always been done. An agreement was recorded many years ago, but only after the practice persisted for several generations."

"So why wasn't I given to a nobleman? Why did Grahar change custom?" I knew the answer from Jesi, but I wanted to hear my aunt's take.

Alette sniffed, displeased. "I can see it from his point of view, but that doesn't mean I agree with it. His decision has been very unpopular. Taking you for his own son robbed another man of the chance. Kings are blessed aplenty; an Elowan bride was a way to bestow favor and share good fortune with a family at court. It was a selfless act in which every king before took part."

"I'm not a thing," I snapped. "I can't be *given* to share good fortune!" Didn't *she,* of all people, understand?

"I know, darling," she quickly apologized. "I felt the same when I came here. But I came to love your uncle-"

"That's different. He gave you a choice."

"I imagine Juls would, if he could. He's a good boy. He'll make a good king."

According to whom? I wondered. *A good king wouldn't force a woman to be his queen.*

But instead of trying to convince my aunt, who couldn't see past her own found happiness, I pursed my lips and played the part I'd vowed to play.

"That's good to know," I lied. "Maybe I'll learn to love him."

A knock on my door interrupted our conversation and Saos poked his head inside the room. "Sorry to cut you short, but Grahar wants to discuss the negotiations. He's in a mood. Can't understand why you came to see Zaria before debriefing, and Oxholde is *definitely* up to trouble."

Reluctantly, my aunt replaced the pie on the table, smoothing her long, blonde hair. "We'll chat again, soon," she promised.

It took forever to see her and now she was leaving so fast. I had so many questions. *What was her life like, growing up on Elowa? Did she get along with my mother? Was she angry when she found out her mother had betrayed her?*

Alette had been promised to the Sea God, just like me. The crown fell to my mother, the second eldest. Only the youngest sister enjoyed a free life, and she'd died in a boating accident before I was born.

I froze, coquina clams creeping up my spine. *Didn't she?*

So many lies, who knew? I had to stop taking information for granted.

"Wait, before you go," I begged, "What was my Aunt Enith like?"

Alette's face paled. In her hesitation, I probed, "She died tragically young, didn't she?"

"It was a tragedy, yes," Alette said, eyes glazed as she stared.

"We've got to hurry," Saos urged from the doorway.

Alette shook her head, giving me a small smile. "We'll chat again soon," she repeated, but her eyes tinged with grief.

As she slipped away, I knew -- whatever happened to Enith, it was more tragic than I'd been told. Alette didn't seem as maliciously deceitful as my mother, but the event was clearly more grievous than she wanted to discuss.

#

That night, a knock on my door sounded and I was surprised to see Lida slip into my room. She wore her usual braid, though wisps of light brown hair fell loose around her face.

"I have something for you," she said, not quite meeting my eyes. "Jesi told me about what happened today."

"Oh." I looked away as well.

"I wasn't able to bring anything here, but I've been meaning to give you a gift. To thank you for helping me stay."

Lida held out her arm and I noticed she grasped a thin piece of paper. As I took it from her hand, I gasped. My lip quivered and I covered my mouth before I whimpered.

Kirwyn. I stared at a picture she drew in Kirwyn's likeness. There was no coloring agent used, but the penciled sketch bore such a resemblance I felt like Kirwyn's clever eyes stared right out at me. She caught the gorgeous shape of his mouth, the devil-may-care fall of his hair, his sharp jawline... even his ears that slightly arched and stuck out just a bit too much.

"How did you do this?" I gasped. If I remembered correctly – if I knew as much as I thought I did – Lida hadn't seen Kirwyn often. Not frequently enough to commit to memory his face in such detail.

Lida shrugged. "My talents were wasted on Elowa."

"Thank you so much," I gushed. "I had nothing at all, nothing to hold, to cling to. This – this is everything. Thank you. And I haven't forgotten about Tomé. I hope you didn't think you needed to do anything to persuade me to help him."

"No, I know you care for your cousin." Lida shifted her weight. "Well. Goodnight."

"Goodnight," I called to her back as she slipped out the door.

That night, I lay in bed, staring at Kirwyn's picture and hoping lightning would strike, hoping I'd figure out a way to escape *and* cease the practice of gifting a Daughter of Elowa to Rythas. But no answer appeared. I counted the growing love of the people as my best resource so far, but I didn't know what to *do* with it, other than to cultivate more of it and save it for someday. For the moment, the more important *I* was, the less likely I could be easily replaced by Jona, should Laz or anyone else try to dispose of me. I ran through a mental list, ticking off what else counted as an asset.

Jesi. She'd proved an invaluable friend.

My ability to swim. I didn't know what I could do with that either, but it was my best strength.

The last two items were harder to consider.

My mind, I insisted. *I'm not an idiot, even*

though I've been treated like one. I can be clever.

Finally, I rubbed my hand anxiously against my neck and thought, *the Elowan way I look.*

It was a double-edged sword. Admitting that my looks were an asset made me uncomfortable... wasn't that vain, proud -- things the Mystics preached against? On the other hand, it was also a danger in a way I never understood back in Elowa. *If Kirwyn hadn't been Kirwyn...*

I couldn't consider it without gulping at the thought.

Before Rythas, it never occurred to me that if he'd been someone else that day in the cave, it could have gone very badly for me in ways I hadn't imagined...

Kirwyn, I thought, before falling asleep. *We'll see each other again. I swear it.*

Chapter 16

The sun shone brightly the next morning, the sky clear and full of promise. It was a new day and I was a new braenese. *Queen-to-be? Young queen? Whatever.*

Staring at Kirwyn's picture while the moon beamed into my room made me feel like I'd absorbed some of his bravery or the power of that shining orb itself.

I had an idea. Like all my ideas I wasn't sure if this one would solve one problem or bring more.

Both. Maybe both. At least it wouldn't risk my life. And though it bruised my pride a bit, it only served to make me look like I'd fallen back in line after my tunic stunt.

"Jesi," I said, finding her already lounging in my chambers as I emerged from a bath. "I need your help. I want to be beautiful. Make me beautiful."

Stretched out like a cat on the couch, Jesi idly pushed back her cuticles with the point of her dagger. "You are beautiful."

"Thank you, but I want to be Rythas beautiful. Like the night of the presentation party. Make me pretty like you are here. Painted. Adorned."

Only half-paying attention, the tip of Jesi's blade dug too deep, tearing a cuticle. Bringing her finger to her mouth, Jesi sucked the blood. "For court today?"

"Yes. But no. I don't want to sit on the sidelines watching Juls. I want to approach like the others. I want to plead a case with the young king."

She narrowed her eyes. "For what?"

"For my cousin. He's... unwell. He needs to leave Elowa. I want to bring him here."

Jesi threw back her head, barking a laugh. "The king will never allow it, no use pleading your case with Juls. Exceptions aren't made. I'm surprised he didn't send your friend back, but I see he had his reasons." Jesi clucked her tongue. "Plus, I think she's making herself useful somehow. She's clever, that one."

She is, I thought, pursing my lips. *Would Lida double-cross me? Offer to spy on me for the king's permission to stay?*

Something to think about later.

Sighing through my nose, I pled, "Jesi, he's withering away. My cousin can't stay there.

Someone broke his heart, badly."

Jesi shrugged, going back to cleaning her nails. "He'll get over it."

"No." I shook my head. "I don't think he will. You didn't see them together. And even if he did, he can't find love again. Not there."

"Lots of Elowans find true love, despite the size of your island."

"No. You're not listening to me," I said slowly, enunciating. "He *can't*. They won't allow it."

Jesi stopped pushing at her cuticles and swung her large brown eyes up to mine once more. She remained quiet a long moment as we stared at one another. Finally, she stabbed the dagger into the little side table where it wedged upright, surely leaving a mark.

"Alright," she declared. "I'll help you prepare. But I have to warn you, it's unlikely to do any good. And even if by some miracle you're granted a favor, think about what that means. You'll be in the Doreste's debt, in their power. I mean, even more than you now are."

"I can accept that. It's for Tomé. He would do the same for me. He *has*."

If I hadn't asked for his help, his relationship might have remained secret. Marcin wouldn't have been wounded and subjected to... brainwashing or whatever happened. It was my fault.

"Okay..." Jesi said, stroking her chin. "I've got an idea, a look."

#

Jesi lined my eyes with black paint on the top of the lids *and* below. She smudged a black paste onto my lashes, darkening and lengthening those as well. She even applied a dark powder onto the lids, subtle in the region closest my nose and deepening in pigmentation as she moved out to the far corners. My already-wide eyes looked larger than ever; dark and mysterious. Jesi lined the outside of my lips with a deep rose pencil, exaggerating the pout to resemble the blood-engorged fullness of... *arousal,* I thought, blushing.

One by one, Jesi unclipped small barrels from my head, a soft curl cascading from each. She ran her fingers through my hair once it all had been freed, fluffing the wave of gold down my back. Then she swept it aside, resting onto one shoulder. Taking sections, she twisted and pinned it to flow over my right side, weaving thin silver ribbons into the style.

"In traditional attire, women often wore gold or silver ribbons in their hair," she said, smiling coyly. "And we're going to want to see your back."

I understood why when Jesi fetched the gown. Indigo with silver trim, the dress cut so low to the rear it would not only display every inch of my bare back, but dip down to reveal the upper swell of my bottom too. Although nothing but a thin scrap of cloth existed to cover the front of my torso, an abundance of material had been added to shadow the dress in a train that trailed at least five feet.

"At least the front's modest," I said, blowing out a puff of air.

Jesi shrugged. "You wanted to command attention."

"Right. Okay."

Carefully, Jesi slipped the dress over my head and slid my arms through thin straps. With my broad shoulders and my swimmer's torso, the material stretched tighter against my skin than its previous owner, pulling the fabric taut across my breasts. *So much for a modest front.*

As a final touch, Jesi slid silver bangles onto my wrists and clipped two silver-and-crystal cuffs on my ears. They ran the whole length of my ear, even extending into a leaf-and-floral pattern resting against my temples.

Jesi let out a low whistle. "I am *good.* The gods wouldn't deny your request today."

I stared at the strange creature in the gazing glass. She *looked* older, powerful, bewitching. "Let's hope so," I sighed. All I needed to do was make sure whatever I said or did matched the façade.

#

Approaching the king's hall from the main

entrance, Raoul immediately spied me and his gaze swept my attire appreciatively. His brown eyes lit with approval and curiosity; his smile came warm.

"I'd like an audience with the young king, to plead a case," I announced, keeping my voice even. "Can you slip me in before the next person? I will be quick; I won't cause anyone to lose a turn today."

"Give me a minute," he replied, "I have a feeling I don't want to miss this."

Raoul disappeared into the hall and I waited, holding my posture proud and strong, like a tree. Back straight, shoulders squared, head high. Thankfully, Raoul returned after a few minutes.

"Room's all yours."

I gulped. Good. *Right?* That was what I wanted.

Raoul opened the double-doors wide, and I strode into the hall with my heart pounding and an ocean roaring in my ears. If people on the sidelines whispered, I didn't hear it. I felt it, though. Their eyes upon me, searing my flesh. I kept my gaze focused on Juls, sitting upon the dais. He wore burgundy today, a thick gold crown, and his mask of power fixed firmly in place.

He does that for everyone pleading a case, I reminded myself. *He can't make special exceptions.*

Still, I would have given anything for one of those jovial smiles often playing at his lips.

As I neared the throne, I heard a few gasps when the nobles saw the expanse of my bare back. *Was it too much?* No, Jesi wouldn't have steered me wrong. This was traditional attire, meant to intrigue or appease or do *something* in my favor today. The heavy gown weighed down upon my shoulders and I heard the whisper of the long train sweeping the floor behind me. Not a soul in the room spoke a word. I didn't spy the king or Laz anywhere, though I was sure what was about to transpire would reach their ears within the hour.

Close now, I watched Juls's Adam's apple bob as he swallowed. Did I make him nervous again? *That's a good sign.*

I swallowed as well – my pride. I'd witnessed so many people of all stations pleading cases over the past few weeks, I knew what to do. Kneeling carefully, I did as they'd done: I laid a gentle, formal kiss upon Juls's sandaled foot. I couldn't help but think of Kirwyn as I bent -- how if I'd ever wanted anything, I'd just ask him in a normal conversation... and he'd do the same with me.

Curiosity danced in Juls's eyes when I looked up. *Another good sign.*

Then, breaking protocol, he extended his hand. He'd *never* done that for anyone before. Tentatively, I grasped it and he helped me rise.

The best sign yet.

"Tell me what it is you seek, young queen?"

I suppressed a shiver. On the other hand, Juls never spoke to me in *that* voice, the young king's voice.

"Mercy," I replied, as I'd rehearsed so many times in my head. "The mercy of Rythas to liberate my cousin from Elowa. To bring him here, under your protection."

Juls cocked his head. "Is your cousin in danger of harm? Has someone injured him?"

"N- no, not physically." I spoke carefully, knowing each word would be parroted to every eager ear throughout High Spire. "But he is unwell just the same and will wither away as surely as if his life had been threatened."

I cleared my throat to steady my voice. "I love my cousin and I ask for his presence by my side. As a... wedding gift." The last part made me gulp. Juls never brought up the topic of our wedding on his own and I knew by now gossip would have reached his ears about what I had awoken to find the other morning.

"Weren't you already gifted a friend from your homeland?" Juls asked, evenly. He didn't sound overly forceful; not like he was pushing back very hard. I licked my lips, studying his words. Was that an intentional thrust he hoped I'd parry, for the sake of watchful nobles?

"She came here on her own – I had no part in her journey. It was just as much a surprise to me as to you," I replied. *Bring the discussion back to him,* I thought. *Us.* "And she is not family. My cousin was – *is* – my closest companion. It would be a tragedy if he weren't here for our wedding."

Juls raised his eyebrows appreciatively, as if I'd made an excellent point to consider.

"I'll speak with the king and you will have your answer tomorrow." He said the words firmly, but his gaze said something else. The way Juls's brown eyes shone brought to life hopeful butterflies flitting about my chest. He waved his hand toward the door; a gentle dismissal. "We must not keep the people waiting."

I tried not to bristle, he had a point -- but the unequal dynamic of the whole exchange left a bad taste in my mouth.

"Thank you," I said dipping my head in a bow. I shuffled toward the rear exits - the royal ones - unsure if it was appropriate to do so but wanting to escape as quickly as possible. I could feel my hands shaking.

Alone in the hall, I threw myself into a wooden chair and let my head fall to my knees.

Oh Keroe, I did it. I think I did it.

My mind raced, picturing Tomé in Rythas. *He'll be so happy here, I know it. We can swim together or spend hours, days, in the library. And who better to help me figure out how to escape?*

I must have daydreamed in that chair for

close to half an hour without realizing it. Juls emerged from the king's hall, jarring me from my thoughts. I jumped to my feet and to my shock, Juls crossed the distance between us in three strides and swept me into his arms, more intimate than he'd ever been before.

"You were brilliant," he praised. "You understood me, knew exactly what to do. We're in sync."

I stared, wide-eyed, while he flashed his dashing grin. *If I understand you, why is it that you don't understand me?*

"If I can be honest, I want to pick you up and spin you right now, but I don't want to mess up this *dress.*" He pulled back slightly to look me up and down. "It suits you. You should wear more traditional attire. Red," Juls said, eyes shining, "I'll get you a red dress to match your ring."

Weakly, I smiled. I'd wear whatever he wanted if it meant Tomé was coming. Juls lifted my ringed hand and kissed it.

"Does that mean my cousin can come? Is your word final? Or will your father refuse my request?"

"He won't. I'll convince him it will look good at our wedding to have someone from your family present. Plus, he's distracted with Oxholde right now." Juls's face fell; his voice turned grave. "One more Elowan is the least of his worries."

I toyed with my hair. "Is it – are we safe here?"

Juls's fingers found the back of my neck, stroking. I tried not to flinch at his touch. I tried not to find comfort or pleasure in it, either. I tried not to think about that confusing possibility.

"Don't worry, my young queen. The castle is the safest place on land."

It was in that intimate pose we were interrupted.

"Zaria," a voice called. I snapped my gaze to see my aunt and uncle coming toward us. Juls abruptly released me, only making it look more as if we'd been caught like lovers.

"Your uncle witnessed your request today," Alette said, smiling between Juls and myself.

He did? I didn't even notice him in the audience. God, I must have been too terrified.

"Well done." Alette winked, but I bit my lip. *Did she think I was falling for Juls, as she'd fallen for my uncle?* "I think you take after me. And we're glad to catch you. Your uncle and I were just discussing fishing tomorrow. Do you want to join us? We have use of a motorboat."

Motorboat, I thought, heart soaring. *That might be my way out; if I can learn how they work.*

"Fishing?" I asked. "You mean… together?"

My uncle cocked his head, laughing. "No, we do it in separate boats. Of course, together! Didn't you fish with your family in Elowa?"

"Uh… fish, yes. Together, no."

My aunt shot Saos a look. "Of course, she didn't," she said, voice low, scolding.

"Well then, something to rectify," my uncle said, still grinning. "We'll take the boat in the afternoon. I'm sure Grahar can spare you for a visit to our place for dinner, too. Oxholde isn't attacking tomorrow and you, clever girl, rooted out your own kidnappers so there's no need to worry. We grill what we catch."

"That sounds… nice. Thank you." It *did.* I'd never been fishing with family before.

"Will your father permit it?" Alette asked Juls.

"My father won't mind," he said, returning to his formal voice. "As long as she brings Jesi along to keep her safe. If you'll excuse me, I have to discuss today's cases with him now."

I watched Juls depart down the long corridor before turning back to my aunt.

She bent her head, low, in a manner I noted was similar to her husband's. "I hear your friend came for a visit. Will she be staying?"

"Yes," I whispered.

Alette smiled. "Good. Why don't you invite her to dinner as well? Your uncle and I would love to meet all your friends."

Friends. Was Lida my friend? Jesi too?

I nodded.

"Wonderful, darling. We'll see you tomorrow."

#

As soon as I returned to my chambers I threw off the oppressive gown and Jesi and I changed into our seasuits. She pulled Lida away from her books in the library tower and found her a suit as well. The three of us wound our way down to the High Spire beaches together – accompanied by a few guards. We spent the long afternoon in the ocean, and I swam to the point of exhaustion. I didn't want to lose my connection to the sea, didn't want to lose my only real strength -- my ability to outswim everyone else. When I'd pushed just past my limits, I dragged myself back onto the beach and lounged beside Lida and Jesi, watching the setting sun.

But I looked down at the sand when it hurt too much... because I wondered where Kirwyn was, and if he stared at the same sunset.

Still, it felt *really* nice to spend the afternoon like that, with friends. The only thing marring my day was spying Laz in the corridor as Jesi and I returned to my chambers. He gave us a dark look, as if we soiled his castle by returning with hair dripping salt water, clad only in short robes.

I slammed my bedroom door behind us, shaking free of my robe and flinging it onto the nearest table. As usual, Jesi plopped on my sofa, uncaring if she wet the fabric. I liked that about her.

"I know you don't worship Keroe, but I'd like to thank all the gods you *do* worship that Juls pushed his way into this world first. Can you imagine if Laz was the eldest son? All that separates me and total despair is a few minutes."

Jesi didn't reply. At her silence, a tingle ran up my arms and I froze. I was getting to know her pretty well.

"What? What is it?"

"Have you heard any rumors about the birth?"

"No. I barely speak to anyone but you." A cold sensation gripped my stomach. "Why?"

One side of Jesi's mouth quirked into a grimace. "The thing is, I suspect they're true. Oh, Grahar's tried to put a stopper in it, but there's always been whispers."

The cold tingle spread to my neck, raising the hairs. I didn't move from my place in the center of the room.

"What. Rumors?"

Jesi let out a huff, tossing one leg over the side of the sofa. "The hermit was present for the royal birth, of course. He's like a spiritual guide, available to anyone who needs advice. He lives in little more than a large hole carved as a cliffside dwelling above Black Sand Beach. When Fersanda lived she relied on him for everything. Grahar has mostly kept the hermit at arm's length since her death."

Get to the point, I thought impatiently.

Jesi let out another puff of air before wincing as she continued. "I wasn't there, obviously, but from what I can glean... I'm pretty sure Laz was born first. And the hermit, in all his mystical wisdom, looked upon the boys and declared Juls would make the better ruler. So he counseled Grahar to claim Juls as the first-born son instead."

The air suddenly left the room. I clutched my midsection as though a swordfish had speared a hole right through me. "Is that true? I don't understand. Why would Grahar listen to some hermit? No, that doesn't make sense."

Jesi shrugged. "Maybe Fersanda persuaded him. And you can see, it worked out. Juls is a much better young king and Laz can be a nasty bugger. Sometimes..." she sighed, "sometimes I think he's meaner on behalf of his brother, so that no one believes the rumors and tries to install him as king. But even if he lays it on thick, he's still a prick underneath."

"I'm going to be sick," I whispered, dizzy. I closed my eyes against the spinning room. But I quickly opened them, to avoid picturing Laz as my groom.

Thank Keroe for this hermit.

For the hundredth time I thought, *as bad as my fate was, it could have been so much worse.*

Chapter 17

As soon as Jesi, Lida, and I reached the king's dock my heart sank.

Too heavily guarded.

A dozen or so boats bobbed in the water - similar to the one in which Singen and Raoul captured me – but the docks swarmed with strongly-armed men and women. *Landdammit.* Even if Rythas came under attack, soldiers would swarm to protect this treasure.

Before I could linger on the thought, my attention was riveted by one huge, wooden ship shadowing the smaller boats beneath it. It was a creation from a fantasy – several stories high bearing three towering masts.

"The King's Light," Jesi said, as I openly gawked. "Named for the string lights you see hanging between the masts. It's a historical boat used for ceremonial activities."

"It's giant," I remarked, staring at the floating mini-mountain. What would the stilt-dwellers of Elowa think of such a wonder?

Shading my eyes against the sun, I caught my uncle waving us over to one of the white motorboats. Despite the slim chances of leveraging the knowledge, I refused to waste an opportunity to learn. When we boarded the vessel, I stayed in the hull while Jesi and Lida shimmied onto the stern to ride with the breeze. I paid close attention to how the anchor was raised, the complex manner in which Saos started the motorized boat, and the strange dials above the steering wheel. As we rode, I kept my questions minimal, silently searing the information into my brain.

There will be other opportunities to learn how to drive it, I told myself.

"Your aunt thinks you and the young king make a lovely couple," Saos casually mentioned, as I stood by his side, stealing glances at the dashboard.

"I-"

"You disagree." It wasn't a question.

I bit my lip. I didn't know if I could trust Saos, but I did trust Jesi, and she trusted him. "I barely know Juls. He's very... noble. I'm sure I'll come to, um, like him more."

Saos laughed deeply, turning the wheel and aiming for some spot in the water he claimed had the best fishing. "You think I don't know what it looks like when a girl's in love? Before your aunt, I had a bit of a reputation."

Panic rose within and I made to protest, but my uncle held up his hand. Without turning his head, he leaned closer and swore, "Your secret's safe with me."

I didn't know what to say so I flashed a nervous grin.

We dropped anchor so far out I could barely see land, and Alette and Saos introduced me to the marvel of fishing in Rythas. Rods and twine and spinning wheels, unlike the spears or nets we used in Elowa. It wasn't long before we spied a pod of dolphins and we all jumped into the water together. The slippery mammals swam lightning-fast circles around us while we twirled, trying to keep up with their spinning. Sadly, I possessed no fins, but the moment was magical. When the dolphins tired of playing with us, I swam laps while Jesi and Lida lounged on the stern, drinking a rum-spiked tea Alette made. Together we ate spicy, cold chicken sandwiches for lunch.

"Blood pepper, just like on Elowa, right?" my aunt asked, smiling. "I like them the same way."

Grabbing another sandwich, Jesi said, "The Fae fête is less than ten days away and you still don't have a costume."

"What should I be?" I asked, not caring in the least about the party, save the opportunity to meet Mal-Yin, hopefully alone where I could try to strike a bargain. Over the past few days, I'd grown fixated on the idea that he might be inclined to help me. Somehow.

"A faerie?" I asked, idly.

"A mermaid, obviously," Lida replied, as if annoyed by the question.

Oh. Well, yes, I liked that.

"What will you be?" I asked her.

"Athena. She's an ancient goddess from an ancient land."

"And you?" I asked Jesi, taking a drink of the rum-spiked tea.

"You'll see," she said, grinning widely.

After we weighed anchor, we headed back toward Rythas, but Saos turned and steered the boat almost parallel to the island. "We'll ride back by the rift," he called out over the roar of the engine. I sat contentedly watching the sea and feeling the spray on my face as we flew at impossible speeds for the next few minutes.

"What's that?" I asked, shooting to my feet when he finally slowed the boat. I stared, wide-eyed at the uneven line of dark blue slashing across the turquoise waters like a lightning bolt.

"Cut waters. A long time ago they bombed here for some reason. Created a fissure in the seabed and made a trench. We don't know why. Could have been for science or a part of some defense strategy in war. We don't even know how far down it goes."

"It's so pretty," I gushed, though it looked eerie as well. "But... how do you cut water?

That's impossible."

"Ah, no," my uncle said, smiling. "It's just an expression. Cut means deep. Cut water means deep water."

"Oh, neat," I said smiling.

Jesi came up behind me. "It's slang. Not just for physical attributes, it can apply to personality too. Like, I'd say Juls is pretty cut even though he doesn't seem it on the surface. It doesn't mean his muscles in this case, it would mean he's deep. Soulful."

"Cut," I repeated, playing with the phrase in my mind. *Juls is cut. The land here runs cut.* Weird, but I liked it.

Kirwyn is cut, I thought. *In both ways.*

His voice popped into my mind, and I froze.

Fort Cuttle, he'd said... *or I'd heard?* Because of his accent and my mind going straight to the cuttlefish.

What if it wasn't Fort Cuttle at all, but Fort Cut... El? L?

My pulse picked up speed. What did that mean? Fort Cut-something? Deep-something? An entire nickname given for something else?

The more I thought about it, the more my heart raced, sure that I was right.

Oh my god. *That wasn't its official name at all, but likely some mainland slang for the fort.*

Oh my god. My efforts up until then were wasted. *The place he'd mentioned he and his uncle had been headed before he washed ashore on*

Elowa... no wonder I never found it on a map.

I'd been looking for the wrong name. I knew that now. But I didn't know where else to start.

#

That evening, we all rode a horse-cart back to my aunt and uncle's house in High Spire. "We've got a country estate in Low Spire," my aunt told me. "On the south side of Rythas. But we prefer the action here."

My uncle roasted the freshly-caught bass over a fire and brought out a lute after we ate. He played songs, and Jesi and Alette sang. I didn't want to enjoy it as much as I did, though I couldn't understand why it bothered me so much.

Before we left their little house together, I hugged my aunt and uncle goodbye. I'd had the idea that Alette or Saos might be able to help get me a key to the Forbidden Texts – they had permission to use boats, after all – but I was reluctant to involve anyone other than Jesi in my plans. I'd learned the hard way not to trust.

To feel her out before we departed, I said casually, "I've been meaning to ask you for days -- what was my Aunt Enith like?"

A cloud passed over Alette's face. "Enith? She was... gentle. Kind. Why do you ask?"

I *knew* there was a lie somewhere in there, but I couldn't guess what she was hiding. "I just want to know, and my mother never spoke of her. Or her husband, my Uncle Volmar. Was he kind too?"

My aunt frowned; her nose scrunched. "He was... I don't think anyone would describe him as particularly kind, no. He was, well, he was a lot like your mother."

Maybe because I'd recently suspected that my mother hastened my father's death, but a *wild* thought crossed my mind. *Did* he *kill* his *wife?*

"Is that what led to their deaths? The boating accident?"

Overhearing us, my uncle came closer and wrapped his arm around Alette's waist. "I'm sorry," he said, "but the truth is we don't know all the details of what happened that day. Volmar's behavior certainly didn't help matters, I'm sure."

I tried to keep my face blank as I scrutinized Saos's words, weighing how much rang true. As he hugged my aunt closer, I could see he'd interrupted as a kindness. Speaking of Enith clearly upset my aunt.

Maybe not dishonest, just emotional, I reasoned. If I pushed, maybe I could get more information from them later.

But for now, I'd keep my escape plans to Jesi and myself.

Chapter 18

Jesi came to my chambers to collect me late the night of the Fae fête. As long as I stayed by her side, we wouldn't be hounded by guards, and Juls sent a messenger telling me he'd meet me later, so I felt freer than ever.

As soon as Jesi opened my door, I gasped. With her skills, she'd pasted red and orange crystals to her face, laced them through the front of her high-styled curls, and placed the rhinestones in patterns along her collarbone, arms, and the expanse of her stomach -- revealed through strategic slashes in her clothing.

"Oh my god, Jesi. This is amazing."

"I couldn't tell you because it *sounds* underwhelming. I'm a faerie, like so many girls tonight."

"Uh... I haven't seen them but I'm pretty sure

you do *not* look like any other girls tonight."

I'd made an effort with the sparkling powder she'd provided, following instructions on where to place the glitter along my cheekbones and around my eyes, but I didn't glow like Jesi.

"No wings?" I asked.

"They get in the way of the dancing. Just *wait* till you see the dancing. It will go on until the sun comes up. The afterparty's in the graveyard. The best one, anyway. Here, drink this to start," she instructed, handing me a glass of something purple with a clear bubble on top – an actual bubble. "I already had one. Just pop it first."

To my delight, I poked the bubble and it burst like magic. Dutifully, I drank a cocktail that tasted like candied violets and ran down my throat with a stinging heat. After, we left to meet Lida by the King's Gate. She wore a loose white garment like a tunic, hanging down to her ankles and embroidered with an owl on one shoulder. She tried to hide it, but I could see by the gleam in her eyes she was excited about the celebration.

Together, the three of us descended the stunning water stairs, taking in the sprawling, shining gardens before us. I could hear and *feel* the palpable excitement in the air before we even entered the festivities. Fountains shone with the firelight of countless candles floating upon the surface, carried by flower-shaped bowls. Glowing orbs in purple and green, levitating in midair, lit the space above. Surely, Spade technology. Or a gift from Mal-Yin? *Where was he anyway?* I could see why Grahar believed the fête would seduce him; it would beguile anyone.

"It sort of begins with the light and dark court as separate, with reverent events and revelrous ones distinct," Jesi explained, as we wove through the enchanting front gardens and into the forest. "By the middle of the night, everything's a jumble."

It already looked like a jumble, to me. Everyone wore a costume – many of creatures real and mythical – most of which I couldn't identify. Musicians played from several different areas, food and drinks flowed, laughter and squeals bubbled from the lips of the partygoers as they chased one other or danced or drank.

"Let's start *dark*," Jesi grinned, raising her eyebrows. She grabbed my hand and directed Lida and I toward the royal graveyard – a small cemetery tucked discreetly behind the hedges of an outlying garden of moonflowers. I'd already been educated on the concept of land-burials in Rythas – it wasn't a shameful punishment like it was on Elowa – but I hadn't yet visited the tombs. Sea-funerals were reserved for kings alone.

We passed groups clustered together,

holding séances, as Jesi had explained earlier.

"Wait, I want to watch," Lida protested, tugging back on Jesi's arm.

"You can watch," I said, still very creeped out by the concept of land-graves. "I want to get a drink."

"We'll meet you in there," Jesi said, pointing to an open tomb, "that's the first bar."

I nodded, finding the concept of drinking in a tomb a bit strange, but it was all a part of the holiday. I also wondered why Jesi so easily allowed me to be on my own, but as soon as I ducked through the doorway and down the steps into the cold, stone crypt, I understood –

-- and immediately wished I were elsewhere.

No other revelers occupied the space except Laz, of all people. And to my total shock, he stood behind the makeshift bar, mixing drinks.

Groaning, I approached the counter. Laz made almost no effort with his costume, except to switch out his usual open-vested shirt for an even more widespread cape-like garment, resting on his shoulders and clasped by a silver chain linking the two halves. No silver bangles decorated his wrists but as always, the silver key mocked from his necklace. *God, did he ever button his shirt if the event didn't require him to do so?*

"I'm not the least surprised to see you skulking in the dark court, but I am extremely surprised to find you serving drinks. Isn't it *beneath* you?" I threw the words, hinting at what he'd said to me at my presentation party.

"No one fixes an *Enchanted Encounter* like me, I'm afraid." Laz held up the smoking, green-colored drink. I wanted to know how the magic worked, but I'd never ask him. "Plus, it gives me an advantage to assess all the ladies' costumes, encouraging those I like to linger and hurrying along those who disinterest me."

My mouth fell. I wanted to snap back something about how it was fun for *him* to engage in intimate activities with other women, but he'd implied a different standard for *me.* Unfortunately, I wasn't fast enough to think of a jab and Laz cut me off.

"Have a drink," he said, looking over my shoulder, bored. "You'll enjoy the fête more."

"Since when do you care about my enjoyment?"

"I don't. But I do care about appearances, and you look miserable."

"I wonder why that suddenly happened," I quipped, rolling my eyes as he shoved a small, stemmed glass across the counter. I didn't move, staring at the ominous, green liquid swirling within, glowing in the candlelight. A menacing, tiny cloud of smoke plumed from the top.

Laz's bare chest rippled with deep laughter. "You think it's poisoned?"

I met his dead-grass eyes, remembering the

suspiciously empty tank, the shark that had suddenly disappeared. "I don't think it would be your first attempt to kill me."

The accompanying tug to one side of his mouth, pulling his lips into a crooked line, sent chills down my spine.

"There have been countless meals since your arrival, little queen. Don't you think I could have gotten my hands on one of them by now?"

I shifted on my stool. He had a point. But he didn't deny wanting me dead by his hands, so there was that.

"As if I'd taint my own masterpiece," Laz said, grabbing the glass and taking a sip to show me it was safe. He pushed the green drink back in my direction.

I looked pointedly at the rim he'd touched with his lips. "Now it *is* tainted. I'd rather drink poison."

The candlelight reflected in the scorched earth of his eyes as if fires raged, burning fertile grounds within. *Too far. I'd done it again.* That quiet came upon Laz I knew too well to read as anything other than the stillness before an attack, like a snake coiling to strike. I braced.

"Oh, but the poisons we keep in the castle wouldn't prolong your suffering, so where's the fun in that?"

I'd vowed to volley back with equal enmity anything Laz said, but his statement, with its fatal assurance, made me pause.

"Is that what this is, Lazlian?" I asked, forcing myself to lean in and pin him with my own hard gaze. I hoped he didn't notice the pounding of my heart or see the sweat on my brow, because his words *did* frighten me. I didn't want to die, certainly not painfully. I didn't have a casual attitude about it, the way Rythasian warriors like Jesi did. "Are you just keeping me alive to prolong the agony before the kill?"

Laz opened his mouth, but before he could answer, a loud group of girls spilled into the room and both Laz and I turned in their direction.

I exhaled, relaxing at the break in tension. Constantly feigning bravery exhausted me. *When would it feel real? How many more weeks, months, until I could figure out an escape plan and breathe easy? Would it be before Laz actually did try to kill me?* Most of the time, all I wanted was to run far away from High Spire and cry. But I would never let myself weep in front of Juls or Laz. *Never.*

Four girls dressed as fairies in differing colors filled the small tomb. To my relief, Jesi and Lida filed in behind them. Oddly, the fairies didn't approach the bar, but stood awkwardly to one side of the room.

Without looking at Laz, I slammed back the drink and left. The liquor burned down my throat but I kind of liked the pain, the thrill of it.

"Omph, how many Enchanted Encounters have you had?" Jesi asked, cocking an eyebrow as I approached.

"One. Why?"

"Good, don't drink any more. That's strong stuff Laz mixes. We're going dancing," Jesi announced, fussing with one of her sticky-crystals. "I'm just going to grab a drink myself first."

"Sure," I shrugged.

As she disappeared to the bar, the empty space she left behind revealed the colorful fairies, stealing glances at me and whispering.

"Is there something on my face?" I asked Lida.

Taking note of my gaze, she titled her head and concluded, "They want to meet you."

"Me? Why?"

Lida's annoyance flared in a way I hadn't seen since Elowa. "You're going to be queen?" she mocked, sarcastic, impatient. "Plus, the way the Dorestes keep you guarded, half-under lock created even more of a mystery about you." Lida lowered her voice, "If they were doing it to check your power, it backfired. You're all anyone's talking about. You and your Elowan ways. Some have called you The Queen of our Hearts."

"But... why?"

Lida shot me an exasperated scowl. "Your

looks, your royal husband, your future! No other reason needed."

I blinked, surprised. I knew tunics became a trend – that was the point. But I didn't know I was the source of gossip or a nickname. The advantage it might provide *did* excite me. Lida's eyes swung between the fairies and myself. "Also, they're wondering if you'll introduce them to Laz. They're hoping to warm his bed tonight."

My mouth fell. *First of all, how did she know so much simply by looking? Secondly...* "He's... Laz," I protested, scowling. "He's not even attractive."

"He's the keylord and the prince," Lida pointed out. "I think that's attractive enough for them."

"Gross."

"He's not *hideous.*" Lida cocked her head, studying the bartender-prince. "He's not hot-hot, but he's ugly-hot."

What?

I spared a quick glance at the grinning keylord. He was pushing his wavy hair back with one hand and leaning long arms onto the counter to flirt with some poor girl who'd worked up the courage to approach him. He certainly wasn't prettily carved like Juls or devastatingly handsome like Kirwyn, but I supposed if he wasn't sneering, he wasn't *repulsive.* He was almost passable. Outwardly.

"Take a deeper look inside," I argued, pulling her by the arm up the tomb steps, so we wouldn't be forced to witness the display. "And how do you know all this just by looking? You're like a genius, Lida."

"Not like. And I told you, my talents were wasted on Elowa."

"Clearly."

"Ready," Jesi announced, coming up on our heels as we emerged into the graveyard.

Together, we wove through tombstones back to the central party. The solemn, séance-like circles had dwindled, giving way to more raucous drinking. Beneath the glowing orbs, we crossed the formal gardens and headed closer to the music by the trees.

My eyes popped out of my head at the writhing clash of bodies on a makeshift dance floor. "What is this?"

Jesi roared her laughter. "The Sea of Flames. Guess that wasn't in your book."

No.

The steps of the dance weren't formal, like a *High Twine.* Couples pressed tightly together without any space, swaying and rocking, hips locked. Partners weren't static, nor did there seem to be any measured exchange, switching in time to the beats. Frenzied, predatory lunges happened at any moment, hands pulling new partners, swirling, rhythmically pulsing. Men grabbed and women giggled away from their companions, or a woman spun out of reach and another man claimed her; an endless cycle of changing dancers. The men led once coupled, but the women could effectively end the pairing by twirling away and pressing onto a new dancer who good-naturedly abandoned his current partner for her.

The lockstep of hips pressed firmly together was like watching another intimate activity, only clothed. *Somewhat* clothed, depending on the costume. My blood heated and my cheeks pinked, both from the liquor and the lustful display.

"Come on!" Jesi said, diving into the crowd.

"Wait!" I called after her, but it was too late. *Was I even allowed to be unattended?*

It was then I spied Juls on the edge of the dancing, dressed as some kind of Fae or elf king in silver and gray. No wings, but he'd donned pointed ears. His long-ish hair fell loose around his ears. Impossibly, he looked more noble than usual.

Seeing me, he gently abandoned his partner and held out his hand.

I didn't know what else to do so I... took it.

In a flash, he pulled me into the dance. The liquor had warmed my blood and I found myself moving, smiling. The long slit of my skirt enabled the necessary movement of my legs but left me even more exposed and the tight chest-to-chest nature of the dance dug the crystalized mermaid bra into my flesh, surely leaving marks.

He's not even sweaty, how is he not sweaty when I can feel my costume sticking to my back?

Yet the alcohol fueled my laughter. It was... intimate, intense. *Easy.* Juls led perfectly. We were matched in height and seemed to fit together well.

Out of nowhere, the William Blake poem popped into my head.

I was angry with my friend;
I told my wrath, my wrath did end.
I was angry with my foe:
I told it not, my wrath did grow.

But at that moment, I wasn't mad. It wasn't anger that shamed me. It was another emotion entirely. I *should* be angry; I had no qualms about admitting such a feeling. Entranced by the music, I switched the words in my head, making it a poem about suppressing... something else.

I felt desire for my friend:
I told my want, my want did end.
I felt desire for my foe:
I told it not, my want...

No. *No.* I cut myself off, refusing to finish the poem in my head.

Instead, I swayed with Juls, a little self-conscious, but *safe.* The way he always made me feel. No one dared cut in between the young king and queen –

-- Until a hand clamped my wrist. I swung my gaze up to find Laz with *murder* gleaming in his wild eyes.

How... when did he abandon the bar?

"No."

I said it aloud, but no one heard above the music. Juls, oblivious to my hatred of his brother or trying to force everyone to get along, let Laz interrupt us... Or perhaps seeing the possibility of me being paired off with another sent girls clamoring to claim the young king before anyone else. It all happened so fast, and we were pressed too close to tell.

Yanking my wrist and pulling my waist, Laz wove us into the thick press of bodies, away from Juls. His steps were less dancing and more tugging as he directed us far from the young king – or from easy escape onto the grass. When we were satisfactorily smushed into one claustrophobic region of the dance floor, Laz switched from his sway-push to moving in time to the lewd dance.

I didn't look at Laz, but I could *feel* him all around me, over me, on me. Laz's long fingers, Laz's thighs, Laz's chest and the crook of his neck. I couldn't possibly have caught his strange sanguine scent amidst the sweat of bodies, but I imagined I could. We rocked, laps pressed tight like every other couple -- except it *felt* more like a dance of raging hate, ready to boil over any minute, so that I wouldn't have been surprised if he brandished a dagger and plunged it into my exposed abdomen right there on the floor. Laz's fingers didn't clasp my hands but dug painfully into my wrists. When I fought to pull away, he tugged me back. Yet neither of us wanted to call too much attention to our mutual distaste so we continued on in a strange half-sway, half-struggle.

What was the point of this?

To my dismay, no one interrupted. Sweaty couples bumped into us and we bumped back. *If Laz didn't hold us up, I would fall over,* I thought with resentment. *Which would be preferable to get me off this floor.*

After a minute, he moved us back in the direction we came. Laz used his superior height or his superior status to part bodies, half-dragging, half-dancing me there. I still didn't understand the point of any of it, when abruptly, Laz shoved me off his body. I felt like a ragdoll he'd played with; one who suddenly bored him. The thought made my hands shake with anger. We were near enough to the edge of dancing that when he stormed onto the empty grass, I stumbled after, rather than risk someone else grabbing me as a spare partner.

"Why did you do that?" I demanded, emboldened by liquor, blood pumping from the exertion of the dance. Though I wanted to shout, I kept my voice low, redirecting all my energy into infusing it with hot rage. "I know you had a point to prove, what was it?"

I didn't expect an answer, but one came... so cold it burned.

"I don't want Juls distracted by you when you might not be around for very long."

I flinched, stopping in my tracks. *Is that what Laz saw? Some affection developing in Juls as we danced? More importantly...*

...That definitely *sounded like a death threat.*

Chapter 19

Laz disappeared into the crowd as I heard Jesi laugh behind me. "Come on!" she shouted, grabbing my hand. Glad for the distraction, I followed her and Lida to a wooded section of the festivities, where a group of mostly-female Fae danced barefoot beneath the trees and around a large fire. *The light court.* Two men sat on the sidelines, beating drums in time. Jesi leapt into the circle as a purple faerie I did not know shoved a sheer scarf into my hands. I mimicked what the others were doing, spinning freeform around the blaze, waving the silk above my head. Behind me, I heard Lida laughing as she followed.

I knew I shouldn't, but when someone offered me a third drink – a white concoction with a sugared rim - I drank it greedily, wanting to forget about Laz and his murder attempts. It smelled of something I couldn't quite place.

I danced until my sandals dug into my feet. I whirled around the fire for one song, then another, and another... when suddenly, I heard the drumbeat slow into a new song, becoming heavier, tense, more powerful.

When the music caught my ears, I stopped. I suddenly recognized the drink. *It tasted of frangipani. Like the trees near my cave.*

I backed away from the dancing -- the laughter had grown too loud in my ears. *Who could think with such noise?* I needed to get away from the music, the shouting, the whirling spin of colors. Stumbling, I headed deeper into the forest, away from the faerie lights and toward the darkness. My feet followed a lesser-worn path, hoping to find silence or maybe...

Maybe punishing myself.

What right did I have to enjoy parties when Kirwyn might be hurt somewhere? Might be putting his life in danger to find me? What kind of person was I?

Walking for several minutes, a tinkling sound drew my attention, accompanied by a soft glow. I thought I even heard high-pitched giggling. I stopped, cocking my head.

Faeries? my liquor-addled brain thought.

I had too much of... whatever I'd imbibed. But curiosity got the better of me and I hurried toward the light. As the trees cleared, I blinked in wonder at an old fountain, half-ruined, half-reclaimed by the forest -- but still aglow with torchlights party guests had carried over.

I saw the source of the giggles. All three of them, barely dressed and vying for prime real estate in Mal-Yin's lap -- easily recognizable from his picture.

My pulse raced. I'd been hoping to speak to him. *He has mainland ties, mainland power. And he toys with the Dorestes. Jesi said he played for himself above all.*

Like Laz, Mal-Yin hadn't bothered with much of a costume, save two small brown horns attached to his head, like a satyr.

He caught my wide-eyed surprise before I had a chance to correct it.

"There she is. Shocked to find others enjoying the pleasures life has to offer?" he taunted, but it wasn't malicious. More... measured. Measuring me? My response? Had my reaction offended him? The artist *had* captured his likeness correctly. His dark eyes were dangerous. A lazy smile played on his lips, as if he tried to distract from them.

How to play this? Shrugging and relaxing back on my heels, I retorted, "I'm only shocked that you've limited yourself to the women of pleasure. Where are all the men?"

Mal-Yin stretched his neck for one of the girls to nuzzle. Perhaps used to an audience, the ladies completely ignored my presence. "Actually, they've been delayed, I'm told. I would appreciate it if you could help hurry them along or find out what is causing the hold-up."

What game is this?

I couldn't tell if he was trying to rile me or if he was serious, but something about his words struck me as contrived. Jesi said Mal-Yin was as slippery as he was cruel. Did he truly possess a hearty sexual appetite or did he use a rakish reputation as a distraction?

Either way, I wasn't likely to find out the truth.

But that didn't mean I couldn't use him to my advantage.

Stepping forward, I readied my queen's voice -- *my mother's voice* -- I thought, with resentment. "I could do a lot for you, I believe." I drew my shoulders back. "But what are you prepared to do for me, in return?"

I had absolutely *no idea* what I was talking about. It was the liquor, nothing more. This game was over my head. But I threw myself into the deep end like the swimmer I was.

Mal-Yin grinned. There was something feline about it. "She *does* have spirit," he said, as if speaking to the air or to himself. "But does she have a survivor's instinct?" He aimed the last question to the girls writhing on his lap and against his back. He did not look at me until he spoke next.

"War is coming to Rythas, young queen.

Who can say if you'll still be in line to be queen when it's over? Who can say if you'll even make it out alive?"

"I- I..." Was he right? *I will survive,* I wanted to proclaim. But I'd never been through a war before. I was already more than half-bluffing and Mal-Yin knew it. I suspected he typically knew a lot more than he let on.

How did I know -- truly know – if I was a survivor, when I'd never been through a battle?

I struggled for something to say in my defense when Mal-Yin drawled, "Talk reaches the mainland, you know. I hear the young king is falling in love with you."

My face flamed. Was I the subject of gossip that far away?

"I hear that half the men in this castle want the love of the young Elowan queen."

Ignoring my heated cheeks, I looked pointedly at the writhing girls and declared, "You and I both know it's not my love they're after."

He raised his eyebrows. "Well, I'm sorry to disappoint you, but the *Queen of our Hearts* is not the queen of mine. I'm more interested in what's in here," he tapped two thin, elegant fingers against his temple, "and what's inside you there doesn't interest me."

Ouch. Is that what he thought I came to do? Seduce him? Both the rejection of my supposed intent and the brutal dismissal of my intelligence stung as much as Laz's barbs. But I forced myself not to react because I *still* couldn't shake the feeling that I was being tested somehow. One of the girls giggled and turned, lowering herself onto Mal-Yin's lap facing him, wrapping her arms around his neck.

I used the diversion to draw a steadying breath and countered, "I'm sorry to disappoint *you*, but I came to see if our interests align. I didn't come here to try and seduce you. Besides, I can see that you have your hands full and I'm not one to wait in line."

Mal-Yin swung his sharp eyes from the girl to me. He whispered something in her ear and she leapt from his lap, beckoning her companions to follow. I watched them wander into the woods.

Mal-Yin crooked an eyebrow at me, a gesture to speak.

"I- I came seeking an ally," I said, palms sweating. "I don't... don't know what it is you seek when you visit here, but I know you want something. Maybe many things. And you can't get what you want from the Dorestes."

I was taking wild stabs in the dark, but Jesi said Mal-Yin played his own game. His face remained calm, but I *swear* I saw a glimmer behind his eyes. I had nothing to sell and didn't know what in the world he wanted to buy. But there was *something*.

"I don't endorse an untested product, young queen," Mal-Yin said slowly, darkly, holding my gaze. I could *not* determine if he'd meant the comment to tease at a sexual insinuation, or if he simply implied that I had not proven myself a worthy ally at court. The lady recently gyrating in his lap made it difficult to keep things straight in my mind.

Probably his intent.

"Talk to me when you have something to offer or have at least proven your worth."

"Then I suggest you keep your eyes on me," I declared boldly. I knew I lied through my teeth and was sure the fraudulence painted itself all over my face. But determinedly, I concluded, "And see what I can do."

Fake, my mind screamed. *You have no idea what you're talking about. Other than inspiring fashion trends you haven't accomplished a thing.*

Although... Jesi and I *had* outwitted the kidnappers. And I made the Dorestes think I'd accepted the marriage. Well, not Laz.

Whether Mal-Yin believed me or whether he was simply impressed by my courage, he looked me up and down, eyebrows raised appraisingly, giving me another glimmer of hope. It wasn't much, but it was enough, for now. I decided to end the conversation on my terms.

"I'll be sure to send the men your way," I said, turning on my heel to leave. I threw my head back over my shoulder. "Unless I find use for them myself."

Mal-Yin laughed, and I knew I wasn't fooling him with false bravado. But it entertained him nonetheless.

#

About a quarter of an hour later, I found Jesi, Lida, Juls and Laz on the edge of the forest, servants helping as they led horses together. I tensed, ready to be chastised for my disappearance, but everyone was too drunk to care. Nearly knocking me over as she collapsed her weight onto my shoulders, Jesi cried, "We've been looking for you. Graveyard party's over, we're headed to the beach to watch the sunrise!"

A boy with honey-colored hair stood shyly behind her. He wore a strange, bronzed warrior's costume. "Zaria, this is Erisio, you'll love him, he's lovely," she slurred, pinching his cheeks and making him crook more of an embarrassed grin.

"I – don't we need guards?" I asked, looking around.

"We *are* the guard," Jesi replied, louder than usual.

"Are you okay to ride?"

"Pfft, I'm okay to fight if need be," she replied. To prove her point, she strode to her horse and slung herself into the saddle with ease.

"N - nice to meet you," Erisio stammered.

"Don't let him fool you," Jesi scoffed. "He's shy in social gatherings, but he's one of our best fighters. We went through training together. Erisio, take Lida with you," she instructed, galloping off to run circles in a streak of red and orange through the night.

Juls came to stand in front of me, leading his tall, gray horse.

"I don't know how to ride," I protested.

"You'll ride with me, of course."

I chewed my lip, eyeing the beast, even taller than the last one I'd been on.

"Am I making you nervous again or is it him?" Juls asked, nodding his head toward the animal.

Both. Not to mention my mermaid skirt isn't built for straddling horses.

"Sit in front. I'll hold you in."

With Juls's assistance, I climbed onto the horse's back as modestly as I could, but the slit in my skirt meant one leg hung bare over the beast and I had to tilt my pelvis to conceal what lay between my legs. Hooking one foot in the stirrups, Juls hoisted himself into the saddle behind me with the ease built from years of practice.

Leaning forward, he whispered, "I told you, you make me nervous too."

He said it like that made everything better. I could hear the grin in his voice. But my body shivered confusingly at his words and his breath on my neck. Nudging his horse beside us, Laz approached scowling -- not that I expected otherwise. The flick of his glare told me my immodest leg particularly disgusted him. Did he think I had a choice?

Juls whispered in my ear, "Hold on," and kicked our horse into motion.

It wasn't a far ride to New Gold Beach, and I couldn't help but grin as excitement thrummed in my blood. I *wanted* to hate all this, to hate these people and my captivity. But... it wasn't that simple. The ride was one of those magical moments, the kind I wanted to clutch to my breast forever. I could hear Jesi's laughter floating on the wind, a fiery Fae on horseback. I watched Erisio and Lida smiling as they rode beside us – a warrior and goddess... even Laz seemed to fit the scene, clad in black like the night itself. Juls completed the picture, some kind of elven-faerie king. Everyone costumed, riding beneath the stars... like a fairytale.

A few minutes later we dismounted at the tree line, tying up the horses and emerging onto the sand one-by-one, gazing up at the sky. The stars faded; we'd arrived just in time.

Juls took a seat in the sand, motioning me to join him between his spread legs -- bolder than usual. *Was it the alcohol or our dancing?* I blinked. Maybe it was just time marching on and him inching us forward.

Either way, the image alone made my heart bleed. *I'd sat like that with Kirwyn. His arms wrapped around me from behind. That's who I wanted. Not Juls.*

But I smiled and did as he bid with surprising ease, like the actress I was becoming.

Despite dancing through the hot night, Juls still smelled of sandalwood and leather. He dared to rub his thumb against the skin of my bicep, but when I jumped a little, he stopped. Jesi and Erisio sang a sweet, happy tune I'd never heard, passing a bottle of something alcoholic back and forth between them. Lida sat, laughing but not singing. Lazlian hovered behind us, like he didn't want to get too close to the sea. *Laz doesn't like swimming,* I remembered Juls saying during our first and only family dinner. Maybe Lazlian didn't like the ocean at all.

The sky lightened to blue as the golden orb peeked above the horizon. I didn't think about Juls, behind me, as I watched that blazing sun hoist itself into the sky. A beautiful sunrise grew before me – dawn; and with it, hope. Mal-Yin might hold opportunity. No one yet set a wedding date. I played my part well.

Kirwyn once compared me to the sun, implying I had the power to burn or warm him. Watching the dawn, I saw something else. The power of patience and tenacity. Rising again, over and over. I would be like that, like the sun.

Beside me, Jesi and Erisio clapped, giddy. "Beautiful!" Jesi cried.

"Juls!" came a shout from the trees.

Heads whipped in the direction of the voice. Raoul dismounted his black horse gracefully, landing on both feet and striding toward us.

"Oxholde is going to attack within days. You need to return to the castle now." He looked up, speaking to everyone. "You all do, for your safety."

I swear I could feel the palpable, immediate tension in our group permeating the fresh, morning air. I shivered and Juls's hands ran down my arms, trying to warm me.

"Something is very wrong. We need to get back and prepare now," Raoul announced. "A battle is inevitable and imminent."

Was an attack the perfect time to escape? Excited fear warred with guilt coiling in my gut at the possibility of leaving without a word. *Jesi, Lida, Alette, Saos… even Juls,* I thought with resentment. *But why should I care if I left him?*

"She can ride with your brother," Raoul instructed, as Juls and I hurried to our horse. "We need to ride fast."

My stomach dropped at the prospect of being pressed against Laz, but Juls shook his head. "She rides with me. We'll be fine. No one is attacking this morning."

"Your father wants to meet, now," Raoul insisted.

"It's fine," I said. "I'll ride with Jesi."

"Sorry, Zaria, but I need to ride back to Navere right away," she insisted, already swinging herself up onto her horse.

"My father can wait a few minutes," Juls commanded.

"No," I protested softly, not wanting to be the cause of problems or earn more of the king's displeasure. "It's okay, really. I'll... ride with Laz."

Nothing about what I just said is okay, I wanted to scream. Instead, I smiled encouragingly and touched Juls's arm. "Take care of what you need to. We'll be right behind you." *Unless Laz pushes me off the beast and rides over me.*

"Thank you," Juls said, staring into my eyes. He looked so perfect in his elven costume; he must have broken many hearts earlier. He really was *distractingly* good-looking, especially when he let his hair fall loose around his ears. Making me blush, he leaned forward and gave me a quick kiss on my cheek.

"I'll find out what the plan is and see you soon," Jesi cried out to Erisio, taking off. Juls and Raoul rode off next, leaving Lida, Erisio, Laz and I to follow.

I'd avoided meeting his eyes as long as I could.

When I finally turned, I saw Laz's jaw clench and his eyes burn with hate. Gulping, I bowed my head and shuffled to his horse.

The next minute was a total disaster. There was no way to mount the horse with any modesty or grace, considering my ineptitude and the mermaid skirt. Juls had been helpful, and it had been dark; neither of those assets were present now. Clutching Laz's thighs and wiggling over his lap were unavoidable. *I understand he's loathe to touch me, but doesn't he understand this makes it worse?*

Lida and Erisio started off without us. I had the feeling she wasn't being inconsiderate but saving me from the embarrassment of an audience.

As soon as I sat myself into the saddle, I felt a new problem. Laz, unlike Juls, wore no proper shirt and I'd only donned the crystal mermaid bra. My bare back now pressed tight to Laz's bare chest. His arms rose on either side of me, holding the reins, and he spurred the horse to action without warning.

Too fast.

Unlike the considerate pace Juls set less than an hour ago, Lazlian urged the horse faster than he should have, desperate to shorten our time together.

The feeling's mutual, but my time is going to be very short if you don't slow down and I fall to my doom.

Maybe that was his intention.

Did he think I'd lean away and risk my death?

I clung to the little upright wedge at the edge of the saddle and pressed tighter against Laz. Trees blurred; we even passed Lida and Erisio on the dirt path.

I hate this ride, my mind screamed, tears pricking my eyes. *I don't want to die like this. With Laz.*

And still he pushed faster.

I squeaked, involuntarily turning my head to my shoulder.

Did he want me to cry out? Ask him to stop? I wouldn't. My heart was in my throat; I couldn't yell if I wanted to.

And still we rode faster. Up toward the castle, racing against the rising sun.

After an eternity, the horse slowed, and I exhaled.

"Are you playing at being the timid princess or are you really the timid princess?"

My eyes snapped wide at Laz's words. I hadn't even realized I'd closed them.

"Do you even know the difference anymore?"

He growled the insult at my ear, mimicking the day I'd called him the insolent prince. Blinking back tears, I saw we'd made it to the gates of High Spire.

"Make up your landdamn mind," I snapped. "Am I too proper or not proper enough? Because you mock me for both at your leisure.

And I'm not - not playing. I don't know how to ride. You rode faster than I could safely remain astride; I could have been hurt and you know it."

"Yet here you sit completely unharmed. Disappointingly. So I'd say I know nothing of the sort."

I didn't reply to the jab because as we rode through the gates, I was riveted by the scene before us.

I saw no trace of the last night's revelry.

Chaos had erupted in its place.

Part Two

Bleed to Survive

Chapter 20

A group of palace guards ran so quickly one tripped and fell, taking down his companion with him. A mother by the stables shouted, arms outstretched, calling her children to the safety of her embrace, likely to whisk them back to the protection of their home. Everywhere I looked, people shoved and hollered.

I spied Juls crossing the courtyard by the stables; we'd ridden so fast we caught up. He looked at us, surprised, then hurried over. Reaching up, he grabbed me by the waist and half-carried me to the ground as I dismounted. Terrified from the ride and anxious about the scene around us, I fell into his embrace. I wasn't playing the timid princess; I was glad to see him.

"Don't worry," Juls soothed, rubbing my back. "It's just the initial panic. Things will calm down soon." Voice straining, he added,

"Then they'll get worse again right before the attack."

Juls, Laz, and I were accompanied by several tense guards as we made our way into the castle to meet Grahar. We found him conversing with Singen by the king's hall.

"Come, we're meeting in the war tower," he said to his sons. Turning to a guard I did not know and waving me off without a glance, he directed, "She goes to her room and stays there."

Wait, no.

I'd hoped Juls would protest. But he read the disappointment in my eyes as fear – and maybe there was a little of that too – when he held my hand to say goodbye.

"You'll be safe there. Nothing is going to happen right now. Let us figure out a plan of defense and we'll come get you for the Offering Ceremony."

What's that? I wondered. Juls leaned forward to plant a little kiss on my cheek – this time closer to my lips than before.

"I'll send someone to get you," Juls promised, breaking away.

"Wait," I cried, but the Dorestes turned and left in lockstep. I had no choice but to follow the appointed guard. He escorted me up to my bedroom, ignoring my protests and questions.

Deposited in my chambers like a wayward child, I stripped the soiled mermaid costume from my body and bathed myself. For a while, I listened to hurried footsteps outside my door and tried to catch glimpses of anything happening outside my windows, but I only faced the sea. Constantly, my thoughts turned to Jesi. She would be equally exhausted and nursing a hangover, to boot. Not having slept the night before, I eventually dozed for a few hours.

I awoke in the evening, resentment rising with the moon. I still didn't know what was going on and no one came to see me. A guard was posted more closely to my door than usual, and he refused to let me leave. Claustrophobia gripped me. It wasn't as acute as when I'd been in my cave's tunnel, but it was worse for the prolonged time passing. My chest and neck flushed red from irritation and rising panic. After about an hour, a servant knocked, carrying a tray with a foul creation.

"What is it?" I asked.

"Goose liver and pineapple pâté," the serving girl explained, before quickly scurrying back into the hall.

It seemed a fancy meal to prepare at such a time and I couldn't help but wonder if Laz was behind it, knowing I wouldn't touch a bite. I nibbled the hard bread instead. Hours stretched endlessly until, somewhere in the middle of the night, I finally fell asleep.

The next day repeated the tortuous bedroom

routine. My frustration and boredom were exacerbated by the tension of not knowing what in all the sea kingdom was going on outside my door. I rubbed my neck even redder, tore at my hair, and endlessly paced. *Shouldn't future queens be more involved in the planning? Had I simply been forgotten?* I thought I'd go mad until Jesi knocked that evening.

"What's happening?" I cried. "I'm not allowed to leave my room."

Jesi sighed, pained. "It's bad, Zaria... I don't know. Laz wants to pull back the ships guarding Elowa."

I blinked, straightening. "Do it! Set Elowa free. We never asked for your protection!"

"Didn't you?"

What?

"Juls disagrees," she said. "He knows it won't make a difference anyway. Oxholde built some kind of large weapon to attack High Spire. Something advanced. But that's not why I'm here."

Jesi placed her hands on my shoulders. "Your cousin arrived. They're sending him up to see you shortly."

"Tomé," I gasped. "Is here? Now?"

Jesi nodded. "He'll be up soon. I'm sorry but I have to go. I'll come get you tomorrow afternoon. From the information we received, we believe Oxholde is planning to attack in two days."

Her words sent coquina clams up my spine.

"There's a ceremony on the eve before any battle where we make offerings to... I don't know," she shrugged, half-rolling her eyes, "appease the gods or something. Ask for favor and blessings in the battle to come. It's tradition and some people take it very seriously, so you'll be expected to be there with the Dorestes."

Good. Anything to get me out of this room before I pull all my hair out.

Jesi left and I paced again like the caged animal I was, until another knock sounded at my door.

I leapt, and my heart leapt with me as I raced to answer it.

Tomé.

His tunic slung off his shoulders like a misshapen sack from all the weight he'd lost. Circles darkened the skin beneath his eyes. Those sea blue eyes were glazed, unfocused, when they should have been sharp and bright, delighting in all the unfamiliar surroundings.

"Tomé," I cried, throwing my arms around my cousin as I'd never before been permitted. "Oh god, I'm so glad you're here but I wish you weren't. I wish you came just a few days later, oh god, I didn't know..."

I felt the small shake of Tomé's head, "It's fine," he murmured. "I'm being contained in a bedroom somewhere. Something about wanting to monitor me or medicate me because I'm not fit to face... in case whatever happened to you when you arrived, happens to me."

I pulled back to look at him, but my cousin looked down, not meeting my eyes. "It's fine," he mumbled. "I just want to sleep anyway."

"Okay, okay," I said hurriedly, hugging him again and nuzzling my face into his neck. Stiffly, he returned the hug, but the tension in his entire body made it feel like he held back a tidal wave of grief that might spill forth any minute. "Stay there," I pled. "Stay safe in your room and when this is all over, I'll come get you."

Tomé, I thought. *I'm so sorry I brought you here now.*

I held onto him for a few more seconds and then guards whisked him away.

It was not the reunion I'd planned.

\#

After a third agonizing day going absolutely mad in my tower, Jesi released me for the Offering Ceremony, just before dusk. By that time, I'd contained my rage to the clenching of my jaw and the occasional tightening of my fists. But inside, I was screaming.

High Spire's largest veranda, overlooking the sea, was crowded with people dressed in white or light-colored attire: shining, ornamental armor and billowing whisps of fine silks. Villagers and nobles mixed to fill the spacious, stone balcony. Grahar, Juls, and Lazlian stood at the balustrade by the sea. Swords dangled from the belts of the Dorestes. *Could they use them?* Curiously, I'd never seen them armed before. More than fifty feet below, fierce waves churned and broke over the rocks, as if the gods were indeed hungry for our offerings. *What we sacrificed today could not be recovered.*

Juls gave me a reassuring smile when I joined his family, but it was brief, and then he replaced his mask of formal nobility. I ground my teeth. Didn't he know I'd been locked away? Didn't he care? Or did he think it was for my own good?

The highest-ranking officials came first, bowing and awaiting King Grahar's nod. Proudly, they'd turn and toss their offering to the sea: a brooch, a hair comb, a gilded bowl. Nobles threw coins and rhinestones aplenty. One pious couple, hands clasped, released to the sea what looked like a very precious mold of a baby's feet. My heart ached as I watched them linger over-long, hugging one another for comfort. Stealing a quick glance at Juls, I could see by the shine to his eyes he was equally moved. Lazlian only smoothed the wrinkles in his white vest, bored. King Grahar's face was firmly molded into stone.

Once the elite made an offering, chosen

soldiers and villagers were given a turn. Parading in a string before the king, they too threw into the ocean beloved possessions, hoping the gods would favor us. The proceedings took so long my feet ached, even in my most comfortable sandals, but the solemn affair worked some sort of magic on me. It would have been difficult to see the respect and fear on everyone's face and *not* feel some of the power and awe for the ceremony.

Finally, the last little boy threw a toy figurine into the waves – a soldier. Though his mother held him aloft, his little arms couldn't muster the strength, and the toy crashed on the rocks below. Though I didn't really believe in the ceremony, even I couldn't deny the ill omen. Waves slammed against the rocks, tossing and scraping the figurine up-and-back as they went, though never strong enough to fully claim or release him.

From my position nearest the railing on the edge of the royal party, only the mother and I could see what had happened. Her nervous eyes flashed to mine, and I did the only thing I could do – encouraged her with a reassuring smile, dismissing the incident.

She didn't look reassured, but gratefully folded back into the crowd.

With a sense of dread, I looked back down, watching the miniature toy tumble about with no hope of finding peace beneath the sea.

Last came the Dorestes' turn. Only I was exempt, having come to Rythas with nothing of value except my mother's conch-and-diamond necklace, but no one knew about that.

"My mother's hair pin," Juls announced, stroking the metal lovingly. Though he had many items from his late mother, I knew it pained him to depart with even one. He watched the jeweled clip soar, then stood for a moment, as if in silent prayer. By the time he turned to re-face the crowd, he'd schooled his expression into blankness.

"My most-prized silver bangle," Lazlian announced, taking his turn. I fought not to roll my eyes. Even I could see the bracelet was old and dinged, and I'd never once caught Laz wearing it. *He probably fished it out of some forgotten box this morning,* I thought, narrowing my eyes.

As if that snake knew *I* knew, he flashed me a smug look before letting it fly.

Finally, stepping forward, King Grahar held a jeweled, silver goblet high above his head for all the crowd to see.

"My great-great-grandfather's favored cup," he declared, loudly.

I tried to hide my frown. Maybe it *was* the favored cup, but I'd seen twenty just like it, so who could say?

"May my sacrifice please the sea. May the gods grant us victory!" Grahar shouted. He threw the chalice into the ocean, hurtling it with impressive strength. It might have landed further out in the water than any other toss I'd seen that day. The crowd watched its arc in silence, until it splashed beneath the surface. Subdued cheers followed.

A terrifying scheme appeared in my brain, as if whispered by Keroe himself.

I couldn't say if I was moved by Juls's sacrifice, frightened by the omen of the young boy's toy solider, or feeling particularly defiant after being driven mad by three days of confinement.

But when I glanced down at my hand, rebellion flared in my chest. I eyed the sparkling ruby.

Don't do it, said a voice in my head. The voice I *should* listen to, but rarely did.

The jewel glittered, temping, taunting. My heart pounded at my own daring. Breathing heavily, I reached for the priceless ruby and slid it down my finger. For several torturous seconds, it stuck on my knuckle, refusing to budge -- as if it gave me a sign, *wanted* me to re-think my insanity.

It's just the heat, I reasoned. *Your fingers are swollen from the heat.*

Which was true, but I'd also lost weight the last few days of barely eating, or else it might not have come off at all – which, finally, it did.

"I too would like to make a sacrifice," I

announced loudly and quickly, before my brain could reason me out of what I planned.

Everyone hushed. Curious eyes focused on me.

I gulped.

Here goes nothing. Correction... *here goes everything.* I'd never addressed the people before. I'd never been given a chance.

"You have all welcomed me here so warmly. It is more than any girl could ask for; you are all more than any queen could hope for."

Out of the corner of my eye, I caught the look on Grahar's face – somewhere between rage and disbelief. *Oh god,* he already knew or suspected what I was going to do. Perhaps he was even just furious I dared to speak.

Don't look, I told myself. *He can't stop you. Not now. Not without looking bad.*

"It would be my honor if I could sacrifice as you have – as my family has," I raised my hand to indicate the Dorestes, though I hardly considered them family. "I should like to follow the example they have set and surrender unto the gods a jewel of great value."

Gasps exploded from the crowd as some guessed my intent. When I held up the huge, glittering ring, everyone quickly caught on.

Oh god, oh god, oh god. What was I doing? Briefly, I closed my eyes.

Don't think about the consequences. Just do it!

"May my sacrifice please the sea. May the

gods grant us victory!"

Flashing my eyes open, I turned quickly and, cocking my arm, I threw the ring as far as I could into the ocean. Feeling half-mad, I watched it soar across the sky in a wide arc before falling and disappearing forever into the murky depths.

For one weighty moment the ocean roared in my ears. Then ear-splitting cheers erupted behind me -- shouts of praise and joyous laughter. Protocol abandoned, people rushed to swarm me, reminding me of the day I'd been betrothed to the Sea God. Only now, everyone could touch me. Only now, they praised me for something I'd *done,* something I'd *chosen to do.*

At my own peril, I thought, though the crowds were blissfully unaware.

Grinning, I stole a glance the royal family. Thankfully, Juls's open mouth was somewhere between shock and admiration. Lazlian bore a murderous expression on the surface, but there was something else going on behind his face I couldn't read. And the king... I gulped again.

Grahar's unrestrained fury blazed in his eyes.

Because I defied him. Because I upstaged him. Because of the celebration I invoked.

Jesi warned me so many times. *You've angered him again, Zaria. Don't get on his bad side.* The king barely paid me much mind since I'd arrived, except to be annoyed with me.

I had his full and frightening attention now.

Grahar would make me pay. I could read the threat in his eyes, and it was enough to make my knees almost buckle; make me wish I could take the whole thing back.

#

I paced my room, unable to sit still after being escorted back again like a prisoner. I wasn't foolish enough to think my actions would go unanswered, but I couldn't fathom what Grahar would do.

Stupid girl, Zaria. You're a foolish, stupid girl.

Collapsing in a chair, I covered my face with my hands.

Was it worth it? Was it the right move? I'd earned more love of the people, but at what cost?

I nearly jumped at the sudden noise outside my bedroom door. When it flung wide, Grahar's imposing figure filled the doorway, causing my stomach to do acrobatic feats.

Don't back away. Don't let him see he scares you.

I managed to stand. No matter what happened, at least I stood. I couldn't control my breathing, couldn't fight the shaking in my hands and creeping up my arms. I knew fear glowed in my eyes.

But I could stand and meet my fate.

Grahar crossed the room quickly and my

heartbeats seemed timed with his footfalls. Rage blazed in his eyes, but his mouth was set in a firm, straight line. I saw Lazlian in that moment. Tall and quick and easy to anger, like his father. Tricky to read. Not to be trusted.

Like most people, I had to look up to meet the king's eyes. He stared down at me like Laz did, like I was something hateful, a beetle that had worked its way into his palace and now needed to be squashed, eaten, or thrown away.

Like he wanted to kill me.

He couldn't. Could he?

With alarming speed and force, Grahar snapped his arm high. My heart barely had time to leap into my throat before he smacked me across the face with a blow so hard I wondered how my teeth stayed in my mouth.

At such a powerful strike, I fell, splaying onto hands and knees. I saw blood splatter across the tiles beneath me – horrifying little droplets. Pain exploded across my face, creeping its way into my brain, reverberating around my head in an intense and instant headache. I didn't have time to assess the extent of the damage before the king grabbed my hair, yanking me to kneel in a move painful enough to equal that of the smack.

"Ow, stop, stop!" I cried.

"You dare to take from me? I will take from you," he spat. "I promise that will cost you, that you will pay for it in blood."

My mind spun wildly, wondering if Grahar would torture me, and how. *Jesi mentioned they tortured prisoners here.* Surely, he couldn't leave scars upon my body? My lip quivered as I tried not to imagine all the ways he could hurt me that *wouldn't* show.

"Stop, *please,*" I cried, holding my hair to brace against his punishing pull.

The wild rage ebbed from Grahar's voice. Instead, his words carried a low, steadied fury. "Your wedding date will be set one month after tomorrow's battle. There will be no grace period following the ceremony, nor following the birth of your first child. I expect my first grandchild nine months after you marry Juls and the rest of the grandchildren in rapid succession. Of which, there will be plenty."

His decree sent chills up my spine. Opening his hand and giving me a disgusted shove, I slumped to the floor. I held my cheek, feeling hot tears pool in my upturned palm.

Grandchildren? I didn't want *one* baby right now, let alone several. And not with Juls, *not ever.*

Sobbing, I watched Grahar leave, slamming my door behind him.

I thought I'd have time... but now I saw my time was quickly running out.

I needed to figure out a plan, and fast.

Provided I survived the battle.

Chapter 21

I cried myself to sleep and awoke to shouting the next morning. Ignoring the pain still throbbing in my cheek, I tossed back the covers and ran to my door, only to find it locked. "Let me out!" I cried, banging. No one responded.

It had never been locked before because the guard was always posted outside. Had he left?

I sprinted to the windows of my room –

- and nearly fainted.

The cause of the screaming appeared to be three large ships with metal hulls, fearsome even to behold. *The secret weapon Oxholde built. But what was it, exactly?* The long boats didn't resemble either the compact motorboats of Rythas, nor the king's wooden vessel I'd seen the day we fished. They had a tattered look, giving them an even more menacing appearance, patched in places with wood, mottled gray and brown.

My chest rose and fell with heavy, panicked breaths. My palms began to sweat. Throwing the widow wide, I cried, "Let me out!" to no one but the sea, and the sea answered only with its ceaseless rush of waves over the rocks.

Quickly, I dressed for the day in the simplest garb I could find – a blue, tunic-like dress. *Had Juls grown angry that I'd tossed the ring?* I wondered, glimpsing my bare finger. *And locked me away in punishment? Yet... he'd seemed to admire the sacrifice. No, this must be Grahar's doing.* I rubbed my hand. It felt lighter, freer for the ring's absence.

But I'd wear whatever the king wanted if it meant I'd walk freely out of my cage.

For the rest of the morning, I alternated between pacing my room and banging on my door, until miraculously, about an hour later, it opened.

Jesi came at me in a rush of comforting arms around my neck. Pulling back, she examined my body, as if to check I that was okay. My bruise must have faded and I had no will to speak of it at that moment. Jesi was dressed for battle and she'd tied her long curls securely into a knot at the back of her head. She deposited a dagger-and-belt combination onto the table nearest the door, similar to the kind the guard wore.

"I'm sorry I couldn't come before. They wouldn't let me," Jesi said, quickly. "You can leave your room now. There's no point in keeping you here. We're not safe in High Spire. They've got some long-range weapon pointed at us that can destroy the whole castle. You're going to have... you might need to escape with the young king if it comes to war. All the guards have been summoned by Navere and I have to go." Jesi's hands clamped my shoulders. "Don't do anything stupid. Now is not the time to try to slip out of Rythas."

She knew how my mind worked.

"Where are Lida and Tomé?" I asked, breathless.

"Lida's in the library, of course, furiously combing through books. Tomé is sleeping in his room."

"You just said we're not safe here! Shouldn't we abandon the castle if it's under an attack like this?"

Jesi shook her head. "Then they'll take it, and we'll lose anyway. Everyone stays. For now."

"What do they want?" I cried.

"Surrender. I don't know the exact terms. I have to go. Whatever happens, stay close to the Dorestes." Jesi squeezed my shoulders. "Listen, you don't understand war yet, but... you can't trust *anyone*, okay? Do you understand what I'm saying?" Her large brown eyes held mine as she spoke. I knew what she implied, and coquina clams raced up my spine. I nodded, tears threatening to spill.

"Just this once, listen to Juls and Laz, *promise me.* If they run for safety, run with them. If they surrender or get captured, *you* surrender or get captured with them."

Tears leaked on my next blink as I nodded, "Okay, okay."

She threw her arms back around me. "Jesi," I cried into her hair. "I'm scared. And I'm scared for *you.* Don't get hurt. I'll promise to stay with the Dorestes if you promise not to get hurt."

"I'll try," she swore. "Here, I have something for you."

Jesi retrieved the belt and dagger combination she'd placed upon the table. "Put this on," she instructed, shoving it into my hands. "I have to go. Stay by Juls, no matter what." She gave me a meaningful look, then took off down the hall, running.

Alone on the threshold of my doorway, I swiped at my tears. I'd been locked up for days and suddenly my cage door had been thrown wide. Part of me was frightened to take a step. If I stayed in my room, someone would eventually retrieve me, tell me what to do. If I went out... anything could happen. I could search for escape. I could locate Juls and stay glued to his side. I could find wine and drink until I numbed myself to the threat.

In a trance-like state, I strapped the belt around my waist, positioning the dagger to my left. Even without any witnesses, the moment felt heavy. I'd never been armed before. Jesi and I never even seemed to find the time for me to train.

Swallowing, I stepped into the stone hall. My heart pounded against my ribcage as I wandered aimlessly – or I thought it was aimless, until I realized my feet carried me toward the war tower. Hearing heated voices within, I pushed the door ajar.

About twenty men and women, most from the Assembly of Elites, sat or hovered beside a long, wooden table. A few guards – mostly palace - also scattered the circular tower.

As soon as I slipped into the room, I met Juls's eyes, standing in command at one end of the table. He flashed a weak smile, meant to be reassuring, but his worried expression betrayed him. He'd unbuttoned the top two or three buttons to his vest and his hair fell disheveled about his ears. Laz and Grahar looked to see what caught his attention, but, surprisingly, ignored my interruption and went right back to debating. With the implicit permission to stay, I pressed myself against the wall and listened.

"We can't get close enough to their ships," a guard said. *Prunson, I'd heard him called.* He was stocky, well-muscled, and possessed sharp blue eyes. I knew, like Jesi, he also wanted a position under Navere as one of the top three. "We approach and they'll launch their missiles or whatever hybrid weaponry it is they've positioned on those decks."

"What are their demands?" someone asked.

"By now, a thousand souls in chains," Prunson said. "Had we accepted when the terms were offered, they claim they would have taken five hundred. Each day we delay, they will increase the demand another thousand. On the third day, they'll attack."

Slavers, Jesi had called them. I shivered.

"We can *not* give them a single soul," Lazlian snarled, one hand fisted upon the table. "Once we give in, they will only return in six months or a year to demand more."

"You are correct, my son," Grahar replied, voice hard.

"And our people..." Juls said. I could hear the agony in his voice. "What we built here would entirely fall apart. Who would ever laugh or love, knowing that at any moment they could be torn from family and forced into chains by their own weak monarchy?" He rubbed a hand down his face. "I will *never* agree. We will not hand over even one."

"You are correct as well, my son," Grahar replied.

"So what should we do?" Prunson asked.

Raoul declared tenaciously, "We take a stand."

"A stand we cannot possibly win?" Juls asked, incredulous. "No, *no,*" he demanded, infusing that one word with a power and authority that rattled even my bones. He leaned onto the table for emphasis, every inch the young king. "We *must* have a better plan, there *must* be a plan."

"We're working on several new traps we can set up throughout High Spire," King Grahar explained, voice grave. "If at certain points we can divert them, trick them into separating their forces-"

"Once they've landed?" Juls asked, disbelieving. "You mean once they've destroyed our walls and killed as many people as they can from their ships?"

Grahar sat back slowly, templing his fingers. "Some lives spared is better than no lives at all."

"With that argument it would be better to bow to their demands and give them our people as slaves! Because we cannot win any battles if they blow High Spire to rubble. They'll take every man, woman and child left standing if we lose." Angrily, Juls ran a hand through his hair. Turning to Raoul, he ordered, "Run it down for us again."

"Three boats anchored by the Bloody Shoals. Not Spade engineering but salvaged from *somewhere.* Ironsides, patched with wood and whatever else they could find. Each laden with a kind of missile-like weaponry, long and barrel-shaped, like cannons. Those might have Spade technology behind them. Either way, capable of reaching High Spire and blowing her to bits. Not a bluff. They were kind enough to provide a demonstration when we sailed out for negotiations."

Bloody Shoals. I knew those. I'd seen them when examining the maps.

Grahar templed his fingers again, staring at something half-obscured from my view by the men around the table. "Three ships built to destroy a fortress and Mal-Yin gives us a dozen handguns and a few bombs."

I craned my neck to see that he gazed at a small metal device resting before him. The object bore the same shiny-silver casing as my Old World egg, but the similarity ended there. This contraption was twice as big and rectangular.

"If he gave any more, he'd be identified as the supplier," Juls pointed out. "And he'd bring the Spades down upon *his* head."

Grahar said nothing.

Prunson spoke up, "But we *have* the bombs. If we get close enough, we can hurl the explosives over the rails of their ships--" He stopped short at Grahar's glare.

"And what if we miss, hm? What if they throw them back before they explode? How will we get close enough? They're monitoring our shores; they have men on watch aboard their decks. They'll spot us and shoot us right out of the water."

Everyone fell silent at Grahar's proclamation. But a thought came into my mind, appearing from nowhere, like the flash of lightning.

Speak, I urged myself.

I folded my lips between my teeth.

Do it! Before the moment passes. Speak!

"They'd shoot us in a boat, yes," I said, voice small, thin. Heads turned in my direction. "But... not a swimmer. They won't be looking for a person coming from the water, and they wouldn't likely spy anyone in the blackness of the sea at night."

By the time I'd finished, all eyes pinned me to the floor. I shifted my weight, nervously, feeling my palms sweat.

"What are you suggesting?" Prunson scoffed. "Someone swim out to the Bloody Shoals? Do you know how far they are? Who can swim those leagues?"

I hadn't measured the distance on the maps, but they *looked* close enough. "I can," I licked my lips. "I think."

Grahar glared at me. "And you think you can just toss a bomb over the rails? Or sneak onto their ships, unseen? How will you escape before it blows? How will you explode the other ships once they know they're under attack?"

Wheels in my head spun, but I had no answers. I looked down, chastised. "I- I...hadn't thought of that," I mumbled, face burning.

Why had I even spoken? What made me think I belonged in this conversation? In the ensuing quiet, hot embarrassment spread onto my neck and chest. *What a foolish girl I was...*

"We'll set a timer."

The voice I *least* expected to hear cut across the room.

I snapped my gaze to Laz, who stared at me. Quickly, he turned to a pile of crates beside the table. Rubbing his fingers over lips, he studied them intently. From my position, I could only see a heap of unfamiliar metal gadgets and spare parts.

"We can wire a timer to each bomb. Set it to go off when *we* choose. I just need some time to engineer it and... everything we've got under lock. Something to waterproof the explosive and secure it to the ship." Laz gave his lips a final tug, then pointed at me.

"I can rig it. She can swim out to the Bloody Shoals."

My heart thumped at his assertion. *Was he serious?*

"We'll blow them to pieces," Laz said, scratching his chin, wild excitement in his eyes. "She can set the first timer, swim to the second ship and third ships and set the others. We'll link them, allotting for a few minutes between each. The bombs will go off in unison and their newfound warships will sink to the bottom of the ocean."

Grahar sat up straighter, staring at his son. "Can you do that?"

Lazlian continued his scratching, moving onto his cheeks and the growing stubble of his beard. Unlike Juls, he hadn't bothered to scrape it. I noticed his silver bangles were missing and his vest, curiously, was half-buttoned. "Yeah, I think so. I need Erisio, he's been studying the Forbidden Texts as well. Prunson, how were the ships constructed? What was the wood-to-metal ratio like? Was there metal at the base of the hull?"

Prunson thought for a second. "Yes. Yes, plenty. They seemed to patch upwards, toward the rails, covering any holes or reinforcing certain sections with whatever they could find."

"Good. We can use magnets. I need Erisio. Now."

Prunson jumped at the order, scurrying from the room to find the boy.

"She needs a wetsuit, dark. Something to protect her skin from the jellyfish and keep her concealed. Tianca, do we have an old one that might fit her?" Lazlian asked, turning to a pretty young woman whose name sounded familiar, though I couldn't remember where I'd heard it.

She paused, pursing her lips in thought, then nodded.

"Good. Go get it."

My heart pounded like an Elowan drum. *Could I really do this?* Across the room, my gaze met Juls's. His eyes glittered, beaming.

For the first time, Grahar swung his head fully in my direction. "Sit," he ordered in his deep, authoritative voice.

Swallowing, I took a seat at the table. If Grahar was agreeing to this plan, that meant he was putting his trust in me to save everyone. A girl he'd struck the day before. He must have been desperate to even consider it. Perhaps he only saw me as the delivery girl, with Lazlian the brains behind the operation. But... it was *my* idea, and, in the end, our victory depended on *my* success.

Not just a doll to dress up and make pretty Doreste babies, am I now, Grahar? I thought, bitterly. *Elowans are clever. You just choose not to see it.*

Multiple conversations broke out around the table. Laz barked orders and people scurried to get whatever he needed. Juls spoke rapidly to Raoul, making evacuation preparations of some kind.

"Come here," Laz beckoned, neither deigning to use my name nor saying "please" as he crooked a finger in my direction. I swallowed my irritation as I rose and crossed to where he sat; now was not the time to start a fight.

"You're going to need to learn some basics, fast," he instructed, sliding a bomb to me. A strange odor caught my nose.

Metal. That was the odd, sanguine-like scent on Laz's skin. *Not blood but metallic.*

"What will happen to the men and women aboard?" I asked, before he could begin any training. "Will they... die in the explosion? Or will the bomb spare enough wreckage to carry them back to their lands?"

I hoped it wasn't a stupid question. It might have been.

"So much better than that," Grahar replied, overhearing. Amusement tilted the corners of his mouth into a slight smile. "They'll swim to safety on the Bloody Shoals. Those who survive anyway, will flee right to those desolate sandbars."

Lazlian, also grinning with malicious anticipation, nodded at his father as he concluded, "And we'll drop by to rescue them."

His voice was like ice in my veins; I shivered. Nothing good would come to these men and women at Grahar's hands. *Torture,* Jesi had said.

And I'd be the deliverer of their doom.

Chapter 22

The wetsuit felt tight, uncomfortable on my skin. Wrong, separating me from the water. But I'd be protected from jellyfish stings and camouflaged in the black sea. Making the swim more difficult, a pack, filled with three bombs, would soon be strapped to my back.

No one but the Assembly of Elites and the guards present at our meeting knew what I was about to do.

"We'll light the fires after we see the explosion," Juls said, pointing to the top of High Spire, where Navere's most trusted guards readied to set a mighty blaze, guiding me back to Rythas in the night. "If for any reason we don't see the bombs deploy... we'll light the fire anyway, an hour before dawn. Their ships have electric lights, but they're dim, so you can't see them from sea level here. But the good news is, you should be able to spy them two or three miles out and it's a straight shot north. Couldn't be better, geographically speaking."

I nodded. "I can navigate celestially. I know the North Star. As long as the currents don't push me too far east or west, I should be within range of sight in a reasonable time."

Juls stood so close I could feel his breath on my face. "What you're doing is nothing short of incredible. We all owe you our deepest gratitude. I wasn't always sure..." He paused, hands rising to cup my cheeks. "But I'm glad it's you." His thumb moved, sweeping my cheekbone, somehow so much more personal, more intimate, than when he'd sucked my finger. My face was my own territory. Kirwyn's territory.

"Are you... glad as well?" Juls asked, searching my face.

"I - " Why was he asking me this *now?* Because I might not make it back? Because we might incite an attack tonight?

"I – yes." In that moment I meant it. Not because I was acting or because I wanted to please him or even out of gratitude that he wasn't a monster like his brother. But because fear, sick and sour, roiled in my gut and I clung to Juls, clung to life or hope or just the nearest human being I could while terror beat in my breast. Shamefully, I said yes because I was scared for what I was about to do and longed for human connection.

If Kirwyn didn't exist, could I love a man like Juls? If I molded myself into what he needed or wanted, swallowed back the parts of me that didn't fit, would I be happy?

It could be worse. It could always be worse.

"I'm sorry about the ring," I said, eyes downcast.

"No apology needed. You did the right thing." Juls smiled, though with the looming threat, it didn't touch his eyes. "I can always buy you a new one, a bigger one."

"No, that's... not necessary," I protested. "It wouldn't... feel like a real sacrifice if I just meant to replace it."

Something in Juls's eyes told me he didn't fully believe me; told me I'd wounded him. Guilt washed over me. *He didn't ask for this either,* I reminded myself.

Yet my eyes rounded when Juls's thumb found my lips for the briefest of moments. His gaze locked upon my mouth, like he wanted to kiss it. Quickly, he dropped his hand, but not before people saw. *What did they see? An intimate parting of lovers? A young king and his... what was I? Bride? Savior? Soldier?*

"Come back to me," Juls ordered, smiling sadly. "That's a king's command."

He left to speak with his father, and I saw my uncle emerge onto the beach.

"Saos?" I blinked, shocked. "What are you doing here?"

"A messenger arrived, thanks to Juls. He told us what you're doing. I sent your aunt to our house in Low Spire, though she went kicking and screaming. She's as brave and stubborn as you are. But it's the safest place for her now. She's not a soldier and it's best if we're separate."

My uncle lifted a flat, rubbery object.

"Put this on. It's a life vest. Don't use it unless you need to. If anything goes wrong at sea, press this," his thick finger tapped a small, black button, "and it will inflate with air."

I nodded vigorously, growing more emotional by the second. *What if something did go wrong? What if I exploded myself somehow? What if I got caught? What if I failed?*

"Okay," I said, still nodding.

To my astonishment, Saos pulled me into a crushing hug. "Whatever happens, your aunt and I want to make sure one of us is around to take care of you," he promised.

Warmth filled me. Suddenly, I wanted to cry, and it wasn't from fear. *Well, not just.*

"Thank you," I said. Maybe it was the life-or-death mission before me, but for the first time ever, I said, "Thank you, Uncle Saos." *He made Alette leave so that they doubled their chances one of them would survive... for me.*

When my uncle left the beach, Laz approached, twirling his finger in a motion to indicate I should turn around. My annoyance jarred me from the threat of weeping. Laz strapped the pack onto my back.

"Just as we practiced," he said. "The first bomb is marked with a *one,* and so on. Seal each to the hull, press the button, set the timer, and swim. Swim fast once you set the last explosive."

"Got it."

"Do you?" he challenged, arching his brows.

I didn't know how to reply. "I mean... yeah, I mean... I think so."

"Everyone's life depends on you. Don't screw it up."

No pressure.

"Did you screw up *your* part?"

Raised eyebrows were my only reply.

I scoffed, "You know, a thank you would be nice. That's all you need to say. Thank you, Zaria for risking your life to save our kingdom."

He shrugged, "Perhaps I'll thank you if you make it back."

#

What an ass, I thought, swimming through black waves. I had to admit I was a little grateful for the distraction. With miles to go, I could see the small firelight in High Spire homes behind me, but no artificial lights from warships came into view.

Head down, breath up. Head down, breath up.

Clear skies guided the way, though the

cumbersome pack made maneuvering more difficult. I swam in rhythmic, meditative strokes, determined not to think on what I was about to do. It didn't matter how much time passed, I swam like I drew my strength from the ocean, not as if it drained it.

Head down, breath up. On and on, just me and the sea. My first love.

Further and further until finally, breaking and blinking, I spied dull lights in the distance, ahead and to my right. The current had pushed me westward.

Turning, I pushed with renewed energy toward the light source.

Head down, breath up. Head down, breath up.

It had taken longer to swim with the pack strapped to my back. Even I felt the passage of too much time; worried how it must have concerned everyone in Rythas. Finally, the ships grew bigger, rose higher, and I slowed down, ducking my head into my shoulders as if the waves would hide me. Maybe they would. Only a sliver of a moon glowed; the sea billowed and waved around me like a dark blanket floating on air.

I switched to a soft stroke, kicking quietly under water as I approached the monstrous war ships.

What if I'm caught before I place the bombs?

I struggled to breathe at the thought.

I couldn't hear anyone stirring in the middle

of the night, but I knew there'd be guards posted. Waves splashed against the patchwork wood-and-iron hull and boards creaked, but all remained quiet on deck.

What if I'm caught? Would I spend my life in chains? Be tortured for information?

I was privy to *some* royal business. Castle fortifications. How the king thought, plotted, and on whom he relied. Important information.

I'm important, too.

Treading water stealthily, looking up at the bobbing, towering walls of the ship, the obvious thought struck.

I didn't have to go through with this. Hurt anyone. I could trade my knowledge, barter for safety...

My heart leapt.

For passage.

To Kirwyn. To find him somewhere on the mainland.

I had no allegiance to Rythas. The king wanted to use me, breed me. Perhaps Oxholde might steal people as slaves, but I was *already* enslaved in Rythas.

Pressed against the first ship, my fingernails dug into a rare spot of slippery, algae-covered wood, scrambling for purchase to steady myself against the waves or perhaps... perhaps preparing to cling to the boat, to climb aboard somehow.

All I had to do was open my mouth. Scream, and someone would come for me. *My enemy's enemy is my friend.* I could be free, could ask to be carried to the North Continent. Maybe I could even negotiate help in locating Kirwyn.

I'd see him again. We'd be together again.

But was Rythas truly my enemy?

If I shouted, everyone I'd come to care about would be in danger. Innocent people put in chains. And many more dead if it came to war. *Jesi, Aunt Alette, Uncle Saos. Lida and Tomé. Even Juls, who'd been nothing but kind to me.*

No. I released the ship, momentarily bobbing lower into the water before buoying up again.

I can't let them get hurt.

Shrugging from my pack, I fished out the first bomb. Before I could change my mind, I released the lever, closed my eyes, and pressed the device to the side of the metal ship, cringing when it made a clamping sound.

Carefully, I reached the top of the bomb, sliding my wet fingers along the rim to find the button I needed.

If everyone had been as cruel as Lazlian, I might not care about betraying them.

I froze; my breath caught.

Lazlian.

Who hated me on sight. Hated me *before* even seeing me. Lazlian, who wished to be rid of me.

Oh no.

Could he have rigged the bomb to explode -- not when I set the timer -- but when I pressed the very button over which my finger now hovered? Was it not a timer at all... but a trigger?

Horrified at the idea, I slid my arm back into the sea.

If I pushed that button, would I die?

I chewed my salty lip, treading water. *Think logically, Zaria. What would happen if the bomb exploded now?*

Lazlian would take down one of the three ships in the process. Perhaps that was worth the sacrifice to him. No one would know what happened. Maybe he would claim it was faulty engineering. Hell, that was still a possibility, even if Laz deigned to keep me alive. For me to push that button meant I not only had to trust that he didn't *intend* to blow me to pieces, I also had to trust that Lazlian knew how to *correctly* rig the bomb.

Landdammit.

I really didn't want to push that button now.

I'd be giving up my chance to see Kirwyn. I'd be gambling that Lazlian knew what he was doing. I'd be risking that he didn't use the opportunity to send me to the bottom of the ocean.

The waves tossed me backwards, as if telling me not to do it. I swam back to the ship, if only to press myself against it for cover.

But… landdammit, all those risks didn't outweigh the risk to the people of an entire land. Innocent people. Including those I loved.

Clutching the ship with one hand, I reached the other back up to the top of the bomb. Before I could change my mind again, my finger found the slick metal button.

I squeezed my eyes shut.

Kirwyn, I thought, praying his name as I pushed.

Beep, beep.

My eyes flew open.

It worked!

The clock glowed in red lights, just as Lazlian had shown me. A countdown clock; the minutes would tick backwards once I set it. With shaking hands, I pressed the numbers, arming the device to detonate in thirty minutes.

That gave me a few minutes to swim to the next ship, secure the second bomb, and set the timer again. I'd have another few minutes for the final ship, and then I'd swim as far away as possible.

Unless…

Oh god.

Unless Lazlian rigged the final bomb to explode when I pushed the button. Wouldn't that be smarter? That way, I'd wind up at the bottom of the ocean *and* all three ships would still explode in due course.

I whimpered, swallowing sea water. Just when I thought I was in the clear, panic seized my gut once more. I had no one to ask, no one to look to for advice. It was only me alone, out in the black sea. My life and the lives of so many others in my hands. How did I know I was doing the right thing?

You've got to keep moving, I admonished myself.

Across the silent sea, I swam to the second ship, heart pounding in my ears for fear I'd hear someone shouting from the decks at any moment. I repeated the process of securing the explosive. My heart gave a little jump when I successfully started the countdown on the device. It was even easier this time, as Laz had linked the clock to synchronize with the timer already in motion on the first bomb.

Suddenly, a bright, narrow light flashed from above. Voices followed, two men perhaps. With a whimper I pressed myself against the hull, trying to disappear. The light moved, searching the sea. I heard the men speaking rapidly, but I couldn't make out what they were saying.

Please, please don't shine the light here.

My heart was going to burst from terror as the light roved. Shaking, I squeezed my eyes shut and didn't breathe.

Oh god, oh god. I'd already set the first two timers. I needed to move, fast. But if I swam, the men above deck would see or hear me. *What should I do?*

I'll wait, I told myself. *One more minute. If the light doesn't disappear by then… I'll risk it.*

Even though the timer glowed behind me, I counted the seconds, trying to calm myself.

Twenty-one, twenty-two…

What if I'm caught, dragged above deck, and I explode with the ship?

Forty-five, forty-six…

I opened my eyes. The light was gone. The voices had faded.

Move, Zaria!

Quicker than before, I swam toward the third and final ship.

But this one terrified me. Trusting Lazlian didn't want to kill me. Yet.

Out of the darkness, his haunting words echoed in my mind.

"Perhaps I'll thank you if you make it back."

I gulped. Oh god, oh god. Why had he said that? Did that mean he didn't intend for it to happen?

Breathing heavy and biting my lip, I withdrew the final explosive from my pack. For a moment, I only stared at it in my shaking hands. But a strong wave came, and it suddenly slipped from my grasp, falling beneath the surface.

No!

Frantically, I dove and scrambled under the

water, feeling in the darkness for the metal.

I had but a few seconds before I'd lose it forever.

Kicking and twirling, I thrashed without aim, screaming underwater all the while.

Suddenly, my hand hit something hard and I grabbed it, clutching the object to my chest. *The bomb. Oh god. I'd almost lost it forever.*

Resurfacing, I gulped deep breaths of air. I couldn't move for a few seconds, needing to calm down. Finally, I kicked back to the last ship.

Now or never.

Keroe, I prayed, when I reached the metal hull. *Don't let me die here. Save me, as you saved Kirwyn.*

With a soft *thwump,* I attached the bomb to the ship.

Let me live, let me find him again.

My finger hovered over the knob.

I didn't trust Laz. I would never trust Laz. But I trusted the sea.

Let me make it through this.

I pushed the button to start the device.

Please, I begged. Taking a deep breath and closing my eyes, I pressed the timer –

-- *Beep, beep.*

It worked!

Oh my god. Thank you, Keroe, thank you.

At my fastest pace I swam for my life, putting as much distance as I could between myself and the three ships. I kicked back in the direction of what I thought was Rythas, judging from the stars. *Thank you, Keroe, thank you,* I repeated.

After five or six minutes, I stopped and turned back toward the warships. With my heart in my throat, I waited, treading water. The sea was deathly silent. There was only darkness and the dull, artificial lights of those ships.

Out of that blackness, three horrifying explosions like I'd never seen before lit up the night. For a moment, I gaped, shocked. Red fire and gray smoke colored the sky. I didn't hear the shouts above the booms. But I flinched, imagining them.

Oh my god, it worked.

I'd done this.

Delivered death. Saved the lives of one land by taking lives from another.

I was going to be sick.

Breathe, Zaria. Swim.

Turning in frantic circles, there was nothing for a moment. Then, I saw it in the distance -- a mighty fire blazed atop High Spire, lighting my return, calling me back. My heart leapt. I didn't want to admit it, but I'd considered the possibility that it might not burn. That Laz would interfere and abandon me to sea.

Swim, Zaria. Just swim back to Rythas and don't think about anything until it's over.

Emptying my mind and letting nothing but the ocean fill it, I swam the long leagues.

But it was a different me who returned in that darkness, a different me who dragged herself onto that shore in the hour before the dawn.

Chapter 23

Bright sun told me I'd slept most of the morning. After a marathon swim like the night before, I wouldn't have been surprised to have slept all day, but my nerves roused me, shocking me awake.

I shot up on the sofa, spying Jesi. I must not have even made it to my bed the night before. Vaguely, I remembered passing out on the beach and being carried to my room.

"What happened? What's happening? Did we attack the shoals?"

She hurried to my side, shoving a glass of water into my hands.

"Yes. You're just in time. Navere is unloading the prisoners by the Bone Gate. He led the attack. More of a massacre, I heard."

"I-"

"Drink," Jesi urged.

Greedily, I gulped the water.

"You weren't there?" I asked, confounded.

Her hair remained immaculately tied for battle.

She shook her head. "I stayed with you. Besides, I knew they'd slaughter anyone who didn't surrender or they couldn't subdue. There'll be other battles to prove myself. Trust me. That's not the one."

Jesi refilled my glass from the water pitcher. I'd never been so thirsty before.

"You'd already done the hero's work. You should hear them. When you tossed your ring into the sea *everyone* started calling you the Queen of our Hearts. They're practically beside themselves with love for you now."

That's what I wanted, right? Having the support of the people was my most coveted asset. I wanted it, just... not like this. I never expected it like this.

"I want to go to the Bone Gate," I insisted. "I want to see."

"Hold on. I want to go too but stay put for one minute. Finish this," Jesi said, touching my glass. "Are you hungry?"

"Ravenous. Ugh, is it wrong that I'm hungry? I'm sick to my stomach but I still want to eat."

"You burned a million calories last night, of course you want to eat."

I drank the rest of my water. "I want to see..." *What I'd done,* I thought. "I want to see the prisoners."

Jesi held out her hand, helping me stand. My

legs were sore and shaky. "Let's go. Everyone else is already there." She grabbed several pies with strange fillings someone had laid upon my table and handed me three. I didn't care if they were sow or squab or dove.

"Eat on the way," Jesi said, as I shoved the first into my mouth.

#

"The Queen of our Hearts!" they shouted as I passed, reverently pressing hand-to-breast. Long before I even made it to the Bone Gate, people swept aside for me, bowed, cheered. Jesi beamed, grabbing my hand and hoisting me up and off my feet. "The young queen," she'd goad them, shouting. "The Queen of our Hearts!"

"They adore you," she whispered as we walked. "You're untouchable. Our savior."

I flashed a nervous smile. I needed the people on my side. Not only did it make me feel safe, but I was banking it for the future. *I just never thought I'd win them like this.*

The sight of so many men and women in chains at the Bone Gate horrified me. Dozens of them, broken and battered on their knees. They resembled Rythasians with different clothing -- informal, rugged, and now tattered.

"There she is!" someone shouted, when Jesi and I approached the expanse of flat stone where Navere crowded the prisoners. It was easy to spy the Commander of the Guard; he possessed a powerful aura and stood taller than most. I guessed him to be in his late twenties; nearly ten years older than Merie. Unlike his sister with darker tresses, he had a head of short brown hair.

Soldiers rushed to my side, pulling me forward and cheering.

"Where's Juls?" I shouted to Jesi. "Where are the Dorestes?"

"War tower," Jesi called back. "They've got their hands full up there."

As soldiers of Rythas celebrated, hooting and calling my name, hate blazed in the eyes of the men and women from Oxholde. They stared up at me, the one who exploded their ships and killed their friends. Some spat.

You would enslave us, I thought. *Enslave children. You left us no choice.*

If I had to do it all over again, I'd still go through with it.

But I didn't want to be paraded around in front of them.

The deadliest stare I'd ever seen sliced through me from a man with a pronounced, sweaty brow, at the end of a row of prisoners. His head turned down, but he looked up, glaring. His hair was shaved on the sides and entwined with three or four braids. Muscles strained the seams of his shirt. I wouldn't want to meet him on the battlefield. Our warriors must have felt the same because he was the only prisoner I'd seen manacled not only by the wrists, but by the ankles too.

All the soldiers wanted their turn to congratulate me. Without much choice on my part, they paraded me up the line, shaking my hand, clapping me on the back, thanking me. In direct opposition to my guilt... a part of me celebrated the way I felt. Proud. Respected. One of them.

"Queen captures queen!" a man roared, and I turned to see that he spoke of a girl in chains, on her knees like the other prisoners.

"That's their commander, Milicena," Navere said, lip curled between triumph and disgust.

I blinked at the girl before me. Quiet rage emanated from her petite figure. Her brown hair bore tiny braids about her face and pale skin peeked through smudges of dirt. She could only have been four or five years older than me, somewhere in her early twenties. *So young.* My gut twisted imagining whatever fate Grahar would sentence her, even as I recoiled, thinking about what she did to those she captured.

Navere pulled me along and by the time I'd worked my way back to the beginning, I needed to catch my breath. Soldiers formed loose groups, chatting, rejoicing, or taunting the prisoners. Not paying enough attention.

That's when I saw the man with the deadly stare rising.

Somehow, he'd gotten his hands on a spare

length of chain. He was still shackled... but his manacles left just enough range to move.

With a roar of rage, he leapt toward me, powerfully swinging the chain. In the heartbeat before he attacked, I recoiled, turning and lunging to protect my head. Soldiers rushed to defend me. But the man struck, and the chain whipped my arm with a force so great I thought it might be broken.

Boom.

I heard the gunshot above my scream and saw Navere standing tall, gun still pointed at the prisoner, now limp on the ground before me.

Boom. He shot again, in the head this time.

The gunshot, like my heart, rang in my ears. Instantly, a sheen of sweat covered my body. I tried really hard not to cry, but it hurt too much. Crouching, Navere scooped me into his arms. He might be brutal or scarily ambitious, but I was glad for his decisiveness. The next thing I knew, soldiers came to aid him, carrying me carefully away from the men and women of Oxholde. I didn't know where we were headed or what was happening – everything had changed so quickly and while these warriors might be used to it on the battlefield, I certainly was not.

"Swallow," Navere commanded, pressing modern medicine to my lips. "It will dull the pain and make you drowsy. We'll get you to the doctor to make sure it's not broken."

Whimpering, I took the medicine, staring up into the flecks of bronze in Navere's hair, trying to distract myself. The sunlight shone through his strands, making them brighter. His face was firm, stern. I couldn't decide if I liked him or if he frightened me.

I'm glad I can be touched at least, I thought, feeling many strange hands carrying me. *Because I don't think I can walk on my own.*

#

It wasn't broken, thankfully, but it hurt like the devil. I'd have black and purple bruises to last the week. For the rest of the day, I dozed off and on, half from the medicine, half from exhaustion. Sometimes Jesi was there in my chambers, sometimes not, and once I even spied Juls in the doorway.

When I awoke for good, the moon shone high, telling me the hour was late. Restless and alone, I gently washed my face and neck, slid on my leather thongs, and opened the door to my bedroom.

At the creaking hinges, the guard at the end of my hall turned. It was Prunson, who'd never before taken a shift.

"I want to go for a walk," I said.

"I could use a walk," he replied.

Internally, I sighed, having thought my heroics might buy me some measure of freedom.

I wandered the halls of High Spire self-consciously, Prunson padding behind me. Truthfully, I wanted a drink. A strong one, or several. I wanted to numb the pain in my arm and... to forget. To not *think*. About what I'd done. I knew I wouldn't take it back but... it haunted me.

Remembering one of the larger verandas overlooking the sea stocked alcohol, I climbed upward and through an arched doorway, emerging into a clear night.

Only one table sat in the middle of the balcony and Laz occupied it. He wore black pants and a black tunic-vest, unbuttoned as usual. My body vibrated with agitation – an effect produced whenever he came into my presence. I spun on my heel to leave.

"Stop," he ordered, as if he had a right.

Now that I thought about it, wouldn't I outrank him soon? Was that how it worked?

Yet I froze, irritated at the command in his tone but too curious not to engage. I turned around slowly, letting my annoyance show as I crossed my arms and raised my eyebrows high, like Jesi often did. Laz sat with one foot propped arrogantly against a chair's edge and gave it a slight shove, pressing back.

"Sit," he said.

I attempted to raise my eyebrows to my hairline.

"You've got somewhere better to be?" Laz challenged.

"Anywhere is better than here," I snapped, spinning again on my heel and hurrying to escape.

"Oh, come, little queen," Laz called. The rough rasp of his voice dripped like honied poison over knife blades. "I'll share the good stuff."

I stopped walking. A drink *was* what I'd been looking for.

He sweetened the offer. "Best of the reserves."

"Whose?" I asked, turning my head over my shoulder.

"Who else? Mal-Yin's."

That *was* the good stuff.

Sighing, I turned around once more and stalked toward the open chair, scowling as I sat. Laz's eyes slid to Prunson, hovering behind me.

"I've got her. Wait down the hall. Return her to her room when we're finished."

I saw red but I folded my lips between my teeth because I *knew* Laz was purposefully being an ass to get a rise out of me. Now, instead of having freedom to walk the castle, I'd lose it as soon as I left the veranda. He watched me carefully, but I refused the bait. I wasn't threatened; all he'd done was show me how my walking about freely threatened *him.*

"What do you want, Laz?" I asked,

admittedly curious.

"A drink. One drink."

"Feeling apologetic? I didn't know a man like you was capable of remorse."

He leaned back, folding his hands behind his head. I noticed he wore the usual silver key, silver bracelets, and I caught the glint of two silver rings lining his fingers. "Not quite. Just curious."

I guess we had that in common. *Wait.* Laz and I had nothing in common. Except his brother.

"Mmm," I mused, non-committedly. "Pour."

At my command, Laz poured the bottle of red wine into a glass and pushed it in my direction. His scorched-earth eyes watched me while I slowly sipped.

"Fine," I sighed, putting down the glass. "I'll bite. Curious about what?"

Lazlian chuckled, folding his arms behind his head again as he leaned back. "Let's have a drink first. Dull the pain in your arm maybe."

"Loosen my tongue, you mean." I took a large gulp, regardless. "I want answers first."

Laz cocked his head, waiting.

"What will happen to the men and women we captured?" I couldn't help but feel pity for Milicena. She was so *young.* "Will they be tortured?"

"Tortured? Not likely." Laz waved a dismissive hand. "We don't need much information out of them now."

Laz's declaration didn't sit right with me. *Didn't we need a lot of information out of them?*

"Navere will execute the highest and send the lowest back to Oxholde, destabilizing command and engendering goodwill amongst those spared, in theory."

"In practice?"

"Milicena, their commander, is the daughter of their clan leader. We'd be no better or worse sparing the highest and executing the lowest. Once her father hears of her death, he's going to vow revenge, which may very well be my father's intent. Anyway, if we return her, she'll attack again. And if we keep her prisoner, her father will attack to free her." Laz's eyes burned in the candlelight. "This isn't the end of a new war. It's the beginning."

I shivered, whispering, "And I started it when I bombed their ships."

"Don't flatter yourself. They attacked first. War is in their nature. Which brings me to my question."

I sat up straighter.

"You swam out to the boats and you did what you said you'd do," Laz began.

"Yeah. So?"

His dark eyes bore into mine. "You didn't betray us. So what I want to know is – is it because you didn't think of it, or is it because you considered it and decided against it?"

I must have taken a second too long to reply.

"Ah, so you did consider it," he replied, smile triumphant.

Restraining myself from slamming my fist onto the table, I spat, "If I didn't consider it, you'd dismiss me as weak-minded. If I did, you'd deride me as selfish and evil. There's no winning with you when you're determined to hate me no matter what I do."

"I don't hate you no matter what you do," Lazlian said. His tongue snaked out to tap his lip, once. "I only hate you when you're... you."

I unclenched my fists, huffing a laugh, "Thanks for clearing that up."

"Is the little queen sore because I don't fall at her feet like everyone else who crosses her path?"

Annoyed, I clenched my fists again and let my eyes flutter shut, because Laz was wrong. Mal-Yin only engaged with me as potentially useful, Juls only went through the motions to do his duty, and Kirwyn certainly didn't fall at my feet when we first met. Unless Laz meant my reputation with the people, and what was I supposed to do about that? Besides, it was the only weapon in my arsenal at the moment.

"You didn't want me here," I declared. "From the moment I set foot upon your island, it was clear you didn't want me to wear the crown. So tell me, what did I ever do to merit such disdain? Why do you revile me in particular?"

Lazlian looked me dead in the eye. "Because you don't love my brother."

It felt like a gunshot rang out at that moment, leaving an eerie silence in its wake. I looked down, guilty. I could say nothing in my defense he wouldn't see through. But Laz had to understand that *I* didn't want this either. Not that he cared.

"And you're not fit to rule," Laz added, casually.

I snapped my eyes back up, scowling. "Oh, like you? Like you are? What would *you* be like as ruler? A hot-headed, impulsive leader with the temperamental arrogance of a royal brat."

"Guilty as charged," he replied. He swung his head, pushing back a section of wavy hair the wind had rustled. "And I can recognize one of my own."

I half-rolled my eyes, refusing to be baited, but my mind screamed, *we are not alike, I am not one of your own.*

"So you don't secretly wish to be king? Resent that the hermit saw the truth of your inadequacy with his mystical powers?"

Laz's expression registered shock; he didn't know I knew. Quickly, he replaced it with a sneer. "The hermit saw a sickly boy who wasn't likely to make it through the first few months of life. He made a cunning decision and proclaimed the younger son, the healthy son, the true heir. That I neither desire nor am built for the throne was a matter of luck entirely separate from his supposed mysticism."

I chewed my lip, wondering how much of what Laz said was true and how powerful this hermit might be. "Did the king consult the hermit on me as well? When he decided not to marry me to one of the nobles?"

Laz's nostril's flared, just a bit. "He did."

"And... what was the outcome? Did the hermit tell him to take me for his own son, to make me queen?"

A crooked grin spread across Laz's face. "He said it was inconclusive. Yet to be written in the stars."

I rolled my eyes. "How convenient."

"My thoughts exactly."

Don't agree with me, I thought. *Ever.*

In the ensuing quiet, it was my turn to study Laz. He sipped his wine and the silver bracelets shimmered in the candlelight. I worked my jaw, trying to work out the question.

"I'm surprised you didn't rig the bomb to blow me up," I said, voice low. "Or did the thought not cross your mind?"

Lazlian's dark eyes bore into mine.

"Well?" I goaded. "I answered your question."

"It wouldn't have been the first time I tried to get rid of you," he hedged. "You're a slippery fish, little queen."

My blood ran cold. "What do you mean?"

"Oh, come now. You've noticed the emptiness of our shark tank. You've suspected it might be the same shark set upon your cove the day of your first wedding pageant."

He tried to kill me. I knew my stiffened posture, my stunted breathing, and my paling face all betrayed any façade of indifference, all revealed how the truth cut me.

"It *was* you," I whispered. "I knew it."

Laz waved his hand in the same dismissive manner of his father, as if it was no matter of consequence. I took a drink because I couldn't breathe. I didn't even know how I swallowed, but I had to do something to buy time. My hands shook from fear or anger.

When I returned the glass to the table, I asked casually, "Did you kill Tolas in some botched attempt to kill me?"

"No."

"Do you know who tried to kidnap me?"

"Unfortunately, no."

I didn't know if I believed him, but then, why would he lie when he'd already admitted to attempted murder? Not to mention all the other veiled threats he threw the night of the Fae fête. I turned the stem of my glass, wanting to do something with my shaking hands. *In what kind of world did a person drink with her captors and would-be murderers? In what kind of world was this the most honest conversation I'd ever had with Laz?*

I put on a mask of regal strength when I asked, "Will there be any future attempts on my life?"

"I haven't decided."

The indifference alone with which he delivered the statement stole my breath once more.

"At least you're honest," I replied, forcing the laugh. "An honest killer. Though I'm surprised you haven't just poisoned me by now – I know you want to take your time, but it'd be slower than an explosion would have been."

Lazlian shrugged. "My brother feels... duty and friendship toward you. He'd mourn your death. But he doesn't always know what's best for him and even when he does..."

"He's not willing to kill for it," I interjected. "Like you are."

"Like *we* are," Laz said, voice deadly calm.

I rolled my neck and shook my head. "That's not – no. What I did last night was different."

"Was it?" he dared. "I bet what stayed your hand when you wanted to climb aboard that ship and betray my family was protecting your family, here."

"I – I don't know." *God, how did he figure out everything in my head?* "And anyway, Juls *will* make those decisions when he's king."

But as soon as I said it, I wondered. *Would he delegate the tougher problems to men like Laz and Navere?*

"I'll... help him," I insisted, lifting my chin and flicking my hair. "We'll help each other."

What was I saying? I didn't intend on sticking around. In the tense moment to follow, I knew it was the wrong thing to declare.

"You think you're beautiful, don't you?" Laz asked, tone dry. "You think my brother will fall in love with you because of how you look?"

"I don't believe your brother could be persuaded to love anyone based on the exterior, if their character didn't match outward appearances. If you think your brother could, then I hold more regard for his intelligence than you do."

I allowed a self-satisfied smirk to touch my lips. Laz's mouth twitched.

"You didn't answer my first question," he said.

"Because it's a trap! I'm not foolish enough to think there's any way to answer it that doesn't annoy you! Besides, you hold so little regard for me and my opinions, what does it matter? Why don't you tell me *your* opinion on my looks so I can simply embrace the same judgement?"

Wait. That came out wrong. Like I was asking Laz if he thought I was pretty. Definitely edging into dangerous territory; I could feel it in the air between us. Maybe it was the wine.

He shrugged. "My brother could do worse. He doesn't seem to mind your muscular figure."

I ignored the barb. "Now who's evading questions?" I reclined as I spoke, and I think the candlelight illuminated my battered left side.

"Well that's certainly not a very attractive bruise," Laz pointed out.

My hand flew to cover my arm. I hadn't seen a gazing glass in the past hour, so I didn't know how bad it might have darkened, and I didn't want to examine it under Laz's watchful eye.

"Good thing they hacked him to pieces. The nerve."

I snorted, incredulous. "Are you serious? Why are you upset that he *hit* me when you've tried to *murder* me? You've *got* to be kidding me. Your own father smacked my face the day before and I doubt you'd have lifted a finger to stop it if you'd been there."

"I've seen him do worse, for less. You got off easy. Besides, I'm not upset," Laz corrected. "I'm affronted. An attack on the young queen is an attack on the Dorestes -- as bold as if the man snuck into High Spire and laid his dirty hands on our jewels in broad daylight. Who does he think he is?"

M outh agape, I asked, "Let me get this straight. It's not okay for him to attack me – because it's an insult to you. But it's okay for your father to smack me, it's okay for you to try to murder me, because I'm... a part of the Doreste fortune? My life or death as casual a proposition as... as..." I caught the glint of his bracelets, "deciding whether or not to don a silver bangle for dinner or to toss it aside to wear another day?"

Lazlian's feral grin instantly raised my hackles, even before he spoke.

"That's unfair. I treat my silver with respect, carefully replacing each piece in a velvet-lined box on the days I decide not to wear one bracelet in favor of another. I don't toss it aside."

As I would you, was the unspoken end to that sentence. *Your corpse. Right into the sea.*

"You're an ass, Laz," I hurled, shooting to my feet. "You don't have to worry about anyone ever tossing *you* aside, because no one would deign to pick you up in the first place!"

Laz's hand shot out, grabbing my wrist before I could leave. "Sit down."

"You sit down!" I retorted, before realizing it didn't make any sense. "Does it bother you, Laz? That I'm not the demure bride for Juls like Merie would have been? The sweet creature who would mold into your family as you see fit? Does it offend you that this isn't what I would have chosen? That this family isn't the one I would have chosen, that your brother-"

Isn't the one I would have chosen.

Landdammit, I almost said it, once again

313

confirming Laz's earlier accusation that I didn't love his brother and undoing my vow to help him rule. I pursed my lips, stopping myself, but what was the point? Laz knew I desired someone else, he'd been very specific about it when we first danced.

I looked toward the arched doorway to hide my face, but after two seconds I grew frustrated.

I am done playing this game with Laz. Whatever it is.

When I made the decision to leave, I realized his hand still clamped my wrist. *Why was his hand still there?* I yanked myself free. Haughtily, I turned and walked toward that beckoning doorway.

"I hear your boy is a *specimen*," Lazlian said, stopping me in my tracks. "Almost as beautiful as an Elowan, and clever too, I'm told. Plotting to get himself off of Elowa... and onto Rythas."

He'd knocked the breath from my body; I nearly doubled over, clutching my stomach.

What did Laz know about Kirwyn? Was Kirwyn trying to get here or was Laz bluffing?

Rage boiled in my breast at the idea that Laz of all people might be informed to Kirwyn's whereabouts. Burning blood raced through my veins and my fingers twitched, wanting to punch him in the face, or worse. Violent fantasies danced in my mind as I imagined breaking the wine bottle – slamming it against the table and holding a jagged piece of glass to Laz's throat -- until he broke down and told me what he knew.

The girl I was before might have done something rash like that. But I was trying to be the woman who knew what an asset patience could be.

Play a long game, Zaria.

I took a breath to calm myself and looked over my shoulder.

"He is." I agreed, smiling on one side of my mouth. "Savagely handsome."

Lazlian's perpetual sneer was back. "Of course he must be, to coax the little queen to open her legs for him."

My cheeks flamed despite knowing Laz intentionally tried to get a rise out of me.

Just like Kirwyn often did, I suddenly realized. But... but... Kirwyn's teasing was playful and... confident. Laz's cruelty stemmed from something ugly -- fear or insecurity somewhere deep inside. I wondered if, perversely, there was something masochistic in it... as if goading me to come back at him harder justified a feeling of... unworthiness? Disgrace? I wasn't sure if that was anywhere *near* the mark, but I knew Laz was hollow, bottomless. Whatever gaped in his soul could never be healed, no matter how much banter I volleyed back to fill it. There was only one way to win with Laz. *Disengage completely.*

"You remind me of him a bit," I said.

"Savagely handsome?" Laz drawled, with mock-curiosity.

I turned and smirked. I could tell his sarcasm belied a burning desire to know what I'd reply, to know if *I'd* comment on *his* attractiveness, as he'd almost commented on mine. Something dark in *me* thrilled in the power I held over him at that moment.

How's it feel to be wanting, to be kept unknowing?

I blinked, one heavy bat of my lashes, still smirking. Then I turned, not answering the question. I scurried off the veranda without looking back.

But Laz's drama only served as a temporary distraction. As soon as I'd ducked through the arches and into the shadowed hall, hot tears stung my eyes.

Was Laz lying or did he know something about Kirwyn trying to save me?

Chapter 24

I awoke to a moody sky, clouds heavy with the threat of rain and wind blowing fiercely. But Jesi arrived, bearing somewhat good news.

"The king has his hands full with the prisoners and planning for retaliation. He's pushed back your royal wedding. Honestly, I don't know how he ever thought he'd pull it off in a month anyway. But he's still bent on going forward despite the upcoming battles, so I'd say this only bought you a few extra weeks, another moon cycle, at best."

"Are you sure?" I asked, deflating.

"I've been asked to help with your wedding gown," Jesi replied. "Preparations for the ceremony are stalled, but definitely underway."

I didn't feel like leaving my room after that, so we stayed inside, windows thrown wide to the storm. We tried lighting candles, but they consistently blew out, and after a while of laughing and racing around to re-light them, we gave up. It was light enough anyway and by the evening, the clouds parted. The pain in my arm lessened – it only hurt when I lifted it. Despite my injury, I insisted Jesi show me some basic moves of self-defense. I was laughably bad with one arm and didn't think two would much improve my technique, but I figured I had to start somewhere. Lida joined us for a late supper in my chambers and, in defiance of the earlier wind, we lit *all* the candles in my room and ate together on the floor. Tomé continued to be quarantined, or healing, or… maybe he just wanted to sleep and didn't want to leave his room. My concern hadn't lessened since he'd arrived, if anything, it was worse.

"I want to show you something," Lida said, still on the floor cushions late that evening.

She turned around, unbuttoned her vest, and dropped her shirt. My eyes rounded. Lida's right shoulder bore the slightly irritated, freshly inked tattoo of Rythas. One crown, with a key beneath. Just like Jesi and Juls and everyone else. *Would Tomé want a mark as well?*

"I've done the research," she said, re-buttoning her vest and turning back to us. "This is a special place."

"But things are so unfair here," I protested. "Well, for me, I guess."

"Everywhere is unfair," Lida replied.

"Perfection doesn't exist. Therefore, some things will always be unfair."

I scowled. "Well, there's levels to it."

"True. But the mainland alternatives..." she shook her head. "Even Spade City, with all its technology, isn't like it is here. This is the best place for me. I know what I'm doing."

"But how do you know for *sure?*" I insisted.

"Because I've done it," Lida replied, flicking her braid. "Ergo, it must be the right thing."

I blinked, frowning. "That's some... cocky, circular logic there," I said. Although I had to admit, I envied her confidence. I felt like a thousand choices barreled down upon me each day and I never knew if I was making the right one. Now I felt more alone, being the only one unmarked, and I'd been in Rythas longer than she had. Although I didn't plan on staying.

"You decided pretty quickly," I drawled, staring Lida down and frowning. Suddenly, I just came out with it. "Are you spying for the king?"

Lida somehow huffed and grinned at the same time. "No. First of all, I feel safer knowing they can't send me back. As for the king... to be honest, I was surprised he didn't ask. He only ordered me to be your companion, as if you needed a doll to play with, to amuse you, to pass the time. But now I understand. He doesn't see you or I as capable of more than play. Certainly not as a threat." Lida's keen eyes bore into mine. "At your own peril, you've been changing his mind. If you're planning something, try to do it with your head down, without drawing attention."

"I've tried! I can't! I can't win the support of the people without, you know, the people. And I need them to like me – it's the only thing that makes me feel safe against the Dorestes and it might be valuable in the future. And if you mean the ships, well, I couldn't save Rythas with a secret swim. But I needed help; it wasn't just me! It was a team. Emissaries who scouted the information about the warships and Laz to construct the explosives and Navere to capture the survivors…"

Lida sighed, "Zaria, I know you're trying to escape. I know you, and the looks you stole at the motorboat's gears weren't half as subtle as you think."

Landdammit, why did she have to be so smart?

"I helped you before," Lida said, "Why wouldn't I help you again?"

"Because that was for Tomé. For a debt."

"And I'm still indebted to you for helping me stay here."

My shoulders slumped. I liked Lida now, but that wasn't enough of a reason to trust her. At least, not with the details of whatever plan I'd concoct.

I replied with a neutral, "Thank you." Half-testing, I added casually, "You spend a lot of time in the library. Have you seen the Forbidden Texts?"

Lida snorted. "I don't have the clearance. But you might. Why don't you take a look at them?"

"Because Lazlian has the key," I moaned, "And he pretty much wants me dead."

Shortly after, Lida left for the night, but Jesi lingered, staring at me quietly.

"I know it's selfish, but do you really still want to escape?" she whispered. "Don't you think you might learn to love Juls?"

"I - no, Jesi. I love Kirwyn."

"But you're a good match. You're impulsive and he's level-headed. You're passionate and he's-"

"Dispassionate?" I quipped.

"Rational, calm. You balance each other out."

There was some wisdom in her words, but...
"I – can't."

Falling onto the couch, my lip quivered and my eyes teared. "You don't understand. When I met Kirwyn... I will never be the same, never. I am marked, Jesi. Not with any tattoo or scar, but inside," I said, beating my breast. "Like – like the rings of a tree. You know how if you cut a tree, you can see where each ring marks a year of its life? And the circle may be thick or thin to record some indication of a drought or some other severe circumstance at a given time? It's like that, inside me. Wherever time is kept inside our bodies, if you cut me open and looked, I'd bear the mark on my soul from my days and nights with Kirwyn." I took a quivering breath, shaking my head and fighting tears. "I bear the brand upon my soul, Jesi. I will never be the same. I have to find him again."

Jesi sighed and sat next to me, wrapping her arm around my shoulders.

"Does that make sense?" I whispered.

Jesi nodded. "I've never felt like that, but yes. It makes total sense."

We sat like that for a few quiet moments. I'd convinced her – for now.

#

Several days passed without much significance, save Jesi sneaking an injection of medication into my room. *Birth control.* I nearly fainted looking at the needle, but she distracted me with tales about the crazy antics of her many brothers back in Mid-Spire. After lying down for a few minutes, the fainting spell passed.

Immediate, immense relief flooded me as I stood. With Jesi's help, I'd bought myself a year of freedom and safety. Unfortunately, I'd prevented moon cycles as well, meaning I'd need to fake the occasional event.

Just as Jesi said, wedding plans continued despite looming war. "Oxholde is always going to attack. If we put life on hold for it, we'd never accomplish anything," she shrugged.

I hadn't earned a seat with the Assembly of Elites, apparently, so instead of meeting with the Dorestes in the war tower at night, I dined with Jesi or Lida. I often wondered what was being discussed about the prisoners. For some reason I didn't fully understand, I wanted to visit Milicena in her cell, to talk to her. She was so *young*.

During the afternoons, I searched the library for variations on a "Deep" or "Cut" fort and eyed longingly the room with the Forbidden Texts. In the evenings, I stared at Kirwyn's picture, always remembering to carefully hide it under my mattress before falling asleep.

Where are you? I asked into the darkness. *Are you coming for me?*

Before the bombing, I almost always dreamed of Kirwyn. Now I often awoke in a sweat, terrorized by night visions of flames and screams.

Nearly a week after exploding the warships, Juls unexpectedly knocked on my door, just after sunset.

"Come," he smiled. "I want to show you something."

It wasn't a request. Kings – even young kings – didn't make requests. But there was a tentative, unsure tone in Juls's voice, and he wore his nervous smile.

I rose to join him, but he protested, "Wait.

No. I'll wait outside. You need your seasuit. If you put it on beneath your clothing, we can go."

Juls quickly departed, leaving me frowning at the closed door. It was late and we were going for a swim? Why?

Rifling through my wardrobe I found several seasuits, slipped into the most modest, and redressed. Juls and I walked down the many stairs of High Spire to a horse-cart by the Garden Gate. Together, we rode an unfamiliar road away from the castle.

"I'm sorry I've been tied up with the Assembly," Juls said, tucking his hair behind his ear. He sounded guilty for neglecting me.

"Oh. That's okay." *I want to be a part of your defense discussions. I don't feel neglected from… dates? Is that what this was?*

"Where are we going?" I asked, as we rode further into the countryside I'd never before explored.

"Somewhere forbidden. No one is allowed to swim where we're going without special permission."

"And, of course, you have it," I noted, rhetorically.

To my surprise, Juls answered. "I pulled some strings with the young king."

Was this his attempt at joking around? Were we playing now?

"Mm," I mused, playing back. "What's he like, this young king?"

"A fine young man, bound to do great things," Juls replied evenly, as if he repeated what was expected.

I tried again, sensing I'd mis-stepped and suddenly feeling compelled to make him laugh. "And what's he look like? I heard an old woman say he's missing several teeth and he spits when he yells, which is all the time. Another claimed he's as fat as a pig and as greasy as the bacon he can't stop eating. Is it true?" I teased. "Is he a frightful monster? Or... could he be handsome? I heard another group of young kitchen maids whispering that he's very handsome."

"Oh yes, he's dashing," Juls agreed, a smile tugging his lips. It was nice to see him joking; it lit his eyes.

"Is that so?"

"You'd swoon."

I threw back my head as I laughed. He grinned and looked down, embarrassed. I'd never heard Juls so at ease. Even when he teased that I made him nervous, he quickly reassumed his rigid, noble countenance.

After a few moments of strained silence, I asked again, "Where are we headed?"

"You'll see. It's a surprise."

"I hate surprises," I said, flatly. *They're never good.*

"I was advised that patience isn't one of your strengths."

My vision went red, despite Juls saying it in a light-hearted manner. The idea that he'd been... briefed on me made me bite the inside of my cheek to keep from saying something stupid.

Even if he wasn't wrong.

Juls didn't understand. I'd spent too much of my life in the dark to care whether someone else deemed a surprise good or bad, to care if another person determined a forthcoming event as fortunate or unfortunate, *I* wanted to know and decide for myself; *I* wanted to prepare. I wanted control.

"Juls..." I began, summoning the courage to ask a question that would undoubtedly be terribly awkward. "Why can't the chosen braenese be touched by a male? My aunt said a man once killed an Elowan who'd touched his bride. Is that true?"

Juls worked his jaw, uncomfortable. "It was a long time ago. He didn't just kill the man, he took a boat over with his friends and was sloppy about it, exposing us. Several generations later, it happened again. This man was quieter but there's some debate over whether or not he even killed the right man. When he returned to Rythas... he was unkind to his wife."

Juls looked out the horse-cart, away from me, shifting uneasily. "It's been law ever since. It's easier this way."

Easier for whom? This law that has nothing to do with the bride, I thought, frowning. *It was all the husband's issue.*

"We're almost there," Juls remarked hurriedly, and I wondered if he sensed some of my frustration.

"Why is this place forbidden?" I asked, cautiously. "Is it sacred?"

Do you understand that I don't fully trust you? That I've been through too much, and a wild part of my brain wonders if you're going to shove me off some cliff? Sacrifice me in a bottomless pit of water?

Juls shook his head. "It's off-limits to maintain the delicate balance required. If too many people did what we're about to do, we'd destroy it. Only the royal family and our guests are allowed to swim here, though anyone can request access and be granted permission, in time."

My shoulders relaxed a bit. "We have forbidden regions, too. The Western tip of Elowa and most especially, Queen's Beach."

Where I found Kirwyn, I thought, even now shuddering to wonder what would have happened if he'd washed up at any other time, on any other cove.

The air was warm and the sky clear when our wagon finally stopped near an inlet. Juls took my hand, leading me around a bend –

– I sucked in a deep breath, eyes wide at the

wonder before me.

An inky bay glowed with billions of tiny blue lights, like submerged fairies dancing beneath the surface. I took it all in, disbelieving.

Juls watched me, not the sea.

"What is this magic?" I breathed, finding my voice.

His deep, warm chuckle sent a thrill through me. "Bioluminescence. It's not magic, at least, no more or less than any other creation in this world is magical. It's a small organism that glows."

Scurrying to the water's edge, I couldn't stop staring.

"A long time ago, there were a few beaches and bays with such creatures, but as the seas became polluted, efforts were made to transplant and cultivate the plankton on other islands," Juls explained. "Out of a dozen, most colonies unfortunately died after a few years. There are only two flourishing transplants from the originals. This is one of them."

A few muted, artificial lights glowed around the bay, but only to illuminate the path, not so bright as to distract from the magic blue creatures shimmering in the water before me like twinkling stars.

"Do you like it?" Juls asked, and for some reason his question made me think of Kirwyn.

What would Kirwyn have done if he'd discovered this? Scooped me up and jumped in, still held in his arms? Made me close my eyes and not open them until I was half-submerged, surrounded by blue starlight?

The idea of Kirwyn surprising me didn't upset me like anyone else. I trusted him.

Inhaling, I pushed the thought from my mind. "It's breathtaking," I replied in awe.

"Would you like to swim in it?"

"I – yes."

We stripped to our seasuits and waded into the surreal bay of stars, kicking out into the middle of the enchantment. I laughed when I turned to Juls. The blue sparks clung to our hair, faces and bodies, sliding about and dripping back into the shimmering water.

"It's magic!" I cried gleefully, waving my hands under the surface and watching the glowing blue fairy light twinkle with the motion.

Juls swam closer, laughing at *my* laughter.

"You know… you caught me off guard the day we met," he remarked.

I grinned, remembering. "I'm sure I made quite a sight."

"Well, yes," Juls smiled, "but I was also thinking of myself and what kind of impression I was making on you. I'd just arisen, and my father had called me to the war tower. I hadn't shaved or combed my hair or cleaned my teeth, which is very unlike me. I wore the previous day's rumpled clothing – something I never do. And suddenly, there you were."

I'd never thought of how he felt. He seemed entirely put-together, to me.

"Look," Juls suddenly exclaimed, voice low. He turned me gently toward the cove.

I gasped, spying two horses of the palest gray, like moonlight, strolling across the beach.

"They're beautiful," I said. *God, this cove* must *be sacred,* must *be something Keroe created specially.* Even after all this time, I couldn't shake the Sea God from my thoughts. It felt wrong.

"Wild horses," Juls said behind me, deep voice next to my ear. "There are bands of wild horses in the countryside."

So beautiful, I thought. *So free. I yearn to be like that.*

"If we're still and quiet, they might come closer." Beneath the bioluminescence, Juls's arms wrapped around my waist, tugging me to him. We kicked softly in unison to stay afloat.

As we watched, the horses did dare closer, uncaring about our presence so far out in the bay. Playfully, one nuzzled the other by the water's edge. For a few minutes Juls and I tread together, observing the frolicking horses until they departed back into the trees.

I spun and looked at Juls, his long dark hair slicked back and threaded with shimmering blue. One sparkle dotted his cheek, right beside his mouth, like a dimple.

His eyes dropped to my lips. I wondered if I had my own blue twinkles there.

The William Blake poem popped into my head again, but with my own distorted lines.

I felt desire for my friend:

I told my want, my want did end...

And then, Juls leaned forward and kissed me, shimmers pressed to shimmers. His tongue swept my mouth and his arms wrapped around my waist.

As the second boy I'd kissed; I couldn't help but compare him to the first.

Kissing Kirwyn had been hasty, hungry. He'd felt... dangerous, desirous. Desiring to dominate, like me. The clashing of hard angles and sharp edges, ready to cut one or both of us if we didn't hold on tight as we struggled, plummeting off some cliff in unison – but not into mortal peril; it was as if we tumbled through air into the sea.

Kissing Juls felt like the comfort of my bedroom in his castle. I tasted security on his tongue. And yet... yawning before me, toilsome years of trying to be someone I wasn't.

And yet...

It was a tender kiss. A sweet kiss.

Not a demon-boy's kiss.

A young king's kiss.

Chapter 25

I couldn't look at Kirwyn's picture that night.

What if he was hurt somewhere and I'd been kissing someone else?

What if he'd forgotten me? What if I was wrong and it was all childishness? Lust heightened by the dramatic circumstances of me leaving?

How did you know, really know, if something was real?

"Jesi, I need to read those Forbidden Texts," I moaned that morning. "I can't... time is running out. The king is planning our wedding and Juls - I can't - I don't know. I feel awful."

"I don't know what you think you're going to find in there. I'm telling you, it's just technical stuff. Laz reads it to learn things like building those bombs."

I gave Jesi my most pleading look; the one I knew she couldn't deny.

"Fine," she huffed, sitting up straight on the

sofa. "I know how you can get the key. It won't even be too difficult." Jesi withdrew her dagger, immediately making me wonder if her idea involved cutting throats. But she banished the thought when she said, "You'll steal it. Laz keeps all the keys in his bedroom."

"But... the royal bedrooms are guarded. Just like mine."

Jesi cocked a wry smile. "Only yours is guarded at the door. The Dorestes share a hall. For... privacy reasons, only the end of the hall is guarded, not the individual rooms. So you can pass the guards and sneak into Laz's room. Find the key while he sleeps."

I threw up my hands. "Um... there's still a matter of the guards. At his bedroom door or at the end of the hall, it doesn't matter. How am I supposed to get past them?"

"They'll step aside." Jesi smiled at her dagger, again making me anxious. Did she want me to threaten them, hold a blade to their throats?

"Right, okay. I'm just supposed to say, 'please let me sneak past and steal the key to the forbidden texts?' Can't you do it?"

"No..." Her wide, lascivious grin made me even more nervous. "It has to be you."

I narrowed my eyes. "Why?"

"They'll let *you* past. If they think you're going to see the young king." Jesi slowly rotated her dagger until the tip pointed upward, imitating the rise of something else. My eyes bulged. "To engage in a little pre-marital indiscretion. In fact, they'll love being the ones to know the gossip before anyone else."

I swallowed. For some reason, the suggestion dried my mouth. "Pretend I'm sneaking into Juls's room…"

"Uh-huh. You don't even need to say a word. Wear something distracting, clearly made to entice. Smile coyly, look up from your lashes, and blush. It's really that simple. Word has already spread about your date last night; it won't be too much of a shock. Once the guards step aside, the hall curves and it's dark on the far end. Laz's room is next to Juls's."

I fell onto the sofa beside Jesi. "I thought I was the only one with the bad ideas. You certainly know your scheming when it comes to… matters of the heart."

Jesi pinched my cheek. "Oh young queen, I'm scheming about another organ entirely."

#

Jesi sucked in a breath. "You look like cake on a plate."

"I *feel* like an offering," I complained, tugging at the back of the scarlet negligee that barely covered my rear. "Can I at least wear a robe?"

Jesi folded her arms. "Do you want this to work? Besides, no one's gonna see you anyway. Except the guards. And whatever stories they spread will work in your favor. The king might even believe them. Probably not. But everyone else will."

Jesi spun me around. "Take a look."

My mouth fell. *Was it wrong if I liked what I saw?* Jesi truly *was* talented with her blade *and* her brush. I blinked at my smoldering eyes, my cascading waves of gold, and bold, come-hither attire.

"I'm glad you approve," she clucked, catching my smile.

"Well, we... didn't dress like this in Elowa."

"Don't accidentally walk into Juls's room like that. He'll do his duty, alright."

I laughed nervously. "Ugh, what am I doing?" I shook my head. "No, I got it. First door is Laz. Easy. I won't forget."

Jesi escorted me past my own guard and down the stone corridors toward the royal tower. "I don't know where Laz keeps the keys, but I know for certain they're in his room, all of them. Take only the key to the Forbidden Texts. We can return it tomorrow night. Hopefully, he doesn't need it before then."

Sweating and staring like a frightened animal, I nodded vigorously.

Jesi chucked. "I'd tell you to relax but looking as nervous as you do works in your favor," she reasoned, leaving me at the corner to walk the last part alone.

Here goes nothing...

The guards looked dissimilar; one wore his

locks tied into a bun and the other's hair was shorn, like an Elowan villager. Surprise registered on the faces of each when I approached, quickly morphing into gleeful curiosity. But Jesi was wrong about not needing to speak.

Both guards smirked in unison and the one on the right asked, "What business do you have with the young king at this hour?"

You know precisely what business I have, you pervert. You just want to hear me say it.

I flipped my hair, imitating Jesi. "No business at all. I was always told not to mix business and pleasure." I tried to be saucy, but I blushed by the end. *Satisfied, creeps?*

Gleeful smiles turned lecherous as they exchanged a look. To my immense relief, they parted. Looking down as I passed, I noticed sweat made the silken nightgown cling to my skin more than before.

Hours. It would take mere hours for this story to circulate the castle. Would it reach Juls's ears? What would he make of it? He'd have to dismiss the guards as lying, seeing as how I'd never arrived. Right?

Tiptoeing down the long hall, I spared one glance over my shoulder to ensure I wasn't being watched. The guards' heads bent in conference, whispering excitedly, surely speculating on what they imagined was about to happen.

With a deep breath, I selected the first door I came to and pushed, quickly throwing myself inside to hide. I cringed at the scrape of wood-on-stone as I pulled the door shut behind me, tensing for a moment, half-expecting a guard to rush down the hall and beat his way in.

Or worse – for Laz to awaken. Gulping, I pictured Lazlian standing behind me, the blade of his sword at my back.

Another deep breath and I turned.

Only silence and shadow surrounded me.

Thankfully, moonlight from the open window and one dying candle illuminated some of the room. I frowned at the dim chambers. The only thing more wrong than being in *Juls's* room at night was being in *Laz's.*

At least his spacious bedroom was more comfortable than the hall, open windows providing a cool night's breeze. I waved my short dress up-and-down from my clammy body, hoping to alleviate the dampness sticking it to my skin.

Laz's room was larger than mine, with an adjacent sitting room and tall windows. Enviously, I eyed what looked to be a private balcony, too. Imposing and centrally placed was a canopied bed, draped in the deep burgundy color so beloved of the Dorestes.

My breath caught. Laz, body half-covered by the blanket, lay sleeping in the bed's center. His arms and legs sprawled, taking up most of the space.

This is crazy.

One move, one wrong move, and he'd wake.

Quietly, Zaria.

I tiptoed across the airy chamber into a darkened alcove. The room wasn't overly furnished or cluttered and with surprising ease, I found a chest of drawers built into the side of one wall. So many little drawers for so many keys. There must have been over a hundred.

The keylord, indeed.

No wonder Laz labeled them -- he'd never be able to keep track. But I didn't understand his system; it wasn't alphabetized. Crouching low, I scanned row after row, pulse racing. I finally found it centrally located, marked in sharp letters.

Library.

Pulling, I cringed at the heart-stopping scrape of the rickety, wooden drawer. But my heart leapt to behold the iron key. Without a sound I removed it. I attempted to hide the prize in a pocket, only to remember my outfit had no pockets. Instead, I clutched the key in my left hand and gleefully tiptoed back toward Laz's door.

Easier than I'd imagined.

But...

Wait. I drew my hand back as if the wooden door burned. I'd accomplished everything so fast, if I opened it now, I'd raise suspicion.

Oh god. *How long did the guards expect Juls and I to... lie abed?*

Whatever they imagined us doing, it couldn't be as short as the two minutes I'd just spent in Laz's room. *Could it?*

I stole a quick glance back at the keylord's sleeping form.

All clear. For now.

The ocean rushed in my ears as I closed my eyes and waited. Every second I delayed was another second I might get caught. But moving too soon would negate everything I'd just done.

Trying to get my breathing under control, sweat gathered under my arms, at the nape of my neck, and in the area between my breasts and my thighs. I counted to one hundred and curled my fists tighter.

Patience, Zaria. Don't open the door yet.

I counted to two hundred, timing the numbers with the beats of my heart, clenching my teeth and tensing my shoulders.

Don't wake up. Please don't let anyone in this hall wake up.

Trying to guess how long... *it...* might take, my mind, totally without my permission, conjured images of Juls and I abed together. It was impossible not to think about. The young king really was dashing... he had such full lips. Unwillingly, I thought about a kiss between us, like we shared in the water... and then I imagined more intimate acts as they unfolded, as he reached for me…

Growing hotter, I shook my head to shake the suggestive pictures right out of it.

Enough.

Heart galloping, I grasped the cool metal of the door handle without making a sound. I knew the scrape of wood-on-stone would scream again when I pulled, but I had no choice.

Just one more obstacle between now and success.

Closing my eyes, I sucked in one last breath.

I tensed my hand, ready to pull –

-- Another hand shot out from beside me, gripping my wrist with iron force.

My heart stopped. I whimpered loudly.

Whipping my gaze up, I saw Laz standing above, his wild stare bearing down. He wore only loose pants, for sleep. His bare chest heaved like he panted. I gaped, wide-eyed with terror, mind scrambling for excuses. *How long had he been watching?* And, oh god – were my lips swollen, my face flushed, my breasts – did I *look* like I'd been thinking about sex because I *had* been thinking about it, moments before?

We were already only inches apart and for a delirious moment, I had the insane thought that Laz moved forward, just a hair, and that he pulled my wrist toward him, just a bit. I might have imagined it, but a squeak escaped my throat regardless. At the same time, I lost my grip on the key.

In one second that lasted an eternity, it fell to the floor with a *clink,* drawing Laz's attention to the ground.

Another tortuous second passed; a surreal moment that felt like it happened in slow motion. I didn't worry about screaming -- all the oxygen suddenly left the room. I couldn't even breathe.

Laz's nostrils flared as he stared at the key laying boldly on the tile between us. His burning eyes snapped back to mine; a snarl affixed on his face. Cruel fingers dug painfully into the delicate skin on my wrists.

"Get. Out."

"Laz I-"

"Now," he growled.

I didn't move, *couldn't.* Helpfully, Laz yanked his door wide and shoved me out into the hall. He slammed the door noisily behind me.

No, no, no.

Both guards faced me, mouths wide. I gulped. *Oh god, oh god. What to do? What would Jesi do?*

I lifted my chin and flicked my hair. Jaw tightly set, I held my head high as I walked down the hall and past the gaping guards.

What else could I do?

Would they think I visited Juls and stopped by Laz's room... after? Would they think I visited only Laz? Perhaps they didn't know for sure from which door I emerged?

Ugh, whatever the guards thought was the least of my worries. Tattletale that he was, Laz would undoubtedly spill in every detail to Juls by morning.

Chapter 26

"It's my fault," Jesi moaned the next day, hovering over me. I knew she felt awful, she hadn't even painted her face, and I'd seen her touch up her lipstick to train. "I'll take the blame."

"No," I protested, speaking to the tiled floor with my head between my knees. "I'm the one who wanted to read the texts and the king blames me for everything anyway. Who knows what they'd do to you?"

Minutes later, I was pacing my bedroom when Lida burst inside, closing the door tightly behind her.

"Zaria, what are you doing?" she cried without preamble. "I've been sent to summon you to Juls. You've long since displeased the king and now you've made an enemy of the prince!"

I see the news spread, as expected. Or maybe Lida was simply informed, being my collector.

"Well what do you want me to do?" I cried, fists clenched. "The king was certain to revile me once he got to know me and Laz hated me anyway!"

"I don't know, Zaria," Lida sighed, shaking her head. "I don't know. You probably aroused something other than hate when you appeared in his room half-naked in the middle of the night."

I squeezed my eyes shut, hands still balled. "Stop it, that's not what happened, you weren't there, you're speculating." Slapping my hands to my forehead, I cried, "And what should I do about all this anyway?"

Lida blew out a puff of air. "Don't lose Juls. Stay on his good side. He's your last ally."

She wasn't wrong. But Juls wasn't my *last* ally, he was always my *only* ally…

…And at the same time, the one person in total opposition to everything I wanted.

#

Juls stood rigidly, one hand on the stone balustrade, looking out at the turquoise sea. Pots of climbing, red Hibiscus flowers framed him on either side. *At least he didn't require me to meet him in the king's hall,* I thought. *Sitting on a throne, looking down.* He didn't hear me approach, so I observed his pensive stare into the waves. He wore a deep maroon tunic-shirt and pants. No crown, no goat's tail. The wind rustled his long-ish hair, slightly.

I'd put on the pink dress from our private dinner together and let Jesi fix two floral hairpins on either side of my head. Shuffling my feet, I made enough noise for Juls to turn. As he took a deep breath and crossed the veranda, nervous fish darted through my gut. If I'd ever upset Kirwyn, he might shout or rage in a fit of temper – and maybe I'd even shout back. But he wouldn't wait to let me know how he felt, wouldn't parade us through protocols or whatever this was.

Straining and failing to keep my voice free of resentment, I declared, "I've been summoned." *Like a child.*

"That's unfair," Juls protested, holding up his hands.

As if anything about this situation has been fair to me.

"You snuck around in the middle of the night, and you broke into Laz's room to steal a key."

Like I had so many other options.

Juls searched my face. "Did you ever think you could just ask me?"

"I – no."

Because your allegiance is with your family. I don't blame you, but it doesn't help me any.

An uncomfortable silence descended. These stunted conversations where we danced around everything that mattered were so different from how Kirwyn and I talked. I shifted my weight, trying to balance confidence and contrition somehow.

"What is it you seek in the Forbidden Texts?" Juls asked, arching a brow.

Maps, I thought. But I couldn't tell him that.

"Everything," I gushed, and it was only a half-lie. "I've had a lifetime of secrets. I want to know everything."

"I'm not my brother, Zaria. I'm not my father."

"I know," I replied softly, head titling down.

You're better than them. You're a good man... in every way but one. The one I need. The one where you stand up to your father and tell him you don't want to marry me.

Unless... unless you do?

Stepping close, it was as if Juls read my thoughts. "Everyone here owes you a debt we can never repay. But if we're going to make this marriage work, if we're going to set an example for the people... if we're going to keep Rythas safe and bring her to greatness..." Juls's hands rested gently on my shoulders, but his words rested heavily. I couldn't meet his eyes. "Then I need to be able to trust you. With my life. With everyone's. With the kingdom."

I felt like a traitor. I couldn't think about it. *Besides,* I argued, *can I trust you? Do you even know your father struck me? Would you take his side if you did? Not to mention you stole me here to marry you without my consent in the first place!*

Juls pressed his thumb and forefinger to my chin, lifting it. Though it never bothered me when Kirwyn did it, the patronizing act annoyed me now. "Look at me, please. I can't do this without your participation."

I can't give that to you.

But I met his gaze. I let my face relax into a pleading look and whispered, "I'm sorry. I should have come to you. I should have asked."

Juls's warm brown eyes lit with something like relief or hope. His thumb edged toward my lips. He leaned closer and I mimicked the act, so that we were pressed against one another.

"Do you want to see the texts?" he asked.

I suddenly beamed, grinning. "*Yes.* Really?"

"Mm-hm," Juls hummed.

Surprising us both, I threw my arms around his neck. "Thank you!"

On some level, I knew what Juls was going to do when I released him, but I shivered with conflicting emotions when he pressed his lips to mine and kissed me while his hands stroked my back.

I had vowed to bend, yet I defied the Dorestes at every turn. *From now on,* I swore, *I will be more agreeable, on the surface.*

Confoundingly, I wished the task were harder. Juls wasn't a terrible kisser or terrible person or even terrible to look at. Pretending to fall in love with him wasn't a stretch.

"They're not as forbidden as you think," he said, when the kiss ended. "Not to *know*. Only to *use*. Access can be granted as long as we don't believe the requester is going to leverage the knowledge to break laws and endanger us all."

At my puzzled look, Juls said, "I'll get the key from Laz. Meet me in the library in an hour."

#

Pulse racing, I approached the solid steel door beside Juls. He turned the key in the lock and we stepped inside.

A small room greeted us, stuffed with books, unrecognizable tools, and small metal devices.

"What is all this?" I asked.

"Technical manuals," Juls said, running his hands down one shelf. "Instructions on modern weaponry," he said, skimming another. "Advanced mathematics," he noted, pointing to a third shelf. "Knowledge the TORR forbids."

"Oh," I said casually. "And maps?'

Juls cocked his head. "Maps? I don't believe we store any maps in here. This is pertaining to the treaty. It's a bit of a gray area. We shouldn't have this stuff, but no one's going to bother coming after us just for possessing it."

My stomach started to sink. "No maps? Are you sure?"

Juls shook his head. "You're free to explore. There's no maps here. Why would that knowledge be forbidden?"

Rocks filled my gut, sinking me right to the bottom of the ocean.

Had it been a stupid, wild hope? Thinking I might find mention of something to lead me to Kirwyn? Where did that leave me now?

Nowhere.

All this time I'd thought my way out was through this room... and all this time I'd been wrong?

"Okay," I said, weakly. "Maybe I'd just like to look around for a little bit. Thanks, I guess. I just wanted to know what was in here."

In the back of the room, a locked display case caught my eye. The glass box held a small, yellow-gold cube.

"What's that?" I asked, hope rising in my chest.

Juls paused, tapping his tongue to his lips. "It was stolen a long time ago. We're not sure the extent of the data, but we know it holds information on some Spade City defenses. Maybe it contains the motherload. Maybe nothing more than secrets to their outer regions, but that's quite a lot."

Furrowing my brow at the metal cube, I asked, "There's information... in there?"

"Mm-hm," Juls said. "We have it, but we don't possess the modern technology to decipher it. It's way too complex to build, not even Laz can do it."

My short-lived hope evaporated.

For the next hour, Juls waited with me, thumbing through various books. When I'd assured myself that the antechamber held nothing of value to help me escape, I let him escort me back to my room. Deflated, I collapsed onto the bed and curled into a ball on my side.

A few minutes later, Jesi knocked. She sat down on the bed beside me.

"You don't look good."

"I've been worse," I replied, speaking half into the downy bedding with my face pressed against it.

"Well, I'm not sure if this will help matters," Jesi began, slowly. "The good news is, the kingdom is in love with you and your relationship with Juls. Stories about your date and your clandestine meeting last night have spread throughout High Spire and are on their way to Low Spire as we speak. Like I said, Rythas loves a good love story and your marriage to the young king is... aspirational. It's a fairy-tale story everyone wants for themselves."

"Yay," I managed, weakly. I bit my lip, waiting for the bad news.

"The guards talked, as expected," Jesi continued. "Rest assured that your love affair with Juls is the dominant story, the one on everyone's lips, but... One of the guards must have wondered if you stumbled out of Laz's door, must have speculated something else. He probably whispered suspicions to someone and... there's a downside to fame. It's unavoidable. And for women, it usually looks like this."

Jesi slid a scrap of paper under my nose.

"I found this in a drinking hall."

My stomach twisted. I felt violated just staring at a crude drawing, clearly depicting me without clothing. On my hands and knees. And right between Juls and Laz.

Chapter 27

I wasn't hoping for an ally, obviously, or any type of beneficial information when I went to see Milicena, the clan leader's daughter and our most important captive. She was doomed and I would never side with slavers. But something akin to morbid curiosity and mutual understanding drew my feet to her cell. We were both very different prisoners in the same place.

And guilt? Some of that too.

As the hero of Rythas, the guards let me speak to her without a fight. Or maybe young queens were permitted; I didn't yet grasp the dizzying protocols. Ever since Juls and I had our little heart-to-heart talk, guards no longer dogged my steps. But wherever I went, I could feel eyes upon me, watching from a distance.

No other prisoners resided in Milicena's underground wing. I walked the cool, dusty hall alone to a cell at the end.

Even filthy she was formidable. Milicena didn't bear as much muscle mass as Jesi or I, but the snarl on her lips, the danger in her eyes, the quickness with which she slammed herself against the bars when I arrived -- all warned anyone to be wary in her volatile presence.

She spat at my feet, showing me no introductions were needed.

What am I doing here? I wondered, pacing back and forth before her cell. Milicena followed me with only her eyes, and whenever I glanced up, I got the disturbing notion that it was *me* behind bars, and I knew it was partially true.

Compelled by forces I didn't understand, I spoke to Milicena. She did not reply. My questions about Oxholde were pointless. My justifications for why I exploded her ships only met with violent madness in her glare.

But over the next few days, I visited her quiet cell each morning. She was so close to me in age... I couldn't help but wonder if I'd been born in her place, as the daughter of Oxholde's clan leader, if I would have made the same choices.

I went on more dates with Juls, too, keeping my vow to appear demure and besotted, and biding my time until some miracle happened, some clue to help me escape.

"There she is. The Queen of our Hearts," people cried, and Juls and I smiled and waved. He

took me to the first established drinking hall in Rythas – thankfully, no illustrations of me naked were to be found. One evening we rode a horse-cart to a cove where dolphins played at dusk. He even took me to one of High Spire's most wonderous creations – the Glass Gardens. Half-enclosed, the wonder spanned several acres. I felt as if I'd been transported into another land of enchantment. It wasn't just the trees – flowers and bushes were designed much larger than usual, so that ambling through a scene gave one a feeling of being miniaturized, looking up to tall, red roses or running hands over blades of grass waist-high. Juls's touch during these public appearances was light but always present upon my hand or forearm. At times he subtly guided with a squeeze or a stroke. It was as if we worked out a clandestine form of communication with signals. *That's good, smile like that,* praised one gentle squeeze or *Don't engage with that man, no good can come of it,* warned another.

Being alone with Juls was more pleasant than dinners with his family, but we occasionally had those tense meals as well. Laz never met my eyes, but I felt his disgust like a hand of phantom smoke, reaching across the dinner table to strangle me.

Each night, I stared at Kirwyn's picture and dreamed of pressing my lips to his, dreamed of him tightening his arms around me.

I should have listened to you. I'd tell him in my dreams. *None of this would have happened if I'd believed you.*

Chapter 28

Hopping from one foot to the other to channel my excitement, I knocked on Tomé's door. A messenger arrived that morning, telling me his quarantine had ended three days prior, to my astonishment.

I blinked as a slight, brown-haired servant of about eighteen or nineteen years of age opened the bedroom door without looking in my direction. I didn't recognize him from High Spire. Though the sun had long since arisen, curtains covered the windows, keeping the room in shadow.

"Tomé?" I asked, wondering if he was ill and there'd been a mistake.

Emerging from his bathing-chamber, Tomé carried wine and smiled when he saw me. It didn't touch his eyes.

"Are you... okay?" I asked, letting my gaze wander across the uncharacteristically messy room and imagining the thousands of questions he must have.

"Getting there," he replied. But it didn't sound like he was getting anywhere at all.

"Have you…" I looked at the unmade bed. Clearly, the servant hadn't attended it yet. "You haven't left your room." I deduced. "Don't you want to see the library?"

"Yeah. Yeah." He took a sip of wine. "Maybe we'll go to the library tomorrow."

My eyes darted to the skinny boy standing by the door.

"Can you give us some privacy?" Tomé asked him.

The stranger nodded, but didn't fully depart, instead crossing into the bathing chamber and closing the door behind him. Tomé took a seat at his table and I sat next to him.

"Talk to me," I urged, leaning into the tabletop and bending my head to look up at him.

"I talk all day, Zaria. I'm kind of talked out."

"Oh."

"Is that what… he does?" I lifted my chin toward the bathing chambers, brow furrowed. "They sent special healers to me once, after I'd been kidnapped. To make sure I wasn't traumatized, to talk it out. Is he…" I chewed my lip. "What exactly does he do for you?"

Tomé lifted his glass of wine, looking at me with his impossibly blue eyes. "Whatever I ask him to, Zaria."

Oh.

I drew one knee to my chest, resting my chin on it, suddenly feeling tired. On the one hand, I envied Tomé's self-imposed solitude, his adjustment period. I was denied those things. On the other hand, a creeping worry for my cousin tickled up my spine. The brown-haired boy didn't seem at all like Marcin – and I didn't mean the color of his locks or the span of his shoulders. His eyes were shifty; never fully meeting mine. I couldn't place it, but he had a negative *aura.* If Tomé headed down a path of despair, this wasn't the kind of man to pull him out. From the state of the room and the dead look in Tomé's eyes, I'd say he was more inclined to help Tomé wallow in it.

But maybe that's what my cousin needed. His own time to sort things out. Being thrust into the world beyond wasn't easy; I knew that first-hand.

I rose. "I'll check on you again tomorrow, okay? And every day."

"Okay," Tomé agreed, sipping his wine once more. "I'll see you tomorrow."

Leaving, I felt as if heavy stones weighed down the bottom of my gut.

That night, Jesi, Lida and I had another of our candlelit floor dinners. Throughout a meal of grilled octopus and pelican eggs, Lida and I discussed Tomé and it dawned on me that all three of us came to Rythas after a heartache. I'd nearly thrown myself out my window and took other dangerous risks. Whatever Lida felt, she suffered in silence. And Tomé coped as he needed right now. But it still left an uneasy feeling in the pit of my stomach. I'd had Jesi to pull me back from the window. My cousin might need the same.

The next morning, I met Juls for breakfast on one of the floral verandas overlooking the gardens of High Spire. I'd tensed at the unusual request, even before seeing Laz already seated.

"My father has decided what to do with the prisoners," Juls announced, standing. "I know you're going to ask about it, I know you're interested in Milicena's fate and so, I just wanted to tell you it's been decided."

Of course my visits to the prisons have been reported.

"And?"

"Enemies are sentenced to death in only one of two ways," Juls hedged.

"Which are?"

"The first - and fastest - is hanging. Publicly, atop the water stair at the King's Gate. It's much more common and preferable to the second. But... that is not Milicena's fate. She'll be dealt with privately and fatally. I'm sorry but, that is all you need to know."

I gave Juls an exasperated look. He stared at me while turning a garnet ring on his finger, then shrugged; a refusal.

"I'm going to be your queen," I said, using my commanding voice, gliding my hands across the tabletop as I walked closer to him. "You have to tell me how things work. It's my job to understand them."

"You're going to be my queen," Juls replied, shaking his head. "It's my job to protect you from brutality you don't need to be a part of."

I crossed my arms, but Juls set his face in an expression I'd come to learn he'd don when leveraging the weight of the crown. Usually whenever he thought he was being honorable and noble.

Laz's voice cut across the room. "If a prisoner isn't hanged, they're sentenced to the Isle of Walking Corpses."

I snapped my gaze toward the dubious prince. Juls sighed, bringing a hand to his forehead, but he didn't silence his brother. Laz quickly continued before Juls changed his mind.

"Though no one's seen anyone in any state – alive or undead - walking about the small island for years. We don't know who created it, or why, but it's a hell on Earth just a boat ride away."

Relaxing into his chair, arm tossed casually over the back, Laz delivered the details with relish. "Utterly infested with Golden Lanceheads, the deadliest snake known to man. One bite will melt the very flesh from your bone. The interior forest is ringed with Manchineels, the ground littered with the poisonous fruit. A snakebite is the most likely cause of death on the tiny island, but there's no source of food or water, so anyone making it past a day or two might be tempted to eat a *manzana de la muerte,* in sheer madness from dehydration. If by some miracle a snake doesn't get you first, any number of other species might kill you instead. Black Titans, as you call them, fire ants, or Brown Recluse Spiders... there's even been reports of deadly traps set within the interior, just beyond the beach -- fake ground coverings hiding pits with spikes."

I shivered, *twice,* as Laz detailed an unthinkable nightmare of an island.

"That's horrible." I whispered. "How can you-"

"Only the absolute worst criminals are dropped there," Juls protested. "It's very small; death usually comes within minutes, if not hours."

"And when this happens, a boat is always stationed nearby, watching to ensure a rescue is never mounted," Laz added, cutting in. "Usually, they'll catch glimpses of the condemned walking, hiding on the beaches, twitching or screaming -- depending on what got them first. That's how the place got its name, The Isle of Walking Corpses. You're guaranteed death if you're sent there but the time it takes varies. Could be an hour, could be a few *days*," Laz said, contradicting Juls. "And the isle is littered with the corpses of those who came before."

"No one should suffer that fate," I insisted, covering my mouth. "It's... barbarian."

"Barbaric," Juls corrected. "Zaria, tell me... if a man kidnapped your child, a young daughter... if he *hurt* her, enslaved her, killed her. Tell me, Zaria, what fate would you order such a man?"

"I – I..." My mind recoiled at imagining the horror, but I couldn't deny the truth that I'd tear any man like that to pieces. Sighing, I said, "No punishment would be too great if he hurt someone I loved." I looked at Juls pleadingly. "But even if Oxholde enslaves people, Milicena might not have had a choice. Juls, she's not much older than us. She was only following her father's orders."

"As I follow mine." Juls leveled his penetrating stare at me.

I fell silent, chewing my lip.

"Her orders would have brought such a fate to children," Juls added. "So there *is* a difference."

I stared at the floor, still chewing my lip.

"What about trading her life for information about who supplied Oxholde with that advanced weaponry? You said before that their soldiers were intentionally kept in the dark, that you haven't been able to get any leads from them. But wouldn't Milicena know *something*?"

Juls cocked his head. "You don't think my father already made that offer?"

"So, she knows her fate?" I asked.

Juls nodded.

She must be terrified, I thought. *Stewing in prison, awaiting a horrible death.*

"I just wanted to let you know that your visits are coming to an end. But my father needs me in the war tower," Juls announced. He stopped, planting a kiss on my forehead. "I'm sorry," he added, before leaving the veranda.

I didn't think he was *entirely* wrong, but why did the execution need to be so extreme? As a deterrent? Tradition? Bloodlust?

Falling into a chair, I grabbed a glass and drank deeply from a bright orange-yellow concoction set upon the table. From the tart bite on my tongue and the burn down my throat, I could tell it was a passionfruit cocktail of some kind.

"Delicious, isn't it?"

I was in such a trance I jumped to hear Laz speak. I replaced the glass on the table, wary, readying for an attack. Laz and I hadn't been alone together since… *that night.*

"I make a killer cocktail, you can admit it," he clucked his tongue. "And we know you like passionfruit. It was in your wedding cake."

I would *not* be baited into discussing my past. "What do you want, Laz?" I scowled, standing.

"What do *you* want?" he countered.

You to disappear from here. Me to disappear from here. Kirwyn to reappear. What don't *I want?*

"You want her hanged instead?" Laz asked, looking up with only his eyes.

I jutted my chin. "Yes." A quick death would be better than an island of horrors.

"Perhaps you can plead her case with my father," he suggested. "There are some advantages to a public hanging, I would think."

"There *are*," I agreed, wheels in my head turning. "Better the people to... be assured of her death than to allow only a few to witness the event from the security of a boat, right?"

Laz flashed his lazy grin, taunting, "Why don't you scurry along and beg of the king?"

Narrowing my eyes, I grit out, "Is that a challenge because you don't think I have the nerve?"

"Oh no, I think our little queen is full of flint, ready to explode."

"Then why are you helping me?" I asked, ignoring the barb. "What trick is this?"

"Because I designed the explosives and because my father thinks you've had enough glory, he's making me claim the victory. That means *I'm* the one who has to do the executing. That's how it works here. And I don't particularly fancy a long boat ride and several boring days at sea."

I chewed on that. I was sure Grahar felt I'd had enough fame already and he gladly handed over the rest to Laz. He also probably didn't trust me to follow orders. *Can't say I blamed him.*

"Well... it would seem we're working together again. We're on the same side," I said slowly, still searching the keylord's cruel face for a trick. "Though for very different reasons."

"It would seem," he said, leaning back and folding his hands behind his head.

#

The king, supposedly too busy in the war tower to see me, agreed to read a message. I sat outside the door and wrote, outlining the reasons Milicena should be hanged -- starting with Laz's suggestion about the public nature of such an execution, the shared *success.* Lastly, I drove home the point that with his son as public executioner, witnesses would be reminded of who masterminded the weaponry.

Waiting long hours back in my chambers, I didn't have much hope my plea would be received. After all, the king had surely already considered anything I could argue. So I nearly fell off my chair when acceptance came by messenger.

Juls is in the tower with the king, I remembered. *Perhaps he persuaded his father.*

At the idea, something warmed inside my chest for Juls and all his noble ideals. Hurriedly, I raced straight to the prisons, wanting to tell Milicena. I couldn't explain it but sparing her somehow felt like sparing myself.

"I have some news..." I told the young prisoner, tentatively. It wasn't *good* news exactly, but, as good as could be expected. "I pled your case to King Grahar and he's changed your sentence. You won't be sent to the Isle of Corpses to die a slow and painful death. You're going to be hanged at the King's Gate tomorrow. I'm sorry. It will be public, and final, but it will be quick."

Fire blazed in Milicena's eyes, and a hideous snarl formed over her face.

Her first words to me nearly knocked me over.

"How dare you!" she seethed.

What?

"I - I don't know what you mean," I stammered. "I'm *helping* you."

Milicena raked her nails down the bars of her cell so hard I think she snapped a few back. "You self-righteous queen of *shit!*" she shouted. "How *dare* you."

I gaped, just as shocked to hear her finally speak as I was to understand what she had to say. "You *want* to be sent to the isle?"

"I want to die on my feet," she cried. "I want to die alone, not humiliated before your people! You've taken everything from me and now you want to take the last right that belongs to me, the manner in which I die?"

"I - " *Oh no.* I didn't know what to say. There was no hope of the king reversing the decree *again.* By now swift preparations were likely underway for the last-minute change. I swallowed, thickly. "I'm sorry. I'm so sorry."

"Get out of my sight!" she hollered.

When it became clear that Milicena no longer would speak, I scurried from the prison with my head bent and my tail between my legs. I *meant* to do the right thing, it seemed like the right thing and –

- Oh. My. God.

That *prick.*

Laz knew, didn't he? He was cruel enough to purposefully manipulate her death into the manner she least desired.

Racing back to the castle, I searched for hours to find Lazlian, but no one knew his whereabouts. It wasn't until nightfall when a servant, frightened at the ill-concealed rage on my face, quickly reported Laz had returned from riding and was now having supper, curiously alone. By the time I reached the hated dining room, I was so enraged I could barely see straight. My arms burned, wanting to punch something. Some*one.*

Storming into the small hall, I found Laz not at all alone. Pressed against the dining table his body was so entwined with a serving girl's I couldn't tell where his hands roamed -- but from her moan I knew he'd squeezed *something* as he kissed her.

On purpose, maybe. Had he heard me enter?

"I want to talk to you," I seethed. "Now."

The girl, wide-eyed, tore back from the kiss, took one look at me, then quickly scurried out between Laz and the table. Head bent, she began re-arranging the plates and linens they'd pushed aside, as if any of that mattered.

Laz held my gaze. For the life of me I couldn't read it.

"Alone," I stated, trying not to growl the command at the girl caught in the crossfire of whatever was about to happen. "Leave, please."

As she scampered from the room, Laz reclined lazily on his chair, assuming his typical insolent pose.

"You knew it wasn't what she wanted!" I cried, as soon as the door shut. "You *knew* it! Didn't you? I knew you were hiding something. You're a snake, Laz, a crocodile just hiding in the brush to attack."

Tossing back his wavy hair, he shrugged. "I told you the truth. I didn't want to make the trip. Why should I be inconvenienced? What the prisoner wants is of no importance to me."

"Because... she fought bravely, she

commanded ships, she is their commander's daughter... we owe her respect."

Laz flashed his teeth. "As opposed to the commoners whom we can disrespect?"

"As opposed to *you* who just disrespects *everyone*!" My hands balled into fists. "And that's not what I meant, you twisted my words! You can't... treat people like this, Laz. Is there even a shred of humanity in you or are you all reptilian at this point?"

At that moment, someone knocked on the door.

"What?" I cried, annoyed at yet another interruption. A young male servant shuffled timidly into the room.

"Yes?" I snapped, trying - and failing - to contain my temper. I was too worked up to feel guilty about it though.

"It's Milicena, my young queen," the man said, not quite meeting my gaze.

My stomach knotted. I caught Laz's face from the corner of my eye. He bore a curious expression I couldn't put my finger on.

"What do you mean? What's happened?" I managed to keep my tone gentle this time, but anxiety crept into my voice.

Encouraged, the young servant spoke louder. "The prisoner is dead. She made a rope from her clothing and hanged herself in her cell."

It felt like the floor moved or the room wobbled. "Are you sure?" I whispered.

The servant nodded. "She's to be carried out the King's Gate with great presentation, so that all are assured she's really dead. Her body will be burned."

Dead? Just like that? I fell into the nearest chair, head in my hands. I heard the servant scurry out and assumed Laz dismissed him. I took a few deep gulps of air and closed my eyes. Then, in a flash of insight, I suddenly puzzled out the look on Lazlian's face when the servant told us the news.

Expectation.

He'd *guessed* this would happen, that Milicena would rather hang herself than submit to a public execution.

As soon as I lifted my eyes – blown wide with fury – I knew I was right. And Laz knew I knew.

"You're a vile snake," I swore, shooting to my feet.

He didn't deny it. I'll give him that.

"It's neater this way," he said, once again brushing back a section of his wavy hair. "Now no one will have to sail to the Isle of Corpses or bother with the stairs in the heat of the afternoon for a long and boring public hanging."

"You're disgusting, Laz." I shook uncontrollably with rage. "You were right all along. I'm not your equal. You're beneath me. I would never do something like this."

"Outmaneuver me?" he mocked, knowing

full well what I'd meant. "No, you'd have to equal my intelligence and you're sorely lacking. You're lacking in every way a woman can possibly lack."

I hated that his insult *hurt.* I saw the crooked, lazy grin on his face, the languid rocking of his chair as he leaned back, one long leg lifted, foot propped on the table's edge...

Before I knew what I was doing, I rushed forward and pushed him. It wasn't innocent, but it wasn't horribly violent either. Not yet. I hoped he'd fall on his rear. A foolish part of my brain thought he might laugh it off in his haughty manner. But he was faster than I expected, shooting to his feet so that only the chair clattered to the ground.

Despite recovering, he pushed me back -- *hard.*

Far harder than he'd shoved me out of his room that night. He pushed with latent, simmering, anger. I stumbled and fell.

I could have stayed down. Maybe he would have laughed over me, walked away. But white-hot anger flared in my brain, burning too brightly to think or feel past its fire. Panting, I shot to my feet and raced forward. I wanted to punch him, but I didn't have the nerve and didn't even know how to throw a proper punch. I resorted to a pitiful slap.

Of course, he caught my wrist before my hand connected -- deep down I wasn't even surprised.

But I was shocked and terrified by what he did next.

Laz's right hand rose high in the air, poised to backhand me. Mad rage rolled off his body; I could feel it permeate the space between us. Instinctively, I cringed, turning my face to my shoulder and squeezing my eyes shut. *He's wearing rings,* I thought wildly, *they'll cut my face.*

The blow for which I braced didn't come. My lip quivered pathetically. In that moment, I was angrier at myself than with Laz. So mad, that when I dared look up at his burning-hazel eyes, I seethed, "You're just like your prick of a father."

"You're just like your whore of a mother."

Why did that hurt? Why did I care about anything Laz said?

"Good. I'm glad." I lifted my chin, ignoring the pooling of tears. Even I heard the wistfulness in my voice as I breathed, "At least I knew love before I came here."

That came out wrong. I didn't mean to drag Juls into it. Or did I?

Juls didn't ask for this either.

But he's not stopping it either.

Just like a warrior whose muscles coil before a physical attack, the flare in Laz's eyes told me he was doing the same, mentally. His hand poised high above my cheek – a warning - but

I knew the real threat was no longer bodily. At least, not at the moment.

"The only reason I didn't rig the last bomb to blow you to pieces is because you're too stupid to trust to have put them in the right order. The next time your life is in my hands, I won't make the mistake of letting you live."

His declaration came low, hard.

I didn't doubt it.

"That's a vow, little queen. And I always keep my vows."

Chapter 29

My wedding day barreled down on me and I couldn't stop it; couldn't find a way to get off the island. It was happening all over again, only this time, it wasn't in doubt about what I wanted. Elaborate fantasies of screaming through the castle, destroying everything in my path and refusing to wed kept me occupied at night.

What if I'd tried to make Juls hate me? Would he have pled to his father to stop this atrocity?

Always, I gulped when that particular idea plagued. *The king would hurt me in private,* I knew. *To ensure I behaved well in public.*

Instead, I stood with squared shoulders when they measured me for my second wedding dress – not white and tiered, with fluffy skirts like the first -- but gold with sheer panels, shooting straight to the floor. I smiled and looked up through my lashes whenever

Juls took my hand, kissing it. I nodded along with Grahar whenever he discussed the guests or the menu.

Kirwyn will come for me. If I can't sneak out, he'll sneak in. Rescue me before the ceremony. This can't really be my fate.

Freer in my movements, I sought my aunt and uncle when I could, to dine or simply converse. As my guard outside the castle proper, Jesi always joined me on those excursions, and Lida sometimes did as well, though Tomé refused. He stuck to his room or mysteriously disappeared half the day. Alette, like my mother, loved beautiful things – but she radiated when sharing them; bringing us coconut cookies she'd freshly baked or discussing a mainland painting she'd acquired. In the evenings, Saos played his lute and sang. As the weeks passed, I even learned some Rythasian songs.

I turned eighteen. It was uneventful.

I knew the king knew it was my birthday, since the day held a deep connection to the tragedy of losing his wife and daughter, but he said nothing and neither did I. I was grateful because if Juls knew, I'd probably have been forced into a party with Laz somehow. I didn't even tell my aunt and uncle. Though I'd grown more comfortable around them, I didn't fully trust Alette until she'd tell me what happened to my Aunt Enith, and I didn't feel ready to ask her yet either, seeing as it caused such grief.

Only Jesi and Lida knew it was my birthday, and they insisted on bringing a layered, pink guava cake into my room that night. We dug into it together without even bothering to cut it and drank bubbly wine Jesi explained resembled pink champagne.

When only seven days protected me from my nuptials, panic rioted in my stomach like a Black Squall. Desperate, the crazy idea to speak with the mystical hermit struck like lighting in my internal storm.

"I'm coming with you," Jesi announced. "You don't know the way and you're not allowed that far on your own."

As we trekked through the forest toward the cliffs above Black Sand Beach, Jesi cautioned, "He's always had a touch of the otherworld, and it's only worsened with age." An additional two palace guards trailed in our wake, so she kept her voice low to avoid their ears. "I don't know if you'll be able to make much sense of him at all. He likes to speak in riddles on a good day."

I rolled my eyes. *Great.* I knew about mystical cults speaking in riddles. The Arch Priestess never said a straight word to me.

You've come to the right place, but you're the wrong person, she'd declared, when Kirwyn and I went to see her.

Who was the right one, anyway? What did that mean? *Wrong for Elowa because I was leaving? Did that mean I was right for here? Or was my being queen in Rythas wrong as well?*

"Jesi," I began tentatively, as we walked under the thick canopy. "I think Laz is going to try to kill me."

I hadn't told her of his threats or what transpired the day Milicena hanged herself. I hadn't even told her about Grahar attacking me. I didn't know why, but I *couldn't* speak of it until then.

Funny though, that the only person I'd ever spoken to of Grahar's assault... had been Laz.

"What makes you say that?" Jesi asked the obvious question.

"Because he told me he would. Multiple times. And because... he almost struck me a few weeks ago."

Jesi's face registered shock. "Laz would never hit you."

"Why? You think he's not capable? Trust me, he made the threat the very night we met."

"First of all, because Juls would be enraged and Laz would never hurt his brother," she replied, wincing. "Also, I'm guessing he most likely wanted to scare you, to even the score, in his mind. For... *that* night." She paused. "But... if you really think Laz is trying to murder you... find me. I won't let him hurt you."

"Wait a minute. Back up. Are you saying he wouldn't hit me but he'd murder me? That makes no sense!"

377

Jesi grimaced. "Well, I can't be sure, but... if he struck you, he can't hide the evidence. If he murdered you, he could find a way to make it an accident. But *please,* don't worry. Do I look worried for you? Laz isn't aggressive like that, he won't do anything to kill you."

"He admitted he stole the shark! He used it to try to kill me before I even arrived! Lured it to the cove where I was swimming somehow and hoped nature would take care of me for him. And he's sneaky. Maybe he wouldn't kill me with his own two hands, but he's proved he's capable of letting someone or something else do the dirty work for him."

Jesi's mouth dropped at the revelation. "Good lord, are you sure? Why didn't you tell me before? That's... I'm sorry, Zaria. I'm so sorry." She pulled me into a hug before letting out a long breath. "Good *lord.* I'm so sorry. But... at least... that was *before* you came. We have to remember that. Juls likes you. Laz won't upset him by hurting you."

"But now Laz hates me more!" I protested, fighting back tears. "Now I've given him reason. Before, I was a faceless entity coming to ruin his brother's happiness or whatever. Now... now I'm guilty of sneaking into his room and trying to steal from him and..."

And whatever happened in that second when he grabbed my wrist, before I dropped the key. I didn't know what it was, but I knew Laz blamed me.

"Tell me exactly what happened a few weeks ago," Jesi ordered.

I related the events around Milicena's death and when I finished, Jesi let out a long breath. "Okay, I think I understand. Laz hates the ocean. I think he nearly drowned as a child and doesn't go anywhere near the water now. So I'm not surprised he'd do anything to avoid having to be the one sailing out to sea in a small boat, watching and waiting for Milicena to die."

He does get weird around the water, I thought. *And Juls mentioned something during our first dinner together.*

"But you didn't see him, Jesi. His eyes were like a madman's. Enraged. Maybe he didn't want to go out to sea, but he used me to make it happen because he despises me."

Jesi nodded solemnly. "For now, keep your head down. Stay close to Juls. And don't be alone with Laz for the time being."

"I don't want to be alone with Laz for the rest of my life if I can help it."

After a few minutes of walking, I said, "There's something else I haven't told you. Grahar struck me the day of the Offering Ceremony."

Jesi gasped. "Zaria what? Why didn't you tell me? I don't understand. Did you tell Juls?"

"I don't know! I was... ashamed somehow. No, I haven't told Juls. I can't. I don't want him in that position between me and his father; I can't risk it when I need him to like me. If I make trouble, it will only make it harder to escape. Please don't tell him. Promise me."

Shaking her head, Jesi closed her eyes. "I'll make you a deal. Just this once, I won't say anything. But if he does it again, you have to tell me and we'll tell Juls. Deal?"

"Okay. Deal," I agreed, hoping it wouldn't come to that.

About a quarter of an hour later, a break in the trees brought us to our destination. Atop the cliff, a gorgeous teal sea stretched before us. Below, a small beach of black sand sparkled. I'd never seen anything like it. I spied a rope ladder secured to the ground, disappearing over the cliff's edge.

Guess it's a climb down.

"I'll wait up here," Jesi said, plopping onto the grass and withdrawing her dagger. She'd probably make a game of tossing it into the dirt or a nearby tree. Ever since Oxholde attacked, I also kept one strapped to my waist whenever I wasn't engaged in formal business with Juls. I still hadn't much skill with it, but I'd gotten a little less pathetic at defending myself under Jesi's regular instructions.

Shimmying over the edge, I climbed backwards down the rope ladder.

I don't expect to learn anything useful, I thought, heeding Jesi's warning. *But I've got nothing to lose.*

About fifteen feet down, I came to the cliffside dwelling – the hermit's cavern carved into rock. The stench of urine and body odor assaulted my nose the moment I stepped inside. Worse – human waste accompanied the scent as a sycophant passed me by on her way to the ladder. She carried a used chamber pot she slung into a knapsack before taking hold of the rope ladder – to dispose of the waste, I assumed.

"You can speak with him, if you like," she said, smiling serenely. "I'll be back in a minute."

The air only slightly improved once she departed.

Alone, I shuddered at the dirty, eerie living space. On a hammock mounted into the low ceiling in the back of the cave, I spied the hermit.

"Hello?" I called into the strange, echo-y chamber, unsure if he was asleep or awake.

No reply came. I stepped closer, moving from light into shadow. He had to be one of the oldest men I'd ever seen, bony, wearing only a garment that looked to have once been loose pants but had been cut off high on his thighs. Though sea breezes cooled the already temperate cave, his stringy, matted hair clung wetly to his head and face.

"Hello?" I repeated, softly. "I – I... they told me I could see you now. I'm Zaria. The, uh, young queen. I was hoping I could ask you about the... future. I guess. Just, um, generally, what it holds."

The hermit grinned without opening his eyes. His mouth held more space than teeth. Without looking at me, he spoke.

From his first sentence, I wanted to scream.

#

"What did he tell you?" Jesi asked, as I climbed back onto the cliff.

"Riddles. Nothing but riddles," I sighed. "Total waste of time."

She laughed, "I told you."

Annoyed that I'd pinned my hopes to a ridiculous notion, the return hike back to High Spire felt even longer. Jesi had a meeting with Navere and I went in search of Tomé. Knocking on his door, I was greeted by the shifty, dark-haired boy I'd often seen milling about Tomé's room. Thanks to the hermit, I was already in a mood and his unctuous grin set my teeth on edge.

"Where is my cousin?" I demanded.

"He's not here," the boy replied, shrugging.

Obviously.

Something straightened my spine at that moment, something I used to possess, but had lost since I'd left Elowa. It came back to me in fits and starts and I struggled not to lose it each time.

"Do *you* like being here?" I asked. It was my old voice, my braenese voice. "Because I can guarantee you won't be much longer if you don't tell me where my cousin is. Right now."

The boy's nostrils flared. Frowning, he said, "He's at a party. The Pepper and the Peach," he said, rolling his eyes. "Down by the brothels."

"Why aren't you there?" I asked, suspicious.

"Not everyone is a social butterfly. I don't much like other people," he declared.

The feeling's mutual, I thought, turning on my heel to leave.

I didn't know what was going on with Tomé, but I knew it wasn't healthy. Jesi saved me from despair when I arrived -- even when she had to physically drag me from the window ledge. It was time I did the same for Tomé, whether he liked it or not. I located a random guard by my bedroom and asked him to accompany me to the brothels -- clustered outside High Spire, I surely wouldn't be allowed to go alone.

I found the venue, The Pepper and the Peach, easy enough, though no celebrations took place in front. Wandering back through a sprawling complex, I followed the sound of music and crossed the courtyard to enter a long hall in back.

Half-naked bodies sprawled across the floor cushions, the chaise lounges, the stone ledges. It looked like a tableau from a Bacchanalian banquet I'd seen in the historical section of *that book* Jesi gave me. I remembered it well because the image colored my cheeks.

I didn't feel timid about any of it now though. I felt angry.

Through a haze of smoke, I stomped across the room, weaving around couples too intoxicated or high on god-only-knew-what to mind my presence. A quartet of lutists played in the corner, and, taking cues from the undisturbed guests, continued the music despite my presence.

I headed straight for Tomé, shirtless, lounging against a sunny window in the corner.

"Cousin," he drawled slowly as I approached. A man shot to his feet at Tomé's greeting, and my eyes bulged to find Tomé was not only shirtless, but pants-less as well. One burning stare at Tomé's companion and he had the good sense to scurry away.

I grabbed a swath of silk from the ground and threw it at my cousin. As he held it loosely over his midsection, covering what should be covered, I could smell the alcohol on his breath

"What are you doing? I know you're upset, but you can't go on like this," I said, straining to keep my voice gentle. "There are better ways to deal with it, Tomé."

He cocked the side of his mouth into a smirk, but one side of his nose scrunched at the same time, so it looked like a snarl.

"If I'm not mistaken you've been known to deal with your pain in much the same manner many nights."

"It's the middle of the day!" I scoffed.

Tomé raised his hand grandly. "Oh, well, I see you've declared that pain can only be dealt with when the moon shines. You know all the matters of the heart, don't you? After all, you are the Queen of our Hearts." He raised a silver goblet in mock toast and brought it to his mouth.

I smacked it out of his hands and onto the floor.

"Stop it. Stop drinking."

"Stop telling me how to feel."

Tomé reached for another goblet, and I pushed his shoulders. "I'm not telling you how to *feel!*"

"No, you're just telling me how to *deal* with my feelings." Tomé pushed me back, but with only one hand free it wasn't very hard. "You can't command my feelings, Zaria. My methods of coping don't bow to your rule."

"I'm not commanding you as a queen. I'm telling you as a friend."

"Friend? Okay, friend, then lay off and have a friendly drink here with me."

Tomé reached for the goblet again and I tried stopping him. The next thing I knew, he grabbed my arms – or I grabbed his – and we were wrestling for the cup. Tomé, nearly naked; me, in a manner not at all queenly as we fell onto the floor kicking and rolling.

Through our swinging arms and legs, I had two immediate thoughts – one, he used to wrestle with Marcin like this -- and two, this is probably how Tomé and I would have fought as children, had touching been allowed.

"You're a bad drunk!" I cried.

"You're a bad friend!" he shouted. His hands scrambled for mine, but I rolled out from under him. Tomé was like a brother; I wasn't the least concerned about his nudity... save for the stares we'd begun to draw.

"If I were a bad friend I would leave you alone to this. Let you become this... mess!"

My ears picked up the silence of the party ceasing around us. People turned, either horrified or enjoying the show. Any two people grappling like dogs on the floor would have attracted attention -- but me, the young queen, and her buck-naked kinsmen -- made a spectacle.

Tomé, bigger and stronger, half-lifted me off the ground. I heard more gasps – no one else would have the audacity to do such a thing. But Tomé was drunk, and I'd been training with Jesi. When he edged toward the small pool, I realized his intentions and released my grip on his shoulders to give him a false sense of security. Then, when he pushed forward, I pivoted, using his own momentum against him, knowing I'd fall into the pool but at least I'd take him with me.

The last thing I heard was the crowd sucking in a collective breath.

I dreaded resurfacing.

I could already hear the rumors. *The foreign braenese and her equally savage kinsmen getting into a typical Elowan brawl.*

Landdammit. I just hoped it stayed there, in the underbelly, rather than float on up to High Spire and the support of those I needed.

By the time I popped my head above water, Tomé was already standing, staring daggers at me. Our plummet seemed to sober him. He climbed out of the pool and whipped a towel off the nearest pile to cover his lower half. Then he stalked from the room, head high, crowd parting around him.

All eyes turned back to me.

I needed to say or do something to contain the damage. Defuse tension. Re-establish authority.

I made myself flash a grin, eyeing Tomé's receding back as he stomped down one of the many side halls.

"Unfortunately, with the departure of my castmate, no encore performances can be expected," I joked, shrugging one shoulder. Nervous titters followed. I sloshed up the pool steps as, thankfully, someone rushed forward with a towel.

"Please – do enjoy the party," I said in a voice both haughty and jovial. I couldn't tell who I was channeling – part my mother, part Kirwyn. Or maybe something in my tone was just *me,* new and unique. I plucked a tart from a nearby tray and took a small bite.

"But I ask that you not include my cousin in any revelry hereafter. I might have to return to claim him. And since he's so reluctant to leave, the next time I come I might need the palace guards' assistance."

I held the eyes of the nearest man to ensure my veiled threat was understood. *Parties may continue. But my cousin is barred entry, or they'll stop.*

The man stared back, jaw set. I smiled. We understood each other.

#

After I cleaned myself up, I headed straight for Tomé's room, taking a page from Jesi's book. She hadn't left me alone when I'd been lost and I was no longer leaving Tomé alone either.

Banging on the door, I was surprised when he opened it, seemingly without his unfriendly companion.

That's... something, at least. The curtains were still drawn, but Tomé was fully dressed.

"Can we talk?" I asked, stepping inside.

"Yeah. Sure. What do want to talk about?"

"You. I want the old Tomé back." *You used to*

be so happy.

"Not something I can give you right now."

I let out a long breath. "I understand. Then I just... want you to be... careful. Show some restraint."

It was the wrong thing to say.

"Like the restraint you showed when you were finally able to touch someone you loved?" Tomé scoffed. "Like the restraint you showed sneaking off to your cave every day?"

I opened my mouth. I shut it.

"How would you feel if you were told you couldn't love the person you love and when you finally get him... only to have him *choose* something else over you?" Tomé demanded. "And then suddenly it's... Everything you ever wanted. You don't know what it's like."

I sat down on his bed. "You're right, I don't know. But I know what it's like to be told I can't love the person I love and to be forced to love someone I don't." Even saying it out loud made a lump form in my throat. "It's not the same, but I know heartbreak. I'm not trying to... I don't want to control you. I envy you, Tomé. You're free. I've been moved from one cage to the next. Rythas might be home for you, you might find your way here. But I can't. Nothing's changed for me. I might as well be back in Elowa."

Kirwyn's face floated in my mind, as it did every hour of every day, whether I spoke of him or not. *The way Kirwyn looked at me. Ravenous, like a starved man. Like he wanted to eat me alive.* Juls's gaze didn't do that. I didn't think it ever could. *Don't cry,* I warned myself.

"I just worry about you, that's all," I said.

Tomé clenched his jaw as he briefly closed his eyes. "I know." He ran a hand down his face. "I know," he sighed.

"Why is everything a disaster?" I moaned, falling onto Tomé's bed. "I don't understand. Who makes these rules? Why?"

Tomé laid down beside me, both of us staring up at the ceiling. "I don't know. People who are unhappy and want everyone else to be as unhappy as they are."

He's right, I thought. People like Grahar. And yet… is that what my mother had done, when she allowed me to secretly be with Kirwyn? Was it cruelty? Or had she truly wanted me to have some happiness? And Juls… he wasn't unhappy. In fact, the more time passed, the happier he became with me. At my expense.

"It's all so complicated," I cried, staring up at the ceiling as if it had answers.

\#

That night, Tomé and I took dinner in his room. It wasn't like old times, but it was a start. Because I had a morning meeting with Juls to prepare for our wedding, Tomé promised to let Lida bring him to the library the next day.

I returned to my room late that evening, feeling a little better that my cousin let me in.

As soon as I opened my bedroom door, I froze.

Someone's been here. Maybe many people. Why?

Hair pins, combs, and makeup from my dresser were scattered haphazardly across the tabletop, some items missing. Chairs were not where I'd left them. A floor cushion was turned over. My bed –

-- my bed!

Sheets lay in disarray. I rushed to lift the mattress.

My heart stopped.

Kirwyn's picture was gone.

Chapter 30

My eyes shifted quickly between Juls and Laz. *They knew. One of them had stolen my picture and I was about to blow my whole besotted braenese routine.* My heart hammered in my chest. *Why else had I been called to this early meeting?*

I'd been summoned to the king's hall where, in three days, our wedding would take place. But Juls didn't sit on his throne, as I'd dreaded. Both he and Laz sat to the side in a semi-circle of wooden chairs, conversing casually until I'd arrived.

"There's a part of the wedding ceremony we didn't previously discuss," Juls said evenly, using his formal voice, handling me with kid gloves.

Lovely. And?

A pause. I'd come to hate that pause. Everyone took it before delivering bad news. It was a warning, a moment of bracing, like the sea pulling back, ebbing before the massive flow of a tidal wave.

Juls continued, gently, "There's a ceremonial knife and... the bride and the groom cut their palms to seal the union with clasped hands, in blood."

Cut? Just the idea made me weak.

I swallowed. "Um... the thing is," I began, already breathing heavy, "I don't like the sight of blood. Especially my own. I don't mean to be weak or cowardly, I try not to, but... I faint. Almost every time."

"I know," Juls replied, waving his hand. The gesture wasn't as dismissive as when Grahar or Laz did it, but it irked me regardless. "We were told."

I clenched my jaw to avoid digging my fingernails into my palms, an act of frustration that would surely be noticed. *How much information about me was passed along before I even arrived?*

"There's a way around it we could take," Juls offered, tucking his shiny, dark hair behind his ear. "If you're averse."

"Averse to fainting at the altar? Yes."

Though I don't know why I'm discussing this anyway. I'm not going through with the ceremony.

"Alright-" Juls began, but Laz, who'd been quietly seething beside his brother, spoke up.

"Royal marriages *must* be sealed in blood. It's tradition." He turned his hazel eyes to me. "The gods know she won't bleed on your wedding night."

My cheeks flamed and I swallowed. I knew Juls knew about Kirwyn, but he never mentioned it. Maybe he didn't care? Maybe he'd been with many others himself? I didn't know, didn't want to know, and didn't want to be having this conversation.

"*Lazlian*," Juls warned, voice sharp and deep, "Zaria doesn't like blood."

"I don't care what she likes," Laz replied flippantly, once again wresting a conversation *about me*, away from me, and speaking as if I weren't there. My jaw-clenching turned to teeth-grinding. Half of me wanted to agree with Laz at that moment, just to frustrate him and also because I knew the ceremony wouldn't get that far. *Kirwyn is coming. I feel it.*

"Do you care that she'll faint and make a spectacle at our wedding?" Juls challenged. "Because I know Father will. And what kind of omen that would be to the guests?"

Laz clenched his own jaw, hate-filled gaze falling upon me. As if this had anything to do with him. As if I were the one to blame for everything wrong in his life.

"She's weak. What kind of Elowan faints at the sight of blood? I thought they were supposed to be godlike creatures of perfection? Do we really want that weakness tainting our bloodline? She's not even marked, Juls.

Everyone here is marked, every commoner, every bride, and especially every Doreste. When is she going to take our tattoo?"

I opened my mouth, but Juls held up a hand to caution me against exploding. I bit the inside of my cheek, hard.

Calmly, Juls declared, "She's not leaving Rythas anytime soon; there's no rush to take our mark until she's ready. As for our wedding, we'll drink from a shared cup and pretend it's been laced with drops of our blood beforehand. It's done in Low Spire ceremonies. It's not unheard of."

"It is for *us*." Laz spat. But Juls only folded his arms, not budging. In that moment, I felt a surge of affection for him. Juls was smaller than his brother but more self-possessed, more in command. The noble way he protected everyone... I couldn't help but respect him.

Laz leaned back, too casually, too measured. He draped one arm over the back of the chair. I knew venom was coming.

"So the little queen won't ever bleed for the Dorestes?"

My eyes fluttered closed against the onset of hot shame once more. *Why did he have to continually bring that up? Why was he so obsessed with who I'd been with before? So concerned with his family's supposed honor? Why did* that *have anything to do with it?*

"She bled for us," Juls said, voice carrying his

warning tone again. "Or have you forgotten the Bombing of the Bloody Shoals?"

"She bled for herself and her friends. It's not the same thing. And if I recall, she returned without a scratch on her."

Enough.

"But I got one the next day," I said, smiling with malice and turning the boys' attention to me. "Don't you remember, Laz? When that man whipped his chain at my arm and bruised it? I'd think you'd remember that, seeing as how we had a long chat about it over wine that evening?"

It was my own warning. I sensed Laz didn't want to discuss that night, that our conversations touched on several matters he wanted to hide. *Trying to kill me, for starters.* And though Laz ran and told his brother everything that suited him, he knew I didn't. I had my reasons, but I danced around the threat that I might break them.

I am a threat to you, aren't I? I'll outrank you, as queen. And I might sway your brother's allegiance. Is that the real reason why you hate me?

Laz's nostrils flared and he pushed off his chair so hard it fell backwards, clattering noisily in the empty, echo-y hall. Without saying another word, he stormed out of the room.

Juls's gentle touch rested upon my bicep, as

if to guide me to stay. "Let him go," he said, standing next to me.

I blinked, shaking my head from the keylord's retreating figure. *What made Juls think I was going to chase after Laz? To further fight him or to make up?*

Juls hadn't... heard about those disgusting drawings, had he?

Of course he has, Zaria, I scolded myself, shame rising anew. *And Keroe only knows what he made of them.*

I forcibly relaxed my tensed shoulders and whispered, "Thank you for understanding about the blood."

It was all the encouragement Juls needed to bring his fingers to my face, stroking my cheek. "Of course. I'd never want to hurt you." Hopeful, but with a touch of uncertainty, Juls said, "I want this to be a happy day for us both."

"I – yes. It will be," I replied automatically. My heart gave a little leap as if to say, *you'd be easy to love,* but at the same time, I thought, *I'm not the right bride for you and deep down, you know it.*

Everyone knows it.

Correction – only a select few knew. Everyone else in Rythas geared up for the royal wedding of a lifetime. Everyone else saw two charismatic young royals united in love and leadership. Saints or saviors; and it all felt like one more big lie, just like Elowa.

Except... it wasn't entirely.

I really *did* care for the people I'd met here, I *did* want to help. Just not as Jullik Doreste's wife.

My lashes fluttered closed as Juls leaned in to kiss me. His soft lips, warm against mine – his hands, stroking my face -- made me reconsider yet again.

Did he feel something for me?

When Kirwyn came, when I escaped, would he mourn my departure?

#

I clutched the rough stone of my window, staring out to sea. A chill came into my room upon the breeze and clouds covered the sky. Sunset wasn't far off but I couldn't see it through the gray. Would it rain on my wedding day? Would it get that far?

Neither Juls nor Laz mentioned the drawing of Kirwyn, so where was it? Who raided my room?

I slid my fingers against the stone, harder and faster, as if to punish myself or to *feel* something. To purposefully experience pain, to see on my flesh the scars and scrapes I felt within. I'd bottled it up since I'd arrived in Rythas, never releasing the scream roaring to come out.

Everything I'd ever been told is a lie. My parents betrayed me. My father is dead. Kirwyn isn't with me. I'm being forced into a marriage I don't want.

Even now, I yearned to wail, to shout out my pain to the sea. But other windows, other verandas, stood too near my own. I suffered silently, scraping my tender palms against the stone.

"Zaria?" I heard Jesi's cautious voice behind me.

"I'm not going to jump," I said, tiredly.

"We know." *Lida's voice.* I turned to see my two friends coming into my room and closing the door behind them.

"Zaria, talk to us," Jesi urged. "Your wedding is only three days away. I admit I hoped… when you came, I thought maybe you'd grow to love Juls. I'm sorry, but it would have been easier for everyone, and I thought if you gave him a chance…"

"He's not Kirwyn," I moaned. "And anyway, Juls doesn't love me. You know that. He loves his duty. He'll choose duty over love every time."

"That's interesting," Jesi chided, frowning. "When we snuck out that day to get you kidnapped… when we snuck a note to Carrington, the guard at the Garden Gate? Do you remember? You told me if he got sacked it was his own fault for choosing love over duty. And now you're saying you can't love Juls because he'd choose duty over love?"

I folded my arms. "It's not that simple,

there's more at play than how he rules and even how he loves. Besides, it was another organ entirely the guard was following that day, not his heart."

"Hey, I get it, no scenario is as simple as it seems on the surface," Jesi said. "But I wonder, what would it be if *you* had to choose?"

"I don't know," I said, hating the whine in my voice. "I guess... guess I'm trying to do both. Somehow."

In the silence that followed, Lida shocked me by announcing, "By leaving?"

I froze. "I-"

"Stop it," Lida snapped. "I already told you, I saw what you were doing on your uncle's boat. I know what you're planning, and you only insult me to protest otherwise. I'm not a spy for Grahar." Rolling her eyes, she added, "Elowans stick together. Just because I bear the symbol of Rythas doesn't mean I forget. We're here to help. And we might have found a way to get you out, if you truly want to leave."

In the silence that followed, I chewed my lip, studying the faces of my two friends. Finally, I took a deep breath. "Okay. I need to tell you both... everything, I guess."

Once we'd lit all the candles and assembled the floor cushions, I said, "I can't marry Juls. I love Kirwyn. I know it sounds silly because we only knew each other for a moon's cycle. But even if I'd never met him, I wouldn't love Juls."

Or would I convince myself I did? I wondered. *Was he doing that?*

"I need to escape Rythas somehow," I continued. "And more than that, I want to stop Elowa from sending the eldest daughter here. I want to stop their lies, everything. But I can't..." I ran my hands through my hair, yanking it. "Even if I try to change things there, I have to change them here first. Rythas has the power. And I don't know what to do! But I can't stay here. I can't... with Juls... and Grahar expects grandchildren!"

Jesi's strong hands patted my back, keeping me from bursting into tears. Swallowing the lump in my throat, I asked, "Lida, do you know what's happening on Elowa? Have the people turned against my mother or has she manipulated them to love her again?"

"Since I left, I don't know what she's doing or what she plans to do," Lida admitted. "You know your mother better than I do. I can't say how to overthrow her, if that's what you want."

That was the problem. I did know my mother. And she wasn't easily outmaneuvered.

"You're a bit like her," Lida added, thoughtfully.

"What? No, I'm not."

Lida shrugged. "What do you want to do? Stage a coup and overthrow the Dorestes? I mean... Navere is pretty shifty if you think you want to align with the army."

Jesi frowned. "That's not... no. Don't say that."

Lida shrugged again, "She has the love of the people and he's got his eye on the crown, I'm telling you. Do you think if Zaria went to Navere and proposed an alliance he'd pass up the opportunity to marry her and take the throne? Not saying he wouldn't think about killing her after, but... she could cross that bridge when she came to it."

"No!" I cried. *"No.* I don't want Juls overthrown."

"Well, you could stay and maybe convince him to help you..." Jesi said, hopefully.

I shook my head. "Juls willingly participated in this arranged marriage, even though he *must* have known what happened the day Singen and Raoul took me. And even if he wanted to change the law, the nobles wouldn't support him. They get first dibs on our Elowan wares, they turn around and sell the goods, lining their own pockets. It's too good a deal. Then once a generation one of them gets the Daughter of Elowa for a bride? They won't give that up."

For a moment, I listened to the calming rush of the ocean outside my window, then sighed, "I don't want to hurt Juls if I can help it. I just want... things to change," I finished vaguely. "Here and in Elowa."

Lida cocked her head and flicked her braid.

"If you want to change things, you may have sway with the Mystics."

I stopped breathing. Even the mention of the Mystics made my stomach clench, but I waited for Lida to continue.

"Pentyr is young, but he wants to become the next High Mystic. If you can offer him change that benefits him, he'll work on your behalf because it suits him."

"What do you mean?" I asked slowly.

"Whatever changes you're envisioning, if it includes allowing the Mystics to marry and bed whomever they like, Pentyr will preach it for you. He doesn't care about compassion, but he does care about his co-"

"Okay, I got it!" I interrupted her.

Lida smirked, wagging her shoulders.

"I don't understand. Why doesn't he just leave? Come here?"

"And give up his position? No, he wants power *and* pu-"

"Stop!" I cut her off again, this time reflexively clapping my hands over my ears. "Gross, I get it. He's slime."

Lida laughed at my expense. "Well, he is. That's true. But not for the reasons you think. Can you blame him? Don't you want freedom too?"

I frowned, knitting my brow. "I'm surprised you're defending him."

"I'm not. I see Pentyr for what he is. More

than anyone. I'm just saying, that's not the reason he's slime. If you want to work with your enemies, you need to assess them with a clear mind."

"Are we working with the Mystics now?" I groaned. "Is that what you're suggesting?"

"I think you're going to have to work with a lot of people you don't like to get what you want."

"Like you?" I teased. "Like us? God, you hated me back in Elowa, yet you helped me anyway."

Lida licked her lips and folded her legs beneath her, quiet for a moment as she gazed into the candle's flame. "I'm sorry. I wasn't fair to you," she said, stroking the end of her braid. "I resented that I had to participate in a charade for you. I resented that you got to leave, gained access to all the knowledge of the world and you didn't even seem to want it. I didn't think it was fair. But I know now that wasn't true, isn't who you are."

Her apology only made me want to cry even more. "No, it's... thank you," I croaked. "But you were entitled to feel that way. And maybe you didn't know me, didn't know what I desired, but I can understand how you felt... more deserving of all this knowledge. I want to *know,* sure, but you, you want to *study.* You belong here."

In the awkward seconds that followed, Jesi piped up. "Well," she drawled, "I think

Zaria belongs here too. But if you're *really* determined to leave..." she slumped her shoulders, defeated "...the only way out is going to be *The King's Light.* Remember that ceremonial ship in the docks? She's large enough to hide on and, on rare occasions, she sails."

My heart jumped at her words.

"But," Jesi cautioned, holding up her hands, "Though you might be able to sneak on, I don't know how you'd be able to sneak off. The Dorestes only use the boat seldomly, and it's rarer still that they dock her on the mainland. Even if you got inside, even if you weren't found, there's no way you'd be able to slip off and onto a mainland shore. There's too many people and too many checkpoints."

I slumped and rubbed my temples, staring at the tiled floor. "Well, maybe I can figure something out... I can only handle one problem at a time. Is there a way to sneak onto the ship and find a hiding spot? Are there plans to sail her anytime soon?"

Jesi shook her head. "Like I said, she's only used for very important occasions."

The three of us stared into the candlelight until Jesi said softly, "I'm sorry I keep trying to make you fall for Juls. I just want you to stay."

"It's alright." I shook my head, biting my lip hard to stop from crying. "It's the easy thing to do. Maybe even the smart thing," I trailed off.

"What's her boy like?" Jesi asked Lida. "I've heard it from her, but I want your take."

"Kirwyn?" Lida laughed, high and haughty, ending on a snort. "Ridiculous. Like, no one like that should exist. The stuff girls' dreams are made of. Dark green eyes, sexy mop of dark hair. He'd cut you with that jawline, no knife needed. You can't blame her for wanting him. Juls is handsome, sure, and he's the young king, but," she sucked a breath through her teeth, "I'm not exaggerating to say Kirwyn looks like a god."

I knew my face reddened to my ears. "It's not just his looks," I protested against Jesi's smug laughter. "I mean, yeah, he's, uh, really attractive, but..." I sighed, "but it's the way he makes me *feel*. Understood. We both, I don't know, were both wild and isolated growing up, in our own ways. He made me feel seen. Heard. Like I was the only girl in his world, the only one who mattered. Like there's nothing he wouldn't do for me. And I feel the same. I haven't changed. I don't..."

I looked down, pursing my lips, and the tears flowed.

"I don't know if he has. I don't know where he is or what's happening!"

Chapter 31

Two days before our wedding, Juls and I sat together to one side of the king's hall for the Ceremony of Gifts. Grahar commanded the throne, and Laz stood before him, acting as some sort of master of ceremonies, greeting emissaries from various mainland clans with ties to Rythas who'd come bearing wedding presents. Since the origins of the kidnapping plot had never been solved, there weren't many visitors granted an audience. We planned a short ceremony.

I'd dressed in burgundy to match Juls, my traditional gown similar to the one I wore the day I begged Tomé's release from Elowa. Jesi helped me style my hair with elaborate pins and we decked my neck and wrists with golden necklaces and bracelets.

I panicked too much to mind the first few representatives.

Two more days. Only two more days until we'd

be married.

It wasn't until a strange tension filled the room that I paid attention to the courtier. Grahar's hands tightened on the balled ends of his oaken throne, skin stretching taut above the knuckles. Juls stared without moving, deep in thought. Lazlian leaned *back,* a move I now understand he made to counterbalance when he most wanted to lean *forward,* or to ready himself to strike.

"Who's that?" I whispered to Juls, without turning my head.

"He's a Spade, a Blackjack," he whispered. "Their emissary."

"Welcome to High Spire," Grahar said, wearing a smile no one could much believe. Only a fool couldn't read the thinly-veiled tension in the air.

The Spade didn't look any different from the men of Rythas, though his buttoned shirt and trousers resembled Kirwyn's mainland attire. I guessed him to be in his late thirties or early forties. He had closely-cropped brown hair and watery blue eyes that saw too much. I leaned closer to Juls and fixed a dreamy smile to my face.

The stranger bowed before Laz, but his eyes flicked to Juls and I. "I come bearing a gift all the way from Spade City," the man announced. Clapping, two other men carried forth a decorative wooden tray, though it wasn't particularly large or heavy-looking. The Spade emissary lifted a velvet covering to reveal a ball of some sort beneath.

"A music sphere," he said, "complete with traditional songs for fêtes."

Once again, the man flicked his gaze over and stared at me – too long.

"Why does he keep looking at me?" I whispered, when the stranger turned back to Laz.

Juls paused a beat, then smiled, threading his fingers through mine. "Why wouldn't he? I'm sure he's taken by your beauty."

"Oh. Thank you." But his explanation didn't sit right with me. I'd been lied to long enough to know when someone evaded.

"Thank you for your generous gift," Laz declared, evenly. "I'm sure it will astound the guests at next year's Fae fête."

The Spade smiled and waved his servants back to him. Readying to depart the room, he slid his gaze to me *again.* Something else caught my attention, as well.

"What is it?" I asked Juls, as the Spade departed. "Why is Laz upset?"

Eerie, that I'd learned to read the keylord so well I knew by the tilt of his head that he was angry. *A survival skill,* I thought.

"He feels it's patronizing," Juls explained, and I could tell Juls shared the sentiment. "A gift of technology we should possess freely, but do not, because of the TORR." Juls sighed. "More importantly, I was hoping for weather-predictive tools, to help alert us to incoming Black Squalls or..." he shifted uncomfortably, "or access to reproductive technology. With their knowledge growing, it's rumored the Spades have treatments for the infertile." Juls shook his head, and his voice grew a hard edge. "We wanted something to help our people. Not to amuse them with mindless entertainment."

As the Spade emissary concluded the ceremony, Grahar rose, but a shout came from the door, stopping him.

"Please!" a girl called. "We want to give our gift as well!"

I looked to see the guards physically restraining a young woman, also in mainland attire.

"Let her through," Juls commanded. Grahar also nodded and the guards instantly released the struggling woman. She shot them a look and jut her chin, before walking proudly to the center of the room. Kneeling deeply, she said, "I've come to present the young king and queen with a wedding present from the Lost Cradles."

Lazlian snorted. "I've never heard of you."

"We are a new clan, small in number but growing strong. We don't have very much to offer in the way of jewels or weaponry, but we are skilled craftspeople. We boast a number of gifted artists in our ranks."

She clutched plate of glass with three colorful leaves pressed within.

"We heard the young queen likes pretty things, so we made her picture of pressed leaves," her eyes flicked towards mine, "from the *forest of colors.*"

The room melted away, ceasing to exist. I saw only the girl and her glass, heard only her words.

The forest of colors?

Kirwyn's forest?

She read the question in my eyes and gave one imperceptible nod. Or did I imagine it? I inhaled a shuddering breath.

Kirwyn – he'd said it in my cave when we'd burrowed through the tunnel to escape.

I'll take you there someday. To the forest of colors.

Autumn. He'd been speaking of a mainland autumn, but I didn't understand it then.

Oh god. This was a message. *He's coming for me!* I forced myself to breathe again.

For one second longer than she should, the girl held my eyes. Then, sweeping into a slow bow, she backed away.

Don't go, I wanted to shout. *Please! Tell me if you've seen him. Is he alright? Why has he given me this picture? Is it a sign that he's coming? What do I do?*

Watching in horror as the glass-encased leaves were swept away with the other gifts, I clutched Juls's arm.

"Wait, no, please. I'd like that picture. She said it's for me and I – I do like pretty things." I titled my head down and looked up, batting my lashes.

"Of course. Laz is just bringing the gifts to be examined for any dangers – chemicals and things of that nature. He'll ensure they're clean and then you can have whatever you want."

"But – but…" I couldn't think of an excuse. My fingers dug into Juls's arm. *But Kirwyn might have sent a note with that glass,* I wanted to scream. *I need it. Oh god, not Laz. Not anyone. I need to see it first.*

"Don't worry," Juls soothed. "It's highly unlikely anything dangerous is present and I'm sure Laz and the palace guards will run all the tests they can think of before passing the gifts along.

"I- I…" I watched my precious leaf-art get carried away, without being able to do a thing to stop it.

My heart sank to the bottom of the ocean.

#

I didn't want to see anyone that day, not even Jesi. I spent hours crying in bed. I had no plan, no picture of Kirwyn, and his message to me had been intercepted -- if that's what it was.

Late that night, a knock came on my door. I opened it to find Juls standing before me.

"I know how badly you wanted this so..." pulling his hand from behind his back, Juls offered me Kirwyn's leaf-glass.

I blinked in wonder at the object, about a foot long and maybe ten inches wide. Three leaves – one red, one orange, one yellow -- had been secured within the glass.

"Thank you!" I cried, throwing my arms around him. "Thank you, it's just... so pretty!"

Juls smiled with a furrowed brow, unable to puzzle out the mystery of my attachment but pleased to have pleased me.

As soon as he left, I threw myself on the bed, furiously turning the glass around in my hands and losing hope with each pass.

What did it mean?

The glass had been sealed, there was no way to open it.

No, no, no...

Had foolish hope made me wrongly believe this came from Kirwyn?

Was this the message and I was failing to interpret it?

Or... had there been a note of some kind? And, if so... had Laz or another guard found it first?

Chapter 32

I was going to be sick. Sick with hope. Sick with worry.

It's my wedding day. Again. I wanted this one even less than the first.

I'd stared at Kirwyn's leaf-art the entire day prior and had no answer to its meaning, though I was sure he tried to tell me something. Even if it was just *I haven't forgotten you.*

No. He's coming. Kirwyn is coming. This isn't real. It's not going to happen.

"I know this isn't what you want to hear and it doesn't help, but my god, Zaria. You look stunning."

"I can't breathe, Jesi," I whimpered, taking great gulps of air. "I can't... I can't run in this thing." My best guess was that Kirwyn would find me in the king's hall, somehow. So many guests and servants and chaos. I'd need to be quick on my feet. I didn't know how we'd get out of High Spire, but he was so clever, we'd figure it out. Kirwyn would have a boat tucked in a cove somewhere and we'd sail far away before the ceremony.

But *this dress.*

Standing in my room and putting the final touches on my makeup, Jesi gave my hand a hard squeeze. It helped with my shaking a little. I'd been waxed hairless on the areas deemed appropriate, though I learned Elowans bore less body hair than most, thanks to the way we'd been *optimally* designed. I'd been scrubbed and polished and painted -- more than the usual makeup. Jesi actually painted my clavicle, arms, legs, and even strands of my hair with a shimmering oil and a dusting of sparkling gold. The wedding dress itself was gold in places covering my skin, though those swathes were minimal. Sheer panels draped from my waist to my ankles and stretched across the flat of my stomach and back. I dripped gold on my accessories as well. A heavy, collar-like necklace crossed my upper torso -- a nod to the customary, decorative metalware. Bejeweled wrist-cuffs that dipped low onto my hands bordered the line between jewelry and armor. Gold earrings and a complicated hair piece resembling a tiara completed my attire.

"You wear gold in royal weddings," Jesi had told me. "The groom wears silver."

It seemed backwards to me; I'd have thought the king would claim the most precious metal, but the tradition originated from some long-ago monarch who preferred the look and carried it down through the Doreste family.

"I can't breathe," I repeated, squeezing my eyes shut. I had to do better than this. Get control of myself and put on my mask. All eyes would be on me today.

Swallow it down, Zaria. Go into that place deep inside yourself and persevere. No matter what happens, you must *pretend.*

Dimly, I heard a knock on the door and Jesi jumped to answer it. As she chatted with someone I desperately tried to meditate like a Mystic. *Swallow it down and pretend.*

After a minute, Jesi closed the door, but she didn't move. "I'm sorry, Zaria. I'm so sorry," she murmured.

"What? What is it?"

"We need to hurry." Jesi grimaced, clearly not wanting to continue. "The ceremony's been moved. Last minute change."

"What do you mean?" I asked, grabbing my neck. "Where?"

She scrunched her lips, face pained. "You won't be getting married in the king's hall. The ceremony and the celebration have been moved to *The King's Light.* Laz's orders."

I didn't need a gazing glass to know the color drained from my face; I felt it. My voice was a whisper. *"Why?"*

Jesi looked at me sadly as she crossed the room. "You know why."

"No, no," I protested, backing up and reaching behind me as if I could hold onto the bed and not move, not be dragged away. "We have to stay here!"

He won't find me. Save me. I'll be married. For real.

Jesi shook her head and reached for my hand, but I pulled it away.

"No! I don't understand. How can Laz... he's terrified of sailing! He hates the ocean! You said so yourself. He *couldn't* have moved the ceremony. That's not possible." I fell onto my bed, pretty sure I heard a seam tear in the skin-tight gown and not caring. Sweat broke out all over my body.

"I'm just as shocked as you," Jesi breathed. "But he did it. You're getting married on the ship and for the afterparty you'll sail up and down the coast. No one was told until now. Servers are rushing to carry the feast onto the decks, guests are scrambling to change shoes or find extra hairpins or scarfs in case of wind."

"No, *no*," I begged, tears welling. "This can't be happening. Did Juls know? I can't... don't royal weddings have to take place in the king's hall?"

"Don't cry," Jesi said. "You'll ruin your makeup."

Oh god, another wedding. This time, with a real groom. Real vows.

Jesi's arms wrapped tightly around me. "Listen to me, Zaria, listen. There's a silver lining. You'll be on the ship all night. If you really want to escape, you can search it. Find a place to hide when the time comes."

Nodding furiously, I mumbled, "Okay, okay, that's something. I can do that, use that... but, but... I'll be married!" Until that moment, I never believed it. Not really.

"I know. I'm sorry. Zaria, we have to leave now. They're waiting to take us to the docks."

A wail erupted from my throat, but I nodded. I had to get it together. Whatever happened, I had to stay strong under my mask. "Okay," I whimpered. "Okay, let's go."

I almost had my breathing under control by the time we made it to the party of awaiting palace guards at the base of the castle.

But one look to the wall nearest where they stood, and my heart stopped.

Oh god, oh god, oh god.

It was my picture of Kirwyn nailed to the wood. Not mine exactly, but a copy.

Beneath Kirwyn's image it read:

Criminal: Level One

Capture Reward: Carte Blanche

Desired Condition: Any

The world spun and Jesi grabbed my arm to steady me. Thank Keroe no one was close enough to see my knees threaten to buckle.

"Jesi, what does this mean? Did Laz find something on that gift? Oh god, are they setting a trap?" My hand slapped over my open mouth.

"I don't know," Jesi spun me and held my shoulders. "I'll find out what I can, okay?"

"What does *desired condition* mean?" I whimpered.

She winced. "It means dead or alive or anything in between."

I fell against the wall to keep myself standing. My world turned upside-down. In a heartbeat I went from desperately hoping Kirwyn snuck onto Rythas, to praying he didn't.

#

Whisps of iridescent silk flowed behind me, diaphanous on the breeze, like gossamer curtains playing with the sun.

This can't really be happening.

I can't really have to go through another wedding.

A sheer gold veil covered my head, sneaking me onto the ship, out of sight by Juls or anyone else. Seeing only the wooden floor below, I shuffled behind Jesi to one of the lower decks.

When she tore the veil from my head, I saw Tomé, my Uncle Saos, and my Aunt Alette.

It was my aunt who gasped. "Oh, darling.

You look like you've seen a ghost." She pulled me into a tight hug. "It will be okay. You look so beautiful. Juls won't... he'll give you time."

I blinked rapidly. *What did that mean? Did she mean... what was supposed to happen after the wedding?*

I didn't know what to say so I turned to Tomé. "You look good," I said in a thin, weak voice. He did. The formalwear of Rythas suited him as much as a tunic. In the last few days, he seemed to have put on some weight. The circles around his eyes faded. The bright blue of his eyes sharpened once more. But he saw through me, and his eyes tinged with sadness.

"Don't," I whispered. "I can't make it through if you say anything."

He nodded, once, sharp.

Please let Kirwyn be safe, I silently prayed. *If guards are waiting for some kind of ambush back in High Spire, don't let them be successful.*

"They're ready for you," Saos said, offering his arm. He gave me what I knew to be an encouraging smile, but it didn't touch his eyes. He understood.

With no father, it was decided Saos would give me away, a custom in Rythas where only a father or elderman walked a bride down the aisle, unlike the Elowan practice of both parents walking a daughter, together.

I took Saos's strong, steady arm. "What your aunt was trying to say," he whispered, "Is that

Juls dropped to us the hint that you won't be sharing a room tonight. He wants to give you time."

Oh, thank Keroe. I was too relieved to blush. Together, my uncle and I climbed above-deck.

The sun shone so brightly, I fought not to shade my eyes. I knew it picked up all the metallic sparkle in my dress and on my skin. Blinking past the assembled guests, I found Juls standing at a podium upon the ship's stern, looking jaw-droppingly handsome. He wore a formal tunic-vest and pants of silver and gray. An imposing silver crown rested upon his perfectly styled dark hair. If I were anyone else, my heart would ache at the sight.

But he wasn't Kirwyn. Only Kirwyn made my heart thump, twist, soar right out of my chest.

Ungrateful. Spoiled.

Out of nowhere, a voice I didn't recognize spat the strange accusation in my head. Maybe it was my imagined judgement from all the assembled guests; seeing Juls through their eyes, seeing myself through their eyes.

The world was on fire. People starved, died, lived out their days in enslavement. And I was being offered a kingdom and a handsome young king and all I wanted was to run away.

Shouldn't I just be grateful? I wondered, as I walked across the ship's sunny deck and to the altar. I had done absolutely nothing to earn this life. Riches, wealth, ease, all of it had been handed to me. *Even affection, if I wanted it.* Juls wasn't like Laz. I could... learn to care for him like a friend or a brother. *It was so much more than most people had.*

And... and... I liked Rythas. Jesi and Lida and Tomé. Saos and Alette. I'd found family here. And purpose. Even revelry.

Shouldn't that be enough? *It was so much more than most people had.* It was everything.

Everything except love, I thought, *and freedom.* Didn't those two things outweigh all the rest? Or, at least, equal them?

Juls beamed as he looked at me, that charming smile upon his full lips, his dark eyes dancing. Saos released my arm and gave it to my future husband. I gulped. To the left, Grahar and Laz stood stiff in matching outfits of silver and gray. Like Juls, they each wore a silver crown. Odd. It was the first time I'd ever seen Lazlian wear one. I wanted to catch his eye, to seethe, to let him know I knew he was behind whatever was happening back in High Spire. But oddly, Laz pointedly looked away, refusing to meet my gaze.

Juls and I turned in unison to face the priest. *Scream. Cry. Run.*

All of those options riled within me.

You will do none of those things, Zaria, I chided, forcing my expression blank. *You will play a long game, like you always planned. Just make it through today.*

I crawled into that space deep inside myself, barely hearing the long wedding sermons or noticing the crowd at my back until we came to the vows.

This can't be happening. I can't be a bride, a wife.

"I, Jullik Doreste, give myself to you, Zaria Freeborn, as your husband and your lifemate, from this day until the end of my days," Juls said, looking at me with a mixture of pride and adoration. I tried to mirror it. "I swear to protect and defend you, honor and adore you. I will cherish you above all, forsaking the love of any other for the rest of my life. I seal my vow with this cup."

Juls took a sip of the cup upon the altar, the one we pretended had been laced with our shared blood.

My heart hammered. Sweat broke out all over my body. I gulped again. *My turn.*

"I, Zaria Freeborn… give myself to you, Jullik Doreste, as your… as your wife and your lifemate, from this day until the end of my days…"

My heart beat against my chest like the wings of a frightened bird, furiously trying to escape its cage. *Oh god, Kirwyn, I'm sorry. I don't know how to stop it. I thought you'd be here to stop it.*

"I swear to protect and defend you, honor

and adore you. I will cherish you above all, forsaking the love of any other for – for the rest of my life…"

Oh god, it's really happening.

"I – I seal my vow with this cup."

My fingers shook so badly as I lifted the red wine and sipped. When I finished, Juls smiled at me and I made my lips turn up into a smile in return. I had to. I would not humiliate him in front of his people. *He's a good man.* Isn't he?

Juls retrieved two small and surprisingly simple gold bands from the altar. Lifting my hand, he slid one onto my finger and handed me the other. I repeated the process, giving us twin bands of gold, a symbol of our marriage.

Juls leaned forward, bringing his lips to mine. I parted my mouth and his tongue swept in, gently. He was always gentle with me, this boy, my… husband.

It's done, I thought, blinking in shock. My own words. I'd spoken vows. *Oh, Keroe, how did this happen? In your realm, of all places?*

I wasn't blessed, I was cursed. Behind me, roars erupted and tears fell from my eyes. I pretended they were tears of joy.

#

The electric lights glowed on the ship, though the sun hadn't yet set. Strung upon the masts, lining the deck, hundreds – thousands – of little, twinkling lights. Gradually and randomly, the tiny bulbs flashed on and off like fireflies in the night.

Any corner of the ship not stuffed with guests in glorious gowns was crammed with food and wine. At the center of a long table sat the meal's highlight, a pair of roasted swans. Everywhere I turned, people chatted and drank. The ship was smaller than the king's hall, some guests had even been turned away, surely devastating them. I was positive Grahar somehow blamed me for the unpopular move.

Like a puppet, I played the part I was supposed to play, all while counting the hours until the ship would re-dock and I could make sure Kirwyn was safe.

He has to be.

In a direct contrast to my Elowan wedding, no one here gave me a moment's peace.

"A toast to the Queen of our Hearts!"

"A dance with the Savior of the Bloody Shoals!"

Every time I turned around, Juls was there, arm wrapping around my waist, head bending close to mine, pulling me onto the dance floor. Night fell and we re-docked in Rythas, but the party didn't end. I needed to get off the ship and find out was happening... but I also had work to do on board. After several dances with Juls, I smiled and said breathlessly, "I need to get some air and use the facilities. Where might they be located?"

"There's a more modern toilet just for us,

deep below deck," Juls instructed, voice low. "Two staircases down, head toward the back of the ship, near the captain's cabin. Well, it's the king's cabin really. You'll see three doors, take the first."

I nodded, paying attention only in case I got caught and needed cover.

"I'll be right back," I said, a bit too loudly.

As soon as I'd descended the first set of stairs and the crowds thinned, I picked up my pace. I needed to find a hiding place on the ship, somewhere to stow away for a long period of time if I ever got the chance. *The bowels, preferably.*

Ignoring Juls's directions, I rushed down the second stair and hurried away from the rear to a large hull lined with paned windows, decorative metalwork, and fancifully carved wood. I opened every door I found, peeking inside to find small storage rooms and the kitchens. Startled servants paused in their work, staring wide-eyed at my intrusion.

Thinking fast, I announced, "I wanted to come thank you personally. The wedding feast is excellent."

The open-mouthed staff barely had time to stammer, "Thank you, young queen, thank you-" before I'd closed the door and doubled back.

I paused only a moment, listening to the strains of string instruments above me.

Flanking either side of the ship's rear were two narrow stairs. I chose the right and nearly stumbled in my race to the bottom. It led to another, longer hull.

No pretty designs here.

I wasn't sure what this area would be used for, but at the moment the long hall was empty, save two people collecting glassware on the other side.

Quietly, I stepped back and continued on to the lowest level possible.

A soft white glowed from the few artificial lights along the walls.

Definitely no ornamentation here.

The air smelled a little pungent; wet or moldy. Barrels lined the narrow walls. Rope and other shipping supplies I didn't recognize littered the dirty, splintered floor.

Somewhere here. I could hide in the dark.

Lifting my long, silken dress, I ran amongst the boxes looking for possible antechambers, but I reached the end of the dark hull finding nothing. There were enough barrels and boxes and shadowy corners where I might hide though. The lower hull was not one large, open area as the upper two hulls had been. Several sections had half-walls built to separate the areas and contain storage.

Quickly, I hurried back toward the stairs when my foot hit a crack and I stumbled. Looking down, I saw an artificial line in the floor, continuing until it disappeared under a barrel. *A trap door?* Grunting, I pushed the barrel aside in two tries, revealing the outline of a what *had* to be a door somewhere.

Big enough to fit a person? I hoped, as I wedged my fingers into the crack and lifted.

To my astonishment, it was.

My heart picked up speed as I eyed the tiny chamber in the floor. It couldn't fit a bulky man, but it could fit *me.* I could hide in this chamber...

...this could be my way out of Rythas.

My stomach flipped, imagining cramming myself into the tight space. My worst fear. My best plan. Quickly, I closed the door and pushed the barrel back on top, concealing the entrance.

Shooting to my feet too fast, I grabbed ahold of the wall to steady the spinning room.

It's the only way. You want to see Kirwyn again, don't you?

Concentrating on my breathing, I fumbled back through the dim light toward the stairs.

"What are doing?" came the sharp demand.

Gasping, I jumped to see Lazlian filling the doorway, blocking it. He'd been curiously missing throughout the entire affair.

"I – I... got lost," I stammered, running a section of my hair through my clammy fingers. "I thought the bathroom might be kept um, out of the way... down here."

Lazlian wasn't buying it. I could tell by his

scowl, by the predatory way he advanced.

He can't kill me, I thought, wildly. It's my wedding. There are witnesses. *He can't kill me in here.*

I *knew* that, logically. But my body sensed a threat all the same. My feet moved backwards of their own accord. Mouth dry, I swallowed several times.

"You came into the cargo hold to find… what? A chamber pot in one of these boxes?"

"No, I- " He'd gotten so close I leaned backwards abruptly –

- *"Ow!"*

I yelped as my bicep hit something sharp, poking out along the wall. Even in the darkness I could see the cut, a line about three inches on my skin, dripping blood. Eyes wide, I grabbed myself under the wound, trying to mute the pain. But the next moment, I loosened my grip as the familiar, hated wooziness rose within.

Helpless, I looked at Laz, whispering, "I… I don't like blood."

He knows that, I thought. But I repeated it anyway.

"I don't like it," I croaked, grasping the wall, looking for purchase and coming up empty. My vision faded around the edges.

No. It's happening and I can't stop it.

"I don't like it," I repeated, arms flailing to find a barrel, a box, anything to grab onto. *I'm going down,* I realized.

Laz only glared coldly.

He's going to let me fall, I thought. Then blackness took me.

#

Blinking my eyes open, I met the unaccustomed sight of the dark and dirty bowels of a ship.

What the...

Waking from a fainting spell always felt like waking from a deep and instant sleep. It took a few seconds to remember where I was, what had happened.

I struggled to push myself into a sitting position.

Dark gray pants... looking up, I saw Laz towering over me. It all came back in a rush. I'd been sneaking through the hull, looking for a potential hiding place. Laz came down and caught me. I'd nicked my arm on something...

As soon as I thought it, the pain returned.

"Ow," I cried, slapping my hand against my skin and squeezing to reduce the pain.

I'd cut myself and fainted.

Whipping my head back up at Laz, I noticed he wound a dark strip of cloth in a makeshift bandage around his hand. I shook my head, trying to clear it. I couldn't feel another bump or bruise. *Did Laz catch me or let me fall? Was he hurt as well? Figures he'd tend himself before helping me.*

A sudden, horrible notion struck me.

"Did you," I breathed, scarcely able to believe I even asked it. "Did you... cut yourself? You didn't..."

I couldn't finish the sentence. *Did you cut yourself to mix our blood?*

Laz's look of disgust told me everything I needed to know.

Oh my god. My mouth dropped.

I swung my gaze back to my wound. Sure enough, I bore the smeared fingerprints from Laz's bloody hands circling my arm.

"You... violated me," I cried, momentarily forgetting the pain. *I* was the one who'd been subjected to a blood-sharing ritual against my will, *while I was unconscious* -- yet Laz had the audacity to sneer, repulsed, as if *he* were the one who'd been violated.

"You've *always* belonged to the Dorestes."

In case I had any doubt as to how revolted the assertion made him feel, he turned his head and *spat.* Then he spun on his heel and left me bleeding in the dark.

"I hate you!" I called after him, too busy squeezing my arm to think of anything better to yell and not having much opportunity as he'd already departed. I pinched my skin as if I could draw his blood up and out. I felt so dirty. *Get out of me, get out of me.* I shoved my fist into my mouth to stifle a furious, frustrated scream.

It doesn't mean anything, I tried calming

myself. *The ritual means nothing to you. It's not like Laz is really inside you.*

But he is, I argued. *His blood. Forever.*

Stumbling up the stairs onto one of the higher decks, I immediately found Jesi. "I hurt myself. Below deck," I said pointedly, holding her eyes. She knew what I'd come to do and pulled me away from curious guests to help me clean the wound. I quickly whispered in her ear everything that happened.

Jesi's eyes widened. "I can't believe he did that, and I don't know how to make it better. You should tell Juls but I know you won't." She shook her head. "Listen, I have news from High Spire that I hope will help." Jesi whispered close against my ear. "He wasn't caught, Zaria. The guards laid some kind of trap, but he wasn't caught."

Kirwyn. My heart soared at her words.

"And from what I can glean, there's only been general speculation based on whispers from the mainland. I don't *think* real evidence was found on that picture. It's hard to say, but whatever Laz knows, he's trying to keep it contained. I imagine he doesn't want rumors of long-lost lovers coming to rescue you staining his beloved family's honor or their image."

You're alive. You're free.

Relief flooded me; my knees nearly gave out. *That is good news,* I thought. The best news I could hope for.

Kirwyn had been spared. But... but...

I was married.

I was Jullik Doreste's wife.

Chapter 33

*T*he young queen, the Queen of our Hearts, the Savior of the Bloody Shoals.

So many titles people shouted whenever Juls and I picnicked in the gardens or visited a drinking hall or strolled the markets.

I didn't feel like they fit. I was just Zaria before. Braenese, yes. But Zaria.

I wasn't even that now. I was Zaria Doreste; my name no longer my own. My *blood* no longer my own. Inescapably, I could feel Laz inside me every time I closed my eyes, every time I saw him across the dining hall. It made me want to claw at my flesh, to tear it and bleed him out. *Was he inside me forever now? Did blood work that way?*

Eternally and *externally,* gold ringed my finger, linking me to Juls.

What was left of me that was my own?

The only silver lining in my sky of gray was Juls's sense of honor. I could have gotten on my knees and thanked all the Rythasian gods for that. Eventually, I did.

Juls and I slept in separate bedrooms on our wedding night and every night thereafter. I didn't know what the king thought of it, and I didn't care. Weeks passed in this manner.

Most mornings, I swam for hours in the ocean. Those were my favorite moments, just me and the sea. I'd pretend I was free, that nothing beyond the waters existed. In the evenings, Jesi continued to train me in self-defense, including a little target practice with arrows. I improved only slightly. During the afternoons I wasn't in court, I toiled away in the library, looking for some indication of Fort Cut-something-or-other. I had a loose plan -- sneak onto *The King's Light,* hide, sneak off once it docked on the mainland and... and... search the wilderness for Kirwyn? Somewhere near the fort? I didn't know, but it was a step in the right direction.

Kirwyn's picture had been removed from the gates, but my original never re-appeared. Instead, each evening I puzzled over the glass art of the three colored leaves. Was I mistaken? Or was it a message from Kirwyn? No one else called it a forest of colors, I knew that now. But if it was his signal, what did it mean?

Always at night I longed to touch him, dreamed of him. I tried not to despair but... in my darker moments I worried...

What if he wasn't caught because... he never came?

Jesi's days were increasingly claimed by Navere's command for strenuous training. After returning some Oxholden prisoners and executing others – Milicena especially – the king expected retaliation in the form of another attack.

I suspected his executions intentionally provoked it, as Laz once speculated. Instead of waiting for Oxholde to rebuild more weaponry capable of mass destruction, he wanted the army angry enough to strike while weakened -- though I couldn't fathom why he didn't sail to Oxholde and finish them off himself. My best guess was that this way, he held the moral high ground by acting in defense. But I had a feeling the situation was much more complex than I currently understood or anyone allowed me to comprehend. Despite my victory and my title, the Assembly of Elites still held conferences in the war tower without me.

The people of Rythas, however, didn't exclude me in the same manner. Many girls I'd seen even emulated me, with golden streaks in their hair becoming fashionable. Some were soft and honied like my natural color, some were bold and sparkling, like my wedding day.

One morning, I'd been in the library for hours when I had an epiphany. Often, I read alone; some days Lida joined me. But I was solo at the long, dark table when inspiration struck.

Slang, came the sudden thought, as if rising from the murky depths of the sea to appear at the surface. Jesi said *"cut"* was slang. Perhaps, I was being too literal? Perhaps the name of the fort wasn't "cut" or "deep" at all... but an indication of its position? Somewhere deep? A fort in a trench maybe?

I slapped my hand over my mouth. *Had I been looking at the wrong documents all this time?*

I didn't need a general reference map...

...I needed a topographic map.

I was about to spring from my chair when I felt the library air shift. I looked up to see the immaculate figure of the king as his shadow crept across the room, bisecting the beams of sunlight. It was as if the happy little dust motes scattered, making themselves scarce in his presence. I swallowed, thickly. I wanted to disappear like the dust as well. I hadn't been alone with Grahar since he struck me.

My palms started to sweat as he advanced. The king wore black and silver with an onyx-and-silver crown. It seemed to match his ash-and-black hair.

"Are you playing games with my son?" he asked in his usual, blunt manner.

"Games?" I repeated, blinking.

"I think you have your own agenda." He spoke with bite and triumph, as if the statement were a severe accusation, as if he'd caught me and brought to light my wrongdoings. *Of course I do,* I thought, *like everyone does.* I blinked once more at the enigmatic declaration. Was I to have no will of my own?

I sat up straight, understanding. *No will that didn't match his son's.*

"Juls has been nothing but generous to you, *I've* been nothing but generous to you, and this is how you repay us?"

Oh no. A fish flopped in my gut and my pulse quickened. *What had I done now?*

A lot, actually. Had he caught me searching the maps? Was Grahar going to mention Kirwyn's picture? Did he know about the birth control?

"I'm aware you haven't shared a bedroom with Juls since your union."

Oh. *That.* Oh no.

"Do you remember what I told you the day of the Offering Ceremony?"

How could I forget? Did Grahar mean he'd been generous because he hadn't enforced his threat that day?

His dark, keen eyes locked on mine. Despite not being an overly large man, he was a formidable king, no one could deny that.

"You have responsibilities as an adult, as a *young queen.* You're overdue for a visit to my son's chambers. See that you rectify that by the end of the week. It would be foolish if you allowed matters to get *out of hand.*"

For a few delayed seconds his order didn't hit. Then I started to shake as Grahar raised his dark eyebrows once, as if to punctuate the command, and left.

I sank to the floor, hardly feeling how I got there, barely aware of the room around me. I pulled my knees to my chest, tucked into a ball, and wept. After some time, I stumbled to the veranda where I'd drunk with Laz the day after the Bloody Shoals. I found an opened bottle of rum and drank all of it.

#

"Oh, Zaria. You stink."

My head flopped back and I peeked at Jesi and Lida through hooded lids. A chunk of something fell in my face, along with my hair. I think it was vomit. "Good. Then maybe no one will want to touch me."

"Is that what this is about?" Jesi asked, voice full of worry.

"What do *you* think it's about?" I countered, wondering if palace gossip spread by now. Nothing was ever secret for long in High Spire.

"Is that vomit in your hair?" she cried, kneeling beside me. "It's… green. What have you been eating?"

I didn't remember so I didn't answer. Instead, I laughed, "So chop it off! Who will copy me then? Who will want me in their bed when I'm bald? Bring me my dagger! Haha, joke's on them."

"You're spewing nonsense. Oh lord, Lida, help me carry her! She needs a bath."

"I'm not... not going in any landdamn bath," I slurred, but Jesi's muscular arms slid beneath my armpits, yanking me to standing.

"Get off me!" I cried, still slurring. Everything spun. I gagged and sour bile rose in my throat and dribbled onto my dress. "You go in a bath! You stink! Let go of me!"

"Ugh, we need to wash her down first," Jesi said to Lida. "Get the pitchers."

Over the next few hours, everything blurred. It began with cool water raining down my body. I wasn't wearing anything so Jesi must have removed my vomit-stained dress. I heard Lida remark something about me being so drunk I'd drown if they didn't hold me up. A few times, I puked some more and they had to start all over again. Eventually, I noticed the moonlight in my room and felt the cool bedsheets upon my hot skin before drifting off to sleep.

When I awoke the next morning, both Jesi and Lida had fallen asleep in my room as well. My head felt like someone had beaten it with a stick. My stomach roiled like a sea storm raged within.

"Easy," Jesi said, when I swung my legs to the tile floor and wobbled. I sank back onto the bed, covering my face with my hands.

"I'm sorry. I'm sorry. Thank you for last night. I owe you."

"You don't owe us anything," Jesi replied in her easy manner. "Except maybe an explanation. Tell us what happened."

Lida called for servants to bring us breakfast and I drank as much water as I could to rehydrate. While Jesi and Lida nibbled a simple meal of mangoes and saltfish, I told them what the king commanded in the library.

Everyone was quiet when I finished. There was nothing to say. I ambled to my window and stared at the beautiful, cloudless sky. Why did it never rain when I wanted it to? My dark mood demanded it; my thoughts were too horrible for such cheerful weather. It should be storming, raging. I needed howling winds so that I could scream my fury into the gusts and my cries would be lost to the storm, hidden by the safety of pounding rain.

Instead… *this.* Always the gentle breeze, the glistening sea, the happy call of birds chirping in the distance.

"I'm going to have to… spend the night with him," I said finally. "He can't… we all know Juls is incapable of lying to his father. Even if he wanted to, Grahar would see right through him."

In the distance, I spied a pod of dolphins. I wished I was out there with them. I wished I were anywhere else, really.

"It's the only option," I said. "I don't know what will happen if I refuse. There was a threat in Grahar's words, I'm sure of it. Either do as he says or something worse will befall me."

"Maybe not," Jesi said, slowly. "Maybe there's a third option."

I shook my head, refusing false hope. "You know Juls can't lie to his father. Even if he went in with the best intentions, Grahar will break him and the truth will spill out."

"Unless Juls believes the truth is that you *did* sleep with him," Jesi said, enigmatically.

I turned from the turquoise sea, frowning, but hoping despite myself. "I don't understand."

Jesi rose and began pacing, turning to meet my eyes every few seconds. "There's a drug. Benzapnol 5, Benny, they call it in Mid-Spire. It can make the user very susceptible to suggestion, very foggy in the mind. Almost like they've had too much to drink, but without the nasty hangover the next day." She looked at me pointedly. "I think I can get some. You could visit Juls's room with every intention of spending the night in his bed – at least, on the surface. But if you dropped a dose of Benny into his cup, if you climbed into bed and made him *believe* that you rocked his world... he'd believe it as well, come morning."

Appalled, I scoffed, "No, I couldn't do that. It

would be a violation... violating his mind. Er, like, the opposite of forced... intimacy. I'd be forcing him to believe a lie of intimacy." I shook my head. "It's wrong."

"So you'd prefer it if you were forced instead?" Lida cut in. "Is that better?"

I opened my mouth, then shut it.

"No, I-" I threw up my hands. "Why is it that all of my choices are horrible?"

"Not horrible," Jesi protested. "Think about it. I'm sorry but, Juls isn't a virgin. That's a good thing. He's never cared that you aren't, either. And he doesn't mean you harm, but... if you rely on him to protect you against his father in this, he will fail you. I know he has a good heart and a strong sense of conscience. But he also has a strong sense of family and of duty. Pit yourself against that and you'll lose. He and Laz can stand up to Grahar better than anyone. But in the end, he'll still do what his father orders. I think your wedding is proof of that."

I plopped onto a chair, needing to process Jesi's words off my feet.

"Does it... would it hurt him?"

Jesi shook her head. "There are fewer side effects than most common drugs. Some people take it just to sleep."

Could I really do it?

"I'm not saying it will be easy," Jesi said, flipping a stray curl off her face. "Frankly, it's a huge risk. I wouldn't blame you if you chose not to, for several reasons. If we're being honest, you and I both know most girls would kill for a chance to spend the night with Juls. Worse fates could befall you. *Especially* if you're caught. I imagine the king wouldn't give you another chance and he'd make good on his threat. I'm not saying it's not a risk; it's a big one. I'm just offering you another way."

I could *not* have Grahar make good on whatever his threat entailed. Just the chance almost made me want to sleep with Juls to ensure it wasn't a possibility.

But I didn't want that either.

Oh, the irony. My whole life, I'd been forbidden from touching a male and all I'd wanted was to do so. To be normal, to not be so isolated, so lonely. Now, I was being forced to be with someone in the most intimate manner possible and all I wanted was to be left alone.

This is total goatshit.

"I'll do it," I vowed, teeth clenched. I sprang to my feet and squared my shoulders. "I'm sorry Juls will have to suffer a little manipulation, but it's the lesser of two evils. He can't protect me, you're right." I clapped my hand over my breast. "I will do what I have to do to protect myself. I *can* protect myself. Well," I smiled sadly, adding, "with your help."

"I can only get you the Benny," Jesi replied. "You'll have to do the rest of it on your own."

I nodded, striding to Jesi and grabbing her

hand. "So what exactly do I... do... to make Juls believe we've..."

Jesi shrugged, "Well, make sure he has wine. After you drug it, you'll wait a bit for the effects to kick in... but this is important – don't wait too long. A few minutes is best. Then lure him to bed and," she shrugged again, "be as intimate as you can without actually being intimate."

"What does that mean?" I asked, furrowing my brow.

"Be creative. Lie with him, beside him. Whisper in his ear. Stroke him. *On his arms!*" she quickly added. "Slip into a negligée and let him fall asleep next to you. When he wakes up, act like you did the deed."

"And he'll believe it?" I asked, incredulous.

Jesi rolled her eyes, "Half the time drunk men don't even remember if they did or did not have carnal relations the night before. With the Benny, he'll believe whatever you tell him. That's not the problem."

I chewed my lip, dreading where she headed.

"The problem is, what are you going to do going forward? You can't drug the young king forever."

Looking back to the sea, I sighed, "I know. But I'll cross that bridge when I come to it. I can only handle one day at a time right now."

Chapter 34

Juls's room was dissimilar to mine in every way. My chambers had been decorated in light colors – pale creams and the faintest blues and greens. Juls's bedding, curtains, and tufted furnishings were upholstered in deeply pigmented shades of plum and red, trimmed in gold. *Future king* the room demanded, making me wonder what the coloring of mine conveyed. The spacious bedroom sprawled as large as Laz's, complete with a private veranda as well.

I had no idea what the first time between a couple was supposed to look like. Kirwyn and I didn't have this problem.

Perhaps this stifling awkwardness between us now was typical in arranged marriages.

"Come in," Juls said, slightly higher-pitched than usual and gallantly trying to hide it. He'd dressed in a loose black tunic-shirt and pants. He didn't wear black often and it suited him. *He looks handsome,* I thought, stepping inside. The door closed behind me with a loud and final *thud.*

No turning back.

I hadn't wasted time. As promised, Jesi procured the Benny from her brothers, and I'd made it well-known that I didn't want to spend the night alone. Castle gossip made everything simple in this case. Juls, agreeable and able to take a hint, sent a messenger to invite me to his chambers two days hence, on the eve of the missing moon. It was that easy. *But then,* I thought, with a twinge of guilt, *everything with Juls was pretty easy. Especially compared to Laz.*

"Would you like wine?" Juls asked raising his arm to indicate the table laden with candles, bottles of red and white wine, and foods reported to be aphrodisiacs: chocolate morsels and ripe strawberries, juicy oysters, succulent rabbit kebobs, figs, dates and plenty of mint to freshen the breath. It almost made me giggle. I was sure the servants did, preparing the meal.

Juls poured the wine with unsteady hands and I bit my lip. *Or had* he *done all this?* Was this his attempt to help ease me into the evening? *While I attempted to drug him?* My hand touched the vial against my breast. I'd worn a white outfit somewhere between a slip and a dress, concealing the Benny within.

I smiled weakly when he pressed the goblet into my hands, his warm eyes hopeful and anxious.

"This is-" he began.

"Weird?" I offered, laughing nervously.

"Not how I'd have courted you, given more time."

I nodded. He always said the right thing. Though truthfully, we'd had months to get to know each other and more time before this night than most young kings would give young queens. *More than someone like Laz,* I thought bitterly. But Juls's and my conversations in getting to know one another had been stilted. He preferred to focus on teaching me about Rythas -- how to maneuver certain situations, customs I needed to understand. When it came to personal matters, he, almost respectfully, didn't pry.

I tugged at the hem of my dress and surveyed the rich furnishings. The room smelled like Juls – sandalwood and leather enveloping me.

"It's nice that you have your own balcony," I said. "To breathe the sea air each night."

"Do you want to step outside?" Juls asked.

"Um, maybe later." I chewed my lip before taking a sip from my cup.

"Alright," Juls agreed. "Later, after we – I mean, before...if you like, tomorrow..." Juls flashed his nervous grin momentarily before smoothing his features. Voice deeper, he stood taller and said, "You're welcome to enjoy the balcony whenever you like."

An awkward silence descended. I fidgeted with my goblet.

"Let's play a game," I suggested, as I'd planned. "A drinking game."

Juls smiled, urging me to continue.

"There's a game we have in Elowa," I explained. *Lies.* Jesi had taught it to me that afternoon. "Never have I ever, it's called."

Juls chuckled. "We have that game here too."

"Oh," I remarked, innocently. "Perhaps we can play another then. I wouldn't want to bore you."

Juls waved his hand. "No, it's a good idea," he grinned.

He sat on the embroidered settee, and I don't think he even had a clue how regal he looked, even executing such a casual move. Head high, one arm slung over the back of the sofa, one foot crossing over to rest upon the opposite knee. All the while his face remained open and honest – a contrast to Lazlian's constant calculation and suspicion. Jul's mouth slid up into a ready smile; Lazlian's quirked, twitched with imminent cruelty. It was always easy to see why the people adored their young king: Juls was born to rule. *He would lie for me if I asked him.* But he was incapable of trickery and his father would see right through any attempt.

Taking a seat next to Juls on the far side of the settee, he looked at me with anticipation.

"Never have I ever… um… broken a bone?"

Juls didn't drink.

"Never have I ever…" he began, "found a pearl in the ocean."

Laughing, I drank. "It was a good day," I sighed. *I'd had many good days in Elowa, before I knew.*

Don't think about her, I scolded, when my mother's face floated in my mind. *About any of them.*

Narrowing my eyes at Juls, I said, "Never have I ever… made excuses to get out of something I didn't want to do."

Juls drank.

"Really?" I asked, raising my eyebrows.

"I regret it," he insisted, grinning apologetically. "I'd just turned sixteen and the court cases were strenuous. Some of the palace guard planned an excursion to Low Spire. I told Raoul I was too hungover to appropriately judge and then I… went with the boys and drank some more. It was just the once," he assured me. "I wasn't ready. My father thrust the duty on me rather suddenly."

I studied Juls's face. *Like now?* I thought. *Like this? What do* you *even want from tonight?*

And interestingly… you are capable of fibbing, at least. Or, you were.

"Never have I ever," Juls licked his lips, "Gone swimming in the ocean without any seasuit. Or anything at all."

Slapping my hands over my eyes and grinning, I drank.

Well this devolved pretty quickly. Fine. Two can play that game.

"Never have I ever had more than one lover at a time."

Juls drank and my eyes bulged.

"Are you serious?" I asked, nearly spitting out my wine as I laughed. I clapped my hand over my mouth this time.

"Just once!" he protested, briefly bringing his own hand to cover his eyes. He shook his head. "A birthday present from Laz when we turned nineteen. How could I refuse? It would be an insult."

"And I'm sure whatever beautiful, scantily-clad women he sent to your door had nothing to do with it." My cheeks flamed to picture it and I drank more wine just for something to do.

Sheepishly, Juls ducked his head.

Oh my god. *Wait.* Juls had turned nineteen right before my arrival. That meant it was a recent occurrence. I grit my teeth. *Laz persuading his brother to love other women, no doubt.* Or...or... *there's no way he could have found out about Kirwyn so quickly and arranged a dalliance for Juls in retaliation?*

"You are full of surprises," I hedged, dying to ask questions I shouldn't.

"And you?" he asked. "I have a feeling you

hide much more behind your beautiful face than people would guess."

I blushed some more and dodged the statement by replying, "Guess you'll have to ask the right questions to find out."

Juls stroked his chin in mock-thought. "Never have I ever… stolen anything."

"Um…" I giggled, stalling. I'd expected something sexual from his lips.

"You *have,*" he accused. "Drink."

I took a sip of wine. "In my defense, it wasn't really stealing. Just borrowing. I fully intended on giving it all back." *Was it even stealing if my mother knew anyway?* And what right had she, had anyone, to claim ownership over the First Feet artifacts in the first place? How silly it all was, revering these everyday objects. *I was a fool. We were all fools.*

When I'd been quiet a moment too long, Juls fidgeted and asked, "Hungry?"

I nodded and he rose to retrieve food from the table. My pulse quickened when I saw my opportunity. I licked my lips. *Should I do it?*

Juls reached for various items, making a plate. *Now,* I scolded myself. *There's no time!*

With his back turned, I shimmied the vial from my dress and uncorked it. Praying he wouldn't turn around, I tipped to contents into his cup.

It's done.

The clear liquid quickly dissipated.

Oh no, now where should I discard the evidence? I hadn't thought of that. Stupidly, I shoved the empty vial back against my chest, instead of under the cushions where I might later retrieve it.

Juls returned, setting a tray of apple wedges, cheese and nuts onto the small table before us. I began sweating when he lifted his wine, tipped the glass into his mouth, and drank deeply.

Would it alter the taste?

Guilt pricked my gut for tricking him. I wasn't like Lazlian; I had a conscience... but I did what I needed to do to protect myself and my loved ones. Just like Laz said that night on the veranda.

Mirroring Juls, I drank deeply from my un-drugged cup.

Now how did I get him to the bed?

Me. I had to take the lead, I realized.

"Actually, I'm not hungry," I said. Swallowing hard, I rose. I crossed the room and sat down on the young king's bed. Juls never took his eyes off me.

What if this were Kirwyn? I thought, heart twisting at the idea. *If he'd been the young king? What if this were his bed, him sitting across from me? How simple my life would have been if I'd sailed here and met him.*

I forced myself not to imagine it. Tucking my chin, I made myself giggle, as if the wine had gone to my head. Juls crossed the room in three strides and sat by my side.

Now what?

"You're so beautiful," he murmured, staring at me. He ran a hand down my arm, and I shivered. "I know Elowans are attractive and Lida is very pretty but... you're heartbreakingly beautiful, Zaria. I don't think you see it but all the people of Rythas see it."

"Thank you," I said, glancing at the floor, feeling my cheeks heat and trying not to furrow my brow. So many emotions warred within me at the compliment. Gratitude that I hadn't been born hideous. Guilt on top of it. Then more guilt because his words made me sad... because I couldn't help but wonder if that's why Juls believed he could love me, why he agreed to go along with the wedding. He barely knew the real me. I felt like I could have been anyone else, inside, and if I came with the same packaging he would desire me.

The idea made me lonely, made me long for Kirwyn. Juls could be taciturn and Kirwyn talked almost *too much.* Yet, we connected. Conversation flowed so easily between us, even when we were fighting. Kirwyn had *seen* me. For all the adoration from the people of Rythas and the ready devotion of the young king, I didn't feel seen.

Well, Laz was uncannily perceptive. He came close.

The unbidden thought appeared, horrifying

me. But then Juls's lips pressed against mine, coaxing them to open and all thought spilled out. I didn't totally *dislike* kissing Juls. But my pulse raced, wondering how far I'd have to go. His hands found my neck, stroking it. He broke the kiss, whispering "*Zaria,*" in my ear, making me shiver. Then he scooted onto the center of the bed, half lying down.

Now or never.

I took a deep breath and lifted the hem of my sheer dress, pulling it over my head tossing the thin garment aside. I wore only a bodysuit, not unlike a seasuit. It held the vial to my chest and served as extra coverage.

I looked at Juls through my lashes.

"So *beautiful.*" He slurred his words and my heart jumped. Scrutinizing him, I could see his eyes were unfocused, lids hooded.

What do I do now? Wait for him to fall asleep?

No, I needed to plant the false memory, make him believe we'd consummated our marriage.

Boldly, I straddled Juls's waist and watched his eyes momentarily widen, then darken. I smiled down at him as I traced his full lips with my finger. Holding his eyes until the last moment, I leaned down and kissed him again.

Eagerly, Juls slid his tongue into my mouth. When his arms wrapped around my torso, I stiffened. *Relax,* I thought. But it became even harder when his hands began to stroke my back. *What was I supposed to do?*

Sweat dampened my brow at the idea that Juls might not pass out before we progressed so far there'd be no turning back. I moaned into his kiss -- or tried to. It came out like a squeak, but if he minded, he gave no sign.

Juls suddenly took control, pushing himself up on the bed and flipping me over.

Oh no. Bad. I needed to maintain our pace.

Rising to his knees, Juls lifted his dark shirt over his head, revealing a slight, but muscular, bare chest. My eyes popped as he reached down, sliding off his trousers next.

Don't look! cried a voice inside my head. *Avert your eyes!*

It was the polite thing to do, after all.

No, he's your husband, you idiot. You're supposed to *look.*

When his undergarments met his pants on the bed, I gulped. My eyes remained glued to the pile of discarded clothes, terrified to look up and see...

Oh, god. I *had* to look.

I shifted my gaze upwards to see Juls, the young king, my husband, naked and proud before me.

Oh, god. I blushed furiously, sweating. He had every reason to be proud.

What was I going to do now? Could I stall him by... touching him? Landdammit, landdammit, what was I going to do?

Juls's molten stare grazed downward along

my body. My heart galloped, my mouth ran dry -- which was not at all convenient because I wanted to scream. Needed to scream. Needed this charade to *stop.*

We'd gone too far and now there'd be no turning back. I felt sweat drip on my brow. Did the young king's room have no breeze? My traitorous, curious eyes snapped downward once more, flaming the heat on my cheeks again. *What was wrong with me?*

Juls reached for the straps on my bodysuit, ready to slide the garment off my shoulders.

I drew in a deep breath, preparing to scream, *stop.* Not only was that farther than I was prepared to go, the vial would spill out onto the bed.

Juls paused. He shook his head, as if to clear it. Moaning low, his eyelids fluttered shut. "I think the wine hit me hard," he murmured. "I need... hold on a second..."

I had just enough time to dodge to the right as he sank onto the pillow. I'd freed my torso, but my lower half remained caged by his.

"I just need a minute," he mumbled, adjusting his head against the pillowcase.

"Juls?" I whispered. "Are you okay?"

No answer. "Juls, are you awake?"

Still no reply.

Gingerly, I rolled him over so that his lower half no longer trapped mine and so that he didn't suffocate against the pillow.

"Juls," I tried again, poking him. He didn't stir.

I titled my head, examining his regal face. He seemed to be in a fast, peaceful slumber.

"Juls, are you awake?" I asked a final time, just to be sure.

Praise Keroe, he didn't reply.

Smiling, I arranged the covers and crawled beneath them. I shimmied close to face Juls, until I pressed against his bare body – avoiding the parts that... poked. It probably would have been more convincing if I removed my bodysuit, but I really didn't want to be naked in bed with my husband. Instead, I laid against his chest and gently folded his arm over my torso, wrapping myself as if in a cocoon of amorous afterglow.

Plausible enough.

I took a deep breath. Tomorrow would be a long day and I couldn't afford any mistakes.

You've consummated your marriage, I told myself, over and over. If I could make myself believe it, I could make Juls believe it too.

Repeating the words, I snuggled into the young king's chest.

Strangely, I fell asleep with surprising ease.

Chapter 35

Nothing happened the following day. Nothing *bad,* and I'd come to read the *absence* of bad, as *good.*

Which couldn't be good. For my mental health anyway.

Grahar didn't bang down my door. No one summoned me. Even my flimsy excuses to stay in the library and avoid family dinner later that night had been accepted.

That morning I told Juls I had a wonderful time -- tucking my chin to my shoulder and blushing. Then I shyly scurried out of his bedroom. Quickly cleaning myself up, I headed straight for the library tower.

Grabbing a handful of books on geography as well as topographic maps, I spread them out onto the table before me and threw myself into analysis, rather than think on my night with Juls and what punishment would be in store for me if I'd been caught.

For hours I thumbed through the books but found nothing. Standing and stretching, I ran my fingers along the coastlines of each map, knowing the fort must be near the ocean. So many defensive structures had been erected and destroyed and re-built over the years, not all of them were even called "fort." I tossed one map aside after the next. Everything documented seemed to be on a large scale, no maps ever noted more minor structural changes in the earth –

-- and then, something caught my eye in the lower regions of the Old Florida on one of the topographical maps. A depression in the ground, maybe a gorge or ravine of some kind. Small, but deep enough to be recorded and bearing a slight "L" shape.

Hardly breathing, I committed the location to memory and ran to find a general reference map. Uncaring about the mess, I tossed everything onto the floor until I found one matching the same region and raced back to my table.

Uncurling it, I placed it side-by-side with the topographic map and traced a line between the point on the first map to the same section on the second.

My eyes widened.

There.

Something stood in the area of the L-shaped, trench-like region.

Casa St. Seodorothian.

It was a mouthful. Perhaps the kind of name people gave a nickname to? Slang?

Could Casa St. Seodorothian be Fort Cut L?

I stared at my find, grinning widely. *Yes.* Yes, it had to be. There was a definite "L-shaped" trench in the ground and a building of some kind within.

Dancing on my toes and alone in the library, I clapped with joy. I now had a general region in mind for when I... figured out an escape. I finally had direction, a goal.

Casa St. Seodorothian.

Are you somewhere around there, Kirwyn?

#

The next few days passed uneventfully. I swam. I practiced using a bow and arrow as well as my dagger. I rejoiced in watching Tomé slowly return to his old self. I even earned a pleased nod from Grahar when I passed him in the hall and at dinner.

But a few weeks after I'd spent the night in Juls's room, I received a message requesting my return. Jesi was able to obtain another dose of the Benny – thank Keroe. But I nearly wept with frustration because it wasn't a long-term solution. I couldn't keep drugging Juls. I felt awful. I didn't even know if I'd get caught this time.

That evening, I arrived at his room in a

pale cream dress, a pale bodysuit, and the drug at my breast. Juls smiled when he saw me, opening his door wide.

"I'm sorry if you had plans this evening," he said, nervously. "My father he... well, he wondered if you'd slept here since..."

Oh.

"No," I said. "I had no plans. I'm... glad you sent your note."

Juls wasn't facing me so I couldn't tell if he'd bought the lie. I was grateful to see a bottle of red wine but no food had been prepared this time. *How would I distract him?*

"A drink?" Juls asked. I nodded and he poured two cups. This time, he sat on the bed.

Guess we didn't need formality any longer.

I joined him, placing my cup on the bedside table. But I didn't have time to drink. Juls cupped my face in his hands and stared at me intensely as he brought me forward for a kiss. To my surprise, his tongue swept in my mouth deeper and more insistent than before. His hands held my cheeks, thumb sweeping my skin every so often.

When he momentarily broke our kiss, he returned that intense stare. What was it? Hunger? Yearning?

I curled my toes nervously against the leather of my sandals. It was as if something in his gaze tried to pull me to him.

A knock sounded on the door and Juls's

eyes slid shut. He sighed through his nose and shook his head. "Yes?" he asked.

"Juls, might I speak to you a moment?"

It was the voice of one of the guards frequently posted down the hall. Juls sighed again.

"One second," he told me, rising to open his door.

As soon as he moved, I slipped the vial from my chest, uncorked it, and tipped it into his glass of wine, just like the last time. My eyes kept darting to his back, but Juls never turned around. He spoke with the guard for a brief minute, then waved him off.

Smiling innocently, I handed him his cup and drank deeply from my own, hoping he'd match me.

He did – but not before a strange pause. Juls stared at his cup, as if debating. When he finally raised it, his eyes never left mine, smoldering over the rim. Then he nearly slammed the goblet onto the table and pulled me back for another kiss. Perhaps the interruption stoked his urgency or perhaps I'd stoked his lust the last time, because Juls kissed me even more ardently than before the guard knocked.

I couldn't help but respond; he swept me up in his need. My distorted version of the William Blake poem popped into mind again.

I felt desire for my friend...

Juls guided me back onto the bed. We lay side-by-side and though I tensed throughout, it seemed he'd gotten so caught up in kissing we didn't progress for a while.

Eventually pulling back, Juls said, "It's funny... I always feel so dreamy with you." He gave a soft chuckle. His eyelids fluttered between open and shut. His head relaxed deeper into the pillow.

Tenderly, I stroked his hair.

"Juls?" I whispered.

No reply. Guilt choked me. And fear. I didn't know if I'd get away with it again and I certainly couldn't fathom being so lucky a third time. I needed a better plan.

"I'm sorry," I whispered. "You deserve better than this. I wish... I wish..."

I wish I could love you.

For a while, I continued stroking Juls's hair. Then, leaning over, I placed a small kiss on his lips. Laying tight against him, I burrowed my head into the crook of his neck and groaned. He smelled of sandalwood and leather and safety.

I'm sorry, I thought. *I don't know what else to do. What am I going to do?*

#

I stayed in my chambers the next day, hoping to make a habit of it. *Visit the young king. Lay abed. Repeat.* Meanwhile, I paced furiously. Bit my nails to the quick. Knelt on my windowsill and made bargains to the Sea God in desperation.

Let me escape and I will build statues to you.

I knew *where* to go, now I just needed the way. But what sort of ceremonial event would make *The King's Light* sail again? Another royal wedding? Could Laz be persuaded to find love? I shook my head. Even if he could, it would never happen quickly, and he'd certainly not marry at sea.

Late that night, I spied the yellow, red, and orange leaf art from Kirwyn, keeping vigil over my bed. How many times had I clutched it, prayed to it?

As if mere leaves could save me. As if somewhere within the leaves lay the answer.

A jolt ran through my body at the thought.

Wait...

Yes, the guards checked the frame, but they could never really examine the leaves without breaking the picture.

Desperate, I grabbed the art and held it beneath the candlelight, examining the colorful trio of leaves as I'd done countless times. But I couldn't find anything new, anything to indicate I was on the right path. I rubbed my eyes and squinted harder.

There must be something.

Slowly roving the edges of each leaf, I gasped to find a small nick on the red one. I pressed the glass nearly to my face to scrutinize it.

Yes. Oh my god. There was a misalignment revealing not *one* but *two* leaves, pressed together to pose as one. Gasping for air, hardly believing what I saw, my finger traced the outline.

Someone had cut with precision a second leaf to match the outline of the first. In all but one area. A nick, infinitesimally small, appeared on the lower left corner of the red leaf.

My heart thumped. *There were two leaves.*

With shaking hands, I felt the edges of the frame for a release but of course, I couldn't find anything different from any other time I'd tried. The leaves were somehow molded inside the pane of glass itself.

Had I been meant to break the glass all along?

Shattering it is then.

Cradling the art in my arms as one would a baby, I raced into the bathroom to conceal the noise. Quickly, I locked the door behind me. I spared one moment to reverently run my hands down Kirwyn's gift. Then, with a pounding heart, I raised the glass in the air and brought it down hard against my water basin table.

I flinched as it shattered to shards in my hands. The glass had somehow been... fused and sealed at the edges only, so that the only way to access the leaves was by breaking it.

I'd expected them to fall, but they stuck to the glass. With the ocean roaring in my ears, I tore the sticky slivers of glass from the leaves. The yellow and orange ones had no secondary leaf behind them.

But the red…

My heart stopped when I caressed the red leaf and felt something thin, but hard, within.

Oh my god.

Carefully, I lifted the false back from the original, pulling the two red leaves apart.

My heart stopped *again* when a brown scrap fell onto the floor. It was thin, but firm, like the thicker stock of paper used for official documents.

It either contained no words or had fallen face-down.

Please let it say something.

With trembling fingers, I lifted the scrap of paper from the white tile. I flipped it over.

Mid-Spire Market. Two days post wedding. Noon.

For a moment, I stared, frozen in disbelief.

It was Kirwyn's handwriting. I recognized it from his book.

Oh my god.

Oh god, no, no, no. Please, no.

I burst into a sob and quickly fisted my hand into my mouth.

It was a message from Kirwyn to meet at the markets *after* my wedding. When the soldiers around me would be light... when the Dorestes' guard would be down... when many people might still be busy cleaning up multiple celebrations after a day spent nursing hangovers... I'd never been to those markets, but I could get there, because of Jesi. Did he know about Jesi somehow?

It was Kirwyn telling me he was coming for me.

It was Kirwyn who came *for me...*

And I'd missed him.

No, no, no. I was going to be sick. I slumped to the ground, pressing my head against cool tile, sobbing.

How could I be so stupid? He came to rescue me and I'd missed it. Oh god, what did he think? That I'd been caught?

Why didn't he try again? Why did he leave me here?

Oh god. Had *he* been caught?

No, surely, Grahar or Lazlian would have taunted that knowledge and Jesi assured me their trap failed.

A stinging sensation began in my hands and grew until I couldn't ignore it. I looked down to find myself bleeding from numerous cuts along my palms.

I hadn't even noticed. Flexing and fisting my fingers, I found no glass embedded in the sensitive skin, but the edges of my vision blurred, as they always did when I saw blood.

No. Not now. I can't faint and risk someone stumbling on this evidence.

Water. I needed cold water. Air.

I shot to my feet – too fast – and felt the world spin. One hand clutched the edge of the bathroom table, while the other scooped water from the basin onto my face and neck. I sullied the bowl with my own blood but I didn't care. I just needed to stay awake. Water dripped down my chest in rivulets while I tried to slow my breathing.

Hang on. Don't faint.

I grabbed a folded towel from the pile and pushed the window wide. I threw myself onto the ledge so hard I almost fell out, gulping fresh air.

Breathe. Don't faint.

He came for me. And I wasn't there.

Oh god, Kirwyn. I'm so sorry.

My mind conjured the hateful image of Kirwyn crouching, hiding, waiting for me somewhere in the Mid-Spire markets. Waiting and hoping and… finally, giving up.

I *had* to escape, to find him, to explain.

Part Three

Burn to Prevail

Chapter 36

The next day, I paced my room, volleying between rage and despair. If a storm had come for cover, I would have thrown my window wide and shouted my fury to the sea. I couldn't do any of it anymore; didn't *want* to. All the waiting, the pretending, the fighting.

I was so *tired,* so *done.*

If I can find Kirwyn, I thought, *maybe it's better to leave forever. Find El Puerto en Blanco and start over.*

In the evening, I bathed, trying to calm myself. I brushed the knots from my hair in an attempt to feel better, to distract my racing mind.

It failed to work.

I went to sleep early…

…and somewhere in the middle of the night, I awoke to screams. Jesi threw my door wide.

"They're attacking!" she cried.

"What?" I asked, struggling to wake. "What's happening?"

"They've come for revenge," Jesi announced, striding to my bed. Across her torso and shoulders she'd strapped armor, *real* armor. "Oxholde brought mainland reinforcements and guns but it doesn't matter, we're leaving the castle."

Prunson poked his head into my room. "Get the young queen and let's go!" he shouted.

"Stop, wait! Why are we leaving?" I cried, stomach twisting. "You said we'd never abandon High Spire."

"Navere's been working on a plan. They're making it look like we're running in fear of something more advanced, like the weaponry they'd had on the warships to take down the castle. Everyone's to flee. Civilians mixed with soldiers, Oxholde won't care, they'll follow and attack,"

Jesi threw clothes at me without breaking her speech. "We didn't expect an attack tonight, we had bad information. But we're sticking to the plan. Navere is leading them into a trap. There's a narrow pass half a mile out. Once our people cross it, they'll turn and fight. Half our army is hiding in the woods to prevent retreat at the rear. Oxholde will have nowhere to escape; they'll be slaughtered."

"I don't understand," I exclaimed, hurriedly sliding the tunic-dress overhead. Jesi used the time to ensure her long hair was securely tied back and out of the way. "Where are we going?"

"You're escaping with the royals, you're not running with the main party. Like I said, we didn't expect this tonight and even if we did, so many things can go wrong. They weren't supposed to be so heavily armed. Hurry up!"

I tied my sturdiest sandals around my ankles, checked my dagger-belt, and stood.

"Remember what I said," Jesi commanded. "Stay with the Dorestes. Don't be clever and don't be stubborn and definitely don't be brave. If anything happens, stay with Juls and Laz."

"No, Jesi," I yelled, clutching her shoulders. "I'm staying with you. You told me the same thing before the last attack and I didn't listen and everything worked out better for it."

She shook her head vehemently. "That was different. This isn't the sea. You can't fight."

"I won't have to! Not if you're with me."

"Let's go!" Prunson shouted angrily from the door.

Jesi grabbed my hand and we fled down the torchlit hall and one set of stairs before slamming into Juls, Laz, Grahar and Erisio.

"Zaria," Juls cried, catching me.

"Where are Lida and Tomé?" I asked, breathless.

"They've already been evacuated with Navere."

My eyes bulged, "No, no." *They're not*

473

Rythasian warriors. They're not... what was this trap? Bait?

Juls ran his hands down my arms. "It's okay. They'll be okay. They're at the front of the line, protected."

"And what of the back?"

"Most are soldiers disguised as civilians."

"Most?"

Juls grit his teeth and shook his head. "This isn't right," he protested, giving his father a dark look. "We should stay and fight."

I know that feeling, I realized, watching Juls quietly seethe. *To want to do things you cannot because people and forces more powerful are commanding your moves.*

"This is Rythas," Jesi insisted. "Everyone fights."

"We gotta move!" Prunson ordered, taking control of our small group.

I followed without knowing where we were headed, listening to shouts within and without the fortress walls. Prunson, Erisio, and Jesi flanked the Dorestes and I, protecting us, armed with guns and swords. Jesi had also strapped a quiver of arrows to her back. The Dorestes all bore swords in sheaths belted at their waists as well. I knew they possessed them; but the only time I'd ever seen the royals armed was at the Offering Ceremony. *Did they know how to use them?* They too carried guns, partially concealed beneath their vests, though

I noticed their outline as we moved.

Under the cover of night we fled east, while most fled west in what I assumed to be Navere's group. A fair number of men and women scattered in all directions. For several minutes we sprinted through a dark path in the woods beyond the gardens -- my best guess being we were headed for a small inlet with a boat. Maybe to sail to safety? But as the sounds of battle behind us faded, new sounds grew.

"Shit!" Prunson cried. "They're here! Double back! Head southwest, away from the castle!"

My heart hammered as we collectively turned and ran diagonally down another dirt path away from both directions of fighting and deeper into the dark forest. But after a few minutes, we saw firelight ahead and only heard more cries.

"How are they here?" Prunson shouted, throwing his arms high in frustration. "Where are they getting all these guns?"

"We've been betrayed!" Jesi yelled. "Someone must have leaked the route-"

Suddenly, several bullets flew, hitting Prunson in the chest and silencing him forever.

I yelped; I couldn't help it. Gunfire erupted from Erisio and Jesi's weapons. Juls pushed me behind him, withdrew his gun and –

-- and the trigger mechanism didn't move.

"What the..." he stared at the weapon. "Laz, can you-"

But his question was answered when Laz cursed, throwing his gun to the ground. "It's jammed. Someone tampered with it!"

True panic set in. *Juls and Laz had no firepower?* A quick glance told me the king couldn't trigger his weapon either. I didn't even possess one. And now Prunson was dead. That left Jesi and Erisio to protect us.

"This way!" Erisio shouted, pulling my hand and leading us in what I realized was the direction of the Glass Gardens. "We have to hide!" he shouted, when we reached the entrance.

Our small party fled for cover in the strange attraction as the sounds of battle crept closer behind us. I could hear *some* of our soldiers, but we were outnumbered -- most of our men and women had been diverted to set the trap. Not enough remained to counter this attack. Turning every few feet and firing, Jesi and Erisio attempted to hold off whoever pursued us.

The fighting spread without any sense of order, trailing down on either side of the gardens, popping up in random patches. Both bullets and arrows flew and we scattered, running for cover deeper into the Glass Gardens, hiding beneath the oversized rows of trees and flowers. The gardens at night were eerie even without the threat of imminent death. Soft, artificial lights illuminated the spooky, overgrown flora, casting creepy shadows everywhere.

We hadn't made it ten feet down the arcade's central path before our group split in the chaos. Juls and his father ducked for cover on one side, Jesi and I on the other, and I didn't even know where Erisio and Laz fled. Jesi and I ran until, breathless and terrified, we found a darkened spot beneath the fake hedges.

"Zaria!" Jesi cried. "I'm out of bullets. I should have grabbed Prunson's gun! Keep your head down!"

I couldn't. I had to know if Juls was safe.

Shots rang out through the gardens, shattering glass with every hit, each one reverberating in my heart.

There! Miraculously, I spied Juls's dark head of hair on the opposite side of the arcade. He turned in my direction, meeting my eyes. *Ever the king,* I thought, contrasting his own stoic, determined mask and alert stare to my panicked expression and wet eyes.

"Juls," I mouthed, half-whispering his name. He might as well have been an ocean away. Bullets flew in the passage between us, we'd never make it to each other. *He's my husband,* I thought wildly.

He opened his mouth, whispering something in return, but I couldn't tell what it was for the tears in my eyes and the distance between us. A shot whizzed past then, so close

I instinctively ducked, covering my head as it shattered an oversized crimson rose not five feet behind me.

This is it, I thought. *This is how I die.* Jesi and I crouched beneath a row of shiny green hedges, huddling close and clasping our hands together. But we had to run, even if it separated us further from Juls and Grahar.

In unison, Jesi and I rose and bolted once more, deeper into the gardens, then crouching again behind another row of glass hedges.

"Where did they get all these guns?" Jesi cried. "I don't want to die. But if I must, not like *this.* Like a pig at slaughter." She breathed fast and heavy, baring teeth… readying. "I want to die fighting, on my feet. Facing my enemy."

"Jesi, no!" I whispered, feeling the tension in her body and fearing she'd stand. "Please, don't leave me." Cowardly tears soaked my face and continued falling into my mouth as I pled. Glass shattered once more, closer now. I'd never been more terrified in my life. "You're not a pig. You're… my protector, my friend. Please, don't run to meet your death."

I clung to the armor on her shoulders, trying not to tremble. "Stay with me! Stay alive. Until the last… the last moment we have."

Suddenly, heavier sounds of gunfire filled the air, coming from the garden entrance and accompanied by shouting.

"Turn!" someone yelled. "They're attacking

from the back!"

I didn't understand what was happening until the rain of bullets over my head died down and rang out in the opposite direction.

Reinforcements were here. With guns!

Screams filled the air and there was twice as much shattering glass as before.

Jesi's mouth twisted into a strange snarl-smile, her eyes glowed with rage, and I knew I couldn't hold her back any longer. Letting go of my hand, she rose to her knees and lifted her bow. Taking aim at the first man, she drew back and let her arrow fly with precision.

My hope for turning the tide of battle was short-lived. I picked up sounds of fighting coming stronger from all the sides of the gardens and now even the rear. The bulk of the shooting rang from the front, but it seemed Oxholde began creeping in from all directions, hemming us in with crossfire.

I'd never experienced anything like it. The screams, the shattering glass, the smoke and *smell* of fear. No – smell wasn't right. But a shared terror permeated the air, suffocating me with every breath. I gasped as a man broke from the thick of fighting, charging Jesi. She quickly drew her sword and raced to meet him, but a second man appeared from the side, brandishing a sword high as well.

"Jesi," I cried.

My hands fumbled to retrieve the bow and

arrow she'd discarded on the ground. Shakily, I picked it up only to have it fall from my hands again.

"Jesi!" I screamed, drawing the attention of someone and only realizing it when the bullet blew by my head, missing by sheer luck as I was already in motion, reaching for the weapon once more.

Oh god, oh god, that was close.

Steady, I cautioned, retrieving the bow and springing back onto my knees. *Steady. You'll only get one shot.*

On my exhale I released the arrow, praying it found its mark.

I heard a grunt and watched with elation as the second man running toward Jesi fell to the ground. I hadn't hit my intended mark – the unprotected area of his face or neck. Not by a longshot. Instead, the arrow embedded itself low in his gut, nearly at his groin. He wouldn't be getting up anytime soon.

Quickly, I pulled an arrow from the quiver and strung my bow once more.

Jesi's war cry came before I drew back. Swords were lost, but she'd tossed her assailant to the ground and straddled him. Wielding a shard of glass she must have scavenged from the shattered bits amongst the floor, she plunged the sharp edge into his neck. The man's head fell onto the floor, blood spilling.

I raced toward the soldier I'd taken down and

raised the arrow I hadn't yet used. Mimicking Jesi's attack, I plunged the tip into his neck, howling my own primal cry. The deadlier move was to pull it back again -- to yank the barbed tip outward, causing even more internal bleeding and destruction.

I wish I could say that's why I did it.

But the truth was... in the heat of the moment... I heard the man's cries and panicked.

On instinct, I cringed, pulling the arrow backward, as if I could undo what I'd just done.

Jesi was right. I wasn't a fighter.

I didn't understand – one second I'd filled with bloodlust and the next, regret. It was so much harder to sort it out in the heat of battle than anyone ever explained.

I did what I had to. I did what I had to.

I ran back for the cover of the hedges, crying and shaking. "Jesi!" I shouted. She sat astride the man she'd killed, grunting and slashing with her shard. "Jesi," I screamed, until she ceased the assault and bolted back to my side, crouching once more under the safety of the hedges.

"You killed him!" she exclaimed in a whisper-shout, laughing with an edge of hysteria. I joined in, crying a mad laugh between exultation and remorse.

I did. Did I want to? Did it matter or was it just one more for my body count?

Jesi threw her arms around me and hugged me. I hugged back, both of us bloodied.

"You save me, I save you," she breathed.

She's right... If I hadn't done it, the soldier would have killed her.

"You save me, I save you," I whispered.

A horrific thought came to mind, and I pulled back.

Where was Juls?

"Let's move!" I cried, and she nodded. Ducking under eerie, glowing Hibiscus flowers, Jesi and I bolted toward the rear of the gardens.

"Laz!" Jesi called.

I whipped my head to see the keylord no more than twenty feet away, running through a glass tangle of Spanish Moss dripping overhead, sword in hand.

Quickly scanning each other for injuries, Jesi cried, "Where's Erisio?" Laz shook his head and shrugged.

Turning, we were about to take off again when something big, something like Kirwyn's grenade, hit the roof above the gardens, causing an explosion.

Glass shattered in the direction I headed, raining down. Hands grasped my waist, yanking me back. With the momentum, I spun into the safety of Laz's chest, tucking my head and clutching him. At the same time, his arms came up around the back of my head almost... protectively. I shivered, never having been in his embrace before. *The battlefield makes strange bedfellows.*

It lasted all of a heartbeat.

Laz bent, retrieving the sword he'd just dropped. Then we took off again, running for a more secure area with the shouts of war close on our heels.

From our right, a solider of Oxholde, a woman larger than most men, charged ahead of the fray and ran straight for us.

"Run!" Jesi cried. But I didn't listen -- instead crouching momentarily in the shadows while Jesi lunged forward to meet the attack. Neither warrior carried loaded guns; swords clashed instead. Jesi moved with godlike strength and speed; I'd never truly witnessed her fight like that before. But the other woman was equally skilled and much bigger. She managed to get in a blow to Jesi's head – not with her sword, but with her fist.

Jesi went down.

I screamed, ready to intervene –

-- when to my utter shock, bullets flew, taking down the woman who'd *just* knocked Jesi off her feet. In the chaos, I didn't even think the shots were aimed at the Oxholden soldier – it was simply *random* crossfire.

Was Jesi okay? Why wasn't she moving? *Oh god, everything happened so fast in battle.* A blink, and someone was gone.

"She's hurt!" I cried, watching the

pandemonium erupt around her, the whizz of arrows and bullets flying overhead. If she stayed out in the open, something was going to hit her. "We have to help her, carry her. Laz, help me move her!"

Panicked, I turned to Lazlian...

...But he was strangely calm.

No, not calm. Hard. Laz stared at me, darkly, unmoving.

"I can't – Laz, I don't know if I can carry her alone and I can move her faster if there's two of us," I pled, tugging his arm. "Help me, *please!*"

His pupils, blown wide, tinged with emotions I couldn't read. Dread filled my stomach as he refused to budge... as I realized he wasn't going to leave the relative safety of the shadows.

"You *coward,*" I whispered, lip trembling. *Or...*

Oh my god.

Was this his vow? The threat he'd made the day he almost struck me.

The next time your life is in my hands...

...He'd promised to let me die.

But... but... I didn't understand. Only minutes before, he'd pulled me to safety when the glass could have injured me, maybe killed me. He'd sheltered me with his own body. Why? Had he done it on instinct or was it a performance in front of Jesi?

I searched Laz's face as he gave a slow,

horrible shake of his head.

Was this cowardice or cruelty? Was it hate or fear I saw glinting in his eyes? Certainly, I found no mercy there.

Tears threatened to spill as I swore, "I'll do it myself!"

Some wild part of me still believed he'd protest. I stepped away from the safety of the shadows, hoping he'd change his mind. Help me.

When Laz simply stared at me with a menacing, dangerous gaze, it hit me like the lash of a flaming whip. It *hurt* and I hated that it hurt. Deep down, I thought he wouldn't really do it and deep down is where it burned.

Instead of crying, I jut out my chin and determined to survive to spite him.

I turned from Laz.

Please god, don't let a bullet hit me.

For a moment I hesitated, waiting for a break in the gunfire, the shouting, the flying arrows. None came. Gulping, I ducked my head down and ran at a full speed toward Jesi's limp body.

"Jesi," I cried, shaking her. "Jesi, please, wake up, wake up."

To my relief, she groaned, lifting her hand to her head. "S'okay," Jesi moaned, soothing both herself and me. "It's not fatal."

"Get down!" I cried, pushing her back as a volley of fire erupted overhead. We pressed ourselves against the ground.

Is this how it ends? I wondered. *Just as it began? I'd pressed myself to the dirt my first day in Rythas when someone shot at Tolas.*

Cringing and clutching one another, Jesi and I remained motionless for several long seconds, waiting for the fire to die down – hoping it would.

Finally, there was a break in the noise.

With my heart in my throat, I helped hoist Jesi up and draped her arms across my shoulder, but she surprised me by standing easily on her feet. "It's okay, I can walk. Let's go."

Running to safety, I saw Erisio had caught up to us again -- which was the only reason I didn't blow past Laz or take Jesi's sword and thrust it right into his belly. Laz didn't look at me. I didn't know if he was disappointed that I didn't die.

"I'm okay!" Jesi insisted, shaking me off. The four of us ran deeper into the gardens, away from the fighting… though it dogged our heels.

"Juls!" I shouted as loud as I dared, catching the flash of his dark head not far ahead.

"Zaria!" he cried, waving us over to him and his father. I fell into his arms as our group formed a loose circle. *Juls is okay. We are all okay. For now.* I looked to Erisio and Jesi for direction, but Erisio cocked his head, hearing something the rest of us didn't.

"They're here!" he cried. "We must have

defeated them at the pass and the rest of our men are here to help! Back up, head to those flowers!" he said, pointing. "Stay there. I'm going to get help!"

Erisio slipped into the shadows along the outer rim of the gardens, racing through the thick of fighting, moving exceptionally fast despite needing to crouch as he ran. The rest of us sprinted toward a field of red glass poppies.

"Behind!" Jesi shouted, as soon as we arrived, leaving us to charge what appeared to be two archers rising to their feet. They weren't skilled fighters, Jesi took out one with a toss of a dagger.

The second was the problem. She didn't have time to reach him, nor did Laz, the next closest, though they both charged with swords in hand. I was sure the archer targeted the king, but his aim was unsteady as he tried to shoot straight and run from Jesi and Laz at the same time. It all happened so quickly. Suddenly, Juls pushed me out of the way and I fell to my knees –

-- and he grunted as an arrow hit him.

With a cry, I looked up from the ground to see he clutched his bicep. No arrow embedded itself in his body anywhere. *Was he okay? Was it only a nick?*

But he didn't have time to react; to duck for cover.

The archer aimed another arrow –

"No!" Grahar cried, twisting to cover his son's body with his own.

The Oxholden man drew back on the bow and I gasped as Grahar leapt, throwing himself in front of Juls. The arrow flew, striking the king's throat. In a blink, the man reloaded and the next arrow hit the king's heart.

Grahar fell to his knees.

Jesi howled her attack as she reached the archer only seconds too late. With one powerful thrust, she shoved her sword into his chest and out the other side. He collapsed, but Jesi still screamed as she pushed one foot against his stomach for leverage, extracting her sword and plunging it again in wild fury.

Grahar toppled to the ground.

No one in our small group made a sound but for our shared breathing. The battle still raged toward the front of the gardens, but I could hear it dying down. I couldn't tell for sure if Grahar lived or died. My heart ached for Juls either way. He crawled to his father, rubbing his hands over Grahar's neck and chest.

The agony crumpling Juls's face answered the question I silently asked.

No one said a word. All I heard was our shared, heavy breathing.

The king is dead.

I met Juls's anguished eyes.

Long live the king.

Chapter 37

Safely distanced from the dying fighting, Jesi fell to her knees, pledging loyalty to Juls.

I moved to mirror her, but Juls grabbed my elbow and kept me on my feet. *Was this normal protocol or was he different?* Had Juls and I just become king and queen on this battlefield?

Laz didn't kneel. He was too busy carrying his deceased father off the ground and onto a bench. But others trickled over as the fighting died down. Soldiers young and old, clean and bloodied, spread out before Juls and I in a semi-circle and fell to their knees. As the distant sounds of battle further muted, more people came and knelt.

I stared, hardly able to process the past hour, let alone the last few minutes. *Was I queen now?*

How close had we been to a different outcome? If our army had only arrived a few minutes faster, the king would still be alive. If Juls hadn't pushed *me* out of the way, Grahar would have never needed to throw himself in front of his son, a move leading to his death.

I couldn't help but feel a horrific irony about Grahar's ending. In his twisted mind, the king always believed I'd give new life to his family. Instead, I'd indirectly brought about his death.

#

We sat amongst the rubble just within the Garden Gate. Juls rested his head upon his fist. Warriors of Rythas moved ahead, sweeping the castle to ensure no soldiers from Oxholde hid within, waiting to assassinate the Dorestes or anyone else.

"We only lost three hundred civilians, give or take. One hundred in the castle and the rest on the trail. It's a miracle," Navere insisted.

"We shouldn't have lost any civilians," Juls growled. "And how many soldiers? Why was the evacuation such a disaster? Why were so many left behind?"

"Battles are chaotic. Some weren't informed, some refused to leave."

I cocked my head. *Some may have been purposefully used as decoys,* I thought. I wouldn't put it past Navere or Grahar – they'd done as much on the trail and this was their scheme, after all.

"They couldn't properly defend themselves," Juls argued.

"This is Rythas," Navere said, soft, but firm. "Everyone fights."

"We didn't prepare them to fight. That's the point. We should have stayed behind and defended High Spire. Instead, my father rigged the gate to remain open, to allow them in."

Anyone inside would have been a sitting duck, I thought, alarmed.

Juls sighed deeply as we surveyed the damage. Oxholde destroyed whatever they'd crossed, spitefully. The gardens of Rythas bore no combative advantage, yet they razed them. The stalls of the market offered no militant advantage, yet they trashed them. The stragglers lingering behind the castle walls posed no threat, yet they killed them.

We were victorious. But Navere saw the cost only in the number of lives lost and Juls saw the cost in the manner, as well.

It was your plan all along, I thought, eyeing Navere. *You knew there'd be casualties on this scale. Were you hoping for more? Are you the one who leaked the escape route and jammed the Dorestes' guns?*

"We didn't give them the chance to die with honor," Juls declared, scowling. "We didn't stay and fight with them." He looked up, eyes hard. "Never again. We will never abandon High Spire again. We will die defending the castle and alongside the people."

Navere bowed to the new king. "We won't

have to. Oxholde will never rise again. We've slaughtered their army. You've become king to a great kingdom in a time of peace."

Raoul stepped forward. "What of the crowning ceremony? Should it be before or after..."

"After," Juls decreed. "After we lay my father to rest." He ran his hand through his disheveled hair. "We should all get some rest right now."

Soldiers and palace officials began to disperse, leaving Juls, Laz and I to speak quietly.

"What of the men who betrayed our escape? Those who sabotaged our weapons?" Laz snarled the words, voice low.

"Too many knew the route," Juls replied, voice heavy with sorrow. "Half the palace guard. Launch an investigation but... the suspects are many."

Navere, I thought. *I bet he plotted it. But... who supplied Oxholde with the additional weaponry? Could Mal-Yin be playing both sides?*

Juls turned and strode to stand before me. Even bandaged and bloodied he looked commanding, though his eyes glazed with grief.

"I'm so sorry," I whispered.

"Are you okay?" he asked.

I nodded, furrowing my brow. "Are *you?*"

Juls took my hand. "I will be. They didn't destroy the towers. We'll rebuild. We'll be more than okay, *I'll* be more than okay, eventually."

He smiled weakly, "With the most beautiful queen Rythas has ever seen by my side."

I quirked a small smile in return, but my stomach sank. Until that moment, I hadn't realized I held onto some wild hope… that with his father gone Juls would… *what? Divorce me? Cast me aside?*

Oh god. Surveying the destruction, the people… looking into Juls's hopeful brown eyes… it occurred to me the opposite was true. He wanted me beside him now more than ever; I was trapped, now more than ever.

"Laz," Juls called over my shoulder. "I'll meet you later to discuss… preparations for father's funeral. Can you help Zaria to her room? We all need to get some rest."

I stiffened. I hadn't interacted with Lazlian since he'd left me to die on the battlefield. Then I groaned, internally, realizing any measure of freedom I'd earned since first coming to Rythas had probably been reversed with the late king's death. Being queen only meant more guards, I'd wager.

Silently, Laz and I walked through the castle and up to my chambers. We did not touch. We did not look at one another. *Was it instinctive or a performance in front of Jesi when you'd pulled me back to safety from the shattering glass? Why did you change your mind minutes later and leave me to die?* My fury boiled, threatening to spill over with each step we climbed. Something else burned in that fire, too, and I despised it more than the anger. That persistent, hateful *hurt* that stung deep inside when I understood Laz planned to abandon me.

Deep down, I never thought he'd really make good on his death threats. Not until that moment.

By the time we reached my room, I couldn't hold back. Before closing the door, I spun to face him, shaking with rage. Down his neck and disappearing beneath his shirt trailed one long, fresh cut he must have acquired on the battlefield, though I didn't know when. I wondered if it would scar. It looked like it hurt. Good.

"Are you a coward or did you hope I'd be killed?" I demanded, searching his scorched-earth eyes. "A little of both?

Laz stared down at me; jaw clenched.

Say *something,* I thought. *Yes, I'd hoped you die. Or no, I'm sorry.*

I'd do it all over again or it was a mistake.

I swallowed. *Anything!*

But Laz did not speak to defend his actions or support them. I fisted my hands, desperately wanting to pound his chest, to make him talk, to demand why he'd done it.

But I couldn't bear losing my composure in front of Laz any more than I could bear his possible answer.

"Guess we'll never know. But I do know one

thing." I gave a haughty laugh to cover the tears welling. "If I ever have the power of your life in my hands, I'll let you die. On any battlefield."

Before slamming the door, I shrugged with feigned indifference and added, "I wish you had."

#

I hated being kept in the dark with anyone, but with Laz it felt extremely dangerous on top of my discomfort. I could rarely figure out what went on behind his burning eyes. It was one more mystery to add to a never-ending list.

Did my mother have a hand in hastening my father's demise, or was that wild speculation on my part?

Who killed Tolas the day I arrived in Rythas?

Who was behind trying to kidnap me?

Did Juls feel anything genuine for me or was he just trying to convince himself he did?

And what really happened the day my Aunt Enith died?

The last question, at least, had an answer I could ascertain. Once I could meet with Alette and Saos again, I'd pry the story from her. My god, I was queen now. It had to come with some benefits.

Just before sunset, Lida burst into my room. "Zaria!" she exclaimed.

"Lida!" I cried in return, hugging her. "Are you okay? Is Tomé alright?"

She nodded. "He's fine, everyone's fine! That's not why we're here."

Behind her, Jesi hurried into my chambers, closing the door tightly.

"Juls is planning on sailing *The King's Light* to lay his father to rest," she said. "A proper funeral at sea, like the old days."

I covered my mouth, gasping. "It's my chance," I whispered. "I can sneak aboard."

Lida held up her hands. "The thing is," she said, wincing, "they're not planning to dock the ship. There's a route taken, an ocean graveyard for kings."

I closed my eyes, groaning. "Where?"

"We don't know exactly, the site is sacred, secret," she explained. "I can show you the general area. But there's no way you can sneak a lifeboat off the ship. She'll be packed with revelers. Apparently, a funeral at sea isn't a somber affair."

"She's right," Jesi agreed. "Royal funerals are celebrated with songs and spirits. And for the king, only men are allowed to attend -- the exception being his wife, if she's living."

"Show me the graveyard," I insisted.

Lida unfurled a map she carried and laid it upon my bedroom table. Running her thin, tapered fingertips reverently over the seas, she circled an empty spot between Rythas and the mainland.

"Here."

I sucked in a breath. It was worse than I'd anticipated.

The middle of nowhere. Keroe's realm. I searched the map for a key, but it had none. It didn't matter because the area Lida circled was pretty wide anyway. But with a pounding heart, I traced my fingers from the graveyard to the closest land.

It's not far from the region of Kirwyn's fort, I thought.

"I don't... I don't know how many leagues it is from there to the mainland, but... that's a big area. If the grave site is here," I pointed to the part of the circle closest to the North Continent, almost hugging the coast, "then... then I can make it. Alone. It can't be too many miles."

Lida's eyes locked on mine. "Zaria. I don't know if it's there or *here*," she protested, pointing to the section farthest from land. "We didn't tell you this for you to consider swimming it!"

I swallowed. "I can do it. I've swum around Elowa plenty of times."

"Under perfect conditions and with the rests, I bet."

I licked my lips to avoid replying.

"Zaria, you're crazy! That's suicide!" Jesi yelled. "We didn't share the information so you could consider a swim, we told you to brainstorm a plan, some Elowan scheming."

Scrunching my lips, I shook my head. "This is my plan. This is my scheming."

"I know you want to escape but think about it," Jesi said quietly. "Is your life here *so* bad? Worth risking a horrible death at sea? I know you don't love Juls but it's not like he's cruel to you."

I fell into a chair, tugging my hair.

"She has a point," Lida chided. "On the one hand, you could be covered in jewels with servants awaiting your every whim. On the other… drowning. Alone at sea."

"You sound like my mother," I replied, frowning.

"Well, you said it yourself. You might be able to do something, as queen," Lida reminded me. "Change the laws. Think about it."

I shook my head. "Juls's father is gone but do you plan to dispose of all the nobles? I'm sorry Jesi, but Navere has his eye on the throne. You can't see it because he's your commander and you admire him. But he's shifty. Someone likely leaked the royal escape route to Oxholde, someone jammed the guns. What if it was him? I don't know what support he's garnered, but I bet he'd use any change Juls tried to enact as justification to gather people to overthrow him."

I can't do that to Juls. I can't cause him to lose his crown, I thought, guiltily. But instead, I said, "And do you really think things would be better for the people if Navere and the army took control?"

Lida frowned. "An accident needs to befall Navere someday. Instead, he keeps getting more promotions."

I shrugged. "Keep your friends close and your enemies closer. Juls won't kill him, he's Merie's brother. Plus, he has no proof."

Striding to my window, I gazed at the turquoise sea as I so often did. I felt Jesi come up behind me.

"I don't want you to leave," she said softly.

"I know," I said, clutching the stone ledge. "I'm sorry. I don't either. I mean, I don't want to leave *you.* Or Lida. Or any of my friends and family here. But I can't stay. I can't keep drugging Juls. He's going to try to sleep with me, Laz is going to try to kill me, and I have to find Kirwyn. I can't... can't live without him, Jesi... it's... hollow."

I'm hollow, I thought. Like a tree, gutted. A façade of strength on the outside only. Empty inside.

"This is so confusing," I murmured.

Jesi let out a long sigh through her nose. "There will be enough commotion the night of the funeral that you *might* be able to sneak aboard the ship," she said.

"And I already know where to hide," I added. "My wedding was good for something."

"But, Zaria... the journey will take more than

a day. She sails tomorrow evening but won't reach the site until the following night. Can you hide that long?"

I felt like I'd be sick. *A full night and day in that dark hole?* I hadn't thought about that. *God, why that? Anything, but that!*

"I don't..." I tried to speak and failed, ending in a whimper. "I'll... have to be."

"And the hard part is the same as it's always been," Jesi protested. "You'd still need to sneak out of High Spire."

"I'm working on a plan for that too," I confessed. "I think... I know a way." The real problem, all along, was ensuring Jesi wasn't punished for my disappearance. And my nights with Juls had given me an idea.

"Tell us now," Lida insisted, "because they're preserving the king the old way, in a barrel of rum, as we speak. Juls is departing tomorrow evening. He's leaving Laz in charge of High Spire and Navere in charge of the prisoners. The ship sails tomorrow, so you better act fast."

Chapter 38

*E*verything changes tonight.
Whether I'm successful or am caught, there's no going back.

My palms sweated, even as I sat, surveying the revelry before me. Despite the casualties, two affairs began – one in High Spire for ladies and lesser-nobles, one aboard *The King's Light*, departing in mere hours to bury the late king at sea.

I needed to escape from the former to make it to the latter.

Leaving the large dinner party as the new queen wasn't going to be easy. The king's hall was jammed with everyone paying their respects in a celebratory, Rythasian manner. As the highest-ranking monarch, I was the host of the affair. Atop my head rested a small gold tiara. To my right, Lazlian wore a silver crown.

He stayed behind to guide me, ruling in Juls's absence.

I didn't plan on sticking around for it.

Throughout the meal, I fidgeted and grabbed my stomach frequently. An act. I'd been waiting for Jesi to return, to get me what I needed, but she still hadn't entered the hall. Time was running out – I was going to miss the departure if I didn't leave soon.

I turned to Singen on my left and announced loudly, "I'm not feeling well, I think I ate something bad. I'm going up to my room to rest for a bit. I'll return shortly." I clutched my stomach as I rose.

Singen grabbed my arm a bit too hard. It reminded me of the day he'd kidnapped me and shot at Kirwyn.

I've never liked you... you charm everyone, but I've always hated you.

"I'll escort you," Singen commanded.

"No need!" I quickly replied, speaking softly now. "Maybe you could send Jesi up instead? I'd rather have someone *female* to help, if you can understand?"

Why are you here, at the head table anyway? I wondered. *Maybe when the king was alive... you were Grahar's friend... but now he's dead.*

Singen released me. "Of course."

"Thanks," I smiled. Making sure not to draw attention to myself, I walked slowly from the king's hall, leaving the revelry behind me. Once alone, I quickened my pace. Raoul was with Juls, Navere combed the woods, looking for any stragglers... that left Singen alone, assisting Laz.

Could Singen be up to something? Could he be responsible for leaking the royal escape route and jamming the guns? I raced down the stone corridors and sprinted up the stairs, considering the idea.

The Dorestes love him because he's cold and brutal like they are.

It hit me.

But they are too close to him.

Just like Jesi was too close to Navere to see his ambitions exceeded military command, the Dorestes couldn't see the bad in Singen. *Was he planning on assassinating me? Laz?*

I was high in the castle, nearly to my chambers when --

"Stop."

Laz's voice, raising instant chills on my skin, called out from behind me. I turned. We stood in a long hallway with arched windows on one side, facing the sea.

"What are you up to?" Lazlian asked, slow and measured.

I gave my best impression of an exasperated sigh. "What's that supposed to mean, Lazlian?"

"You lied back in the hall," he said slowly, advancing. He wore black, in mourning, and had actually buttoned his shirt all the way. "You're hiding something. I just can't tell what it is."

Warning bells rang in my head. Being alone in High Spire with Lazlian, without Juls's protection, was a terrifying prospect.

I narrowed my eyes, feigning annoyance. "Why yes, I am, if you must know. I didn't really eat something bad. I have my monthly cramps." The lie rolled off my tongue so easily, just as it had with Singen. *How skilled I'd become.* "I just didn't feel like announcing it to the guests. Would you mind if I went and laid down now?"

Laz stepped closer, ignoring my request. "Are you hiding someone back in your room? A lover, perhaps?"

I shot Lazlian a dark look. He stood only a few feet from me now.

"With the king at sea, maybe you're planning something?" he mused, making my heart race. *What did he know -- or suspect he knew?*

"Is this your moment to stage a coup of some kind? Have you persuaded the guards to assist, to strike while the throne sits empty and place you on the chair in my brother's absence?" Laz asked. "It's an old story, isn't it? The queen offers her body to the captain of the guards in the hopes of using his power over the army to affix the crown on her head – perhaps both their heads."

Lazlian stood much too close now. His silky voice slithered through the space between us, full of barely-concealed venom. "Are you hatching a plot to betray us, little queen?"

"Absolutely not," I grit out, thankful he was on wrong path so my lie came easily once more.

Standing over me, Lazlian scrutinized my face. "Then why is there guilt in your eyes?"

My stomach dropped. I wouldn't fool Laz the way I fooled others; he was predisposed to hate me. Finding fault with me came as naturally to him as it had his father. Laz was out for my blood before I even stepped foot on shore.

A picture of me physically attacking the keylord floated across my mind. I ruled it out. Even with my dagger he was bigger, faster. The preposterous image of me fleeing down the corridor also came to mind, but I knew I'd never make it ten feet.

Not fight or flight then.

But I needed to outwit him, distract him, *something.*

I made a quick decision before I could back out.

"Enough!" I roared, in a manner that reminded me of Kirwyn's temper. I withdrew my dagger from the belt at my waist. "Here. Take it."

Lazlian didn't move, eyeing me suspiciously. "Take it!" I demanded, shoving the blade into his hand. Cautiously, he wrapped his fingers around the handle, but only because the alternative was to let it crash to the floor.

With both hands, I reached the neck of my

black gown and tore, ripping it open enough to expose the first third of my bare torso. Reflexively, Laz raised the blade – a move to defend or attack, I wasn't sure. The hallway was so quiet I could hear the sea, far below. I held my dress wide, heart pounding frantically as I puffed out my chest, offering a clear strike. *Right to my heart.*

"I can't do this forever," I panted, sweat running down my neck. "Look over my shoulder all the time. Fear every morsel of food I put to my lips. Wonder if I'll wake in the night to find you over me, ready to kill me in my sleep."

Holding Laz's savage glare, I tugged harder at the seams of my dress, pulling it wider. "You think I mean to betray you? You want to kill me?" I goaded. "Why wait another minute? The king is dead. No one is here but you and me, Laz. No one will ever know it was you. This is what you've been waiting for. *Do it!*"

I closed the few inches between us to meet his outstretched arm, pressing my chest to the deadly tip of the dagger with feigned boldness. *What was I doing?* Such a dangerous, foolish gambit. This wasn't Kirwyn or Juls before me. Lazlian didn't value human life -- or any life -- other than his own.

Is that the sea I hear? Whispering on the wind, calling me home?

Would he strike?

My heart pounded so wildly beneath my ribcage I wondered if Laz could somehow *see* it. But I forced myself to snarl, "Push the blade into my heart, Laz. Do it, and let's be done with this game."

Lazlian's eyes narrowed. I winced when I felt a slight prick of the tip against my unprotected flesh, but I didn't look away. If he planned on taking the offer and killing me, I wanted to at least look him in the eyes -- to look death in the face.

This is a fool's game, cried a voice in my head. *A deadly game.*

I hear the sea at least, I told myself. *If I die now, my last thoughts will be of Kirwyn, and the sea, calling me home.*

I wasn't surprised by my rapid breathing, by the deep rise and fall of my chest – but I was shocked by Lazlian's. No other sound echoed in the hall, but for our panting in unison. Laz's jaw remained clenched; his dark gaze filled with an intense emotion I couldn't determine. Wild hatred? Burning rage? Fear? Did he worry about getting caught?

Why had he paused so long?

He's going to do it. He wants to do it. Maybe he's warring with himself or maybe he's just... plotting an alibi.

I forced myself to stare into Laz's pitiless eyes, fearing that if I closed my own, I'd make it easier for him. Agonizing seconds ticked by as

I held my dress wide, baring my breast to the dagger. To Laz. To death.

The tip of the blade pressed harder and I gasped.

Against my will, my eyes grew wet. *Not because I am scared of dying,* I lied to myself. *Because I'd been staring too long.* I needed to blink, that was all. But if I blinked, a tear would surely fall. Maybe that's all this reptile would need to tip the scales in favor of killing me.

I drew in an audible, shaky breath and, even though I kept my eyes open, I couldn't prevent that tear from trailing down my face.

I'm not pleading with you for my life, I swore. *I just can't help it.*

I flinched when Laz's other hand reached out and touched it, long, bare fingers brushing against my cheek. He lifted the tear and stared at his wet fingertip for a moment. Did it amuse him? Disgust him?

When his eyes flicked back, Laz's cold stare pierced me, much like the dagger would any second. *This is it. He's going to kill me.* My chest trembled against the sharp blade. I licked my lips, swallowed, and raised my chin to meet my doom with some strange combination of defiance and acceptance.

I'm so tired of fighting, I thought. *And I'm so scared to do what I'm about to do. Maybe it's easier this way. If you kill me, I won't have to hide in that awful hole and make that arduous swim.*

Looking at Laz, it occurred to me again how easily everything could have been different. Or would it have ended the same? If the hermit hadn't made his declaration and Laz had been the young king...

Strange...

...Why had I never wondered what *he* thought before? Why had I never asked? Even a fool would consider it and Laz was far from foolish. Surely, the thought crossed his mind.

"You could have been king," I whispered.

Laz's eyes flashed at the unexpected declaration.

"Would you have slain me sooner? Or would you have spared me? If I'd been..." I swallowed. *"Yours?"*

I didn't like the way the word sat on my tongue. Or I did, and I didn't like *that.* Everything was too confusing with a dagger at my heart.

Laz didn't reply and I was unable to read his cryptic face. Fires blazed in his scorched-earth eyes. He worked his jaw; clenched it. Agonizing seconds passed. Then suddenly, the pressure on my skin abated as Laz drew his arm back, just a hair. I gasped.

Nothing happened for several long heartbeats.

Had my ploy worked?

"Go to your room, little queen," Laz said, narrowing his eyes.

I tried not to let too much relief flood my face. Slowly, Laz turned the dagger around and handed it back to me. As I grasped the hilt, Laz's other hand clutched mine, crushing my bones.

"*Ow*," I whispered, panicked.

"If you ever try to betray us, I will kill you," he vowed. "And no love from the people or pleas from my brother will save you."

Laz's hand squeezed mine even harder. "Do you understand me? I will kill you so slowly you'll be begging to die for days – *weeks*."

I gulped, trying not to cry out from the pain. "I believe you," I whispered. "It's a good thing I don't plan on betraying anyone."

Lazlian searched my face one last time, heating it. It was as if his eyes burnt a trail in their wake. Finally, he released his excruciating grip on my hand.

"Go to bed. Now."

I didn't need to be told twice. I scurried to my room.

Chapter 39

"Jesi!" I whisper-cried, closing my bedroom door behind me. "I don't have much time."

Eyeing her up and down I noted she carried the rope, a bag, and a bundle of clothing. Lida waited next to her, stroking her long braid.

"Zaria. Are you *sure* you want to do this? I don't... don't want this to be the last time I ever see you. I'm scared for you." Jesi wrinkled her brow. "And I can't remember having been scared of anything in a long time, outside of battle."

"I'm sure," I whispered, lying. *I'm sure I have to find Kirwyn. I'm sure I can't stay here. I'm sure I have to do something to stop the Daughters of Elowa being sold like prized goats.*

I'm not so sure this is the right way to do any of it.

"But Lida, I need you to do me a favor. Can you get back to the hall and keep an eye on

Singen? I don't trust him. I don't trust Navere either, but I have a feeling Singen may have sabotaged our escape. I can't shake the feeling he might try something tonight, with Juls at sea. I wonder if he'll try to... murder Lazlian. Can you watch him and... warn Laz?"

"You want to help Prince Lazlian?" Lida asked, brows raised.

"No. Well, yes." *Did I?* I'd *just* vowed the day before that I'd let him die if I ever held his life in my hands. I told him I wished he *had.*

"I don't want anything bad to befall Juls," I said, truthfully, carefully. "And that includes his throne and his family. Please, I know you know people. I could be way off, but please keep an eye on Singen and tell Laz if you have any suspicions?"

Lida nodded and hugged me. "Okay. And Zaria... Thank you for letting me stay here. Be safe. Kiss your sexy god-boy for me," she teased, trying to make light of the moment.

"I will," I replied, stifling my tears.

And then she was gone.

"Jesi..." I moaned, softly. "We have to hurry."

She shoved the clothing at me and said, "Alright. Here's what you asked for."

Tearing off my black dress, I stripped to my undergarments and quickly yanked on the men's tunic-vest and loose trousers. Meanwhile, Jesi fixed two glasses of wine. She poured a clear vial into one of them.

Her own.

Placing the goblets on the table, Jesi sat in one of the sturdy, high-backed chairs.

There was so much I wanted to say to her, and no time left to say it. I took a drink to fortify myself. I passed the other chalice to Jesi and when our fingers touched on the goblet, neither of us let go for a moment. Everything I could say felt insufficient. I owed her a debt so mountainous I could never hope to repay it.

"I can't-" I began, before breaking off. I took one shaky breath. "Jesi, I don't know how to ever thank you for all you've done."

"You can start by making it to the mainland alive."

I nodded. Her words only made me want to cry more.

"If it wasn't for you, I'd never escape this cage."

"I'm only helping you unlock the door. It's you who must fly. Or in this case, swim," she joked, but her smile didn't touch her eyes.

Jesi lifted the chalice to her lips and drank, keeping those large eyes locked on mine. She finished the entire dose as I hurried to fetch the rope. Tense, Jesi watched. For someone so used to trusting her body, so used to being able to rely on its strength, it must have been difficult for her to let go. I wound the rope around her torso, stopping to knot it throughout.

"I'm sorry," I apologized when she grunted.

"I have to make it tight."

Crouching, I secured her thighs to the chair's seat.

"We might not ever get the chance to speak again," Jesi said, after a long moment of silence.

"I know," I whispered. "But I hope that's not the case."

"I have to confess something before you leave," she whispered. "It's not... I just didn't ever want you not to trust me, to think me a liar. I'm *not,* you know how I feel about that. Except. I was, sort of. Once. Except I was really something worse-"

"I don't understand what you're saying."

"I'm a murderer." Jesi closed her eyes, wincing. "It wasn't intentional, but it wasn't entirely innocent either."

"What do you mean?"

"I visited my family before you arrived. My brothers, I've told you... we're all so different. Lucio is the youngest. He wants to be a doctor, he's such a good kid, so studious. Izan is the eldest and he looks after everyone, in his own way. Like me. I send money home, Izan... protects us. We all take care of each other, we're family. The night we drank together, I let it slip that I knew about Tolas and plans for your arrival. I don't... know what I was thinking. I'm scared to think about it."

Jesi gulped, meeting my eyes. "The next day, Tolas was killed and I took his place."

I didn't move. *Jesi's brothers.* Who always got me what I needed – birth control, drugs to prevent me from having to sleep with Juls, even whatever Jesi just imbibed. Had her brother stepped in to get Jesi what she needed too? What the whole family needed – her promotion, her income?

I couldn't think about that now. *Except -*

"Jesi, did you stage my kidnapping?" I gasped, wide-eyed.

"No, no!" she insisted. "I swear I had nothing to do with that. I don't know who those men were. But I did... let Navere believe they were connected to Tolas's death. To steer the search away from Izan and clear the way for us to leave High Spire."

Her face crumpled. "I'm sorry. I swear it's the only lie I ever told you and I don't even know how much of it is a lie and I don't want to know, don't want to look into it too closely. Do you understand?"

I nodded. It was done. I wouldn't weep for it now, that wouldn't change anything. And... even if I could change the outcome, would I? What would have happened to me without Jesi? If Tolas had been my educator, my companion?

No time to think on any of it.

"And one more thing," Jesi said, taking a deep breath.

I met her wide eyes and braced. I hated

this moment. Bad news always followed. Something to hurt.

"I don't like boys, Zaria. I like girls. A lot."

For one moment I said nothing, then I burst out laughing. "Yeah, I kinda figured that out a while ago."

"What?" Her wide eyes widened. "But you never said anything! And I couldn't tell, with the way you were raised and all…"

I shrugged. "I figured if you wanted to discuss it outright, you would."

"I didn't know how you'd react, coming from Elowa."

She had a point. I rocked back on my heels. "I'm not the same girl I was when I arrived. Besides, I think Elowans are full of it. I can easily guess what the Fire Maidens are doing up there on their mount."

Jesi laughed as tears pooled in her eyes. "I'd like to see it someday. Elowa."

I didn't know what to say. Would I ever want to return?

Suddenly, I remembered my mother's conch-pearl and diamond necklace. The one I'd worn at my first wedding and had since forgotten. I raced to the drawer to fetch it.

"Jesi," I said quickly, waving the pink pearls in the air. "Take this. I don't want it. Take it and give it to your brothers, sell it, whatever. Are you listening?"

"It's starting to take effect," Jesi said softly,

shoulders relaxing.

"Here," I said, stuffing the necklace into one of her inner pockets – the kind she used for hidden daggers. "Take it. Sell it. Okay?"

She nodded sleepily and I hurried to finish tying her feet.

"Zaria…" she whispered, struggling to speak. Briefly, I looked up, but didn't stop in my work. When I'd completed the final knot, I glanced up again to see Jesi's eyelids flutter shut.

"Don't die," she whispered before she slumped, head falling against her chest.

I whimpered. *It's done.*

Hopefully, guards would find Jesi before she awoke, making it look more realistic and limiting her suffering to a few stiff joints. If not, she'd have to attempt to escape by smashing the chair and alerting others, which wouldn't play out as nicely and might cause some minor injuries.

It had to be my fault.

I'd drugged her, I'd tied her up. Otherwise, she'd be implicated in my escape and suffer… I couldn't think about what Laz or Navere would do to her.

No time. I hugged Jesi's sleeping form and raced to my bathing room, facing the gazing glass.

Withdrawing my dagger, I hesitated.

I couldn't do it. All those years I wanted to cut it to the roots, and now, when my life depended on it, I couldn't make my hands move. *The irony.* I felt as if something mystical wove itself through the strands of my hair, like tales of mermaids whose power lay within their long locks.

I made my hands work, tying my hair into a tight goat's tail at the nape of my neck and picking up the dagger once more.

Not all of it, I bargained with myself. *Only what falls beneath the hair tie.*

Pulling my hair taut, I raised the blade.

You have to hurry. It will grow back.

With a deep breath, I hacked the first section of golden locks, cringing. My strands were too thick – it would take another cut, if not more, to finish the job.

Quickly, I worked my way through the hair spilling out below the tie, chopping until all of it piled into my wash basin. Holding up my lost strands felt surreal.

Hurry.

Turning in the gazing glass, I looked at my stubby goat's tail in disbelief. My blonde locks now fell only to the nape of my neck. Even though I knew I had done it, I felt around the blunt, uneven edges to confirm it was real. *My hair. My beautiful hair.* It was as if I'd lost a limb.

There's no time, I scolded. *Hurry!*

Gathering the fallen strands, I tied them into a sheer scarf and stuffed them into my shirt. I would dispose of the strands in the sea to hide the evidence... and because a superstitious part of me felt like that's where my hair belonged. Using a brown powder, I dusted a coating on my cheeks, chin, and above my lips, making it look like the shadow of a beard and moustache. Lastly, I checked the side bag to ensure it was stocked with leather skins of water, dried fruit and salted fish, my wetsuit, a flotation device, and a compass. Then I slung it across my chest, letting it hang by my waist.

There. It was...

...*awful.*

I frowned at my reflection. No one would be fooled in the light of day. But the night was dark and, by the docks, maybe I would pass for a boy.

I just had to make it out of the castle first.

What looked like a snippet of hair sticking out beneath the wash basin caught my eye. I was about to bend down and pick it up when I heard a voice behind me --

"You look hideous."

I jumped, turning to see Tomé standing in my room.

"Tomé!" I cried. "You scared the sea out of me. What are you doing here?"

"Jesi told me everything. Don't be mad at her. She thought you might need help sneaking out of the castle. I can see you need more than that," he said, frowning. "Here, let me fix... whatever that's supposed to be on your face."

"Stubble," I protested, tears leaking anew.

Tomé strode into the bathroom and picked up the brown powder. I stood still while he worked, brow furrowed, trying to give me a more masculine look.

"I can help you get out of the castle, but you'll have to sneak onto *The King's Light* alone," he said.

"How?" I asked. "I was going to wait for a crowd at the Garden Gate, to sneak out behind them..."

"With me. The Bone Gate. The guards posted tonight practically jump out of their skin to avoid me. If I escort you out, it looks like I'm escorting someone who's visited my room earlier..." Tomé said, holding my eyes to convey his meaning. "They'll prefer to pretend we don't exist."

I threw my arms around my cousin. "I'm sorry, I thought things were better here."

"Better, yes. Perfect, no."

I nodded slowly against his neck. "I'm so sorry I didn't tell you I was leaving. Jesi was supposed to give you a message after I'd gone... but I didn't want to trouble you with worry or the burden of lying. I didn't know what to do! It was for her to decide how you were faring and what to say..." I trailed off, crying hard. "I'm just so happy we can touch. It was all so silly growing up Tomé, wasn't it? I really hope you're happy here. I hope you understand that I can't be. But you can."

I forced myself to stop my rambling and, full of gratitude, gazed up at my cousin. He looked like his old self. Tall, strong, charismatic. The turquoise sea in his eyes and the bright sun in his smile. He wasn't smiling now, but I felt like the old light was back, beneath, and I knew if he grinned, he'd beam.

"Don't forget your scarf," he reminded, handing me the black cloth from my basin. I tied it around the top of my head and knotted it at the base of my neck, concealing some of my hair and hoping to blend.

Before we left, I stopped one last time to kiss Jesi's temple, running my hands along her curls. "Thank you," I whispered.

Tomé took my hand, an act I wondered if I'd ever get used to, and we scurried out of my room and through the dark castle halls.

Chapter 40

The night air was sweet and balmy, sticking the shirt to my skin with a sheen of sweat. Tomé was right; not only did the guards neglect to scrutinize us, they averted their eyes. Playing it up, Tomé held me tight, like a lover, planting a kiss on my lips when we parted. *Chaste and yet a damnable offense in Elowa.*

"Stay safe. Swim strong," he whispered, poised on the rocky path leading to the docks, just around the corner from the guards' view. "May Keroe protect you."

I blinked. "After all this, you still believe?"

He flashed a sad smile. "There are worse things to worship. Plus, if the Sea God listens to anyone, it's gotta be you."

"I don't want to leave you, Tomé." *God, this is so messed up.* I had to go, but I didn't want to abandon everyone I loved. Like my cousin. Why had I never told him before?

Because Braeni don't typically show affection so freely.

"I love you, Tomé. You know that, right?"

"I know. I love you too. Now don't cry. There's nothing to cry about because you'll do what you intend and we'll meet again."

That was the Tomé I remembered. Confident, optimistic.

I wiped my tears with the back of my hand. "Okay."

We hugged tightly one last time and I scurried around the narrow path leading to the harbor. I had to run to make it on time. When I finally reached the docks, men busily loaded supplies for the two-day journey aboard *The King's Light.* Crouching in the shadows by the rocks, I watched for a few moments as servants carried barrels, bags, and trunks onto the ship.

Now or never.

I thought I'd scream in terror as I willed my legs to straighten, walked behind one of the bigger men, and picked up a bag. I padded up the gangplank with my head down and my heart pounding.

To my astonishment, not a single guard stopped me or even deigned to look at me. I could hardly stifle my smile.

Everyone sees what they want to see, I realized. When I'd snuck out the Bone Gate with Tomé, the guards looked away in fear. When I snuck up onto the ship, the men's eyes skirted over me, seeing a mere servant.

I'd never been invisible before. It was jarring, but freeing.

In my wildest dreams hadn't I imagined escaping High Spire and sneaking onto *The King's Light* would prove so effortless, in this part at least. But never in my life had I been someone else. Unidentifiable. Unimportant. A blank slate.

If I was blank, I could write whatever I wanted upon the slate.

The idea intoxicated, sending a jolt through my body.

Still carrying the large bag to obscure my face, I snuck below deck. My heart stopped when I heard a familiar voice.

Juls.

"Open the best bottles now," he said. "My father deserves a toast as we depart."

I winced, forcing my legs to keep moving. *I'm sorry. So sorry.*

Padding down to the lowest hull, I found myself happily alone. I discarded the bag and raced to the hiding spot I'd found on my wedding day. The trap door was still intact and luckily still difficult to spy in the dim bowels of the ship.

Now or never.

I gulped and folded myself into the darkness.

#

Hell.

I thought a lot about the concept in that hole. *Did it exist? Could it be worse than I suffered now?* Sweat dripped off my body and I continually fought fainting. I struggled to breathe, to hold onto life. Minutes passed, but they might as well have been hours. A small beam of light shining through the cracks and the dim noises of celebration high above were the only things keeping my sanity.

Why, of all the tortures to endure to find Kirwyn, did it have to be this small space, tight as a coffin and seemingly alive... like a malicious, hungry thing eager to swallow me up, to eat me, to turn into an actual tomb encasing me forever.

I fought another wave of nausea. Was it my imagination or did the walls shrink, ready to immobilize me eternally? The air alone pressed upon my organs, crushing them, making each breath laborious.

Kirwyn, I'm coming, I repeated, over and over.

Eventually, a listlessness so great settled over me, I couldn't tell if I was awake or asleep. My head bobbed, my eyes glazed, and drool dribbled onto my chin. I didn't care. I was only half-alive.

Sometime later, I caught the sound of voices close by. Boxes were moved and to my horror, I heard the scrape of wood just above my hiding spot. What tiny beams of light I had coming through the slats disappeared, plunging me into darkness.

Oh god, someone had shoved a box or a barrel over my hiding spot.

I clapped my hand over my mouth to stifle the squeal.

Please don't let the door be stuck, please don't let the door be stuck.

Sweating and shaking, tears streamed down my face as I waited for the sounds of footsteps to recede. Every fiber in my being shouted at me to scream, to announce my position and seek help.

Oh god, oh god. What if no one ever comes down again and I die in this dark hole?

Once the hull quieted, I made myself count to ten, crying all the while. When I hit *ten,* my hands were already banging on the trap door.

Stuck.

Another wave of nausea hit me and this time, I threw up on myself. I'd barely had anything to eat, it was just stinging, sour bile. In total darkness, I pounded the wood with my fists, uncaring if I blooded my knuckles. I had little room to kick my legs, but I tried, scraping them as well.

Stop, Zaria, you have to stop, to wait.

Oh god. Let me out!

Your only choices are to wait in silence or to ruin your escape.

Fear gripped my heart so tightly I thought it would burst. I retched again.

Kirwyn, I thought, drawing his image to mind: green eyes piercing me like they could see through to my secrets, the cock of his impish smirk, his strong arms reaching to enfold me. I wanted him more than anything. If I could just *not die,* I might find him...

I froze at the sound of boots hitting the floorboards nearby. Scraping noises above resumed, closer and closer, until narrow beams of light filled my tiny chamber once more. Another wave of nausea – this time from relief – dizzied me.

Hours of torture passed. It was a hell designed for me, personally, much like when I'd crawled through the tunnel in my cave. Only this time, Kirwyn wasn't there to guide me. I was utterly alone, sweating and shaking. As much as I feared the dangerous swim ahead, I'd take it any day over the stifling hole.

Finally, silence fell upon the ship.

I could barely contain my exuberance in pushing the trapdoor wide and springing free. *The first night's celebration is complete. Everyone is asleep.* Hands still shaking, I sat in the dim hull beside my hiding space. I uncorked my water and drank. I nibbled salted fish I fought to keep down. Without straying too far, I stretched my arms, my legs, and paced. I was exhausted but refused to return to the little prison. Not until I heard the first stirrings of men in the late morning.

For hours I sat in darkness, scared, but strangely content. As long as I wasn't in *there,* I was okay.

The horror of men waking for breakfast condemned me back to hell. With my stomach roiling, I re-tucked myself into the tiny prison.

For Kirwyn. For all the future brides I can save. For myself.

It wasn't any easier than the first time. The only saving grace was that my body was so spent, I fell asleep for the entire day, awakening only to the noisy celebration on the second evening. I wasn't sure, but something told me at least ten hours had passed, maybe twelve.

Was it too soon? Where were we? I needed the men drunk, the hour late.

"A good man was the good old king, a good old man was he..."

Beneath the floorboards, I heard the chorus of song coming from inebriated servants fetching who-knew-what from the dark hull. Jesi was right, funerals – at least, royal ones – were celebratory affairs.

Once alone, I found my water and carefully took a few sips, still curled into a ball on my side.

I can't stay in here much longer, I thought. *I'm going to scream.* I forced the dried fruit into my stomach despite its resistance. I'd need my strength for the swim, and it helped to focus on something other than the creeping terror of the walls closing in on me.

Get out, get out, get out. My heart seemed to beat the command.

I couldn't take it. *Now's as good a time as any.* I pushed the trap door wide and left the horrible hole forever, gasping for fresh air.

No matter what happened, I wasn't going back in that hole. I'd rather return to Rythas.

First, I needed to figure out our location as best as I could. I wasn't sure the time or the ship's position and assuming either could prove deadly. Securing my scarf around my head, I crept onto the deck above, trying to look inconspicuous in case anyone returned. The air was so much cooler, sweeter outside the bowels of the ship. I found a darkened corner and crouched. As I moved, I heard the music flowing louder.

If I waited too long to jump, I'd spend too much time swimming in the daytime. The burning sun would beat relentlessly down on my body, making every stroke harder. I doubted I'd make it to shore in those conditions.

But if I jumped in too soon, we'd be too far from the coastline, and I'd drown from exhaustion before seeing land.

And if I didn't move soon, I might get caught, and all my preparations would be for nothing.

Who could guess what punishment I'd suffer? I honestly didn't know what the Dorestes would do to me, but I knew I'd never get another chance.

The song ended and I hadn't moved a muscle, clinging to a wooden column rising up in my shadowed corner. Another song began, a little more upbeat. I pictured Juls and wondered if he'd pasted a smile across his face, put on a show of bravery for the men.

Of course he did. He's Juls.

What face would he wear when he found out I was gone?

He's kind to me, I thought, guilt and fear rooting my feet to the spot. *I could find him and confess, say I changed my mind. Live out the rest of my days as queen to a noble king. With my family and friends.*

It's not so bad. It can always be worse.

Kirwyn's face floated across my mind, sending a terrible ache to my heart.

But, I thought... *it can be better too.*

Under dark skies, Kirwyn had thrown himself into the Blue Beyond for me. I could do the same for him.

My ears picked up the drums beating loudly, encouraging raucous singing. The songs had taken a more upbeat melody since the night before.

It's done, I thought. *They'd buried the king at sea.*

Which meant we were either at or near the gravesite or... heading back to Rythas?

Before fear could freeze me again, I slid from my corner. I'd need to make it up one level to reach the windows.

Carefully, sticking to the shadows, I ascended the stairs. My heart pounded and sweat gathered around my neck and under my arms. Any second someone could leave the celebration. To relieve themselves or take a break or gather more rum or any number of reasons. Impossibly, my heart beat even harder as I pictured someone catching me as I snuck about, as I imagined having to explain my presence with no reasonable excuse.

I exhaled a sigh of joy when I made it to the next deck and found it empty.

Hurry!

Retrieving the rope from my side bag, I slung it around the nearest pillar. Rushing to the nearest window, I pulled the lever and pressed, trying to push it open.

Stuck.

My heart sank. I pressed harder, without success.

Stupid. I should have tried the windows before.

I moved down to the next window in line, pulled the lever, and found it equally jammed.

I pursed my lips against the cry rising up from my throat. Tears welled in my eyes and when I blinked, they fell.

Stupid, stupid. Maybe all the windows had been sealed shut, and the only way out would be to break one -- which would surely be heard.

I moved to the left side of the first window I'd tried and pulled that lever, only to find the window just as stuck. Crying freely now, I buried my face in my hands.

There had to be another way off this ship.

My heart stopped as I heard a noise from above.

Someone is coming.

I darted aft, abandoning my sack along with the rope, hoping no one would notice it or think it looked out of place. Making myself as small as I could, I pressed into a dark corner and hid behind one of the barrels lining the wall.

I heard footsteps grow closer. A man, heavyset by the sound of it.

I pursed my lips tighter, hugged myself, and tucked my head into my knees. Tears streamed down my face. *Please slow down,* I tried to convince my heart. *He's going to hear your beating.*

The man came closer, when suddenly, his footsteps stopped. My breathing stopped with them. A tear dripped from my chin onto my shirt and in my fear I imagined he could hear the splash. A scraping noise sounded two feet from where I hid, and I realized he was pulling out the barrel next to me.

Relief washed over me. *Rum. He came for another barrel of rum.*

And, thank Keroe, he'd chosen one I wasn't hiding behind.

With a grunt, the man lifted the barrel. His footsteps, now even heavier, pounded against the floorboards as he huffed back toward the stairs. I heard him take the steps, slowly, until he'd made it to the top.

I wiped my tears, exhaling at the passing danger... but the man paused. Straining my ears, I heard him chat with another man passing by and then the *thump* of the first man dropping the barrel onto the deck.

Landdammit. He had no intention of moving anytime soon.

Now what do I do?

The windows on this deck were locked and these men had settled into a long talk. Closing my eyes, I pictured the boat in my mind.

The king's cabin. Grahar's room. *Now, Juls's room.* Surely, those windows would open.

If I could make it there.

If it remained unguarded.

Creeping and half-crouching, I slid from the main hall and worked backwards, feeling my way along the wall until I came to a doorway. Pulse racing, I peeked out beyond the frame.

No one was coming.

I bolted through the open space, up a small flight of stairs, and down a corridor. The door to the king's cabin was obvious – ornate and the standing alone along the back wall. Cringing, I pushed it open and slid inside.

Juls's room.

The large chamber bore dark woods, intricately carved. It had been richly appointed with heavy curtains, gold sconces, sculptures and art along the walls. Deep shades of red, like the Dorestes preferred.

I can smell him in this room, I thought. *Or is my mind playing tricks on me?*

Shaking away the guilt, I noticed with glee one of the windows was already ajar. I sprinted across the room, pushed the window wide, and grinned as I breathed in the salt air, the scent of freedom.

I pulled myself back and paused, catching Juls's scent again.

Sandalwood and leather surrounding me, I was sure of it.

More guilt washed over me. Too heavy to carry while I swam.

Before I could second-guess the decision, I raced to a pile of charts, maps, and other documents spread on the table in the room's center. I tore the corner from one uninteresting piece of paper and fumbled around until I found a modern writing utensil to compose a final note.

Thank you for being kind to me. I'm sorry. I hope you find happiness.

It was... pathetic, *Zaria,* I thought. Certainly not an eloquent goodbye, but it was all I had time for.

I folded the paper and looked around the room until I found what had to be Juls's robe, hanging on one hook in the corner. I slid the paper into the pocket on his left side. Juls was right-handed. I wasn't sure he'd use the robe's pockets that night, but if he did, he'd favor the right side. I didn't want him to discover the note immediately, for fear he'd turn the ship around and hunt me down.

At the thought, I glanced at my own left hand. I still wore my gold wedding ring. In all my frantic planning, I'd forgotten about it. *What to do with it?*

I didn't want to make the journey with it on, to leave a tie to Juls on my body. Besides, what would I do with it once I swam ashore?

I didn't want to toss it into the sea. Such an act felt disrespectful, and I still bore guilt from the first time I'd done that to Juls.

Sliding it off my finger, I winced as I hovered above the pocket of his robe. Would it be like a slap in the face if I returned the ring in this manner?

But what else could I do?

You never asked to marry him, I reminded myself. *He knew he stole you away from the boy you love, and he did it anyway. If you hadn't been quick-thinking, he would have forced you to...*

535

I dropped the ring beside my note in the pocket of Juls's robe.

A fish flopped in my gut as I heard voices from the hallway outside the lavish cabin. I scurried back to the window and quickly reached for my side bag, only to find nothing but air beside me.

Oh no. *Oh no.*

I'd left it in the main hall. *No, no, no.*

Big mistake.

Not that I had time to tie a rope to help me down from the tall ship, but my wetsuit, flotation device, and compass were in that bag.

The voices came closer.

I'd have no protection against the jellyfish stings and no back-up plan to help me stay alive if I ran out of energy.

Terrified, I scrambled onto the window's ledge to avoid getting caught.

I had no choice. Except the choice to give up.

Carefully, I slid through the open window, standing on the small ledge and clinging for all I was worth onto wet wood above. I pushed the window back into its original position, half-open. I could distinguish the voices now, giving my heart a little pinch. One was a man I didn't recognize.

The other was…

Juls.

Oh god. If I jumped, they'd hear the splash. I needed to hold on until they left the room. I shimmied to the side of the window, digging my fingernails into the sodden and slippery beams. I pressed myself flat against the ship, both to keep balance on the little ledge provided and to decrease the risk of being seen.

"I'll be out in a minute," Juls said, and I heard the other man leave.

I sucked in a breath as he strode to the window. *Please, no. I'd come so far.*

Panting, I squeezed my eyes shut as Juls pushed the window wide. I tried tucking my head into my shoulders as if I could make myself disappear. God, he was *right there.* Unknowing I stood mere feet from him.

I heard Juls sigh, staring out at the dark waters. It sounded... pained or wistful. *My* heart ached for the heartache *he* must feel, losing his father and inheriting a kingdom in the same moment.

I could reach out. Take his hand and forgo this dangerous swim.

He'd forgive me. That's the type of man he was. He'd hold me and soothe me and forgive me.

I hated to admit that it was appealing for all the wrong reasons. It was so much easier than what I was about to do.

Juls, I thought, *I do love you... in a way.*

He gave another long sigh, then pushed back from the window.

The moment was gone. I heard his footsteps

recede. I folded my lips between my teeth to keep from calling out after him.

The door swung shut.

I was alone again.

I glanced down at the black sea, rollicking beneath me.

What if it all was a lie and no mainland existed? What if our guesstimates were wrong, and it was too far to swim? What if I cramped and couldn't move? What if a shark or some other sea creature caught sight of me and thought I'd make a tasty meal?

Once I leapt, there'd be no going back. I couldn't change my mind, couldn't hope anyone would save me. Everything depended on how long and how far I could swim. Alone.

I looked down. My clothing would only impede my strokes and the thin material wasn't sturdy enough to fill with air and use for floating. Still clinging onto the slippery wood with one hand, I shimmied out of my shirt and slid my trousers down and off my legs. I didn't want them discovered drifting in the waves, so I bundled them up and tucked the pile under one arm, along with the scarf containing my hair.

I had nothing now.

No crown, no clothes, no crutch.

It was only me and the sea.

Standing in my thin undergarments, I bore no protection against morning's blistering sun and myriad sea creatures lurking beneath the surface. Most dangerous of all, I carried no compass to guide me and no life vest to save me should my arms and legs tire.

Oh god.

I was entirely alone and dependent upon myself.

I closed my eyes and jumped.

Chapter 41

Not a cloud crossed the sky, and the moon was but a sliver. Clear and bright, stars shone upon the world, lighting my way. The sea was as calm as could be expected.

Keroe was on my side in this, at least. If the waves rolled rough or the heavens hung heavy with rain, my escape would have been over before it began.

Treading water, I watched *The King's Light* drift away, feeling as if a rope tethering me to everything I knew, everything I was, pulled taut, stretched until it frayed and snapped.

Gone. All of it gone forever.

What have I done? A small part of me wanted to scream, *come back.*

Opening my hands I released my clothing, watching it dance as it briefly floated, before waves carried the soft shirt and pants further away and under. Losing even that wet, flimsy bundle felt like losing my last layer of protection, the last physical connection to my old life -- save the undergarments I wore, though they were but a scrap. I untied the scarf bearing my hair and let it disperse in the black sea as well; strands of gold eerily waving and sinking.

Take it, Keroe. I watched it disappear like an offering. *Take it and keep me safe.*

Turning away from the fading boat, I steeled myself for the arduous swim.

Keep swimming toward the abalone cluster. I looked up at the sky, first finding the North Star, then turning to the string of stars resembling the holes on the iridescent shell. Mainland lay somewhere in that direction. I needed to move before the stars did.

With a deep inhale, I took my first stroke.

Head down, breath up. Head down, breath up. Rhythmic, meditative. My solace. Before Kirwyn -- before Juls and Laz and any of it -- it was me and the ocean. I began with the sea. If I died this night, if the black waves enfolded me in a fatal embrace, there was a macabre symmetry to ending with the sea.

Head down, breath up. Head down, breath up. How many miles had I swum? It wasn't long before I felt the first jellyfish sting across my thighs. Wincing, I prayed, *please don't let this be a large cluster.*

It wasn't... but the threat remained. A

smack was the appropriate term; and fitting. If I hit a smack of too many jellyfish, I'd become tangled, the stings overwhelming and drowning me.

I didn't want to break my pace, but I stopped every so often to read the stars. Time was difficult to judge -- it seemed not to exist this far out in the middle of the endless ocean. Sound barely existed as well. It was otherworldly.

Keroe's realm. Forbidden.

I found it all too easy to imagine the stories I'd been raised to believe were true. That if I kept going, I'd find myself in the jaws of a terrible sea monster, or I'd be pushed right over the edge of the endless waterfall, falling into an abyss but never reaching the bottom.

If I thought too much about it, it became difficult to push myself forward. Stroke after endless stroke in the vast ocean, in the never-ending swim.

Head down, breath up. Head down, breath up.

Then I'd picture the threats I knew to be real. Sharks. Exhaustion. Heat stroke. The second jellyfish sting was quickly followed by the third. I stopped counting after that.

Head down, breath up.

Hours passed and my arms ached. My lids grew heavy. Who knew if I even headed in the right direction? Who knew if mainland was real?

This is endless. Impossible. Maybe Jesi was wrong, and the ship sailed another course, far from the coast. Maybe my swim was hopeless before it even began.

There is nothing, I thought, treading water again and spinning in circles. How many hours had I been swimming? It wasn't yet light; it couldn't have even been more than six. And yet it felt as if each stroke forward was a stroke into nothingness.

I'd die out here in this vast ocean. Maybe that was Keroe's plan all along. The skies had been cleared and the waves were calmed to lure me out, beyond the realm of men and into his domain. When my legs tired, when my arms could move no more, I'd fail. I'd sink to the bottom of the ocean and into his arms, as I was destined all along. *His* betrothed, *his* bride.

Don't, I scolded myself. *Don't despair. That's what distinguishes you from everyone else, that is what you* can *control. Not the waves or the weather or even the strength in your body to make this swim, but the* determination *to do it.*

Maybe I'd gone a little mad when I started talking to Keroe. Not just praying, but actually carrying on a conversation.

I'm sorry I didn't want to marry you. I'd make a poor bride anyway. You know that, right? I certainly wasn't what Juls wanted, though he tried hard to convince himself. Laz vehemently despised me. Come to think of it, Mal-Yin merely humored me, tolerated me at best. I seem to rub men in power the wrong way, Keroe, so I doubt you'd be any different. My running away saved you a headache.

I imagined the Sea God sitting on his coral throne beneath the waves, listening.

Kirwyn is the only boy who matched me. Help me find him. Please? He wasn't a man in *power, but he* was *powerful. If that makes any sense? If by circumstance he'd been born as Braeni or as young king, he'd have done well. I think we can do well, together... Just help me survive, please.*

Conjuring Kirwyn's face in my mind, I narrowed my eyes at the blackness ahead and pushed on.

The sky lightened.

Don't fade, I begged of the stars. *I need you to guide me.* But I was sure of it now, gray tinted the world above. Light came from behind me, chasing me. I beat the waves faster, as if I could outswim the dawn. With the sun at my back, at least I knew I headed in the right direction.

Suddenly, I gasped, blinking.

Land.

I could see what I guessed to be palm trees and the slight rise of soft hills beyond.

Unless... it was a mirage from madness. My head pounded, the muscles in my arms and legs screamed, and my skin burned with stings all over my belly, thighs, and even my neck. The worst were in the sensitive underside of my arm, rubbing painfully with each stroke.

No, no... I spied land ahead, I was sure of it.

Oh Keroe, how horrible it would be to fail now, when I can see my goal. My muscles begged me to stop, my cracked lips pled for water, my lungs screamed for a break.

Even my heart was too tired to give anything more than a small leap at the miraculous sight.

You must go on, Zaria. You must.

Keeping my head above water seemed a monumental task. It lulled and rocked, wanting to soften, to sink.

Keep going or you'll die.

Behind me, the sun had fully arisen, and I suddenly remembered the dawn after the Fae fête, when we'd all gathered on the beach, to watch.

I'd vowed then I'd be like the sun, determinedly rising again and again.

And pushing on, I thought. *I must push on across the sea as the sun pushes on across the sky.*

No one in the world could stop the sun from burning. And no one could stop me either.

I grit my teeth resolutely, though my strokes were no longer strong, capable. I flailed like a floppy, uncoordinated child first learning to swim. I beat the water and kicked wildly, without grace or power. Every so often, I sank and wasted effort swimming back *up* instead of forward.

But land came closer. Real. Strange and

wonderous and full of promise. Wider and bigger and right in front of me. I could hear the cry of dinbirds; watch their swoops and dives.

Until finally, my toes scraped the seabed on one of my kicks.

I could touch it. Land. Mainland. The North Continent.

Half-crawling, I dragged myself onto the shore, cutting my hands and legs on the sharp edges of shells as the waves pushed me along like a ragdoll. I was too tired to fight them. It didn't matter; they were nothing compared to the lashes trailing my body from all the jellyfish stings.

I slumped onto the beach, waves lapping at my feet. *Was it high tide or low?* I couldn't make my eyes focus enough to tell. The sun shone too brightly.

Higher, I begged myself. *Crawl higher up the beach or else you'll die if the tide comes in.*

But I couldn't. My body no longer heeded my commands.

I blacked out before my head even hit the sand.

Chapter 42

Nothing made sense. Not at first. I couldn't remember what I'd done -- I barely knew who I was. It came back to me in pieces, like waking from a deep and troubling dream.

Only I'd dreamed none of it. Juls, Laz, Jesi and all of High Spire were real -- though miles away and separated by Keroe's realm.

I'd made it to mainland.

Somewhere else. Somewhere new.

"Shh..." a woman above me soothed, wringing out a rag and wiping me down. I wasn't on a beach, as I last remembered, but inside a stifling hut of some kind, similar to those in the village of Elowa. The woman wore Kirwyn's style of clothing. She had Kirwyn's accent. Groaning, I tried to focus on her appearance, but my eyes clouded and I made out no more than wispy brown hair and a middle-aged face.

I *had* to know where I'd landed. *Was it close to where Kirwyn once traveled? Was he there any longer?*

"Casa St. Seodorothian," I rasped, or tried through my swollen tongue, and the woman soothed me again.

Time passed and my vision cleared, but my head never pounded so hard before. I lifted it when the woman poured water into my mouth, and I gazed down upon my body. Every inch of my flesh was mottled with bruises and welts as if I'd been beaten and whipped. The jellyfish stings no longer burned, but they itched. My twitchy muscles were too sore to use -- I attempted to lift my arms and failed. I caught a tremor in my hands and felt my legs shake at odd intervals.

I believe I slept an entire day or two. I heard mainlanders enter and leave the stifling hut for a long time before I could fully focus, speak. Once I regained some control over my body, I studied the modest surroundings. The hut was sparsely furnished and contained two cots for beds – one of which I occupied.

New land. New world. New people. The same queasiness I'd felt first stepping onto Rythas washed over my stomach again.

It's terrifying, but you must keep going.

"Where am I?" I croaked. Judging by the hot sun baking the hut it was late afternoon.

"Shreelos," the woman replied, wiping me

down with the cold, wet rag, then applying a cool ointment of some kind on my skin.

The word meant nothing to me. If I'd seen it on a map, I didn't remember it.

"Who are you?"

The woman stiffened. "It is perhaps better that you do not learn our names. Safer for everyone."

"How long have I been here?"

"Three days since my husband found you on the beach. You're lucky it was him. You're lucky it wasn't further up, near the village. We reside on the outskirts."

Found me? *Like Kirwyn,* I thought, heart aching. He'd washed ashore and I'd saved him. Now someone repaid the kindness.

"Casa St. Seodorothian," I rasped. "Is it far?"

"Is that where you're from?" the woman asked gently.

"I – no." *How much should I confess?* She was helping me, after all. But it wouldn't be wise to reveal more than necessary.

"I… lost my group in that area," I lied. "I'm from the west."

"Clanless," she remarked half-question, half-statement.

I nodded. No point in denying it when she could see I bore no mark.

"I… there was a storm at sea," I explained, using Kirwyn's story. "I fell overboard and washed up here, I guess."

Her pursed lips alone told me she didn't believe me.

Your accent, you idiot. You don't sound like you're from the mainland.

I shrugged, sheepish. She smiled, indulgent.

"The fort you seek is maybe thirty miles from here. But the Spades are sweeping the region, you'll never make it without getting caught."

My heart careened wildly against my breast. The odds Kirwyn lingered in this area were slim, but it was *something.*

For several days I dozed, healed, ate and drank when food or water were pressed to my lips. After about a week, a man entered the hut, followed by what I gleaned to be the adult children of the couple – a son and a daughter. All possessed the same light skin, light eyes, and light brown hair. All eyed me warily. I caught the clan mark on the right shoulder blade of the boy: a basket filled with what looked like bread and fruit.

When I could easily sit up without aching muscles, I looked over several sets of mistrustful eyes and announced, "It's been over a week. Thank you, but I am well now. I should go, I *must* go."

It was a stupid thing to try or even to say. I had no plan. No supplies. No map. It might be suicide. But it was no crazier than jumping into the sea in the middle of the night.

"The Spades are crawling all over the area," the mother tending me cautioned. "Stay put. They'll depart in a few weeks, maybe a few months. If you leave now, you'll be captured. They don't raid our village, we're one of their suppliers. If you stay, you'll be safe here."

"Or we can hand her over and be rewarded," her son said, folding his arms. "No one is safe if they find us hiding a freeborn."

"She's not one of us," the daughter agreed, scowling. "Think about it. What if they take revenge on all of Shreelos for harboring her? Is she worth the risk to Delosor's new baby being stolen, enslaved?"

The mother rubbed her hand over her heart, silent.

"I can leave," I offered, quickly, guiltily. "You've done so much for me, please. I don't want to trouble you further."

"No one is *going* to find out about her," the father commanded, glaring at his children. "The Spades won't billet here, they'll want better accommodations. She stays put, we stay quiet, and they'll never find her."

Huffing, the younger boy and girl departed the hut. It was settled, but I knew I couldn't hide there forever and with the use of my body returning I was eager to move on.

"Thank you, but I cannot stay for moon cycles," I protested.

"Just one," the woman urged, laying her

hand upon mine. "Just one, then."

"Might I be able to walk? Anywhere? I need to get my strength back. I cannot stay cooped up in here for weeks. And... wouldn't it be better if I slept elsewhere?" I asked, eyeing her husband.

She followed my gaze and shook her head. "He's sharing the children's hut right now; he's fine."

"Thank you, but... I cannot stay inside for a moon's cycle," I pointed out. Claustrophobia pressed down on me again and more importantly, I *needed* to work my muscles. I was also growing bored staring at the sparsely furnished hut. There were no books, no art, no objects much at all except cookware.

The woman looked to the door, anxiously rubbing one shoulder. "I suppose you could walk south. It is, sort of unofficially our land, our forest and beach. No one from the village trespasses."

"Please, yes," I begged her, "I don't like to be far from the sea."

"You can't swim; you'd be spotted," the father said. "But you can exercise in the woods and on the beach, if you must."

Over the next few weeks, a funny thing happened. Instead of becoming friendlier with my rescuers, as one would expect, we all grew quieter. A strange time of solitude passed until I realized I was all but swimming in a Sea of Sorrows, not speaking unless it was necessary.

The family tolerated me, and the woman cared for me, but everyone tried to interact with me as little as possible. I was thankful for it. The quietude helped me process everything that happened in Rythas, and it suited me after being endlessly paraded in front of a swooning crowd. I tried to keep out of everyone's way except when I cleaned the hut – both for something to do and to repay the family in any small way I could.

Whenever permitted to safely walk, I explored the forests and beach to the south – never north. Every evening we ate fresh fish. I couldn't spear my own without entering the ocean, but I found bushes of deep, purple elderberries within the wood and I often brought clusters of the hanging fruit back to the hut for our meals. By the beach I found pigweed growing in patches and I gathered leaves for a salad. I spied plenty of grubs and beetles, but I stayed away from collecting them. Kirwyn didn't eat insects and neither had anyone in Rythas.

The family gave me clothing like their own – cream-colored short-pants and loose white shirts. Mainland clothes.

Every day, I stared at the sea and thought about Jesi. I hoped she wasn't punished in any way for my actions. I worried about what Juls felt when he'd learned I'd gone. Did he believe me dead? Did everyone? I debated whether or not I'd guessed correctly and Singen was planning to harm Laz somehow. I even thought about my mother. Would word reach her that I'd disappeared?

Mostly, I wondered about how to find Kirwyn and how to request supplies without revealing too much of my purpose. I wished I had something to give the family in return for saving me, but I'd washed ashore with nothing to my name – without even a name. Not one I could use, anyway. Who was I now, here? Not a braenese. Not the Savior of the Bloody Shoals or the Queen of our Hearts or even Zaria Doreste.

Although... I was, wasn't I? By law, I was a married woman wherever I went.

Days turned into weeks, and I couldn't stop reaching for my phantom hair. The mother helped even out the trim one afternoon, cutting a better line than I had with the hasty hacking of my dagger. I could always feel the freshly-chopped ends grazing my shoulders as I turned my head. On the one hand, cutting my hair felt liberating, as if I'd freed myself of past traumas. On the other, I missed my long, golden locks. It was such a silly thing to mourn after all I'd risked, but I pined for it to grow anew.

More than a moon cycle passed in this quiet manner. Inconsequential days and nights. My favorite times were alone, staring at the ocean. I'd hug my knees to my chest, wrestling with my feelings about Rythas and everyone in it. It had changed me, whether I liked it or not... and more confusingly, I often couldn't even sort out what I did and did not like. Half my emotions I couldn't understand, or name.

I'd cut my hair and swam somewhere new, but it didn't undo what was done. *Juls and Laz.* I was bound to one brother by matrimony and the other by blood. Even being separated by all of Keroe's realm didn't change that.

But the sea soothed me. The sea, it seemed, was where all things began and where all the answers lay. For me, at least. We were connected, the ocean and I. Whether or not Keroe lived below and answered my prayers, the depths swirled with fathomless magic. I didn't need to understand how. I didn't need the Mystics to tell me the means to worship it. I didn't need to explain my feelings to anyone. What I felt was between me and the sea.

One unimportant afternoon like any other, I stared at the waves, sitting on the sand not too far from the tree line. But northward, something dark caught my eye.

A rider on horseback, moving fast down the beach.

Coming straight for me.

My blood ran cold.

Scrambling to my feet, I noticed the rider wasn't wearing clothing from Shreelos or Rythas.

A Spade?

I'd been found.

Gulping, I thought, *I can't outrun a horse.* But I ducked into the forest and sprinted at full speed.

Seconds later, I heard the Spade follow.

Even at my fastest, the hoofbeats pounded closer behind me.

Oh god, I should have never sat so conspicuously on the sand. Would it have made any difference, or did they know where I was anyway?

Darting south, I headed toward a small ravine on the desperate hope the Spade wouldn't see me or wouldn't be able to steer the beast into the little gully where a fresh-water stream ran to the ocean. Half-tumbling, I threw myself down the slope, sloshing into the narrow brook. Stumbling to my feet, I ran along the edges of solid dirt, heart careening against my chest and pulse racing.

Behind me, I heard the horse *clop* into the ravine.

No!

My ears picked up the curious sound of the horse *halting* and the rider dismounting.

Encouraged by the Spade's bad decision, I pressed my legs to pump faster.

"Stop!" the voice hissed on the breeze.

Or else what? I cringed, expecting an arrow in my back. But I kept running for my life.

The Spade chased. His legs were too long and too fast; I couldn't outrun him.

What could I do?

Rocks!

I spared only a few seconds to find the best one, bent down and scooped it up –

- and felt the full weight of the Spade slam into me from behind.

Not just slam -- he half-picked me up off the ground. Holding my arm aloft to keep the rock from hitting his skull, he twisted me around and at the same time swept me off my feet and onto the dirt.

My mind was wild with fear. I couldn't focus; couldn't think. The Spade climbed on top of my body. With one hand restraining my arms above my head, the other clamped over my mouth.

In my struggles, I glanced up –

-- and the world fell away.

Kirwyn?

Keeping his hand over my mouth, he whispered, "Shh…"

Chapter 43

*T*his isn't real, Shreelos isn't real. It couldn't be. I'd never made it to the mainland. I'd drowned at sea and had been wandering around some purgatory until that moment.

If that was the case, I was glad. Now I'd entered some charmed afterlife.

I must have.

Because it couldn't be Kirwyn pressed against me.

Impossible.

The only alternative to having died was to accept I'd gone mad, envisioning such ridiculousness. And if that was the case, I'd be devastated when lucidity returned and he disappeared.

At that moment, death was preferable.

Wide-eyed I stared, forgetting to move or blink or breathe. The rock tumbled free from my limp hands.

It can't be...

I was looking into Kirwyn's face.

My god, he was even more jaw-droppingly handsome than I remembered. Dark hair falling toward deep green eyes. Sensuous lips, surrounded now by several days' stubble.

"Shh... there are others just behind me."

My heart stopped beating. It *couldn't* beat -- it had exploded at the sound of that voice. Kirwyn's voice. I blinked, rapidly, making sure he didn't disappear. My lip quivered and a solid lump formed in my throat.

Oh my god. He was here! How was this possible?

My heart was going to burst with joy. Hot tears pooled in the corners of my eyes and on the next blink, they fell.

"I'm going to move my hand now, but don't shout. Zaria, be very quiet, they're not far back. Nod if you understand."

How can this be?

I nodded. But Kirwyn didn't let go right away. He was *staring* at me, and I noticed his eyes were wet.

"We've got to stop meeting like this," he grinned.

I started to laugh-cry, remembering the first time we met, in my cave back in Elowa. Kirwyn let go of my wrists and mouth and leaned down to kiss me.

Everything faded. There was only *us*. I

couldn't hear the stream or the birds or the sounds of anyone in pursuit. Nothing else existed. The world was so far away it felt like it never was.

I used to think I'd swoon if I ever saw Kirwyn again. I thought my body would forget how to function and I'd fall to the ground in a sobbing puddle of boneless flesh.

I *was* sobbing. But that's all the reality had in common with the fantasy. I lost myself in Kirwyn's kiss. Tugging at his hair, his shoulders, his back -- it was like I couldn't get close enough to him, like I wanted to melt into him.

"Kirwyn!" I whispered, tasting the tears falling into my open mouth.

"Zaria," he whispered in return.

Real.

Breathlessly and as silently as possible, we tore at each other. I kissed his lips, his cheeks, his forehead and even his eyes until he held my head still so that he could kiss me all over my wet face as well. He kissed me like he didn't believe the moment was real or as if it would slip away and he had to imprint all the kisses he could before then.

I think that's how he felt because that's how I felt.

"Kirwyn, Kirwyn," I breathed.

It can't be; it can't be real.

He ran his fingers through my hair and held

my face between his hands. He was almost entirely the same. Too beautiful to look at without hurting. His torso was still lean, still boyish, though the stubble made him appear older. Shaking, I ran my hands over his solid chest and the muscles in his arms to be sure he was truly holding me, and my mind hadn't snapped and imagined all of it.

"Zaria," he whispered. *"My* Zaria."

Seven moon cycles. I'd waited seven moon cycles for this moment.

"How is this possible? Is this really you?" I murmured, inhaling deeply. I remembered that woodsy smell. *Him.*

"It's me," he replied, before claiming my mouth again.

I knew those lips, I loved those lips. He was the same – his voice, his face, his hair...

Oh god, what did he think of mine now?

Suddenly, Kirwyn broke our kiss.

"Are you hurt? Did he hurt you?"

Confused, I muttered, "No. No, I'm... fine."

Am I?

Kirwyn leaned back, cocking his head, listening.

"Zaria, we have to go. Now."

"Go?" I asked, confused.

"They're looking for you. *Everyone's* looking for you. A small army came from Rythas to search for the missing queen, then the Spades received reports of a freeborn hiding in

Shreelos."

"What?" I whispered. "How do you know? I don't understand. How did you find me?"

"I can explain everything later."

Kirwyn sprang to his feet, ducking to keep his head beneath the rim of the ravine. Extending his hand, he pulled me up.

"Hurry," he whispered, half-dragging me toward his horse as I stumbled to keep up with his long strides. Kirwyn helped me into the saddle and a familiar fear crept cold through my breast as the beast was a lot taller than it seemed at first. It was a long way to fall. Kirwyn paused, listening again for sounds on the wind. Satisfied, he swung himself up behind me.

Is this real? My mind repeated, even as I felt the security of his solid chest behind me.

"Hold on and lean into me," Kirwyn ordered, grabbing the reins. I didn't have anywhere else to go and not much to hold onto but the edge of the saddle. My heart nearly stopped when Kirwyn kicked the horse and we took off down the ravine and then up the small hill, running through the woods at a breakneck speed.

"Try to keep your head low!" he instructed, turning off the path and into thicker growth, unable to avoid the branches still whipping our arms and legs.

We'd only ridden a minute or two when I heard the sound of men shouting on the beach behind us.

I gulped. *They're here.* Kirwyn was right. Rythas had come for me. Or the Spades. I'd been mere minutes away from getting captured and dragged back to High Spire... or enslaved.

With a nudge from his legs, Kirwyn urged the horse *faster.*

Please don't let them catch us, I prayed, cringing at the pounding *thump-thump* of horse hoofs upon the dirt. *Would it echo through the trees?* Sweat broke out all over my body. Whatever happened, I refused to be parted from Kirwyn ever again.

I'm not going back. They can't make me.

Tensing, every minute I imagined voices behind us. My stomach endlessly flipped while Kirwyn steered us on what I gleaned to be an intentionally confusing path, backtracking and doubling over the stream. Costing us time, but worth the risk.

Please don't let them find us, please don't let them find us.

"Hold on," Kirwyn said, turning our horse in yet another direction and preparing to run. "Get low."

I ducked and he steered us into even thicker foliage. My heart pounded wildly as we darted farther away from the beach.

I refuse to return. They can't make me.

I jumped at every sound... but it was only birds or animals we sent scurrying from our path. After fifteen or twenty minutes of hard riding, Kirwyn pulled the reins to slow our horse. We cocked our heads, listening above our panting.

"They're not following – yet. By now they must know you're gone and will begin searching." Kirwyn slid onto the ground and reached up, assisting me off the horse. I immediately threw my arms around his neck and he pulled me close. Still pausing and listening, he said, "We can only spare a few minutes. Stretch your legs, catch your breath, take a drink."

"How are you here?" I cried, searching his face. "What's happening?"

"It's a long story," Kirwyn said. "There's dozens of Rythasian soldiers scouring the settlements along the coast, looking for the kidnapped queen. Then I caught word of a beautiful freeborn girl hiding in the village here. I figured out they were one and the same," he said, cupping my face. "You."

"Kidnapped?" I repeated, shocked. "Rythas thinks I was kidnapped?"

"Yes and no. Stories conflict," he said, reaching into his saddle bag and retrieving a canister of water. He handed it to me and I drank quickly, deeply, before handing it back to him.

"But – how do you know all this?" I asked, holding onto his waist as if he'd disappear if I let go. "I don't understand! How are you here, now?"

Kirwyn drank a few sips, then returned the water to his bag.

"I've been helping them," he explained, nudging me to re-mount. "When I heard about the kidnapped queen, I offered my expertise as a scout. I've been guiding your army through the territory. I'll explain everything later. I want to put more distance between us and them."

I pulled my hand free, covering my mouth as I gasped. "Offered who? Rythas? The guards? Kirwyn, no! They have your picture, they know what you look like."

Kirwyn's brow furrowed. "How would they know what I look like?"

"They got a drawing of you, it's a long story..." I stared at the ground, shaking my head. "I don't know who's here, but the palace guards saw your picture. At least, for a day..." I trailed off, remembering how Laz was keen to take it down. "Oh Kirwyn, I'm sorry! It was my wedding day and then... I'm sorry I didn't come to meet you. I can explain, I got your message too late... it's another long story."

"Tell me later," he said, "we don't have time now." Kirwyn tried to seize my waist, to hoist me up.

"Wait, stop!" I said, pushing his hands away, feeling sick. The weight of it all settled deep in the pit of my stomach. *I am a married woman.* "Kirwyn, I'm sorry, I didn't have a choice. I – I'm married now." I couldn't meet his eyes.

Kirwyn's hand touched my chin, lifting it. "You're not anything you don't want to be. You're free. But we need to leave *right now* if you want to stay that way."

This is a dream, I thought. *It can't be real that he found me so easily.*

"I can't just leave. I have to say goodbye. I have to explain. The people who took me in, who helped me, they've been kind to me."

Kirwyn shook his head impatiently. "No, they betrayed you. Someone informed the Spades you were hiding there."

"No! Well, maybe but…" I pictured the young boy and girl who didn't want me in their hut. "I know who it was, and I don't blame them, not really. But the woman who helped me…"

"There's no time."

"Kirwyn, I can't just leave her with no warning or explanation!"

"You'll only put her more in danger," Kirwyn cut me off. "The less she knows, the better."

I didn't move, considering.

"Zaria, listen to me. You're in my world now. Please, just trust me. You need to listen to me, to do as I say. Didn't I listen to you in Elowa when you knew best?"

"No!" I scoffed, throwing up my hands. "Absolutely not! You never listened to me!"

Arrogant, infuriating, and we were arguing in less than a minute. Definitely Kirwyn. Definitely not a dream.

Yet just looking at him sparked a reaction in my body; all of my nerve endings alive and yearning. Seeing him made the blood rush to my lips, eager to kiss him; it made my fingertips tingle, longing to touch him. The pull I felt toward Kirwyn was like the force of gravity and I was just as helpless under its command.

Kirwyn began looking anxiously over my shoulder. He had one hand on my waist and one behind my head, protectively.

"Right, well, I was wrong. I should have let you lead when you knew what you were talking about. We're in my world and you need to just trust me and get on the horse. Now." His muscles tensed and I knew he was considering how best to put me on the horse quickly if I didn't climb there myself.

"Well, that's convenient for you to suddenly admit," I said, voice dripping sarcasm. But I gave Kirwyn my hand to assist in hoisting me onto the horse's back. I closed my eyes, feeling a pang of guilt to leave the woman who'd been so kind to me, as well as terror that I'd put her and her family in danger.

As if reading my mind, Kirwyn said, "They turned you in. The Spades won't hurt them, don't worry."

I relaxed a little.

"It will take longer but it's safer to ride inland, then north. We don't have to run but we need to keep a good pace. Are you okay to keep riding?"

"I'm with you, Kirwyn," I said, still hardly believing any of this was real. "I can ride all day and night if you need us to."

His arm wrapped around my waist and from behind, Kirwyn planted kisses along my neck and shoulder, leaving gullflesh in his wake. I must have tasted of sweat but he didn't seem to care. Heat flooded my veins.

You're here, I thought. *You're really here. I'm with you; we found each other.*

"But where are we going?" I asked.

Chapter 44

Kirwyn abruptly stopped planting kisses. I could hear him wince as he said, "I can't explain yet. There's... a lot to tell you. I know you have a lot to tell me. But not yet. Tonight, when we camp, we can talk."

There's so much to tell you, I don't even know where to start.

"I had to cut my hair," I moaned, though it was obvious. Of all the things to say, that's the only one I felt ready to talk about.

"It's perfect," Kirwyn said, running his nose up the side of my neck. "Easier access to this spot." He kissed somewhere sensitive near my ear, and I shivered.

"The one I remembered you liked," he said, grinning against my skin.

I smiled too and more tears leaked. Was it possible to die from happiness? Because I felt like I might at any moment.

He urged the horse forward once more and I settled into Kirwyn's chest, trying not to fret about his perplexing refusal to tell me more and our pacing, which prevented conversation. Instead, I studied the interior mainland as we rode. It didn't look too dissimilar to Rythas or Elowa or even the coastal wood. I'd seen images of cold places in the library tower. Mountains and snow. Forests of color and bare, brown ones. Spade City and nearby towns. But if I didn't know better, I'd think Kirwyn and I could have been riding in the untamed wilds of Rythas. I couldn't decide if that made me feel safer or more anxious. I couldn't believe any of this was real. I kept expecting to wake up.

After what felt like more than an hour, we finally stopped to stretch our legs and drink once more. When Kirwyn swept me up in his arms and began kissing me again, nothing ever felt more right in my life. I clung to him, clawed at him, feeling like I tried to climb *inside* him.

But I was terribly confused by his refusal to share our direction.

When he broke our kiss I pled, "I can't keep riding like this. I need *some* answers. For starters, how did you convince my mother to let you leave Elowa? And what have you been doing all this time? And where are we going?"

"I swear I can answer all your questions soon," he said, pulling me close by my waist again.

"Kirwyn, *please*," I protested, backing out of his grip. My head was bursting with questions. *We finally found one another... everything is going to be okay.*

"I'm not going one step further until you tell me where we're headed." My foot stomped, my teeth grinded, and I placed my hands upon my hips.

Kirwyn fisted his hands, eyes briefly closing. "I can't."

Was he angry with me for getting married? For failing to come when he tried to rescue me?

"Why not? We said no more secrets between us, remember? We said total trust."

He sighed, running his hands through his hair. "I know. But it's not my secret to tell. It's not... what you should hear from me. Not my place to..." he fisted and flexed his hands again. "Yes, total trust. And I need *you* to trust *me*. Just get on the horse, Zaria."

I crossed my arms, debating.

Kirwyn laughed, licking his teeth. *That grin.* It was demonic and irresistible all at once. I focused on his canines; I'd forgotten how sharp they were, giving him a feral, menacing quality.

"Get on the horse."

I didn't move. Kirwyn raised his eyebrows, tensed his muscles, and I *knew* what was coming. Quickly, I threw up my hands in surrender, "Okay, okay, I'll get on the horse."

Despite my proclamation about riding for

days, my backside ached, my thighs burned, and even my feet were sore. I wore leather thongs I fought not to lose as we galloped. The only reason they stayed on at all is because the woman who'd taken me in, who'd given me everything I now wore, had gifted me shoes a size too small and I hadn't the heart to tell her they pinched.

Kirwyn mounted the horse behind me and coaxed us forward, this time down a dirt trail. We rode through the forest for a few minutes before I stiffened away from him – half-playfully, half because I really was frustrated that he refused to tell me anything. With a huff, I jut out my chin.

Kirwyn switched the reins to one hand, snaked his arm around my waist, and pulled me back, his breathy laugh warming my neck.

I turned my head toward his bicep and bit – maybe a little too hard.

"Ow," he growled through clenched teeth, sliding his hand under my shirt and squeezing my bare waist until I was forced to release my bite.

I yelped, letting go and grinning, my heart ready to explode with happiness. *I remember you. I remember this. I remember us.*

"The mainland monster shows his true colors."

"The savage princess shows hers."

I snorted, meaning to sound haughty but

of course it came out unrefined, sullen. It didn't matter. I'd never been so happy in my life. Nothing else mattered; we were finally together again.

"I thought I was a demon," Kirwyn murmured, nuzzling my neck.

"Demon. Monster. Same thing."

He chuckled, "I suppose-" Kirwyn cut off abruptly and stiffened. "Zaria," he whispered, pressed tight to my ear.

Just the way he said my name froze my heart.

Worse -- he squeezed again where his hand rested at my waist. It wasn't playful like before. It wasn't anything like what Kirwyn would ever do. It hurt enough to startle me. At the same time, his arm locked too hard across my waist, making it difficult to breathe. I whimpered, speechless and confused.

"Don't say anything," Kirwyn whispered directly into the shell of my ear, low and hurried. "Just this once, please, listen to me. Not a word no matter what."

Fear rose in my gut, both by his tight grip and the worrisome plea in his voice. I didn't understand it. But I trusted him. I folded my lips between my teeth, bewildered but quiet. Kirwyn relaxed his grip on my waist, but his arm still crossed my midsection, pulling me tighter than before. I could feel his body, rigid with tension behind me.

In the deathly silence that followed, I heard

the sound of people ahead and my stomach dropped. Stepping from the trees and onto the dirt path...

Men. Maybe six or seven in total. Too many for us to fight off. Kirwyn had a dagger strapped to his waist and I suspected more weapons in his saddlebags, but we couldn't handle this many opponents on our own.

Oh god, please don't be Juls's men. Please don't take me back. Not after finally finding Kirwyn again. Not after all I suffered to get here.

"Well, hello there!" a man greeted. The mainland accent would have made me sigh in relief, if it wasn't for the deep sarcasm embedded within his tone. My heart leapt, then sank. Especially after two of the men aimed crossbows at us. "And where might you be going?"

"Spade City," Kirwyn replied, smooth as silk. "I'm taking her back where she belongs."

Oh god, oh god, what was happening?

"A slave, then?" the man asked. He was fairly well-built, had a head of wavy, dark blonde hair and dark eyes. He looked to be in his mid-twenties, but the rest of the group ranged in age. From the dirt coating their ragged clothing and the slight grease in their hair, I guessed they were travelers of some kind. Each man had a horse saddled with plenty of gear. Some, like the leader, had dismounted. All blocked our path.

I gulped.

"She has other notions, but yes," Kirwyn said, jovially. "She managed to escape before being marked. I've been sent to collect her."

"You're far from Blackjack territory," the blonde man pointed out. "How'd one girl make it so far?"

"She's good at making friends and allies to help her along," Kirwyn replied.

The man stepped closer. "I can see why."

I fought the urge to duck my head, instead focusing on steadying my breathing as I counted... eight men in total. We definitely couldn't fight them off.

"She's a pretty slave," the man remarked.

Kirwyn laughed his agreement. "You can see why I'd been tasked with chasing her so far."

"Let's see your mark?" the leader requested, though we all knew it was an order.

Oh god, I thought, *this is it. This is how we meet our end.*

I expected Kirwyn to protest, to give some fast-talking excuse. But he loosened his hold on my waist to reach around and pull aside the top of his shirt.

Why? What was there? Had he joined the Spades or some other clan? Is that why he wouldn't tell me where we were going?

The leader stepped around to look at Kirwyn's shoulder.

"He checks out," he called to the other men.

How...

But the blonde man didn't make any move to let us pass. He returned to the front of our horse, stroking the animal's head and taking a hold of the bridle – a subtle message that we weren't going anywhere.

"Give me one good reason why we shouldn't kill you right now and take the girl back to Spade City ourselves. Claim whatever reward is being offered for her capture and enjoy the... spoils."

"I can give you two good reasons," Kirwyn said, calm, but cold. "Upon her return, she's going to be punished for escaping. Even if she wanted to protect you -- which I have a feeling she isn't inclined to do -- she won't hold up under whatever torture they inflict. They're going to get the full story of how she managed to run in the first place, who helped her along the way, and what transpired during her rightful return. The Spade she belongs to won't take kindly to you killing his best bounty hunter or *spoiling* her."

The man stared up at Kirwyn, eyes like coals. A long pause drawled as he studied us both, nodding his head side to side, as if volleying between believing Kirwyn and killing him right there.

"And the second reason?" the man asked.

Kirwyn reached into a saddle bag – a motion that made the men holding the crossbows tense. One of them bared his teeth – or what remained of them. Four or more black spaces revealed themselves in his mouth as he snarled. Very slowly, Kirwyn withdrew a small, velvet pouch. He tossed the black bag onto the dirt at the leader's feet. It landed with a curious jangle.

"Spades are generous to their allies. Just as they never forget those who insult them, they always reward those who aid them."

The man leaned down in one quick, graceful motion and scooped up the pouch. Untying it revealed more than a handful of strange metal coins. I caught his eyes flash, though the rest of his face didn't move a muscle. He took one coin between his teeth and bit it. Turning, he tossed the bag to a short, portly man who caught it with one hand. Everyone watched as he fiddled with the coins, holding them up to the light, feeling their weight and performing other tests or examinations I couldn't figure out.

"Looks real," he finally concluded. "Spade tokens."

"There's more where that came from," Kirwyn said, smug as sin.

"Well men," the leader said, turning, "We've got ourselves an escort job!"

They cheered. My stomach flipped. *Escorting us? Where? To Spade City?*

#

I didn't need to act terrified as we rode; I could barely calm my sputtering heart. Kirwyn kept his arms tight around me – assumingly to keep me close as his prisoner but in reality to keep me calm as his...

What were we?

Lovers on the run? Outlaws? Headed for El Puerto en Blanco or... *what was I going to do if we survived this?*

I'd come so far. And I still had no plan. It seemed minor compared to our life-or-death stakes, but it bothered me that I was married. I knew it didn't mean anything, not really, not if I didn't want it to. But it felt like a mark upon me, a tattoo forced on me somewhere *inside.*

With miles between our location and Spade City, our pace was merciless. But no matter how I slumped in the saddle, falling into Kirwyn's chest and using him for support, he rode stiffly behind me. I remembered how he used to keep horses near his library, growing up. He'd probably been riding since he was a child. Posing as a scout must have come easy to him.

We stopped at dusk to set up camp and I watched in wonder as men drew modern equipment from sacks and assembled it before my wide eyes. Shiny tents, sleek cookware, and barrier devices of some kind. Metal disks, half-buried in the ground, made an invisible perimeter against intruders. I watched as one of the men set up the wide circle around us. Anything larger than a rabbit, their leader explained, tripped a device strapped to his wrist, alerting him of an intrusion. No one could sneak into our area without him knowing.

No one could sneak out either, I realized with a sinking heart.

"Farip Fabroni," the leader finally introduced himself, handing Kirwyn a spare tent. "Everyone calls me Fabroni."

"Corlis," Kirwyn replied, jolting me back to Elowa in my mind.

I'd used that fake name to introduce him to my mother, the night of my wedding feast.

Fabroni's men helped pitch the tent on Kirwyn's chosen site -- as far away as possible from everyone else, where we'd have *some* privacy. Throughout it all, we exchanged weighty looks, but I remained silent. If I spoke, I feared my accent would raise questions.

One of the men cooked dinner over a central fire, and ravenous, we ate a watery, vegetable soup in silence. Only when we'd rested and filled our bellies did conversation begin – mostly aimed in Kirwyn's direction.

He wove a long-winded tale of his efforts in tracking me and I listened like everyone else, enraptured. I'd forgotten what a gifted storyteller he was, having grown up in a library. With all the clever details and funny anecdotes he invented – seemingly on the fly – I almost believed him. Everyone laughed along...

...Everyone except the large, toothless man. Too often, he stroked the hilt of his dagger, eyeing me.

Kirwyn justified traveling alone by alluding to the idea that he'd snuck off and rode ahead, tricking the men he'd traveled with and wanting to claim the Spade reward for my capture himself. I think he said it purposefully, the duplicity endearing him to like-minded men.

"So what's it like, being a Spade?" Fabroni asked.

"Well, the food's better," Kirwyn quipped. "No offense."

"None taken," the cook laughed. "We haven't been able to buy better ingredients in a long time. With your tokens we'll have a feast as soon as we can trade."

"I've spent some time in hiding, just outside Spade City," Fabroni remarked. "Which part are you from?"

Kirwyn hesitated for a beat. Sitting so close to him, I could feel the tension in his body.

Oh no. He doesn't know how to answer.

The beat dragged unnaturally, painfully long.

He doesn't know Spade City at all, I realized.

We need a distraction.

Something to capture everyone's attention…

Without stopping to reconsider, I leaned over and grabbed the dagger from Kirwyn's belt. I jumped to my feet and ran to the edge of the clearing before anyone could stop me. Turning, I held the blade out before me, thrashing wildly at the air, as if I'd never wielded a weapon before. "Stay back!" I cried, inflicting my voice with fear, with an unnatural high pitch to distract from my accent.

The men gaped… then laughed, all tension forgotten. Which made *me* laugh on the inside.

"I – I want a horse!" I shouted with exaggerated desperation, trying my best to mimic their manner of speech, breathless and squeaking to mask what I could not. "Give me a horse!"

"Do you hear that?" Fabroni shouted, grinning. "The girl wants a horse!"

Kirwyn rubbed his chin, as if equally amused – in truth, I think he *was.* Or he would have been, were the situation not dire.

"Do you have rope I can borrow?" he asked, standing casually. "I seem to have left mine with the men I left behind."

I allowed my eyes to widen, as if in fear.

One of the men fished a coil of rope from his pack and tossed it to Kirwyn. Kirwyn slung it through his arm and over his shoulder, then locked his deep, green eyes on mine. I knew what he intended, and he knew what I'd done. I loved that we communicated without needing to speak.

"Thanks for your assistance," he told the men, mouth cocked into a half-smirk, just for me. He titled his head down and looked up, eyes dancing with both delight and menace. Retreating, I repeated, "Stay back, I mean it," waving the dagger sloppily, stabbing at air.

My god he was faster than I remembered.

Kirwyn charged, grabbed my arm, and pressed my wrist, forcing me to drop the dagger to the ground with just enough pressure not to hurt. I didn't have to fake the squeal as he picked me up and tossed me over his shoulder. He carried me across the clearing to our tent as I kicked my legs and beat his back – putting on a show for the echoes of laughter behind me.

"I'll see you in the morning," Kirwyn called to the men.

Ducking through the flap, we entered the relative privacy of our little shelter at the edge of the campsite. Kirwyn stood still in the center.

"Why aren't you letting me down?" I whispered.

"Why are you still hitting me?" I could hear the grin in his voice.

I continued to push at his back. "Because

you're not letting me down."

"Because you keep hitting me. Someone's gotta yield first."

"Oh my god, you're *impossible*," I whispered as loud as I dared. "I'd forgotten how impossible you are. Bloody incorrigible."

"Likewise. You know I can do this for-"

Changing tactics, I lifted his shirt and pinched his side, much as he'd done to me earlier, but even harder.

"Ow," he cried, shifting me and setting me back on the ground to rub out the spot I'd pinched. "Savage. Did they teach you that in princess school?"

"No," I smiled, stretching up to wrap my arms around his neck. "I had to learn how to deal with demon-boys like you all by myself."

"Well, you're doing a fine job," he whispered, still rubbing the skin I'd injured. Kirwyn slid the rope from his shoulder and I stiffened.

"You're not really going to tie me up, are you?"

He flashed that impish grin – the one that weakened my knees. "Not unless you want me to."

I blushed *furiously.* "Incorrigible! I told you."

Kirwyn leaned down and kissed me *very* quietly. I threaded my fingers through his dark hair, clinging to it. I couldn't believe he was really there, holding me.

"Can you blame me?" he nipped my lip.

"You're adorable when you're angry."

I rolled my eyes and quietly, we sank to the tent's floor, facing one another. I scooted into Kirwyn's open legs, unable to get close enough to him. I feared if I were too far, we'd be ripped apart again.

Settling against him, I whispered, "Kirwyn, I'm scared. How are we going to lose them before we get to Spade City?"

"I'm working on it."

"How did you get marked? Did you join the Spades?" I asked, bewildered.

"No. It's a fake. It's not permanent."

"And they believed it?"

"You can't tell the difference and besides, no one ever impersonates a Spade. If they catch you, they'll flay the mark right off your body and the rest of your skin along with it. It was a risk, but I figured this far south I'd be more likely to encounter other unfriendlies. I didn't know so many Spades would be scouting the area on some mission to clean it out."

"Have you... did you find your uncle?" I asked, tentatively.

Kirwyn's face fell as he shook his head.

"I'm sorry," I breathed. "We'll keep looking. Where did you get the tokens?"

Kirwyn's mouth twitched. "Your husband."

I blinked. "What?"

"He's funding the mission to find you. It's my payment for guiding. Half when I took the job, half once complete."

"I'm sorry. I didn't mean to get married. I didn't have a choice." I gazed at the floor.

"Hey," Kirwyn said, lifting my chin back up to meet his eyes. "I know. I'm sorry, too. Do you... want to talk about it? What happened over there?"

"No," I said, surprising myself. "Not yet. They took so much from me. All of them. My mother, the Mystics, the Dorestes. I don't want them to take any more. Not now. If something happens... if we don't have much time together for any reason, I don't want to spend it talking about what happened in the past. Does that make any sense?"

"Total. But it doesn't need to. You don't have to justify your feelings to me. You have a right to feel... however you feel."

I tried not to frown at his cryptic reply. It was gallant and yet... there was a hidden meaning I couldn't glean.

With night upon us, Kirwyn unrolled a small mat for sleeping and I nuzzled into the safety of his arms, sighing contentedly for the first time in moon cycles. Surely, if anyone opened our tent for any reason, it would only look like he was keeping me close as his prisoner.

You're here, my mind repeated. *After all this time, you're really here.*

I wanted to stay up all night talking but after the long day's ride, we fell asleep holding each other.

Where I'd longed to be. Where I'd dreamed of being so many lonely nights in Rythas.

#

I awoke, needing to relieve my bladder. Sliding out from Kirwyn's arm, he did not stir. Surprised, I realized I had no idea how long or far or hard he'd ridden before finding me. For all I knew, he'd gone days with little to no sleep.

Not wanting to disturb him, I crept from the tent, blinking at the dying light of the fire. For a moment, the scent of woodsmoke in the cool night air brought me back to Rythas, to the night of the Fae fête. A strange pang shot through my heart.

It wasn't all bad, I thought.

I headed into the brush and toward a slight slope on our side of the camp, trying not to make any noise. I went as far as I dared without crossing the perimeter and did what I needed to do, yanking my short-pants back around my waist and returning to the wooded incline.

I heard the snap of a twig behind me, but before I could look, a hand clamped over my mouth and arms yanked me clear off the ground. I screamed behind the large, fat hand and pulled fruitlessly at it. Someone dragged me backwards, away from camp, farther than the artificial boundary. Had it been disabled?

Thrashing wildly, I couldn't free myself, but I

managed to free my mouth.

"Kirwyn!" I cried, kicking and punching as hard as I could. *"Help!"*

A dagger pressed to my throat. I instantly froze.

"Scream again and I'll slice you," he said. Even from behind, sour breath assailed my nose. Without moving the rest of my body, I slowly turned my head to stare up at the livid face of the toothless man – the one who'd held a crossbow at us earlier.

I gulped and drew one quivering breath --

-- Suddenly, his weight disappeared from behind me as someone crashed into him, sending me tumbling to my hands and knees in the process.

Kirwyn.

He was there – shoving my assailant off me and knocking him onto the ground. He straddled the man's massive waist, though he wasn't quick enough to pin his arms. Kirwyn grabbed the hand holding the dagger, but the man's other arm swung, connecting a painful-sounding punch to Kirwyn's jaw that sickened my stomach.

I realized Kirwyn hadn't deflected the hit because he was busy grabbing his own dagger. He shoved it into the man's bloated belly. With stunning speed, Kirwyn withdrew the blade and sliced the man's neck. If there was any doubt as to his death from the first stab, there could be none now.

"Kirwyn," I sobbed, struggling to my feet and running to him. I buried my head against his chest and felt his arms cradle protectively around me.

After a moment, I noticed Kirwyn stiffened. The eerie quiet made the hair on my arms stand on end. I lifted my tear-streaked face to see that we had an audience.

Fabroni. His men also watched, twenty paces back.

Oh god. We'd killed one of their own. He's going to kill us now.

"He attacked her," Kirwyn said coldly, hands tensing around me and angling himself in front of me. "I was protecting Spade property."

I trembled -- both from the shock of the assault and from the terror that our mutual death sentence would be pronounced any second.

Or … what if they killed Kirwyn quickly but a fate worse than death awaited me?

I'd die before I let that happen. Before they laid a hand on me or tried to return me as a slave to Spade City...

"Go back to camp," Fabroni announced sternly, slowly, without even bothering to look over his shoulder. "There's nothing for you to see here but a lesson on what happens to men who disobey my orders."

I blinked through my tears.

Was he letting it go?

Kirwyn pulled me even tighter as Fabroni strode the rest of the way downslope, coming to stand before us. He eyed us intently while behind him, his men dispersed. No one spoke for several seconds. My heart thudded. My labored breathing was the only sound.

"Curious that you're returning the girl to her masters, yet she calls to you to save her... and clings to you even now. Kirwyn, was it?"

I pulled away from Kirwyn, but it was too late. He and Fabroni stared hard at one another. I looked anxiously back and forth between the two of them.

"I don't think you're returning her anywhere. My guess is you were either sent to capture the girl and fell in love with her on the way, or you escaped with her at the beginning." Fabroni volleyed his head side to side. "Which is it?"

Before Kirwyn could even attempt a lie, the blonde man's eyes narrowed. "She's not even a slave, is she? Caught in bed with another man's wife, were you? Thought you'd run away together? Maybe stole some tokens before you left?"

Miraculously, he wasn't far off.

"Yeah..." Kirwyn breathed. "Something like that. Let us go and I'll give you more tokens. I have another pouch hidden in the false bottom of my bag."

Fabroni stroked his chin. "There are only two possibilities for running. The man you stole this girl from is either a friend and guilt made you leave... or he's more powerful than you. Richer. Either way, I return her myself and I bet he'll reward me with more tokens than you've got." Fabroni narrowed his eyes, musing almost to himself. "But why is she unmarked?"

"You don't know what you'll find in Spade City. You might get no reward at all. They might just as like take you a prisoner," Kirwyn countered. "Better to claim the prize you know than risk more for the one you don't."

The man volleyed his head again. "No, I don't know what I'll find because I don't know what's really going on here. I bet if I start torturing one of you, the other will start talking. Real fast."

The man stopped his head volley and flashed the hint of a grin.

He opened his mouth, as if to call his men...

I have to do something. Quickly.

"Stop!" I cried. "Wait!"

Fabroni's eyebrows rose, but he didn't shout. Kirwyn stared hard at me, shaking his head, but I shook my head in return, looking up with pleading eyes. *Please understand.*

"I am not a Spade of any kind," I said, taking a deep breath. "I am a queen."

"A queen?" Fabroni chuckled.

"*The* queen," Kirwyn quickly added. "If you

haven't heard of the search by now, you will. There's an island, Rythas. She is queen."

"Rythas? The Spade playground? I've heard some strange rumors recently..."

Kirwyn nodded. "They're true. Look at her. Have you ever seen anyone so beautiful before? She's the missing queen they're all looking for."

The man resumed his head-tilting again, debating whether or not a lost queen truly stood before him. I could easily guess where his thoughts would head if he determined we spoke the truth. *Riches. Rewards.*

"Let us go and we'll be indebted to you," I declared, using my most regal tone. "You'll be rewarded with something far better than gold or Spade tokens. You'll be owed a queen's favor. What is more valuable than that?"

"A king's favor," he quipped.

"Depends on the king. Depends on the queen."

Wait... what was I saying? Did I imply I was going to go against Juls somehow? Was I declaring war of some sort? I didn't know, but I couldn't go back to him, and I couldn't let Rythas take another Elowan bride. I had to do *something*.

"Bold words," the man remarked.

"She's a bold queen," Kirwyn replied.

"She'd have to be to be doing..." Fabroni circled his finger at us, "whatever it is you two are doing."

What were *we doing? What was I hinting at to*

Fabroni? To gamble on *me* over *Juls* because…

"And you're a clever man," Kirwyn added. "Clever enough to realize that banking on her favor is better than anything else you might want. She doesn't have the power to grant it now, but if you let us go, she *will.* She won't always be a queen on the run."

I furrowed my brow, looking up at Kirwyn. Did he know what I considered? Or was he bluffing, as I often did? *How* could he know?

The strange head-volley returned as Fabroni stared at me. "I have your word, as queen. I let you go, you owe me one favor. Whether it's in the backlands or if I journey to Rythas or wherever we meet again. Whenever and whatever I ask. No favor is too big."

"You can't ask me to hurt anyone," I hedged. "Including myself."

A quick head-tilt, then, "Deal."

"Deal," I agreed. "One favor. You have my word as queen."

What had I gotten myself into?

"You should leave, now," Fabroni dismissed us. "If I ever see you in these woods again before you have the power to grant my favor, I'll expect three times the payment to let you live," he said, looking at Kirwyn, "and I'll return her to her king myself."

Kirwyn nodded, once, curt.

"But leave that extra bag of tokens you've got hidden in your bag before you go."

Nodding again, Kirwyn ushered me up the hill toward our horse. I expected an arrow in my back at any minute, especially as the men stared, disbelieving their leader allowed us to depart. Stopping only to grab his bag from the tent, Kirwyn retrieved another small pouch of tokens and tossed it to one of the men. We remounted his horse and quickly rode away from the campsite and into the misty pre-dawn of the forest.

"Are you okay?" Kirwyn asked, once we put enough distance between ourselves and the men. I nodded, but it was a lie. I tried very hard not to think about what would have happened if Kirwyn hadn't been there.

"You saved me," I whispered.

He nuzzled my neck and hummed softly. "It's my job to protect you."

Warmth spread through my chest, but, disbelieving I asked, "Why?"

"Because I love you," he whispered in my ear.

The warmth fanned into a heat. It flooded my veins with a giddiness, as if I were intoxicated.

I'd been so worried in Rythas that you'd forgotten me or reconsidered. Thought it might be a youthful infatuation.

"Then it's my job to protect you too," I replied.

"You just did. And by my count you saved me at least twice on Elowa. I'm sorry I... failed you in Rythas."

"You tried," I argued, though deep down it nagged at me why he didn't try harder, or more often, as I would have for him. "I failed *you*. I'm sorry I didn't understand your message sooner."

"It's not your fault," Kirwyn quickly dismissed. But something in his tone worried me. *Did he disbelieve me?*

I sighed. Thinking of Rythas made me very tired. I'd finally found Kirwyn. All I wanted was to stop running, hiding, fighting. We had each other; we didn't need anything else. And the rest of it... Grahar was dead. Juls wasn't like his father; he would never take Jona in my place. She was most likely safe, at least.

"I want to leave, Kirwyn. You were right. It's dangerous here, far more so than Rythas. I don't want to do this anymore. I think we should find El Puerto en Blanco and just *go*."

"Not yet," he insisted. "I need to show you something first."

"What is it?" I demanded. "Where are we headed?"

Chapter 45

"**Z**aria, I don't want to blindside you. But I don't think it's information I should have had before you to begin with."

"I don't understand," I cried, frustrated. "Stop managing me. You're not making any sense."

"I know. But you've trusted me this far. Can you trust me a little bit farther? We'll reach our destination by nightfall. And then... you'll know everything."

I sighed through my nose. What choice did I have?

"Okay," I whispered, resigned. "I trust you, Kirwyn."

Of course I trusted Kirwyn. Above all others in this world.

Except... except... why didn't he try to rescue me outside of one failed attempt? Why was he being... off?

We rode, but I felt a wall between us, and I didn't like it. Things Kirwyn wasn't saying, things I held back. Partially because we were too exhausted and partially because we both wanted to get somewhere safe before having any meaningful conversation... and partially because I could tell he wanted to show me something first. Something that might change things.

Sometime during the hot afternoon, I fell asleep in the saddle, leaning against him. Kirwyn roused me only to nibble some fruit and bread he'd stored in his bag. Later, we hitched our horse to a tree and waded into a wide stream to cool down and wash off, but we couldn't linger more than a few minutes.

Every nerve in my body was on edge by the time dusk fell and we approached a large white house, nestled in the forest. It rose two stories high behind botanical gardens and guarded gates. The men atop the guard posts weren't Steel Guards or Rythasian warriors; they bore mainland guns more menacing than any I'd seen before – long-barreled and complex.

Was this a clan?

To my surprise, one of the guards nodded at Kirwyn, letting us pass. Kirwyn nodded back.

My heart picked up speed. "Kirwyn? What is this place?"

"It's where I've been most of the time you were in Rythas," he said, voice heavy. "It's where we'll be safe. If you want to stay."

"I don't understand. Where are we?"

"Home. Sort of," he murmured, sliding off the horse and reaching up to help me. Looking around, I forgot all about my sore limbs. The estate was stunning. Ponds with floating white lilies and gardens of deep crimson roses flanked a house glowing with soft, modern lights.

Kirwyn approached the front door and moved to open it.

"Wait! Shouldn't we knock?"

"By now the guards have radioed that we're here. They'll be waiting for us."

"*Who?*" I demanded.

Kirwyn ran a hand through his hair. His soulful green eyes swam with concern, which only made me more nervous.

"People important to you. Maybe more important than anyone," he said.

What?

"Kirwyn, no. No one will ever be more important to me than you."

His eyes searched my face and he leaned down to kiss me once before opening the door.

Nervously, I followed Kirwyn into the house. It proved as gorgeous on the inside as it was on the outside. Luxurious furnishings decorated the floor and beautiful artwork - both old and more modern – adorned the walls and tabletops. Taking my hand, Kirwyn led me through one parlor into another, further toward the back of the house.

My eyes rounded and I gasped at the three people standing, waiting for me: an older man and woman and a young girl.

Elowans. *Braeni.*

No, I realized, cupping my mouth, stunned.

Relatives. All Braeni could link family members by only a few degrees of separation, but the faces before me were strikingly similar.

Family.

Who were *these people?*

The girl, about my own age, stepped forward. No – *exactly* my age, if I'd had to guess. It was as if I looked into a gazing glass that had been slightly altered, as if someone painted my portrait but got a few of the features wrong. The picture reflecting back was my own and yet different. Her eyes were the same blue in the same round face, but her rosebud mouth was a bit smaller and her forehead a little higher. She stood a few inches shorter than me, and her frame was thinner. The three Elowans wore mainland clothing of the finest material. The man had on white shirt and cream colored trousers, and the two women wore white dresses.

"Who – who are you?" I asked, breathless and instinctively backing up against Kirwyn.

The girl smiled, sadly, sweetly. "I'm Aewna," she replied. "We've been wanting to meet you for a long time."

"Have a seat," the man said. "We have much to tell you."

"Father," the girl gently chided. "Please. We agreed it's best if I do the talking."

I cocked my head at their accent. It wasn't Elowan but it wasn't mainlander either; it was somewhere in between. My eyes fell upon the man she'd called father. He too bore a resemblance to me, or I guessed it would be better to say I bore a resemblance to him. His face held a strange expression I couldn't read, but something like concern or calculation colored his furrowed brow. Put out, he crossed arms at his daughter's reminder but held himself back from saying more.

Somebody better start talking, fast, I thought.

The girl extended her arm, inviting me to sit. "Please," she said softly. Her mannerisms were different than mine too. *More graceful,* I thought.

I looked at Kirwyn, bewildered. He nodded.

Speechless, I took a seat, never letting go of his hand. Kirwyn stood above me, his other hand on my shoulder, as if protecting me from whatever was about to be said.

"Would you like anything to drink?" Aewna asked, settling into her chair and smoothing her skirt. "Maybe some-"

"I'd like you to start telling me what is going on," I demanded, squeezing Kirwyn's hand for reassurance.

"Okay. I will tell you everything to the best of my ability, but please let me know if it's too much. I'm going to start at the beginning," the girl said. "Before we were born."

We? So we are family?

"Our parents," Aewna said, turning my world upside-down. "Or really, our grandparents."

The girl looked up at the older man. "Please father, let me tell it as true as I can."

Turning back to me, she said, "Our grandparents didn't mind when their third child was yet another girl, the High Braenese and High Braenar were ecstatic and all of Elowa celebrated. The first born, smiling little Alette, would marry the Sea God, as was custom, and live out her days in Rythas. The second, clever little Pama, would reign as the next High Braenese of Elowa. And the third, sweet little Enith, was free to do as her gentle heart desired."

The young girl before me spoke slowly yet I fought to keep up.

"After the chosen braenese, Alette, sailed off to meet her groom, Pama was expected to marry," she said, carefully. "Pama chose Volmar."

Volmar? I thought, flinching. *My uncle?*

"But Volmar had fallen in love with young Enith. The king and queen urged her to choose another, but Pama was insistent. In her mind, Enith had all the freedom, being the third born, and now she was taking the man Pama loved as well. Denied, Pama fled the palace and found Volmar on the beach. If she couldn't convince her parents, she hoped to bring him back alongside her, and that together they'd persuade the High Braenese and High Braenar to allow them to marry. Volmar spent a lot of time with her younger sister, but Pama didn't believe he loved her."

Aewna tucked a strand of her blonde hair – so similar to my own -- behind her ear. "Pama told Volmar she wished for them to marry, but he said nothing in return. To Pama, that was worse than if he'd cruelly refused her. Pama fled in tears. It was the last time she'd cry for many years. She did not even shed a tear when Volmar and Enith were married the next moon cycle."

I blinked. *My mother had wanted to marry Volmar?*

"Pama, the middle child, the heir, refused a husband until she could refuse no more," Aewna said. "Her parents bade her choose or threatened to choose for her."

I can't believe my ears. I'm not hearing this.

"She chose Darius. Young, malleable, Darius. He was as good as any other. Better -- for his adoring eyes never left Pama and he hung on her every word."

My father? I could tell Aewna spoke with exaggerated slowness and still it felt too fast.

"They were married in three moon cycles," she said. "Days after the wedding, the High Braenar and High Braenese died of a strange sweating sickness. Some whispered the timing was cruel -- if she'd only delayed her wedding a few days, Pama could have avoided it altogether. Others whispered that she poisoned her parents herself."

My blood ran cold. *Why was it that when it came to my mother it was impossible to sort out whether a horror befell her or whether she brought terror upon someone else?*

Aewna drew a deep breath. "Nothing happened for several moon cycles. But on the first night of the Solstice Games, the celebration grew wild. Sea wine flowed like never before. A rare shark was found and killed, and everyone shared in the meat. The games had been close, exhilarating the crowds. Even bottles of Old World wine were brought out for the royals and their family. Strong wine, whose potency dwarfed that of the Elowan wine, making it impossible for the Braeni to bide their intake. Hardly anyone had a clear memory of what occurred that fateful evening. Many men and women slept where they passed out, in the grass or on the beach."

Behind Aewna, the man tensed. The woman covered her eyes, letting out a soft whimper.

"Pama sought out Volmar. That is certain. What happened when she found him beneath the palm trees is *unclear*," Aewna insisted. "No one knows the real story, no one was sober enough to be sure."

The man behind her impatiently shifted his weight from foot-to-foot.

Aewna took another steadying breath. "Nine moon cycles later, braenese Enith and her husband, Volmar, were expecting a baby any day... and so were the High Braenese Pama and her husband, Darius. Two sisters, two royals, pregnant at the same time."

I scrambled to catch her meaning. No... I knew what she implied, but I couldn't believe it. Any of it. The tale was too fantastical; it couldn't be true.

Yet long ago words whispered in my mind...

Darius was a strange choice for your mother...

When you were younger, the royal family didn't make public appearances for many years...

Even what Nasero said before he died... that I didn't know what my mother had endured. *Or was that his biased opinion?*

Most troubling of all, Kirwyn's free hand stroked my neck, attempting to soothe me, as if he believed this story. Dizziness washed over me. Could he tell?

"Enith and Volmar had a daughter they named Aewna. A few weeks later, Queen Pama had a daughter she named... Zaria."

No…

The man became jumpier, wanting to cut in and trying to restrain himself. I shook my head, but Aewna continued. "Pama was in a… state after the birth. It happens to new mothers sometimes. Eventually, they almost always return to health. But the High Braenese was out of her mind when she ordered her niece, the baby Aewna, seized by the Steel Guard."

Aewna's face crumpled in pain as she spoke. Not for herself, I think, but for what she relayed next, to me.

"More alarming still was when Pama handed her own newborn, baby Zaria, over to the guards."

No, no, my mind screamed. *Stop talking.* I wrang Kirwyn's hand, fighting the urge to slap my hands over my ears, to stop hearing this awful tale.

"Two guards, each carrying a naked babe, waded out in the surf by queen's command," Aewna whispered. "They stood far apart. Volmar was brought onto the beach with a sword at his throat."

My heart galloped. Air left the room. *Stop talking! Stop lying!* I wanted to shout. But I had no breath in my body.

"*Choose,* Pama said to Volmar. *You can only save one. You'll never make it to both. Choose.*"

I gasped, clapping my hand over my mouth and shaking my head rapidly. *No. None of this is true, stop lying!*

"Each guard held a babe high above his head... and then each dropped a newborn into the ocean."

Chapter 46

"**I** tried to save you both!" the man behind her cried, unable to contain himself any longer.

Volmar.

I understood now I was looking at my Uncle Volmar. I blinked. Unless... unless what Aewna suggested was true. *Was he my... father?*

"You have to understand that, know that, believe that. A father cannot help but try, even if the odds are against him, even if it's an impossible task," he declared passionately. "The current ran to you, I chose to swim to Aewna because I thought I could get her and use the current in my favor, to swim faster to you next. I didn't believe your mother would kill her first born child, after all! And I was right! You see, you see, I was right!"

What I saw before me was a very defensive man. More so than a remorseful one. *Was he claiming to be my father? Could my mother have truly tossed me into the sea, to drown?*

"She made us all believe, but she never had any intention of killing either of you," Volmar decreed. "Perhaps I should have given her what she wanted and swam to you first. But I'd lost hold of my sanity. You cannot imagine what it is to see your children like that, about to be murdered."

Your children? I blinked. Kirwyn rubbed the area between my neck and my shoulder again, attempting to soothe me.

"Nearly two decades have passed and your aunt can hardly make it through a moon cycle without having a nightmare and she wasn't even there!" Volmar added.

I clenched my stomach, feeling ill. "Are you saying you're my… father?" I croaked. I kept my eyes on the strangers before me but all I really wanted to do was tuck my head between my knees to stop the room from spinning.

"I wasn't sure back then, no one was sure. I doubt your mother even knew for certain. But as you grew, we received information. Travelers from Rythas spoke of your beauty. Reports make their way mainland, if you know who to ask."

Even staring wide-eyed at the man, I didn't know the answer. I'd always resembled my mother over my father, Darius. And Darius and Volmar didn't look distinctive enough for me to tell. Elowans looked similar, Braeni even more so, and I had a feeling my mother chose Darius for an even greater resemblance to Volmar, if any of the story was true. They both possessed blonde hair, broad cheekbones and wide shoulders. Tall, with the same blue eyes. The main difference was this man had a short beard and a strange accent.

I looked at the pretty blonde girl my own age. "Aewna?" I asked, tentatively. "You're saying you're my... half-sister? No wait, that's not right. You're my cousin, my first cousin once removed? No, I- I don't know. What are you?"

"Both, really," she replied. "If my father is indeed your father as well."

"I am," he boasted. "I am the father of the Queen of our Hearts."

What did that have to do with anything?

"I don't understand," I said, looking at my timid Aunt Enith, clutching the chair's back nervously. I studied my uncle... my uncle-father... whatever he was. "Everyone was told you both died in a boating accident. What happened? How is it you came mainland?"

By now Volmar had wedged himself in front of Aewna to command the room. "She never intended to hurt either of you, only me. She's a vicious and vile woman, your mother. I wouldn't give her what she wanted, you see. I wouldn't give her the satisfaction of swimming as she wanted. And I was right. As soon as I took off in the surf, her guards retrieved you from the sea."

Why were we talking about him again? Volmar hadn't answered my question.

"The High Braenese banished our family, or freed us," Aewna explained softly, peeking her head around Volmar and shrugging. "Depending on your point of view. We have a kind of... asylum here, diplomatic immunity."

Unblinking, I stared at my lap. How much of this was true? Who was really my father? Was I the product of love or... an attack? By Volmar or my mother?

Sweat dripped down my brow. *Why was this room so hot and where had all the air gone?*

Looking back up at all three of them, I asked, "What really happened that night?"

"Did she claim I attacked her?" Volmar demanded, face contorted. "Because I didn't."

"No, she hasn't claimed anything!" I cried, throwing up my hands. "This is the first I'm hearing of all this!"

The more Volmar spoke, the more he rubbed me the wrong way. But he finally relaxed his shoulders, running a hand down his face. "She came to me, your mother. I can see her in the night, standing above me so clearly, but," Volmar shook his head, "even that memory I don't fully trust. It is like... a memory of a memory."

I didn't know what to say. At that moment, I wished to be anyone else. No matter what my future held – even if I was a High Braenese, even if I ruled as a queen -- this stain remained. I could never wash it from my past. I wished more than anything to not have been borne into this family with its endless lies. *There are other families out there that look after one another, that care for each other,* I thought. Families like Kirwyn's or Jesi's. I had to admit even the Dorestes loved and protected one another. Why did everyone in mine have to be so selfish?

"Did you love her?" I asked. Eyeing Enith, pale and stricken, I added, "Ever?"

Volmar gave a soft smile, much like Aewna's, but it didn't touch his eyes the same way. "I couldn't help but love her, though I don't know if love is the right word. Admire. No one could help but feel a sense of admiration for your mother. She was horrible, yes, but extraordinary too. Tough. I think she didn't want you to have to be that way. Part of her wanted to protect you, to coddle you so that you'd never experience pain as she did. But another part of her wanted to harden you, to make you in her image."

"How do *you* know?" I demanded. "You weren't even there."

"From your friend's stories," Volmar said, lifting his chin in the direction of Kirwyn.

I glanced up at Kirwyn with accusing eyes.

"I didn't say any of that." A look of irritation

passed his face. "We'll talk later."

I hated everyone knowing more than I did, as usual. My mother lied to me my whole life, *again.* Landdammit, others must have known or suspected and lied to me as well. Servants whispering behind my back in the palace.

How deep did the lies go? Was everything I'd known a lie?

I wasn't proud to be the daughter of anyone involved. I didn't want to be like any of them.

I thought I kept my face blank, but Kirwyn read it.

"I'm taking Zaria to her room. She needs rest." He wrapped his arms around me, and I let him coax me to standing.

"We care about you Zaria," Volmar said, reaching out his hand. "Everyone in this room loves you. We're all here to help. We only want to help you."

"Loves me?" I asked, anger rising. His words sounded empty. I recoiled from him. "You don't even know me."

At that moment I realized I already *had* a father -- a father I could choose. And it was neither the one I'd been raised to believe was my biological dad, nor the one standing before me now, who claimed that role.

It was Saos. I had a mother too, and it was Alette. They were the parents I wanted. The only two to truly care for me. The only two I truly respected or aspired to be like.

I miss them. What will they think when they've learned I've gone?

Even if I came to know Volmar, even if I learned to... love him somehow... I didn't know if I could *like* him. His story had too many holes, too many gray areas. And the narcissistic way he concerned himself more with how he appeared, than me, the one whose world was just turned upside-down by this information... It reminded me a lot of my mother.

I stared at the bearded stranger. If by some miracle I spoke to my mother and got her side, I'd still never really know. She believed her own truth, much like Volmar.

Oh my god. It suddenly occurred to me... all my life, my father hardly paid any attention to me. I'd always thought it was because of the sacred law and maybe some of it was, but now I knew the main reason. *He suspected I wasn't his.*

"We're going to our room for the night," Kirwyn said, ushering me out. "Zaria will speak to you again in the morning." He declared the last part sharply, like a warning not to disturb me.

As Kirwyn escorted me, I stopped one last time and turned.

"Is this all there is? Or are there more secrets?" I cried. "Because it's been eighteen years and I'd like to get it all out now, thank you very much."

"There is no more," Volmar insisted, shaking

his head.

Not that I believed him.

#

"Please, I need air," I said, when Kirwyn tried to lead me up the stairs of the fancy house.

Nodding, he led us through a back door into the rear gardens. They weren't sprawling, like High Spire, but they were pretty and well-cultivated. I could smell the night air heady with roses.

I didn't want to have an audience but nowhere gave the privacy I desired. I stopped walking when we reached a back entrance, guarded by armed men atop high walls.

"You didn't tell me," I whimpered. "I rode with you for two days and you didn't tell me."

"It wasn't my place, Zaria," Kirwyn insisted.

"So your loyalty was to them. These people I don't know. Over me."

"No," he said, grabbing my wrist. I tried to pull away, but I couldn't break his grip. Deep down, I didn't want to.

"It's to you, it's always to you. But they are your family. You deserved to hear it from them. Not me. Even if I don't think Volmar..."

Kirwyn glanced up at the guards and lowered his voice. "Volmar can be challenging. But you had a right to make up your own mind about him and your family's plans. And your... Aewna is like you. Well, she's not at all like you

613

really, but what I mean is – she seems to have risen above what her parents taught her. Her father has been grooming her for a future, but she's developed her own mind. Once you get to know her, I think you'll like her."

"I don't understand. How did you find them?"

"The Arch Priestess told me when I went to see the Fire Maidens. When I was trying to get off Elowa. I wanted to tell you but there wasn't time. They had very little recent information, but they had enough for me to use. Enough for me to locate Enith and Volmar. I struck a bargain with your mother. She either didn't know where to find them or wanted to get close but couldn't. I agreed to deliver a note to Volmar, and she helped me leave." Kirwyn's eyes kept flicking toward the guards, though we remained out of range for them to hear our whispers. "It was either that or kill me and I don't think she wanted to do that. When I came here… we thought we could get you out of Rythas sooner. The longer we were apart, the longer I had kept the secret from you, the less I felt it was my place to tell you."

I couldn't speak; didn't know what to say. Worlds continually crashed down on me. That's how it felt.

"I need to get out of here," I declared, stalking toward the back gate.

"Zaria, I don't want you out there by

yourself," Kirwyn said, grabbing my bicep. "It's not safe."

I looked up at him, confused. "I assumed you're coming with me?"

What was it? Why was there this wall between us now?

Exiting the grounds, Kirwyn followed me into the dark forest and the more we walked, the more I could tell something was wrong. When I felt sure no one could hear us, I stopped and turned.

"Talk to me, please. What is it? Something is different and I don't understand. Why didn't you come for me again? You just gave up after one try. Why not sooner? Later?"

Nothing would have stopped me from trying again and again... and the Kirwyn I knew... thought I knew...

Kirwyn shook his head. "I couldn't."

"You could. I know you could."

"Get in? Yes. Get the both of us out? Impossible. You don't know how much orchestration went into that attempt. Even if it were possible... I *couldn't*."

Kirwyn reached for my arm, but I yanked it away and stepped beyond his reach.

"What aren't you telling me? What does 'couldn't' mean?"

Kirwyn's face fell. I had a horrible thought.

"Are you in love with her?"

"Who?"

"My... sister. Cousin." I cringed. "You know who I mean. Aewna."

"What? No. Why would you ask that?"

"Because you've been off! Something is going on and you're not telling me. There's a wall between us that wasn't there before, despite all the reasons there should have been one when we met!"

"Are you in love with *him?*" Kirwyn asked, and I could tell he fought not to snarl.

"What? Of course not! He was terribly cruel."

Kirwyn cocked his head. "By all accounts your husband is renowned for his benevolence."

Oh god. Oh no.

I slapped my forehead, shaking it. "No, wait. I-"

I had imagined Laz. What in the world would make me do *that?*

"I thought you meant someone else."

"Who else is there?" Kirwyn asked slow and calm, but his eyes blazed like they could set fire to the trees around us.

"No one."

"Then who did you think I meant?"

"His... brother," I winced.

Ironic. All that time Lazlian believed Kirwyn would interfere in my relationship with Juls... and it turned out somehow Lazlian was interfering in my relationship with Kirwyn.

"It's a long story," I breathed. "I don't know

quite how to explain it." *Even to myself.*

Suddenly, the William Blake poem came to mind. And there in the dark wood, I finally finished my distorted version of *A Poison Tree.*

I felt desire for my friend:
I told my want, my want did end.
I felt desire for my foe:
I told it not... my want did grow.

Oh god, I'd grown a poison tree inside me. Except, the poison wasn't hate but... misguided yearning of some kind. Somehow, Laz managed to poison me without sneaking anything into my food, as he'd once threatened but with... with... words.

But *I* did this, too. I watered the tree with tears and smiles and bore the apple for him to enjoy, laying outstretched beneath the branches. All those times I'd willingly engaged with Lazlian, even sought him out... I was in a very dark place during my time in Rythas... and the darkness in him called out to the darkness in me. I'd spiraled downward in shame, let myself get sucked into a whirlpool of toxicity.

I finally understood why his cruelty hurt so much. Because I *knew* Laz was poison, yet a foolish, naïve part of me wished he wasn't. And woven into that mess, I'd refused to acknowledge a latent... attraction... to some part of Laz. I expended so much effort trying to suppress it, I somehow made it bigger than it was... until I bore a landdamn poison tree of misguided desire inside me.

And I despised Laz all the more for it.

Is this... could this be what he *felt?*

More importantly, how could I explain it to Kirwyn?

Kirwyn was quiet for a while. His shoulders tensed, his hands fisted, his jaw clenched. "You don't owe me an explanation."

"Then why do you look like you could kill someone right now?" *Me.*

"Because I'm thinking about it!" he roared. "Because I've been imagining murdering your husband ever since I last saw you. And now I want to take his brother down with him. I want to burn that whole damn castle to the ground!"

"Then why didn't you?" I cried. "All I wanted was you. I spent so many nights alone in that castle, dreaming of you, praying I'd see you again. I still don't understand... anything! And I don't know what to do going forward!" Hot tears pricked my eyes. "But I don't care about that right now because you're here, you're finally here, and all I want to know is why didn't you come for me? Why didn't you rescue me and burn all of High Spire to the ground? Take me away to El Puerto en Blanco where we could start a new life, a life for ourselves?"

My lip quivered. "What do you mean, you 'couldn't?'"

Chapter 47

"Zaria..." Kirwyn groaned. "Once I met your family, I understood. They have plans for Elowa. Bigger than us. Plans I knew you'd want to be a part of."

"You knew? You *knew?*" I growled the words between clenched teeth, growing angrier by the second. "After all I'd been through, you thought I'd want to be a pawn in someone else's game again? If you think that, you don't know me at all! You let me be used – some shiny bauble for the Dorestes to play with. You're just as bad as they are! You're all the same. The Mystics used me, the Dorestes used me, my father wants to use me, everybody uses me! How could *you?*"

Kirwyn reached for my arm, but I whirled away. He grabbed my waist and spun me back around.

"Just tell me! Why *couldn't* you come for

me?" I shouted, pounding his chest with my fists. It was a childish rage, misdirected, but I'd bottled it up for so long. Wasn't I allowed *one* moment of being something other than in control, wearing a mask, pretending to be a queen? I was tired, so landdamn tired of it.

Kirwyn pulled me tight to contain my flailing as he whispered close to my ear. "Zaria, not just *our* game. *Yours.*"

I heard Kirwyn, but he didn't make sense.

"I've known. *We've* known. Your family and I – we heard the news about what you were doing over there. We watched you rise to become the Queen of our Hearts. You won them. The people love you. Maybe it's your destiny – the destiny *you* forged for yourself. Not whatever your mother or Nasero wanted you to be, not whatever Grahar wanted to shape you into."

"Don't you understand?" Kirwyn begged.

No, I thought madly. *I don't understand what you're saying at all.*

No... that was a lie.

Only this time, I was lying to myself. I did understand. I courted their love. And I feared it too. The power. What I'd do with it. What would happen if I failed. What would happen if I succeeded.

"If I took you away from that, I *would* be no better than the rest of them. And for what? A life in hiding like we'd have here?

Always looking over our shoulders? Or finding El Puerto en Blanco and running? Knowing you abandoned Elowa and Rythas? Could you live like that? Knowing your sister, your kin – knowing they'd meet the same fate as you?"

I didn't want to listen. He was making sense and I didn't like it. I didn't want logic, reason, the greater good. I wanted to erupt and incinerate everything in my path. I wanted to think about *my* needs, what *I* wanted. My rage burned like a fire, and it called out for fire in return. Not water to douse it.

"You're all just cowards," I accused, uncaring if I was being wildly unfair or not. "Cowering like little boys and letting me do the work."

Kirwyn's hands fisted around my biceps, hard enough to hurt. "You think I cowered like a little boy? Are you kidding me? Do you know how hard it was for me to watch you over there? But what kind of man would I be if I stole you from your plans to suit myself? To put *my* needs over *yours.* Could you love someone like that? Because I don't think I would like myself very much. You didn't have to tell me, and I understood what you wanted, even separated by the ocean. So why can't you understand me right now? If you think I wouldn't have risked my life in a heartbeat, if you think I didn't want to raze that whole place to the ground, then *you* don't know me at all."

"Maybe I *don't* know you," I said, not

meaning a word of it, just feeling utterly explosive. My rage was misdirected, I knew that. I was angry about many things, but most especially the bomb my possible father dropped on me that night had me hurling anger like shrapnel. Kirwyn was merely nearest, bearing the brunt of it. A part of me, deep down, even knew he could handle it and adored him all the more for his skill. Kirwyn wasn't like Juls, who'd be aghast at such an outburst, or Laz, who'd manage to make it worse. It was as if Kirwyn had a power to manage it, to safely redirect my energy.

But… I had changed; we'd both changed. And what if it *had* been youthful fancy between us? Kirwyn and I had only known each other for a moon cycle.

"This is crazy," I whispered, searching his beautiful face. "Think about it. We barely spent a month together. We were so naïve back then…like children. I know it wasn't that long ago but so much has changed since Elowa. You don't know what I've endured. I don't know what you've been through. Maybe I don't know you."

With a shaky breath, I stepped away from Kirwyn and deeper into the forest. I didn't have any real direction, didn't have a plan.

I was shocked to feel Kirwyn's hands grip my waist and yank me back to face him. Before I could blink, one strong arm slid around my shoulders and the other, behind my knees, lifting me off my feet and carrying me deeper into the woods.

"Oh, I know you," he said, almost chuckling. "I figured out exactly what you're doing. When you're scared, you argue."

I frowned, fighting the heat on my cheeks. *Was he right? Well... Maybe.* But I recalled at least once when *he* started a fight for no good reason back on Elowa.

"I think you like to run so I will chase you," Kirwyn smirked, laying me down in a clearing while I tried my best to scowl. "And if you don't think you know me..." he said, twining our hands together and holding them against the grass on either side of my head. "Then let me remind you."

Whatever flimsy anger I possessed was quickly supplanted by need when Kirwyn's body pressed to mine. His mouth swooped down on me like a bird of prey, swallowing any protests.

God, the way he kissed me. Each lap of his tongue, like stoking a fire. *It never felt like this with Juls.* The heat began in our mouths and spread throughout my whole body, setting fire to my blood and melting the wall between us. With the barrier gone, our connection resumed, locking into place.

I remember you, I thought. *I remember this. Us.*

I had sudden, tantalizing ideas about where

it could lead. Fierce desires. I unclasped our fingers and tugged at Kirwyn's shirt. But to my disappointment, he stopped me, taking my hands in his. A feeling of rejection flared in my chest. Kirwyn broke our kiss to nibble my ear, hot breath against my neck.

"Keep your hands here," he rasped, raising them back to either side of my head. "Can you do that for me?"

His deep voice alone did funny things to my body. I nodded.

"Go ahead and fight me again in a bit, as hard as you'd like. But let me do something first. Okay?" As he spoke, Kirwyn slid down my body, relieving me of my clothing.

"What – what are you doing?" I had an inkling. No... I knew *exactly* what he was doing. I'd read about it, heard about it. But having it happen *to* me was something else entirely; the moment too surreal to be believed.

"Something I've been thinking about these past seven months. Maybe you're right. Maybe we were childlike when we met." Kirwyn's husky voice gave me chills. "We're not anymore."

In case I had any lingering doubts, he leaned down.

"What are you *doing?*" I whispered, even though I *knew*. I just couldn't believe it.

Kirwyn paused, backing up. "No?" he asked, cocking one eyebrow.

I swallowed, hard.

"Yes," I breathed, looking down one last time.

Kirwyn's grin was diabolical.

He kissed me where I'd never been kissed before.

#

Trees blocked the stars but that was fine – I saw enough of them behind my eyes by the time Kirwyn fell down next to me and pulled me into the circle of his arms. I rolled at his tug, nuzzling against his chest. My heartbeat slowed to a normal pace as my senses returned. I could hear the nighttime sounds of the forest. Insects chirping, the slight rustle of leaves in the trees.

"That was a dirty trick," I grinned, surprised to find my mouth so dry. My face quickly heated. Had I been too loud, too vocal?

"Are you going to stop arguing or should I do it again?"

"No!" I protested, cheeks flaming. I needed time to process what just happened -- I didn't think I could handle more.

How did he know me so well? Know what I needed or wanted or how to handle anything, everything? It scared me a little, as did the intimacy of what we'd just shared. I couldn't stop marveling at it.

"I don't understand…" I began. "You'd do *this*

with me, but you would let him... touch me. Against my will. What do you mean by you 'couldn't' come? You said no god could keep you from me, but a boy-king could?"

Shoving up to look at me, Kirwyn's eyes flashed and, in a heartbeat, he sprang to his feet. I scurried to stand with him, yanking my clothes back on.

"I meant what I vowed, *nothing* could. Nothing in this world -- except you." Kirwyn's hands raked through his hair and then his arms stretched wide. It was his turn to erupt as he shouted, "You think it didn't kill me? Every second of every day I thought I might go insane. I thought I might kill someone, kill everyone on that whole damn island and save your precious young king for last and do it slowly. Day after day I combed those beaches and talked to everyone I met, risking capture and enslavement, just to learn everything I could about Rythas. I thought of *nothing* but rescuing you, thought of *nothing* but his dirty hands on your body and my bloody hands tearing him apart."

By the time he'd finished, Kirwyn's shoulders were pushed back and his hands were fisted, as if readying for the imagined fight. Breathing deeply, his nostrils flared until his voice calmed into lower, more controlled anger.

"Your family is the *only* thing that stopped

me from making a huge mistake. When I found them and understood and listened to the reports they received. They have people in High Spire, Zaria."

People? What did that mean?

"I didn't believe any of the reports at first. But all the stories I gathered corroborated his information. Volmar receives news from those inside the castle. Spies. They tell him what they're able because he pays them what he can and because they're vying for favor should there ever be a change in power. But it was a one-sided hell. No one dared pass you a message or risked revealing themselves in case your loyalty lay with the Dorestes, then or in the future. They merely threw information at us in bits and pieces, like scraps to a dog. Only when I learned about the young king did I calm down enough to function. Only when I was assured he wouldn't touch you. We heard... that you kept separate bedrooms. That he is a *good man*." The last two words came out through clenched teeth.

"They told us the marriage would never be consummated unless *you* went to *him*."

Oh no. My heart stopped beating. Silence drawled between us. Kirwyn's face flitted between fury and agony as he gritted out, "And then we received word that you did."

I drew in a quick breath, the only sound between us for several long moments as we stared at one another. Never in a million years would I have imagined the choice I made that night would reach Kirwyn's ears.

Kirwyn's throat bobbed and his eyes closed as he said, "We heard... heard you were happy. That you'd found family and friends. That you were the belle of every ball, dancing all night with nobles and emissaries. That the young king and queen were very much in love. That it wouldn't be long before... that the late king would get those grandchildren he wanted so badly."

My own eyelids briefly fluttered closed.

"You thought I loved him," I whispered.

"I didn't know! Were you playing a game, or did you want to stay in Rythas with your king? I thought if I could just get you alone, talk to you..." A muscle in Kirwyn's cheek twitched. "I hoped you'd show up at the markets but I didn't know if my message would be intercepted. I didn't even know if I was in Rythas on a rescue mission or a kidnapping plot anymore. Though I would have... returned you. If that's what you wanted."

And I never came. Possibly confirming his suspicions.

Kirwyn shook his head. "I came back without you. And then I heard about your... visit. To his bedroom."

"I'm sorry," I said quickly. "Nothing happened. It wasn't like that. It's... another long story. But I promise you, it's not what you think." I licked my lips. "How long were you in Rythas?"

"Three days. I was there the day of your wedding. Your husband set a trap. Arranged a decoy for you and the young king, a couple that looked like you. And he was there, the young king's brother. It seemed legit."

I blinked. *Laz? The day of my wedding?*

"Where?"

"Some gardens made of glass."

Oh my god. Is that why I never saw Laz during the celebration? The ship had sailed close to the coast... I'd assumed it was because Laz was afraid of the ocean or even for the views. But maybe he'd taken one of the rowboats and slipped off without me even noticing? I'd been crowded on the dance floor so long, I wouldn't have seen him depart or return. *That can't be right.* I couldn't imagine Lazlian in a small boat. Though it was technically feasible... *Wait.* The ship didn't depart until the ceremony was over and *oh my god.* Laz only showed up again after we'd docked. *Maybe he'd been gone the whole time?*

"They set up a fake ceremony," Kirwyn explained. "Small, intimate. They must have found a wig for the girl and makeup. She was you, at a glance... but I knew she wasn't you."

"How?" I breathed.

"She didn't move like you. When you're in

a situation that makes you uncomfortable you might look down, or you might catch yourself and stubbornly jut out your chin. But you're never neutral, you wear your emotions on your face. At least, you did before. She was too... blank. I don't know how to explain it. She wasn't you."

Oh, Kirwyn. I hated picturing him looking for me, waiting alone.

"And then I saw you."

My mouth dropped at his words.

"I followed people to the docks. The crowds when you disembarked were too thick, they couldn't contain them. And you were waving and smiling and kissing your king."

I let my eyelids flutter shut again. *Ugh... it meant nothing to me.* I didn't even think about it.

"I... had to," I insisted shaking my head. "I didn't mean it."

"You were very convincing," Kirwyn said, voice low. "I left, still unknowing whether you played a game or had fallen in love with him."

What a mess, I thought. *God, Kirwyn was right there when I came ashore, and I never knew it. So close.*

"I returned to your family's house not sure what to do next, especially after hearing about your night with... *him.* Then suddenly, out of the blue, word came that you'd been kidnapped. I *still* didn't know what to believe.

When the first of the Rythasian soldiers came to the mainland, I pretended to be a guide with intimate knowledge of the region and clans. I led them in the mission to find you, though I've been leading them in circles." Kirwyn half-rolled his eyes. "I listened at night, heard them talk. Heard them speculate that the queen wasn't kidnapped at all. There'd been rumors she plotted her own escape, jumped off a ship and swam to shore. No one wanted to speculate too loudly, for fear of the Dorestes' wrath. And besides, it made no sense. The queen loved her people as they loved her, and she loved the king, as he loved her."

All this time... My heart ached for what Kirwyn must have gone through.

"But I knew it then. That you'd done it, that it was your choice. Which only made me feel despicable for ever suspecting otherwise or worse... that something awful happened and you changed your mind. That he... hurt you. Long after the soldiers fell asleep, I stayed awake, wondering what you endured in Rythas and hating myself."

"Kirwyn," I breathed, stepping close to cup his face with my hands. "It was always you. I... there were times when I doubted... it all happened so fast. But it's *you.* It's always been you."

He leaned down, grabbing my waist and kissing me possessively. Making my knees melt.

"Just no more secrets between us. Please," I begged; forehead pressed to his. "Don't hold back because you think I can't handle it. I don't want to hear about my family from strangers. I know they are my family, technically, but you're my family more. You mean more to me than they ever will."

Kirwyn worked his jaw, flinching as if pained.

Oh no. I had that image again -- of the sea ebbing, as it does before releasing a powerful wave. The forest around us seemed too quiet, seemed to draw an anticipatory breath.

"There's just one more thing you don't know. When I came, it wasn't the first rescue attempt."

His voice made the hair on my arms stand on end. *What did he mean?*

"We sent in a team for you. Volmar put it in motion before I arrived, and it was botched from the beginning. He picked the wrong men, word leaked. Your sister tried to plant rumors of a kidnapping attempt for ransom money to cover up what was already being whispered. She wanted to throw anyone off your family's trail, to send the Dorestes in the wrong direction. The men were sent to rescue you, but you..."

The ground ripped out from beneath me and my stomach dropped. In my mind, I went back to when I first arrived in Rythas, to that day with Jesi in the shack.

"My... kidnappers?" I whispered, furrowing my brow. "They were there to... rescue me?"

Oh my god. I slapped my hand over my mouth and stared at Kirwyn with wide eyes. "I killed them. They would have taken me but I..."

"You didn't know," Kirwyn insisted. "They didn't want you in more danger than you already were."

"I killed them, Kirwyn. It's my fault."

"No, Zaria, no. And they weren't good men to begin with. Volmar has some clever ideas, but his execution is..." Kirwyn made a pained face. "Not always as wise."

"It worked," I breathed. "Aewna's rumors. The Dorestes thought someone was after money, but they never figured out who was behind the plot."

"We never knew exactly what went wrong. We didn't know for sure if they kept you in the dark, as planned -- at least, initially -- or if they *did* get around to telling you and you..." Kirwyn shook his head, "...didn't want to go."

Two rescue attempts, both thwarted. Oh god, *if I'd just let them take me, they would have taken me straight to Kirwyn.*

"Oh god. I think I'm going to be sick."

None of it would have happened. My entire time in Rythas...

And all these deaths. *Solan, Nasero, Tolas,*

the young boy the Mystics believed had touched me, these kidnapper-rescuers, hundreds in the Oxholde army, Milicena... So many deaths upon my head, I'd lost count. I was a harbinger of death.

I didn't want this. I'd never asked for this.

All of it, all the pain I suffered in Rythas could have been avoided if I'd only just gone with those men. I could have been with Kirwyn months ago!

"I'm going to be sick," I managed, before doubling over and throwing up in the grass.

"Let's go," Kirwyn said, patting my back. "I'm taking you back to the house. I'll draw a warm bath. We're safe there."

#

"Modern plumbing," Kirwyn explained, though I wanted no parts of the strange levers and knobs at that moment. I was unfazed. Was it possible to be so continuously bombarded with so many impossible wonders that a person just numbed themselves, at a point? Miraculously, water flowed, filling the tub, but I didn't care to ask about the magic.

We stood in the adjoining bathing room to our bedroom in the elegant white house, nestled within the wood and guarded by men with intimidating weaponry. My... family... read or slept or did god-only-knew-what just outside our door.

Kirwyn's deep green eyes searched my face. Was I pale? When I thought about the kidnapper-rescuers, I felt like the wind had been knocked out of me again, the world ripped from beneath my feet. There was nothing I could do about it now. It wasn't even anyone lying to me, this time. But the fact that I could have avoided... all of my time in Rythas... if I'd *only* gone with those men...

But one of them tried to assault you, I reminded myself.

You don't know what would have happened to Jesi if you fled...

And what if... it wasn't all for nothing? What if you have a purpose, a destiny to do something?

"I'll leave you alone to bathe..." Kirwyn said, reluctantly. "I'll be just outside the door."

Hands resting on my shoulders, he kissed my forehead and departed. I stripped out of my dirty clothing and stepped into the hot water. But I didn't move or bathe, not for a long time.

#

I don't know how Kirwyn knew to return to the strange bathing room before I finished. I'd drawn my knees to my chest and wrapped my arms around them. Maybe I took too long. Maybe he heard me. I was crying pretty hard.

He wore no shoes, but the rest of his clothing remained. Kirwyn didn't bother taking anything off when he quickly stepped into the bath, sat down, and drew me into his arms.

"Don't," I whispered, but I didn't mean it and he didn't listen.

I *really* let go then. Ugly-crying against his chest, snot-nosed and wailing. I hadn't sobbed that long and hard my entire time in Rythas. He made me feel so safe. How long had it been since I truly felt safe? Juls had given me some security; he'd been the lesser of two, *no* – multiple, evils. A life raft in the stormy sea. But Kirwyn was solid ground underfoot. Stubbornly unyielding, but sheltering, too.

"I've got you," he said, rocking us slightly and making something flutter inside me. His strong hands rubbed circles on my wet back.

"I'll always find you and I'm never leaving you," he swore.

For a long while, I did nothing but bask in the comfort of his vow. Finally, I whimpered, "It can't have all been for nothing. I won't let it."

Teary, I looked up at Kirwyn. God, he was so handsome, he made my heart thump, even in the midst of a breakdown. He was soaking wet and still fully clothed; his shirt clinging to his muscles. How did I get so lucky? That he washed up on *my* shore, that *I* found him?

"What do you want, Zaria?" he asked. "The choice is yours. You have freedom. We can leave tomorrow if you like and search for El Puerto en Blanco. No one will blame you. No one will say you're walking away. You've endured more than your share and you deserve your chance at happiness. Everyone does. If you want to stay hidden here with your family and let them continue their plans for Elowa and Rythas, I'll support you. I'll stay with you here forever if that's what you want."

I wiped the tears from my cheeks. He hadn't said it. What we'd danced around with Fabroni -- the idea Kirwyn hinted at when he said I played my own game. What I dually courted and feared.

"And if I want the third option?" I asked, tentatively at first, but voice growing stronger. "What if I want to fight my own way? What if I want to risk my life, risk all our lives?"

"I told you once you're a goddess to me." He grinned as he spoke, caressing my face and giving me a playful wink. "I'll follow you into battle."

I laughed, but it was sad. "What if I lead all of us to our deaths?"

"Your family is already invested. Volmar wants Elowa and that means he has to deal with Rythas. They're doing this with or without you. So stop worrying about them."

For several moments I concentrated on my breathing, gazing down at where Kirwyn and I connected in the water. Finally, I looked up.

"I can't leave them," I whispered, becoming more animated as I spoke. "Juls would never take Jona, but I'm not sure he could stop someone else from doing so, when she's older. And the next girl... it has to stop; lives can't keep being sacrificed. I can't walk away, knowing I left them to that fate. That I did nothing to help stop it."

I frowned, clutching the edge of the tub. "And I don't think it's fair that Elowans are being lied to." I huffed, shaking my head. "I don't know. I want change."

I'd come so far from that night on the beach with Kirwyn, when he told me about planets and, as an Elowan, I didn't believe him. Now I knew so many truths and... maybe I wanted the people of Elowa to know them as well.

"What did the words mean, Kirwyn?" I asked suddenly. "The Gaelic ones you said that night we spent together? You said if I left with you, you'd tell me."

He chuckled softly and raised his eyebrows. "Technically, you never left with me."

"I tried. Eventually."

"I'll tell you what. You and I make it out the other side of... whatever it is you're scheming, and I'll tell you then. What is it? Because I know that look. You're deliberating something."

"I'm working on a plan," I admitted. "It's a longshot but it's all I've got."

"Whatever you're working on, it's bound to be better than Volmar's notions," he said, tucking a wet strand of hair behind my ear.

"What do we need to do, princess?"

My heart skipped a beat whenever he called me that. *I'd rather be your princess than his queen.*

"We need to find Mal-Yin."

Kirwyn's eyes widened. "Mal-Yin? Why? So he can kill us?"

"I know him. He won't kill me. He trades with Rythas, helps them."

"So everyone in the world is looking for you and you want to deliver yourself to your enemy's ally?"

"Rythas isn't my enemy. Nor is Juls, not truly. That's what makes this so difficult. I'm also not sure if Mal-Yin is playing both sides… he might have armed Oxholde against Rythas. But he won't betray me to them. Not if we can persuade him to help us. Not if we give him something else he wants more."

"And what's that?" Kirwyn folded his arms in what I knew to be a firm refusal. Even soaking wet he looked formidable.

"I don't know yet," I confessed, wrapping my arms around his neck. "I'm working on it. Do you know how to find him?"

"Yes," he admitted, while shaking his head *no.* "But we're not going there. My answer is no."

"You're so bossy! Which is it? You just said you'd follow me, now you deny me?"

Kirwyn scoffed, "It'd be easier to sneak into

hell and back."

"Well, then." I let my breath fall across his beautiful mouth, stretching up to press my wet lips to his. "Who better to lead us into hell than a demon?"

The End

A Poison Tree

By
William Blake
Songs of Experience 1794

I was angry with my friend;
I told my wrath, my wrath did end.
I was angry with my foe:
I told it not, my wrath did grow.

And I waterd it in fears,
Night & morning with my tears:
And I sunned it with smiles,
And with soft deceitful wiles.

And it grew both day and night.
Till it bore an apple bright.
And my foe beheld it shine,
And he knew that it was mine.

And into my garden stole,
When the night had veild the pole;
In the morning glad I see;
My foe outstretched beneath the tree.

About The Author

Elora Morgan

Elora spends her free time pursuing fantasy. Nothing engages her mind like a fantastical new world -- except when that world contains lovers who initially despise one another. She reads and writes these angst-filled pairings from the East Coast of the U.S.

YA ROMANCE | DYSTOPIAN | SCI-FI/FANTASY | ENEMIES-TO-LOVERS

is no other land in all the ocean.

BUT WHEN THE SCOUNDREL AWAKENS, HE HAS THE GALL TO AMBUSH ZARIA.
As three pageants leading up to her wedding turn unexpectedly deadly, and the enigma of its true purpose looms, Zaria is torn between her long-desired fate as Sea Queen and the infuriating boy who tells her that everything her people know is a lie.

Borne To Salt And Sin: Fated

THE KING WANTS HER BACK
They call her the Kidnapped Queen, but King Juls is a beautiful liar. Zaria risked her life to escape an arranged marriage she never consummated and never wanted. Now, without better options, her husband is determined to hunt her down under the guise of a rescue.

THE BOY FROM BEYOND WANTS HER SAFE
Reunited with the one she chose, Zaria has her own plans -- if she can find support. She'll capture the castle, force Juls to change the laws, and protect the next chosen bride. Fleeing together through the deadly backlands, Zaria and Kirwyn will first need to survive.

But she's not the only one with a burning goal,

and the clash of desires might save or destroy entire kingdoms.

THE KEYLORD WANTS HER PUNISHED
Before the battle's over, two things are certain: Zaria needs to stay close to the boy she loves...

...and far away from the prince she hates.

Because the king's cruel brother swore to make her beg for mercy if she ever betrayed his family. And Prince Lazlian always keeps his vows, especially when they concern the little queen he despises.

He hates her so much, she's all he can think about.

Made in the USA
Monee, IL
19 November 2022

18124373R00374